E

KARA DALKEY

To Will, Emma, Pamela, Steve, Nate, Pat,
Terri and Val, for the usual,
and special thanks to Denny Lien
for service above and beyond the normal duty
of a college librarian.

PROLOGVS

A SHAFT OF LATE WINTER SUNLIGHT stabbed like a golden sword-blade into the dark interior of the Temple of Jupiter Capitolinus. Within the brilliant light, a veiled woman entered. To any of the supplicants offering sacrifice, or the senators discussing politics, or the priests helping the ill who came for healing, the woman seemed the most modest of Roman matrons. She wore her palla low over her forehead, and her veil covered her face in the style of Parthian women. Her garments were of plain, homespun wool and even the tips of her sandals did not show beneath the hem of her pleated stola.

As she walked down the central colonnade of the temple, those who happened to notice her might have nodded their approval of her graceful and proper deportment, or paused a moment to wonder who she was before returning to their business. Those who watched longer might have noted that she did not proceed to the enormous gilded and painted statue of Almighty Jupiter, Father of Rome, that dominated the far end of the temple. Nor did she turn to her left to cross to the aisle guarded by Juno, Holy Wife of Jupiter and patroness of all women, wives and mothers. Instead, the modest woman crossed the inlaid marble floor to the right, to the aisle of Minerva.

There were few supplicants to the Goddess of Wisdom, Art and War on this day, and the modest woman was able to walk up to the pedestal of the statue with no one to block her way. The woman stared up at the seated figure; the sculpted

Minerva stared back with stern benevolence, a spear in her right hand and plumed helm covering her head. The modest woman placed a bag of coins at the feet of Minerva, and lit two sticks of incense. Then she stood back with her hands upturned in prayer.

But after a few moments, there came a disturbing change in the pious scene. The woman began to tremble, then shake noticeably. Her sculpted hands balled into fists and she began to beat upon the feet of Minerva as if she could bring the statue down with her blows. Flakes of flesh-colored paint flew off with each strike of her hands. The woman threw back her head and cried out in Greek, "Cruelest Pallas Athena! Have you no mercy? Have I not suffered enough?"

Her wails brought priests rushing to her side, to see if she were ill or possessed by a daemon. But though she still trembled, the modest woman seemed to recover and gently pulled herself out of the priests' hands. Holding her palla tightly around her, the woman rushed down the aisle, ignoring all offers of assistance. She did not look to the right or left, but went straightway out the great entrance, as if impelled by the stares of the curious, leaving in her wake bewilderment and a great deal of talk to be shared at the noontime baths.

PRIMVS

G NAEUS CORNELIUS SCIPIO HISPALLUS, praetor peregrinus of Rome, strode into his Palatine home, bringing the dismal atmosphere of the morning rain in with him.

"Appropriate weather for a visit to the Temple of Storms, my Lord," said the slave who took the praetor's damp wool cloak.

"Perhaps," grumbled Hispallus, "but not comfortable for a man my age to be out in." *My age,* thought the praetor. *Cousin Scipio Aemilianus is forty-six, only two years younger than I. Yet he could stand for hours in front of the Temple receiving the adulation of the crowd, with no sign of discomfort.*

Aemilianus had just returned from an embassy to Greece and the lands of the East. He had gone to the Temple of Storms, which had been built by an ancestral Cornelius Scipio more than one hundred years earlier, to give thanks to the tempestates for a safe voyage back. *He is considered a hero,* thought Hispallus, *like his grandfather Africanus. I, too, am a Scipio. Yet what have I done that has received the notice of Rome? Nothing.*

"May I take your toga also, my Lord?"

"Eh?" said Hispallus, his reverie broken. He fingered the purple and gold border of his toga praetexta thoughtfully.

"No. It is time for the morning salutatio. Go see that the gates are opened and my visitors admitted."

"My Lord, your guests already await you in the atrium."

Hispallus frowned and walked down a short corridor, the slap of his red leather sandals seeming unnaturally loud. He came to the threshold of the atrium and stared across the wide expanse of mosaic floor and down the rows of delicately carved columns. There were only a few men standing here and there in the great hall.

"Marcus!" called Hispallus. A gangly young man detached himself from a group of lictors and came running.

"My Lord?"

"Are these all the *clientes* who have come for salutatio today?"

"It would seem so, Magistrate. One awaits you in your tablinum. He says he is a former slave of yours named Daedalus."

"Ah. That would be Thessalus's son, come to ask about his bridge." Hispallus's gaze was drawn to the far wall of the atrium. Along its length were deep niches, each of which contained either a bust or a statue of an illustrious member of the Scipio family, of the gens Cornelia: Barbatus, conqueror of Lucania; the brothers Gnaeus and Publius, who died gloriously in Hispania; Africanus, who defeated Hannibal; Asiaticus, who put down the Antiochan uprising; Nasica, who had welcomed the Magna Mater to Rome; and Aemilianus, now a censor, who had razed Carthage, and had been the youngest man ever to be consul. *All men of great deeds. And all I am given to do is to disappoint a boy architect about his bridge.*

Hispallus turned and went to a pair of bronze-plated doors that stood ajar. Before entering, he stopped, looking at the scene within the tablinum. A young man, eighteen years of age, with dark, curly hair, sat slouched, leg over the chair's arm, in an adolescent posture of relaxed defiance. In one hand he held a chalice of Anatolian silver that he was studying as

EURYALE

if he wished to determine where one blow might do the most damage.

What disrespect is this? Not wise in a young man in need of support. Hispallus gave a loud cough and, pushing the doors open, walked in.

"Scipio!" The young man jumped up, arms spread wide.

"Salve, Daedalus." Hispallus gave him a brief embrace of greeting.

Daedalus stepped back, his face warm and hopeful. "So tell me, Scipio, how much does Rome give me for the Pons Daedalus Magnus?"

"I am sorry, Daedalus. Rome gives you nothing."

Daedalus's face fell. "Nothing?"

"The censors have rejected your request. They will give you no money to build your bridge."

"The cens— Don't be so pompous, Scipio. One of them is your cousin. Could you not influence him?"

"Aemilianus has only just returned from the East. He has more pressing matters to attend to. And may I remind you that a bridge was built across the Tiber only three years ago."

"Yes, a plain, dowdy lump of brick. Did you show them the plans?"

"Indeed." One of the quaestors had stared with amazement at the proposed conglomeration of arches, columns and statuary, calling it the most ornate monstrosity he had ever seen. "They felt your design was too expensive and elaborate. They could not, in good conscience, spend the City's money on such a project."

"Elaborate? Expensive?" Daedalus turned to the wall and spoke as if delivering an oration to the nymphs and satyrs painted thereon. "Gold flows in daily from the plunder of Macedonia, and Rome cannot afford a bridge? I would think they would want to flaunt the might and glory of the Republic!"

"Calm yourself, Daedalus. You may still have hope. The consul Piso privately advised me that he approved of your design. If you could find the funding from some other source, he implied he would see that the land is allotted for your use."

Daedalus turned and regarded the praetor, his eyes smiling but cold.

Hispallus found the young man's expression unsettling. *As though he has just made a decisive move in a game of Twelve Lines. Did he expect to be turned down?*

"Well," said the young architect, "what better source for private funding than my former master Scipio Hispallus?"

Hispallus shook his head. "I am sorry, Daedalus. I do not have the funds available."

Daedalus's eyes narrowed. "Ah, but I am forgetful. Your money is currently tied up in the furnishing of your wife's villa in Ostia. The same villa my father designed for you when I was a child."

"I do not mean to appear ungracious, Daedalus. I held your father in high esteem—he was a good slave and a good man, and it would not displease me to help his son. But I cannot offer you what I do not have. I would think it would please you that I am embellishing your father's work."

"Please me!" Daedalus's eyes blazed anger. Then he suddenly cooled. "I think you will find the money for me, Hispallus. I know a great deal about that villa, with its hidden passages and underground rooms. I watched my father draw the plans, and as I child I played in the foundations as they were built."

"What are you saying?" asked Hispallus. *What does he know?*

"What do you think the opinion of your *clientes* would be if they knew what their praetor's wife used those rooms for?"

"As your father knew," Hispallus lied, "the villa was built for my wife's health, on the advice of the priests of Aesculapius. The underground chambers were built to house special baths."

"I know what my own eyes have seen, Hispallus. Or are you implying that your wife's love of wine is so great that she bathes in it? Perhaps that is the style among Bacchantes these days."

He knows. Iupiter Invictus help me, he knows. The worship of the God of Wine had been outlawed half a century before, when the ecstatic rites he inspired proved to be fertile ground for intrigue, immorality and murder. The interdict did not, however, prevent the determined from continuing to worship him secretly. "Have a care with what you say, Daedalus. No one would believe such slander."

"Not even if your own son corroborates my words?"

"My . . . son?"

"He has proven to be a most excellent drinking companion."

Ah, Cnaeus, my son, what a disappointment you have been to me. Was it your mother who ruined you so? "I see. And you, who grew up in our household after the death of your father, you to whom I gave freedom and a start in your career, you would make Cnaeus publicly shame his family because I could not give you money for a bridge?"

Daedalus gave the praetor a smile more chilling than his former anger. "There is no need for such histrionics, Scipio. I know you will give me no reason to let slip your family secrets." The young architect picked up the Anatolian chalice and, placing it on the small table next to him, spun the cup on its base across the table surface.

Hispallus leaped forward and snatched the cup away. The table, whose top was constructed of the finest imported hardwoods laid out in the signs of the zodiac, was one of his most prized possessions. He glared at Daedalus.

"You will find the money, Scipio," Daedalus said with a smirk. He went to the bronze doors and looked back at the praetor. "One more thing. Do not have your lictors follow me in order to send their knives up my back in some alley. I have an associate who knows what I am doing. Should I not return to him, he will, within a day, post announcements of your wife's activities all over Rome. I will speak to you again in two days—"

"No! I . . . I have duties as a decemvir sacris faciundis. I cannot possibly find the money so soon."

"Ah, yes. You've become a politician-priest now. You know, if you did sponsor my bridge, you could, in truth, become a pontifex."

"I do not find this sacrilegious talk amusing."

"*Vale,* then, Scipio. Send word to the Taberna Romana when you have the money. Then we will speak again." With confident steps, Daedalus left the tablinum.

Hispallus sat heavily on his ivory curule chair of office. *Iupiter help me. First I feared I would have no glory. Now I must fear infamy instead. There is property I could sell, but it would doubtless take longer than the time he will give me. He must have known the trouble this would cause me—he must have wanted it. Why? And why didn't I see that this could happen. Why didn't I stop Clodia while I could—*

"Magistrate?" Marcus stuck his head into the room. "Are you ready to see another guest?"

"In a moment," Hispallus said, rubbing his face. "Come in and close the door behind you, Marcus."

The secretary did so and approached the praetor with concern. "My Lord, are you all right?"

"Mmm? Merely worried, Marcus. The young man who was just here needs funding for his project and I feel . . . compelled to give him what aid I can. Yet my own assets are tied up. Any suggestions?"

"Could others of your family not lend you the money, Magistrate?"

Hispallus shook his head. "The other Scipios would think it a folly to spend so much for a bridge. They would want to know why, and for private reasons I prefer to keep that to myself."

"Well, my Lord, you have many *clientes* who owe you favors."

"Yes, but they usually come to me for money, not the other way around. *Clientes,* as a rule, are not wealthy people."

"Hmmm. There are wealthy foreigners who fall under your jurisdiction. Perhaps for one reason or another you could coerce one into assisting you. I have heard stories of wealthy widows who come to Rome to spend extravagantly, and to be courted by estate hounds. Just a little while ago, I overheard one of your guests out there speaking of such a woman—a Greek lady who apparently has money to throw away on philosophers and other riffraff. He claims it was she who sent him to you."

"Really? Send the fellow in. Perhaps he has useful information."

"Yes, my Lord."

Marcus left and returned quickly, followed by a short, fair-haired man whose face beamed with excitement. "Paraithos of Megara, my Lord," said Marcus, who then leaned against a wall with his arms crossed on his chest.

"Welcome, Paraithos. I—"

"It is as foretold!" Paraithos exclaimed, dropping down on one knee and raising his eyes toward the heavens. "The stars told me I would soon be in the presence of the most wise and powerful man in Rome, and it has come to pass!"

"Perhaps you have confused me with someone else," said Hispallus with a wry grin. *And I would not clothe children in such transparent flattery.*

"No, my Lord Magistrate, the stars do not mislead. You are a Scipio, are you not? Then I am well guided and Fate has brought us both to this meeting."

"No doubt. I have a question for you, Paraithos."

"Ask anything, Magistrate. But, of course, it will be the divine stars that answer. I am only their vessel of instruction."

Hispallus frowned and rubbed his chin. "What manner of philosophy is this that makes the stars to be gods?"

"It is the ancient wisdom of the Chaldeans, my Lord. They who first watched the movement of the heavens and learned of the awesome truths the stars have to offer Man. And I am a chosen descendant of those Chaldeans."

Hispallus looked the man over. "Megara is a Greek city, the last I had heard. And you seem too fair to be Babylonian."

"In spirit, my Lord, in spirit! The knowledge has spread through Greece and made all those who accept its truths Chaldeans."

"I see."

"Have I answered your question well, my Lord?"

"Actually, I had intended to ask something else. Marcus has told me that you were sent to me by a Greek woman of wealth. Tell me about her."

"Ah. A kind woman, if misguided, my Lord. She lives on the Aventine, and is quite old, yet seems to have kept her health. She is always veiled, though, so it is hard to tell. Anyway, she says she will pay a great sum of money to anyone who can answer a certain riddle. The riddle is: 'How can stone be brought to life?'"

"And could your stars answer this riddle for her?"

"They answered, my Lord, but the Domina Euryale was not satisfied with the reply. Her elderly maidservant nearly laughed me out of the house. Stones come to life in the natural order of things, being ground by wind and rain into the earth that sustains life. But the Domina said this reply was not useful to her, whatever that means. Yet she was kind enough to give me a small sum for my pains and suggest I come to you. In this, she was wise indeed, for what magistrate does not need an astrologer to advise him of the path Fate has laid for him?"

This magistrate does not, thought Hispallus. "There is only one piece of advice I would ask of you, Paraithos. Do you think this woman—Euryale, did you call her?—would she be willing to give money to support another project other than this riddle of hers?"

A sly look came into the astrologer's eyes. "And it was foretold that your first need of advice would be concerning money. I can tell you the best source, my Lord. "He leaned forward. "There is a man on the Via Latina by the name of Culeus, who has helped many with such a problem."

Marcus coughed loudly behind his hand.

"Marcus?" Hispallus glanced at his secretary who came forward and whispered in the praetor's ear.

"My Lord, I have heard of this Culeus. He is a notorious moneylender who has been the sorrow of other nobiles. Don't fall into his trap."

Hispallus cleared his throat. "I see. My problem, Paraithos, would be best solved by someone other than a money-lender. And I see that advice would be best sought from someone other than an astrologer. You are dismissed. Fare you well."

The astrologer stood frowning, looking back and forth from Marcus to Hispallus. "Culeus, of course, had jealous rivals who slander him—"

"Enough, Paraithos. Get you gone."

With an exasperated snort, the astrologer turned and walked out the doors, his quick steps echoing away in the atrium beyond.

"Should he, perhaps, be arrested?" asked Marcus.

"For what? Giving bad advice? Of that charge, Marcus, half of Rome could be found guilty. No, forget him. Instead I want you to seek out this Domina Euryale and have her come to see me three days hence."

"Yes, my Lord. Shall I send in another guest now?"

"Is there one out there who is a friend, or even a close relative?"

"No, Magistrate. I believe your friends and relatives have all gone to the house of Aemilianus to welcome him home."

"Yes, I see." Hispallus rubbed his face and covered his eyes. "I understand."

SECVNDVS

D EINO PUSHED A STRAND OF GREY HAIR back from her face as she shuffled quickly into her lady's tablinum. She squinted and saw, with her blurred eyesight, that the other servants had finished setting the furnishings. In the center of the room stood a large bronze brazier, whose three legs had been cast in the form of entwined serpents. In its bowl were heaped glowing coals to help banish the chill evening drafts. Between the brazier and the front entry stood an elegantly carved chair. This indicated that a female guest was expected—if the witch they awaited were male, a cushioned couch would have been set out instead. Between the brazier and the far wall stood a tall screen with a cedarwood frame and panels of polished white chalcedony. Oil lamps of bronze hung in the corners of the room, illuminating frescos of pastoral scenes on the walls.

The rustle of shifting fabric came from behind the screen and Deino realized her lady must already be present. Clearing her ancient throat, Deino approached the screen.

"Who is there?" Euryale's low, musical voice called from behind the screen. "Deino?"

"Yes, Despoina Euryale."

"What is it? Has the Marsi witch arrived?"

"No, not yet. But a messenger came with a letter."

"A letter? From near or far?"

"From here in Rome, Despoina. It is from the praetor peregrinus, Scipio Hispallus."

"A praetor? What would such an exalted personage want with us? Let me guess—there is to be some new law concerning what foreigners can wear in Rome, or where we might live, nai?"

Deino unfolded the papyrus in her gnarled hands. From a pocket of her peplos, she took a large, scratched crystal lens. She looked at it a moment, then shook off the horrid memories the lens evoked in her. Holding the lens before one eye, Deino scanned the note. "No, Despoina. The praetor wishes to invite you to his home, to discuss 'matters of mutual interest.'"

"Oh? As I recall, the main concerns of Roman magistrates are war, politics and the chastity of their women. Hardly interests of mine."

"He says you may be in a position to achieve recognition for your contributions to the greater glory of Rome."

"Ah. It's money he wants, then. A donation toward his reelection, or another call for aid to legions hard-pressed in foreign lands. A pity I shall have to disappoint him."

"Yes, Despoina. I'll send the usual excuses."

"No, Deino. It would not do to snub him. Our position in Rome is precarious enough. No, invite him here instead. Cite my 'infirmity' as the reason."

Deino allowed herself a smile. "Yes, Despoina. What day should I suggest?"

"Whatever day he has chosen, or the nearest auspicious day. You know my schedule."

"Yes— Ah!" Deino started, hearing the bell at the gate.

"Well, if Tyche smiles, that will be our witch. Go show her in, Deino. Hurry, now. I hear witches can be frightful when crossed." There was laughter in Euryale's voice, but Deino's misgivings prevented her from joining in her lady's amusement.

The old woman turned and walked as swiftly as her aching bones would take her through the colonnaded atrium. At the far doorway, Caecus, who was fully blind but knew the house well, was leading in a tall, thin woman.

"Are you the Marsi witch?" said Deino, putting the lens to her eye.

The woman drew herself up and stared imperiously. "I am Simaetha saga magica. I trust you are not the Domina Euryale."

Deino frowned and noted that below the deep folds of the witch's palla, Simaetha's eyes were a bit too wild and bright. *Hah,* thought Deino, *are you one of those reckless Dionysians or did you need some mystic potion to give you courage?* "I am not. I am her maidservant Deino."

"That you are still a maid at your age does not surprise me. Take me to your domina forthwith, or face my wrath for your delay."

They are all so proud, these magi that my despoina consults. So proud and so useless. Why does Euryale bother? "This way," Deino snapped. Dismissing Caecus, she turned and led the witch into the tablinum.

Euryale had moved the screen and sat openly, but completely veiled, on the far chair.

"The magia Simaetha, Domina," Deino announced with distaste and stood aside.

"Welcome, Simaetha," said Euryale. "Please be comfortable and tell me of yourself." She gestured toward the other chair.

But Simaetha did not sit. The witch pulled back the palla from her head to reveal a mass of unkempt, unbound hair. Deino noticed something strange about her untamed tresses and squinted to see more clearly. There among the snarly locks were the skins of snakes twisted around the witch's head.

Blasphemy! thought Deino, with a sharp intake of breath. She clenched her teeth and fought to keep her anger hidden. She looked at Euryale but the veil hid whatever reaction her lady might have.

Simaetha walked slowly back and forth in front of Euryale like a lioness examining suspicious prey. "Why are you veiled, Domina? Do you fear my evil eye?"

Ha! thought Deino. *Rather you should fear hers, you insolent harpy.*

"Not at all, Simaetha," said Euryale.

The witch paused. "Are you a priestess, Domina?"

"I once held that honor."

"What god did you serve, and where?"

"I served the goddess of my people, in Epeiros, near Thessaly."

"Thessaly?" Simaetha hissed.

So, thought Deino, *you think perhaps my lady is a rival witch, from the country famed for witches, eh? Do you fear that she will test your power? Well, I will not tell you otherwise. I'll let you sweat.*

"If you are from Thessaly, why do you call upon me?" asked Simaetha.

"Even the skill of Thessalian witches was not enough to help me. It would seem their reputation has been enhanced by distance and legend."

"Ah, and your goddess bade you to search in the hills of the Marsi for the powerful one you seek."

"My heart bids me seek everywhere for one who knows the answer to my question."

Simaetha gave a knowing nod. Suddenly, she turned and pointed at Deino. "You! Have you dreamed lately?"

Taken aback by the question, Deino said, "Well, yes. I dreamed this past night of an owl flying across a river, an olive branch in its talons."

"You see, Domina. Hecate herself has sent your servant a vision, saying that She of the night shall send one to bring peace to your soul."

Fool! thought Deino, *any Roman worth his amulets thinks the owl is an ill omen. And it is truly ill for my despoina, as the owl is a bird of Athena, who torments her so. The dream bodes ill indeed, if she chooses to listen to you, you Esquiline bitch.*

"Yes, perhaps an auspicious sign, Simaetha," said Euryale. "Which brings us to the question at hand. Can you turn stone into living flesh?"

Simaetha raised her thin arms dramatically toward the ceiling. "Domina, you see before you one with the power to command the winds of the skies and the waters of the seas. I can call the stars from the heavens, bring the moon down from the sky and conjure the daemons from the depths of Hades. Shades of the dead speak their oracles at my command and—"

"Yes, yes, I know all that," Euryale said gently, "but can you bring stone to life?"

Simaetha lowered her arms and glared at Euryale's veiled form. "The gods know there is nothing I cannot do. But tell me, for such a simple question you might ask a philosopher or an alchemist. Clearly there is more to this matter than mere transformation of substance. Is this a matter of healing? A matter of . . . love?"

Hmph, thought Deino. *Perhaps there is some intelligence to this creature after all.*

Euryale replied, "Your surmise is close to the truth, Simaetha."

"Ah! That is why you have summoned me, for spells of healing and love are a specialty of the Marsi witches."

Deino rolled her eyes heavenward and sighed.

"I am pleased to have my information confirmed," said Euryale. "So, since you have implied that you can accomplish this, please tell me by what methods you would turn stone to flesh."

The witch paused, warily. "Since you have not yet contracted me to your service, Domina, I am not obligated to reveal to you my secrets."

Euryale sighed. "The gist of it then, if you please. And speak carefully, for from your words I shall weigh your knowledge and skill."

Simaetha gave Euryale a measuring stare. "Very well. Listen, then, and judge me as you will.

"First, certain herbs must be gathered when the moon is dark, and others when it is in its fullness. These, along with the proper parts of bats and dogs, along with the ground bones of those who have died for love, shall be given into flames consecrated to Hecate.

"Then we must have blood in abundance, for flesh without blood is lifeless as stone, therefore stone requires blood for life. We will find a young boy, a patrician would be best. Then we will bind him, and place delicious food before him, but not allow him to eat. Slowly we will drain the blood from him and bathe the stone in it, and his hunger shall become the hunger of love transferred to the stone. Then we will cut out the seat of his soul, his liver, and—"

"Enough!" Euryale stood, her fists clenched. "I'll hear no more of this murder. I'll not waste a life to gain one. Begone! And be glad I do not inform the authorities of your evil."

Simaetha's eyes narrowed as she flung her palla back over her head. "So. You do not have the courage for true witchcraft. I will go. But for your insults you shall hear my curse."

Deino saw Euryale's hand stray toward her veil and Deino gasped in anticipation.

"Go on," Simaetha taunted. "Show me the face you hide behind your veil. Let your eyes meet mine and feel their power."

But Euryale's hand paused, then dropped. "Curse me all you will, Simaetha. I am already cursed by the gods themselves. You can do no worse."

Deino rushed to Euryale's side and placed an arm around her shoulders. To the witch she said, "Begone, and be grateful my Despoina has spared you. You would find the gaze of her eyes far worse—"

"That is enough, Deino," Euryale said wearily.

Simaetha stared, frowning, at Euryale for long moments. Then, without a word of farewell, the witch turned and walked out. Deino did not deign to escort her to the gate.

Euryale stood bowed, her hands kneading the wool of her stola. "I could not do it, Deino. Not even for love. I'll have no more ghosts to haunt my dreams."

"I understand, Despoina. You made the wisest choice."

"I only hope *he* would understand." Euryale sighed. "I will go walk in the garden, Deino. I will see no one else today." She turned and left by a side door that led to the garden path.

Deino did not follow. She only shook her head and sighed. *Ah, Despoina, he understands nothing, and it would be best if you could leave it so.* Taking a nearby ewer, she poured water on the coals in the brazier. With a mighty sigh to match her own, the coals released a writhing, grey column of smoke and steam. With the rising mists, Deino sent a silent prayer.

TERTIVS

MORE ENTANGLEMENTS, thought Scipio Hispallus, as he watched his lictor run back across the mosaic-tiled plaza, delivering his reply to the servant of Euryale. The lictor spoke briefly to a squinty-eyed boy at the edge of the plaza and the boy turned and ran off. *I had hoped to handle this discreetly. Now I learn that because of her age and infirmity, I must go to Euryale myself.* Shaking his head, Hispallus readjusted the fold of his toga that covered his greying head.

Hispallus felt footsore, weary and cold. Februarius was a month of purification, in prepetration for the new year which, in older calendars, had begun in Martis. It had been no surprise that the Sibylline Oracles, which his college of priests had the honor to consult, had called for an amburbium. But this ritual procession of priests and citizens around the walls of the city had only made Hispallus more acutely aware of his age. He had spent the long walk brooding on his problems rather than praying to the gods for the cleansing of Rome's evils. *Mars, forgive this former soldier. I have different battles to fight now.*

In the middle of the plaza stood an enormous marble altar, already prepared with boughs and coals for burning. Beyond the far edge of the plaza rose the stairs to the Temple of Jupiter Capitolinus. This most ancient and revered of Rome's temples dominated the hilltop, as well as the city itself, its triangular roof thrusting into the pale sky like a blunt spearhead.

The members of the procession arranged themselves around the altar. The six Vestal Virgins, dressed in stolas of brilliant white wool, stood on the temple steps. The sixteen *flamines,* caretakers of the temples, wearing their pointed caps and laurel wreaths, stood around the edge of the plaza. The sixteen augurs stood, heads draped with their togas, in the southeast corner of the plaza. The Pontifex Maximus brought forward a torch and lit the boughs on the altar.

At this signal, Hispallus and the other nine members of the decemviri came toward the altar, bringing the victims to be sacrificed; an ox for Jupiter, a pig for Juno and a sheep for Minerva. A slave with a huge mallet struck each animal forcefully on the forehead. As each went down, a pontifice came forward with a knife and a bowl to drain the blood.

Hispallus felt strangely detached from the proceedings. No awe for the gods, no pride in taking part in this event filled his spirit. He was aware of the movement of people around him, and he appreciated the warmth of the altar fire, but he performed his own duties as if walking in his sleep.

Hispallus helped the pontifex mix the blood of each animal with milk, honey and wine. Three silver bowls, each filled with the sacred mixture, were set upon the altar. The pontifex raised his arms in prayer, Hispallus and the other decemviri did likewise. The prayers were not said aloud. Such aspects of the state religion were state secrets, as was the identity of the true patron god of Rome and the true name of the city itself. Who knew what foreign sorcerer might use the knowledge to gain mastery over the Republic? Hispallus had doubts this was possible, but he put it from his mind. Now, when the priests wished to gain the attention of the gods, was not a good time for heretical thoughts.

As the pontifex poured the contents into the altar fire, the only prayer in Hispallus's mind was *Gods, grant me wisdom. How I surely need it.*

Huge, foul-smelling plumes of white smoke billowed out of the charred wood as each silver bowl was emptied. This ended the ritual, and Hispallus was about to turn away, when a bright flash of light on the altar caught his attention. He narrowed his eyes and thought he saw, within the smoke, a great white owl with black eyes like coals staring at him. Above the hiss and crackle of the fire, a harsh female voice whispered, "Beware, Hispallus! Beware the serpent's eyes! Two faces has a coin, and two has Janus. Blood and treachery stains what money buys!" The owl then faded and disappeared.

Hispallus stared into the smoke until his eyes teared, but he saw no more manifestations and the voice did not speak again. He felt a hand on his shoulder and looked around. A cowled augur stood beside him. Beneath the folds of the hood, Hispallus recognized the handsome face of Scipio Aemilianus, which now wore a frown of concern.

"Did you see the owl, cousin?" Hispallus whispered. "Did you hear it?"

"I saw nothing, cousin. But I grew concerned at the way you stared at the fire."

The pontifex turned from the altar and stared at them both. "What is this disturbance?"

Before Hispallus could replay, Aemilianus said, "The good praetor was overcome with smoke, but he has recovered."

The pontifex narrowed his eyes. "Did he not say he saw something?"

Hispallus paused. Any irregularity would mean the entire ritual would have to be redone. If the vision was deemed a divine visitation, it would have to be shared with all of Rome, for it occurred during a ceremony of state. His life would be closely examined to determine why the gods would grant him such an honor. "No, pontifex. I only felt dizzy from the smoke."

"Of course," Aemilianus put in, "I do not think a mere *decemvir sacrorum* would see anything of importance in fire. They see their oracles in books, not smoke." This elicited mild laughter from some near bystanders and the face of the pontifex darkened more.

"Must we begin the rites again?" called out one priest.

Hispallus's legs ached at the thought of taking a new ox, pig and sheep for another walk around the city.

"The ceremony had ended before I spoke with my cousin," Aemilianus said. "I see no reason that his discomfort should bring trouble to the rest of us. I have no doubts that the gods are satisfied with our efforts. Let us be done and declare the city sanctified for the year!"

A few cheers came from the assembled citizens and priests. The pontifex growled, "This is a holy altar, not the Rostrum of the Forum." He looked to the Vestal Virgins, the eldest of whom nodded her head and held open her hands. "Then it is done!" thundered the pontifex, and he swiftly strode away from the altar.

For once, Hispallus was grateful for the great popularity of Aemilianus. "I owe you thanks, cousin."

Aemilianus smiled. "I presumed to imagine that if the gods have chosen to give you hints and portents, they were for you alone, else we would all have seen them. And what the gods intend for you, the world need not know, eh?"

"No, Aemilianus, indeed not."

After a pause, Aemilianus went on, "I have heard rumors that all is not well with your family. I sincerely hope the gods have given you guidance. If you should ever care to discuss this smoke-reverie, and the problems it attends on, you'll find me a most attentive listener."

"I will remember, cousin." But as Aemilianus squeezed his arm in farewell and walked away, Hispallus thought, *Do you think I could speak frankly of my shame to one so highly favored by Rome and Fate? By Pollux, may it never come to that.*

QVARTVS

Sevisus ran down the Capitoline Hill toward the Forum Romanum, his wool cloak billowing out behind him. He dodged colorful blurs and dark shapes, repeating the praetor's reply to himself to memorize it. One more errand to run for the Domina and then he might spend an *as* or two for a sweetcake or some fish pickle. He squinted out over the red-titled rooftops, bringing the streets into sufficient focus to choose his route, then continued on to the dark level of the streets.

Here he slowed a bit, listening for the clatter of horse hooves or the cries of rich men's runners. The streets were narrow, and an approaching chariot or litter meant a leap to the walls or else be overrun. The overhanging upper stories of the shops and houses presented dangers as well, as various pieces of crockery and the contents of slopjars might come flying out of the windows onto the heads of those below. Sevisus didn't mind the hazards. There were rewards to be had for even such mundanely dangerous errands.

He paused at an intersection to get his bearings. From his left came the thick, sweet odor of grapes and vinegar, marking the presence of a wineseller. From his right came the faint acrid odor of a cloth fuller's shop. Knowing he was on the right street, Sevisus continued. He stopped at the entrance to a dim, even narrower alley whose walls seemed a channel for the strident voices of orators in the nearby Forum. With an expectant smile, he stepped into the alley. Though it took him out of the way, Sevisus could not pass this street by.

Midway up the alley, amid the moneylenders, ironmongers, cobblers and bakers, was a particular stall to which Sevisus was drawn like a fly to honey. The stall belonged to Joseph the Bookseller, and to Sevisus it was the most magical place in Rome. He leaned his elbows on the front counter of the stall and stared dreamily at the shelves in the back. They were crammed to the rafters with papyrus scrolls, wax tablets and leafed paper codices in every language in the known world, or so Sevisus imagined.

The Domina had only one library and it was small. But it contained books of many languages, including a roll of picture-writing that Deino told him was from Egypt. It was in this library that Deino had taught Sevisus to read, explaining that it would make him more useful. And it was there that Sevisus had found a book of philosophy. Sevisus had been enamored of books ever since.

"Ho, there! You! Get your filthy arms off my— Oh, it's you, Sevisus." Old Joseph came bustling down the stall, his wiry black and grey hair and beard sticking out from his face like the rays of a dark sun. "Has your domina decided what book she wants yet?"

It had been a convenient fiction when Sevisus had first found this place to claim that his owner wished a book. By now he was sure Joseph knew it was Sevisus himself who was the hopeful customer, but the bookseller was too kind to say so.

"No, sir. Please tell me what you have in stock today, so that I can help her decide."

Joseph gave a broad smile that made the corners of his dark eyes crinkle. "Today we have a copy of 'Mostellaria' by Plautus, if your lady enjoys drama. And some works of Pacuvius and Accius. I have a rare copy of the work of Anaxagoras, and a book of Plato's philosophy by Dionysius. And I have a somewhat used copy of Cato's 'De Agricultura,' if your lady ever decides to own a large estate. Also, I happen to have the latest verses of Terence. And there is a volume of the *Histories* of Polybius. Do any of these interest you?"

"They all do!"

Joseph smiled again. "God blesses those who read by giving their minds the eyes to see the world. Here, I will give you something. Does your lady like riddles?"

Sevisus nodded. He knew of only one riddle that interested his Domina, but he liked them a great deal.

"Here is a scrap, sold to me by an astrologer down on his luck. I have been unable to sell it, though." Joseph bent down to rummage in some hidden shelves beneath the counter. Sevisus leaned over and got a glimpse of edge-worn papyrus before the bookseller had rolled it in a clean linen rag. "It may be nothing, but perhaps it will bring joy to someone, eh?" Tying a piece of yarn around the roll, he presented the gift to Sevisus as if the boy were an honored patrician customer.

"Thank you." Sevisus held the gift close to his chest.

"You're quite welcome," Joseph murmured. Then, louder, "Be off with you, boy! Can't have non-buying layabouts like you taking me away from honest customers."

"Yes, sir." Sevisus grinned and left the alley, placing his treasure in a pocket of his tunic. He ached to look at it, but there was one more errand to be done before he could take time for himself.

He hurried down the broad Street of the Etruscans, whose sides were lined with every kind of merchant's shop: perfume sellers and silk merchants, fruiters and bakers and fishmongers. It was said that the merchants of this street were so full of eager avarice that they would probably sell themselves, given the chance.

His sandals slapping the flat paving stones, Sevisus trotted past the Palatine Hill topped by the temple of the eastern goddess Cybele. The avenue curved west past the Great Altar and narrowed, losing itself among four-story tenement houses. If Sevisus had turned south, he would have come to the Circus Maximus. But the boy had no interest in the place or the Games . . . he had gone once, only to see distant blurs moving about in the midst of spreading scarlet stains.

Instead, Sevisus continued west, stepping watchfully. The walls of the tenements leaned precariously over the street, blocking all sunlight. The air was redolent with the smells of close-packed humanity and the nearby cattle market. Children in ragged tunics watched him pass, their eyes wide. He could almost feel their envy. The fact that he served a wealthy household was obvious by the garments he wore.

Sevisus hurried on, rounding the small Temple of Hercules Victor. Beyond this he came upon the muddy Tiber, which flowed swiftly with meltwater from the far-off mountains.

Following along the southwestern curve of the river, Sevisus came to a group of ramshackle houses clinging to the bank. It did not take him long to find the door he sought. Even if he had not been there before, and even if there had not been the symbol of a snake biting its tail on the lintel, the house of the alchemist Olerus was distinctive by its rotten-egg, sulfurous smell. Sevisus knocked on the weathered wooden door.

The man who answered the door seemed more like a baker than a scholar, large and round and sweaty and jovial, but Sevisus liked the alchemist all the better for it. "Sevisus! Good to see you! Come in, my boy!"

"Thank you, sir." Sevisus stepped within, surprised to find the house nearly as dark and gloomy as the last time he had visited—which had been at night.

"Have a seat and rest awhile." Olerus pushed Sevisus amiably to a bench beside a rough-hewn table. "No doubt you've come to find out how I am proceeding on your Domina's problem."

"Yes, sir." As Sevisus sat, a plate of bread, cheese and sausage was placed in front of him. He wished he felt like gobbling up the food, but the atmosphere seemed to chase away his appetite. He heard someone moving in the shadows across the room, and he squinted in the darkness. He knew in that direction lay a wall covered top to bottom in shelves filled with books—it had made him burn with envy when he first saw it.

Then a figure entered what few rays of dim afternoon sunlight penetrated the room. He seemed tall to Sevisus, and his eyes were dark. His hair and beard were black and curly and thick, and cut square at the ends. His robe was long and had a multicolored yoke and sleeve edgings. He sat slowly across the table from Sevisus and said, with a slight accent, "Greetings and good afternoon, young man."

"Afternoon, sir."

"Decided to join us, have you?" Olerus said to the newcomer. He sat heavily on the other side of Sevisus's bench. "Archidemus, may I present Sevisus, a most intelligent servant of the Domina Euryale. Sevisus, this is my house guest Archidemus." Leaning confidentially closer, he added, "He's a *Chaldean*."

"I'm . . . honored to meet you, magus. Are you an astrologer?"

"Worse than that," Olerus muttered. "He's a Stoic."

Archidemus smiled gently. "While it is true that astrologers tend to be called 'Chaldeans,' not all Chaldeans are astrologers. Though I am cognizant of the movements of stars and planets, I do not tell fortunes by them."

"But you are a sorcerer, are you not, magus?"

"I am a teacher." Archidemus looked away. "That is to say, I once was."

"What happened?"

"My homeland has been overrun, Sevisus. Parthians have captured Chaldea. They have little respect for priests or philosophers. My school in Nineveh was destroyed a year ago. I have come to Rome seeking a better place for my teaching."

"I'm sorry, magus." But along with the pity, Sevisus felt some disappointment. "Then, you are not really a magus, are you?"

Archidemus raised an eyebrow, then smiled. "It is danger-ous to make such quick assumptions, young man. I believe I am entitled to that address. You see, I am a theurge."

"A what?"

"A heretic, boy," Olerus cheerfully put in. "He summons gods in order to speak to them. Damned hubris, if you ask me."

Sevisus frowned, a memory begging his attention. "I remember reading that Stoics have no gods . . . they are atheists. How can you summon what you do not believe in?"

He felt a nudge from Olerus's elbow. "Don't get him started, lad. He'll talk your ear off with his philosophy."

Archidemus ignored the alchemist's jibe and answered, "That is a common misconception, but your source is in error. Stoicism teaches there is a divine power in all things, though it may take different forms. This power has always been and will always be, and it makes all things in the universe one. Is this not similar to your own learning, Olerus?"

The alchemist grunted.

Archidemus went on, "We simply choose not to personify the divine powers, as the Hellenic and Roman faiths do. To us, Thoth, Serapis, Enki, Vohu-Manah, Ganesha, Athena and the alchemical Hermes Trismegistus are all visions of the same informing spirit. I became one with this spirit through ritual, while you achieved this state by poring over your books, but it is the same thing."

"So that is why you are not an astrologer," Sevisus said. "To you the stars are not really gods, as some say, but only parts of a bigger god."

"The sun, the moon, the stars and planets with their heav-enly fire are certainly the most impressive manifestation of the divine power. But they are so distant from our world, their movement so grand in comparison with the mortal reckoning of time, that it seems ludicrous that they should be tied to our petty concerns below. If I could predict the movement of these dust motes," Archidemus placed his hand in the ruddy shaft of sunlight, "they might tell me more of the future of human affairs, at least in this vicinity. But even the mathematics of my people could not calculate exactly where these motes will be in the next hour, let alone a month or a year. You seem a bright lad, Sevisus. What brings you to this bookworm's lair?"

Sevisus noticed fuzzily out of the corner of his eye that Olerus was giving him a dissuading scowl. But the alchemist clearly had no answers to the Domina's problem yet, else he would have said so already. And Sevisus could not help hoping the foreign magus might be more knowledgeable. "My owner, the Domina Euryale, has a question to which she seeks an answer."

"From alchemy?"

"From any science, magus. She wished to know how one might turn stone to living flesh."

Archidemus leaned forward, stroking his beard. "A . . . challenging question, to be sure."

"And one aptly suited for alchemy," said Olerus. "It is clearly a mere matter of transformation."

"Ah, have you then solved this riddle?" Archidemus asked.

"I am proceeding toward a solution, you might say. Well you might say, for I am sure it will involve water and earth somehow."

"I see. Is your Domina a philosopher, Sevisus? Why does she ask this question?"

"I truly do not know, magus. Though I have lived and worked in her house for some years now, I know little about her. She is always veiled, so I have never seen her face. She rarely goes out or has visitors. All of us who serve her are close-sighted or blind, even Deino who's been with her forever, it seems. The Domina has a special little temple for the worship of her family gods that no one but her may enter. And at night, when she thinks no one watches, she speaks to a statue in the garden."

"Truly? What does she say to it?"

"I have not dared to go close enough to hear, magus."

Olerus began to chuckle and his belly shook. Suddenly he burst into roaring laughter. "So! The lady has fallen in love with some carved Adonis and would have me bring him to life for her. Well, well!"

Archidemus frowned. "I think the situation is more complex than that. I would like to speak to your Domina, Sevisus. Do you think she would agree to an audience with me?"

"This is not your sort of problem!" Olerus objected.

"If you are certain of that," said Archidemus, "then there is no reason to think me a rival in this matter. Well, Sevisus?"

"I will tell her of your interest, magus. I'm sure she'll be pleased to speak with you."

"You will, of course, also tell Euryale," Olerus said sternly, "that I will soon have her answer and she need not seek further."

"I will tell her of your progress, sir. If you will excuse me, I'd better be getting home. I've heard the residents of this neighborhood become quite . . . unfriendly after dark." Sevisus rose to leave.

"Don't forget! And—" Olerus stood, the bench beneath him groaning with relief, and put a paternal arm around the boy. "Tell her if we can't make her statue return her affections, I'll make her a nice homunculus that will serve her as sweetly as she could wish. Tell her, eh?"

"Yes, sir."

"There's a good lad. Good evening to you."

"And to you, sir. And you, magus." Sevisus stepped into the dying sunlight and hurried toward the Aventine hill and home. He could hardly wait to give the Domina the pleasing news. She might reward him generously. Perhaps he might have the evening off, and get a chance to see what the bookseller's gift might be.

QVINTVS

INTEMPESTE NOCTE

SIMAETHA SAT BOLT UPRIGHT IN HER BED, her heart a pounding drum in her chest. Wind rattled the thin wooden walls around her, shrieked through the cracks in the roof. But Simaetha was still entranced by the spell of her dream—lost in the cries of night owls and the flash of shimmering scales. It was not the chilling drafts that set her hair on end.

"Hecate, can it be? Are the visions you send me true?" she whispered. Throwing aside her blanket, Simaetha jumped from her bed, her thin stola fluttering around her. She staggered in the dark to a table in the middle of the hovel. Her hands scrabbled around the table top like startled crabs until they found a cluster of chicken bones near one corner. Simaetha raised the bones, then let them fall. Carefully she felt the table top to determine in what pattern the bones had fallen.

"Yes!" she breathed, as her hands gave her the answer. "So. The Domina Euryale is more than a witch. What power you offer me, Hecate. What temptation to a healer and a sorceress. Do you test your servant?" Simaetha shuddered and groped about the room for her palla. Finding instead her worn wool cloak, Simaetha wrapped herself in it and sat upon the bed.

If the Domina Euryale is as you have shown me, Hecate. I might become the greatest of witches. My people will have

*power far beyond that of the priests of Athens or Rome. Is this
what you offer your servant, Hecate? Then I will not fail you.*
Banishing sleep from her mind, Simaetha sat long into the
night lost in thought.

Cnaeus, Hispallus the Younger, felt no cold himself,
blanketed as he was by the warm haze of wine in the blood. The
noise from the last of the drunken brawls in the taberna below
his garret had ended, and all felt peaceful and calm. Through
a small window, he gazed up at the lights of the homes on the
Palatine Hill—their flickering lamp and torchlight shining
like stars come down to earth. *Somewhere up there sits my
father. I wonder if he is working late. I wonder if he thinks of
me, or have I shamed him so that he forgets he has a son?*

Cnaeus heard the door behind him open and he swung his
head around. "Daedalus?"

The young architect's face, pale as he entered into the dim
lamplight, responded with a tight smile. "Cnaeus, this is unfair of you! You have started without me."

"You're late," Cnaeus accused with a wavering finger.

"I have a career to look after."

"Is that a slap at me because I do not?"

"Nonsense," said Daedalus, pulling up a stool beside the
window and sitting. "I'm merely envious of your idleness."

Cnaeus coughed a laugh. "Since when have you envied
me, my favorite of Fortune? Looking at us now, who would
guess which is the former slave and which is the son of a great
patrician? But don't keep me waiting. Is my father going to pay
for your bridge?"

"Yes, I believe he is, one way or another."

"Ha!" Cnaeus slapped his leg. "I knew it. I told you he
would think of you as another son and treat you like one. You
are well on your way to wealth and fame, my friend. When
they make you an *eques* and give you the gold ring, will you
accept me as your poor, humble client?"

"There is no need for such talk, Cnaeus. Your turn for Fortune will come."

"You forget, Daedalus, I have been censured by the Senate for the 'disgraceful life' I have led. That is doom to the public life of any man."

"Don't be so morose. They merely turned you down for the one post. You didn't really wish to be propraetor in farther Hispania, did you?"

"I hear the weather in Gades is excellent this time of year. No, Daedalus, you are fated to rise above me. At our deaths, your ashes will be entombed in a grand mausoleum of your own design. I, however, will be found pickled by wine beneath a table in the taberna downstairs. I shall die so full of spirits, I will haunt this place forever."

"Stop this. I tell you what, Cnaeus, I will see that one of the statues adorning my bridge is modeled after you. Then you will have immortality. How does that sound?"

"Would you?" Cnaeus broke into a grin. "Which god or hero would you make me? I'm not old and stern enough for Jupiter. I haven't the form for Hercules or Mars. There's only one choice of course . . . I'll be Bacchus!"

Daedalus scowled and stood suddenly, knocking over his stool. He turned away from Cnaeus and paced into a dark corner. "Don't mock me!" he growled.

"I . . . I meant no offense, Daedalus," said Cnaeus, reaching out an unsteady hand. "I'm sorry. I keep forgetting you suffer from my mother's strange practices too. I remember you told me once you had actually watched one of her rites. You were a braver child than I. The screams and noises were bad enough for me—I always ran and hid under my bed."

"Enough!"

Cnaeus turned back to the window and its Palatine view. "He deserves a better wife, Daedalus. You asked me once whether I might denounce my father, tell the Senate how he condoned my mother's rites, in order to regain some status as a good citizen. I'd never do it, Daedalus. All these years he could have had me imprisoned, sold into slavery, even executed for all the disgrace I've brought him." Cnaeus shook his head. "But he has not. Instead, he sends a lictor by from time to time with a little money and questions as to how I'm faring. Then he lets me be. And now he willingly gives aid to your career, so it is as though you never lost a father. He deserves a better wife . . . and a better son." This last ended in a whisper.

"Silence!" Daedalus hissed. "Let us speak of something else."

SEXTVS

Hispallus was bounced and jostled in his litter as his slaves bore him down the Palatine Hill. He had hoped to make this visit as discreet as possible, but certain rules of decorum had to be followed. Before his litter, six lictors and several *clientes* ran ahead to clear the path and announce his passing. He had told them not to shout, but they were in full voice today, as loud as braying mules. Hispallus kept the curtains of his litter closed, hoping the people he passed did not become too curious.

He occupied his mind mulling over the myriad possible meanings of the oracle in the sacrificial fire. Two faces and treachery seemed obvious—it described Daedalus's behaviour. But blood . . . *Whose, and how spilled? And why the mention of serpents' eyes? The trouble with oracles is that they might mean anything. And when we mortals misjudge the meaning, the gods have the final laugh.*

Hispallus's small procession wound around the Aventine hill and up a slope just beyond it that abutted the ancient Servian Wall that dated back to the time of the Alban kings. On this crest were temples of lesser and foreign gods, and the houses of wealthy folk who did not mind living far from the center of Rome. The homes were large and set farther apart than usual. The slaves set the litter down at the gate of

Euryale's domus and Hispallus climbed out, adjusting his toga and tunic as he stood.

The plain, cedarwood gate was set in a high wall of reticulated stone, and the house itself could not be seen from the street. This was quite unlike the normal style of Roman houses, and Hispallus wondered at the secretiveness it implied.

The gate opened, and a servant holding the inevitable leashed dog stood waiting for them. "Praetor Hispallus? Please enter."

Hispallus and his retinue passed through the gate, the dog straining at the leash to catch their scent. The praetor paid little mind to the servant until he noticed some of his lictors making the sign of the fig to ward off the evil eye. Hispallus turned to chide them, not wishing Euryale's household to be insulted, then saw what they saw. The servant's eyes were completely white. *He is blind.* Hispallus felt a shiver of irrational fear. Yet he was relieved that the servant could not see the reaction he caused.

"Welcome, Magistrate," said a voice at his elbow, and Hispallus jumped a little. He saw a young lad of perhaps fourteen years squinting up at him, and he recognized him as the slave who had brought Euryale's message to the temple. "Your lictors may rest here in the garden. Please come with me to where my domina awaits."

One of the lictors caught the praetor's arm. "I don't like this, my Lord. You should not walk alone in . . . this place."

Hispallus patiently pushed the lictor's hand aside. "I fear no harm from the Domina Euryale or her household. You and the others will wait here, as requested. And you will take care not to offend any of her servants, slaves or kin. We want her good will."

"As you wish, praetor." The lictor stood aside, shaking his head as if facing obstinate insanity.

"Then lead the way, boy," Hispallus said to the squinting slave. "What is your name?"

"I am called Sevisus, sir. This way, if you please."

The slave led Hispallus down a path that passed tall hedges of myrtle, laurel and bay, bare elm, cypress and peach trees, and beds of budding roses. The praetor was amazed at the extent of the gardens and could easily imagine how beautiful they would be at the height of spring. The usual Roman house had no gardens at all, though some of the Cornelian clan and other patricians who had been to Greece had adopted the style. But Hispallus had seen nothing like this, not even in Hispania. *It is like having a house in the country while remaining in the city,* he thought, and he resolved to walk more through the gardens later.

They passed through a peristyle of simple, unfluted doric columns on which twined thick, bare vines. Entering the house itself, Hispallus was struck by the uncluttered openness and tasteful embellishment of the foyer and the atrium. Patricians who boasted of "Hellenic" décor in their homes often meant an overabundance of elaborate artifacts of dubious origin that cluttered every available space. Euryale's home had clean, white-washed walls with only an occasional fresco depicting sprigs of herbs, flowers or sprays of wheat. The floor of the atrium gave him a moment's pause, for it depicted a complex composition of entwined serpents. But even this was spare in detail while remaining elegant in design. The more he saw, the more Hispallus respected the taste and sensibilities of the Domina Euryale.

The praetor followed Sevisus into the tablinum. This room Hispallus also found pleasant, with its lovely pastoral scenes on the walls. A guest couch had been set out for him, strewn with pillows for his comfort. A modest table was spread before the couch, offering stuffed dates, sweet cakes and fish pickle with flatbread, and a ewer of wine. A brazier with legs were shaped like entwined serpents held warm coals on which had been set incense to give the room a subtle, pleasing aroma.

As Hispallus seated himself on the couch, a woman entered from behind the tall screen. She wore a simple stola of homespun wool the color of cream. Her head was completely covered by her palla and her face veiled by woolen gauze. Hispallus had heard that many Hellenic women went about veiled, but he didn't think it included the eyes also.

The woman sat as Sevisus introduced the praetor. The boy then bowed and left the room.

"Welcome, honored magistrate," said Euryale in a low, melodious voice. "Please be comfortable."

Hispallus stared. Seeing the veiled and cowled woman beside the smoking brazier gave him a sudden feeling of disorientation, as if he had been transported magically and now sat before the Sibyl at Cumae or Delphi. He felt at a loss for words as he waited, almost expecting her to intone an oracle for him.

"You seem disturbed, Magistrate. It is my unusual appearance, no doubt. Please forgive me, but I am quite old and . . . disfigured. This covering is for your sake as well as mine."

"Apologies, Domina. I did not mean to seem rude. My mind was momentarily elsewhere. I find not fault with your kind hospitality." *Odd that the astrologer mentioned no disfigurement. And her voice and carriage seem quite vigorous for one who is elderly.*

Then, as Euryale leaned forward to pour the wine, her palla slipped from her hand, revealing smooth, unbent fingers that could be no more than thirty years. The praetor started in surprise. Then she settled back in her chair and the hand was obscured once more.

"What is it, Magistrate? What surprised you?"

"Er, it is the wine, Domina. Falernian, isn't it? A surprising extravagance for an informal visit such as this." Hispallus could not imagine why Euryale was perpetrating such a ruse. Politeness and the practical need to do business with her, however, were reason enough to let it pass unmentioned.

There came light, embarrassed laughter from behind the veil. "But you are a most honored guest, Praetor. And Falernian is not beyond my means, as I am sure you know. Else you would not be here."

"Ah. Yes. You have a perceptive mind, Domina. You refer to the reason I am here. Well . . ." Hispallus described Daedalus's plans for the bridge. He used the most impressive terms he could think of, but he could not tell if the face behind the veil was moved by his oration.

"An interesting project," Euryale said. "I am usually asked to donate funds for the building of temples, not public works. Owing to my . . . origins, and the faith of my people, I generally decline these requests."

As she leaned forward to take a stuffed date, Hispallus noted the one gold bracelet she wore was in the shape of a serpent wrapped around her wrist. Sunlight winked from the serpent's ruby eye. The praetor felt his throat tighten. *Could the oracle have meant her?* "I cannot help but notice, Domina, that you have a liking for images of snakes. Does this have a relation to your family faith?"

Euryale paused a moment. "The serpent is a symbol of nature and the earth. In this way, it relates to the faith of my people, yes."

"Ah, then you are a follower of Ceres, or Demeter."

"In a way, yes."

"Well, the bridge could be dedicated to whatever deity you choose. Daedalus has no preference. And he is, like yourself, of Greek origin."

"I believe you have been misinformed, Magistrate. Though I am from Epeiros, I am not of Hellenic descent and I feel no affinity for the Doric people."

"Oh. My apologies."

"The misunderstanding is forgivable. But it does not matter, as the money I might give to such a project is already set aside. As you may have heard, I am offering 250,000 sesterces to whoever can answer a certain question. Until that question is answered, or I am convinced there is no answer, I will do nothing with that money."

"I see. Dear lady, forgive me if I seem contentious, but is it truly worth throwing such a sum after an intangible when it might do much good for the Roman people and bring honor to your name?"

"I pursue this 'intangible' for the sake of my honor . . . and more," said Euryale, hardness creeping into her voice.

"Very well, then I must apologize again. But will you not at least consider my request?"

Euryale sighed. "I confess that I have become disillusioned lately. I have asked witches and sorcerers from half the known world how stone might be turned into flesh, yet each answer seems preposterous or evil. There is one more who offers me an answer, and my hope bids me give him an interview. But if he proves false as well . . ." Euryale turned her hands palm up. "Then the money might as well be thrown across a river."

Hispallus attempted a hearty chuckle. "I would hope you think better of our project than that, Domina Euryale. After all, it would earn you the goodwill of all Rome."

"Of course. I understand."

"When do you expect to know the outcome of your 'final hope'?"

"He comes in two days. I shall know in three. Does that suit you?"

"It would satisfy me. I only hope it will sit well with my architect, who is naturally impatient to begin work. But it will please him to hear that you think well of his plan. Yes, it should do."

Hispallus steered the conversation to other, more trivial comments, but found the veiled lady opaque in her responses, even concerning simple questions as to her health and her family. When the praetor gently pointed this out to her, she answered:

"Forgive me, Magistrate. You see, the only family I have in the world is one sister who is far away. My parents are long dead, and my other sister was . . . brutally murdered by an adventurer from Argos. Forgive me, it was long ago. I should not speak of it like this."

"I understand, Domina. The sorrow can feel fresh for a long time. My own father died when I was quite young, and he still visits my dreams. But what of your more distant relatives?"

"Long dead, also. My village, you must understand, had seen much of war."

"Ah. I see." Hispallus remembered that during the suppression of the Antiochan rebellion, his kinsman Asiaticus had had many Greek cities put to the torch and plundered. He hoped Euryale harbored no ill will toward his family.

Fearful that he might say something more offensive, Hispallus stood to go. "Well, I regret to leave you on such a sad note, but I do not wish to tax your hospitality, and I have other business to attend to. I thank you, Domina Euryale, for your kind attention and your willingness to consider a donation to our public works."

"And I thank you for thinking of me in relation to this noble endeavor," Euryale said, standing in one smooth motion.

Hispallus could not tell if there was irony in her voice, so he simply smiled and inclined his head. "Good health to you, then, Domina."

"And to you, Magistrate. Sevisus will see you to the gate."

The squinty-eyed boy appeared at the sound of his name. With a final nod to Euryale, the praetor allowed Sevisus to guide him into the atrium. But there he turned and said, "If I may, I'd like to return by a different path. I greatly admire what I saw of the gardens as we passed them. I would like to see more."

Sevisus paused, clearly torn between obedience to his owner's private wishes and fear of offending a high-born personage. "As you wish, sir," he said at last.

Hispallus followed the boy out a side door of the atrium onto a smooth, graveled path. The gardens seemed to stretch the entire length of the house, and were artfully laid so that he could not determine their width. Sevisus turned at a perpendicular path and headed toward the front gate at a walk suspiciously faster than comfortable. *He will let me have my way, but no more.* The praetor deliberately dawdled behind.

He noticed just beyond a stand of poplar a thatched roof, similar to those that were said to have covered ancient houses. "Sevisus," the praetor called out, "what is that building?"

The slave turned, looking to where Hispallus pointed, and blanched. "Oh, no, sir, please! I cannot show you that. That is the home of my Domina's lares."

"Ah. Fear not, Sevisus. I've no wish to disturb your lady's family gods." The praetor thought it curious that a whole temple might be built for their worship. Normally, a Roman household devoted only a large cabinet or at most a room to their protective spirits. *Perhaps it is a Greek custom,* he thought. Hispallus turned and let Sevisus lead him farther down the path.

Beyond a line of bare peach trees, surrounded by low evergreens, stood a statue that made Hispallus catch his breath. This time he was not deterred by the slave boy's protesting gesture, but walked right up to the base of the statue to examine it.

It was of a nude young man with handsome, Semitic features. He stood in a pose of shock and surprise that was vaguely disturbing in this otherwise peaceful garden. But it was the quality of the stone which most caught the praetor's eye. The marble was a beautiful ivory hue, and cut so skillfully that the dark veins seemed to match exactly the visible vessels of a living man. "What exquisite artistry," Hispallus murmured, stroking the smooth marble foot. "Do you know the sculptor of this piece, boy?"

"No, sir. The Domina has never mentioned a name."

"Well, I shall ask her when I next have a chance." The praetor had not yet had a bust of himself carved for an atrium niche. *Perhaps Fortuna has directed me here for good reason.* Smiling, Hispallus turned and let Sevisus guide him, without further interruption, back to his men at the front gate.

"A BRIDGE! DID YOU HEAR, DEINO?"

"Yes, Despoina. Such foolishness." Deino waited patiently beside the dressing-table as Euryale sat before her on a bench with cushions of golden silk.

"No, foolishness is not the right word, Deino. This bridge, or something about its construction, is very important to the praetor. He nearly begged me for my donation. And there must be some urgency in the matter. I think normally a quaestor would be making such a request. Something is very odd here, don't you think?"

"Surely it is not our concern, Despoina." Gently, Deino unfastened the upper corners of Euryale's veil from the palla and lifted it away. As Euryale's face was revealed, the old woman thought it a great pity such beauty must remain hidden. With centuries-deep affection and respect Deino regarded the high cheekbones, full lips, straight nose . . . and the eyes. The eyes that none but Deino could meet. The irises were a deep emerald green, edged by a thin circle of crimson. *Such beautiful, deadly eyes.*

"Don't you think the praetor might make it our concern?" said Euryale, lifting one delicate brow.

"Perhaps, if he has learned something of our secrets. Perhaps he was spying."

"No, he knows nothing . . . his face showed too much bewilderment. And if spying is his business, he would have sent a lesser man. There is something more that binds his fate to me."

"Let us hope it does not bind him too closely to you . . . for his sake."

"Speaking of bindings, please let us remove this turban. My scalp aches so."

Deino slipped the blanketlike palla off Euryale's head and folded it, then set it aside. She turned her attention to the wide band of thick, soft brown wool wound around Euryale's head. Deino discerned ripples of movement underneath the cloth. "Your little ones are restless, Despoina."

"Yes. It has been a while since they were unbound. And I'm sure they sense my discomfort with the praetor."

Deino carefully unwound the turban, not touching what lay beneath. As the second layer was revealed, the head of a small, green serpent, no thicker than Deino's thumb, popped out between the cloth strips. Its scarlet eyes blinked and its tiny red tongue lapped the air. Then another green head slipped out beside it . . . and then another.

"Patience, little ones!" said Deino. "Give me a moment." Soon the last layer of wool came off, revealing a writhing mass of little green snakes crowning the beautiful Euryale's head.

"I am so sorry, my little ones," said Euryale affectionately. "I did not mean to keep you bound so long." She ran long, slender fingers into the sinuous mass. The serpents entwined themselves lovingly around her fingers, touching them with their flickering tongues. "Are you hungry, my little ones? Shall we feed you at last?"

"The meathouse was well stocked three days ago, and there should be flies a-plenty," said Deino.

"Good. See that the others are given work elsewhere. I wish to walk through the gardens."

"Nai, Despoina." Deino went to a covered bowl and pulled out a cloth pouch that was filled with cedar chips, cinnamon and cloves. The aromatic sachet would mask the odor of the ripening meat for the sake of Euryale's delicate nose, as her little snakes feasted on the flies the meathouse attracted.

Giving the pouch to her lady, Deino excused herself to see to the servants' safety, and the gorgon stood and stepped out to take her walk.

SEPTIMVS

Hispallus stood in a dark corner of the Basilica Aemilia, waiting. *Do the gods mock me, by having Daedalus ask to meet me here—in this hall, built by the family of my most enviable cousin?* He stared up at the vast arches of brick-faced concrete that spanned the great meeting hall. Voices from the Forum outside echoed in the dark upper reaches of the basilica, as if angry ghosts and daemons harangued each other there.

There was no one else in the hall, there being no administrative meeting today. Hispallus's only companions were the occasional bird and bat. At one point some slaves entered bearing laurel wreaths for the Kalends of March, but Hispallus hid behind an enormous column and they passed him by.

It had taken much coaxing for his lictors and attendants to agree to remain outside. Hispallus remembered an old saying of his father's: "When a man enters public life, his life is public ever after." Hispallus had no wish to share the shame of Daedalus's extortion with anyone, if he could avoid it.

"Salve, Scipio," said Daedalus just behind him and Hispallus jumped. Turning, the praetor saw the young architect leaning carelessly against the pillar. "Did I frighten you, Scipio? A powerful man of justice like you? You flatter me."

"Flattery was not intended," Hispallus growled. "What do you want?"

"You know what I want. Do you have the money?"

Hispallus took a deep breath. "I am making arrangements."

"You don't have it. I can tell by the look on your miserable face."

"I told you I am making arrangements! My source . . . needs time."

"Your source." Daedalus leaned back against the column and closed his eyes. Black curls framed his thin, handsome face, and in the dim light he nearly seemed a marble decoration attached to the pillar. "Would that, by any chance, be the Domina Euryale?"

"How did—"

"Your lictors see to it that your whereabouts are widely proclaimed."

Damn them, thought Hispallus, *my very fame will ruin me.*

Daedalus smiled. "A wealthy Greek widow. How delicious. I have made a mighty Scipio become a legacy hunter. She will have to die soon for you to receive the benefits of her will. Is that the delay? Does she cling too dearly to life?"

"It is not that!" Hispallus clenched his fists and took a step toward Daedalus. "She is no widow, and she will donate the money freely if that is her choice."

"You have allowed her a choice? Clearly you have not been persuasive enough, Scipio."

"What would you have me do? Euryale is a lady of quality and deserving of respect. I will not interfere in her decision any further."

"Well! A paragon of womanhood, is she? I shall have to meet this Euryale myself. Perhaps my good looks and smooth tongue will make me more persuasive that you."

"You will do no such thing! I forbid it!"

"You forbid . . ." Suddenly the young architect's face twisted into a smile and he pointed at the praetor. "You like her!"

Hispallus felt his cheeks redden and he scowled. "The Domina Euryale has the right to live as she wishes, so long as she breaks no Roman law. I will not press her. Nor will you."

Still smiling, Daedalus looked down the dark nave of the basilica, toward the Forum. "You know, I find that place out there fascinating. In the center of the Forum stands the great Rostrum. On that platform any man may stand and speak to the crowd whenever he likes and they will listen. If I, or my friends if I am not available, were to get upon the Rostrum and speak, do you think Rome would listen to me?"

He bends me to his mad will as if I were a lump of lead. Disgusted with himself, Hispallus said, "I will find the money elsewhere."

"No. I will deal with this woman. After all, she is also Greek and I owe my countrywoman a visit, don't you think? Yes, I will speak with her."

"Why?"

"Because you so badly wish me not to. I must see this creature who has captured your heart."

"I see." Hispallus felt a cold knot in his stomach. "It isn't the bridge at all, is it? You do not care if any monument is built. You only want to torment me."

Daedalus's face became very serious. "The bridge means more to me than you can know."

"Then you should take care, Daedalus, that you do not take such steps for your bridge that you fall from its height."

"You mean if Euryale proves unmoved by my charm?" He shrugged. "Then you will seek the money elsewhere, as you have said."

And where will it end? "Why this madness? Why do you hate me so?"

Daedalus arched one eyebrow. "You cannot guess?"

"Please enlighten me."

Daedalus barked a bitter laugh. "Either you are the finest actor who never graced a theater, or you are the stupidest man in Rome."

Hispallus shook his head. "And what manner of man are you? Surely not Thessalus's son. I treated your father well, and in return he gave my family friendship and loyalty. Thessalus was a good man. But you—"

Daedalus's eyes narrowed. "Don't make me ill, Scipio. You though my father was a sheep. Fit only for sacrifice."

Ah. Is that it? "You hold me responsible for your father's death, don't you? I was miles away when the fever took him, Daedalus. Clodia told me she had the wisest men she knew looking after him. The gods take who they will, Daedalus, despite our earthly efforts."

The architect crossed his arms tightly on his chest as if holding himself together. "You don't know. Or perhaps you are lying. Either way, you will pay. You let it happen. Now I must go . . . I have business to attend to. Vale, Scipio." Daedalus turned on his heel and walked swiftly away.

Hispallus took a few steps after him, trying to think of some way to deter him. But Daedalus was gone, swallowed by the darkness in the depths of the basilica, the echoes of his footsteps ringing hollow overhead.

OCTAVVS

S EVISUS STARED AT THE PAPYRUS on the table in front of him, disappointed. Sighing, he plucked his elbows on the table, resting his cheeks on his fists. *And he asked if I liked riddles. Hah.* The text was a riddle, all right—a random-seeming mixture of Egyptian hieroglyphics, Greek and Phoenician letters, and symbols Sevisus did not recognize at all.

"Sevisus? Are you in there?" Deino called through the door.

"Yes, Deino."

The old crone opened the door and walked in, carrying a large basket. "Good. You must—what is that?" Before Sevisus could answer, Deino had snatched up the papyrus fragment. Pulling the round crystal from her pocket, she closely examined the writing. Sevisus had once asked to look at the crystal, but Deino had cuffed him and he never dared ask again. "Where did you get this?" she said.

"Joseph the Bookseller gave it to me. He said it was useless to him and I could have it."

"I can see why. It's pure gobbledygook."

"Can you read it?"

"Of course not! Doesn't look like anything meant to be read. Looks like a madman was practicing his letters. There's things here that aren't letters at all, in any language." She tossed the papyrus. "Perhaps you can use it to wrap fish with, or to wipe your bottom. Anyway, do you remember what day this is?"

Sevisus desperately thought. Was he to take the laundry to the fullers today? Was it time to pick up the repaired shoes from the cobblers? Market day had been just two days before, so—

Deino gave him a disgusted sigh. "I see you do not. It is the Despoina's 'Day of Sorrow' and you are to remain in this room the entire day." She set the basket down on the table. "I've brought you bread, cheese and fruit, and a small wine-skin, so you won't starve."

Sevisus now remembered the day from previous years. One had to stay indoors sunrise to sunset, never even looking out doors or windows. It seemed an odd sort of ceremonial observance, but Euryale was a foreigner. Sevisus wondered if slaves in other foreigners' households were made to join in their masters' strange rituals.

"I recall it now, ma'am, but if you please . . ."

"What is it?"

"I would prefer to spend my day in a different room."

"No." Then Deino frowned. "Why?"

"I wanted to go to the library, ma'am, to try to decipher this papyrus. If you let me stay in there I shall be so wrapped in my studying I will not even to tempted to look outdoors. Please? I can do nothing in here."

Sevisus waited while Deino regarded him with narrowed eyes, her bent fingers tapping the edge of the basket. "I'd want to cover the windows," she said at last. "And then you'd have no light to read by."

"I'd light a lamp."

"And burn expensive oil?"

Sevisus compressed his lips, then said, "You may take it out of my pay however you wish."

"Don't you want to be saving your money for manumission? Or do you want to be a slave forever?"

"Deino, please! It can't cost that much, can it? I could stand being a slave a little while longer, but I can't stand being cooped up here with nothing to do."

"Hmm. I could take this basket away and let you go hungry as your payment."

"If you wish." Sevisus had known days of hunger under earlier masters. It was preferable to a day of going mad from boredom.

"You are determined. The scrap is that important to you?"

"I think it must mean something. At least today it will not interfere with my other duties to try to find out."

"Well. If it will keep you occupied. Let us go to the library now before I change my mind."

Sevisus wanted to kiss her wrinkled cheek. Instead he just grinned. "Caecus can have my food basket."

"No he can't. He has one already. Besides, we can't let you become weak and sickly just because you are stubborn. Get your scrap and come along."

INCENSE HUNG HEAVY IN THE MOTIONLESS AIR of the little temple, where Euryale knelt before an ancient, weathered limestone statue. The rough carving depicted a muscular woman in a tunic cut short to midthigh. The waist of the statue was girdled by entwined stone serpents. Serpents were carved among her limestone ringlets and serpents she held in each hand. Folded wings flowed over her back as if they were a feathered cloak and on each side of her a watchful stone leopard sat, keeping eternal guard.

Euryale set a dish of flaming oil on a flat slab of marble before the statue. Beside the dish she placed a piece of sheepskin, a feather, a fish's tail, and, closest to the statue, a dry snakeskin. Then she sat back, holding out her hands in prayer, speaking to the statue in a language that had died centuries before.

"Great Mother Medusa, for whom my sister was named, Lady of Beasts whose womb and heart are the earth and its creatures, hear me. Let me not forget my years of service to you. Let me not forget the conquerors who would banish you.

for you. Let me remember all, that I may worship you through memory."

Euryale closed her eyes and with the aid of the incense fumes sent her mind reeling back through the centuries. She remembered her sisters, as they appeared long ago; young and beautiful, with faces that gave only pleasure to look at and long, brown hair that flowed like rivers. She remembered the day they were consecrated before the golden altar in the temple of Medusa—how excited and awed they had been. With great solemnity they had sworn to serve Her and protect Her temple. And so they did, with the aid of their servants Deino, Enyo and Porphredo who were but a little older than they.

Euryale remembered when the strangers came: Hellenes from the east, who offered to protect her people from invaders—and then proved to be invaders themselves. Strange gods they brought, who lived on mountain peaks and had the temperaments of spoiled children.

Temples to these gods were built, to the displeasure of Euryale and her sisters, in their village, near the temple of Medusa. The strangers did not destroy the native temples, but they laughed at the gods of the Pelasgoi. Particularly they laughed at the goddess Medusa, and they carved her likeness on their shields, claiming her ugly face would frighten away all enemies.

And Euryale remembered her sweet, brave sister, namesake of the goddess, going to the temple of the one called Athena and proclaiming that the beauty of Medusa was greater than that of any foreign goddess. This blasphemy horrified the foreign wizard-priests, and their vengeance came quickly. Through the priests' evil arts, the sisters were cursed to resemble the goddess they served . . . with one horrible difference. Whosoever they gazed upon would be turned to stone. And their servants, Deino, Enyo and Porphredo, were made eternally withered and old.

Euryale remembered the horror of seeing her family, as they rushed to her aid, transfixed by her gaze and turned to stone before her eyes. In shame, in sorrow, Euryale and her gorgon sisters and their servants fled to the village and hid among the hills, far from the sight of people.

Euryale remembered how, for a time, they indeed lived as monsters, stealing from unwary wanderers. In time, Euryale and her sisters amassed enough wealth that such horrid practices were no longer needed and they moved to the far western edge of the world, to Mauritania, where they could live in remote splendor. And it was there that the Lady of Beasts showed that she did not desert her namesake entirely. For Euryale's sister Medusa, one last gift was granted . . . the gift of death.

"Was my service unworthy, Lady, that I am still made to suffer this life? Should I have defied the strange gods as my sister did? What may I do to earn again your pleasure? Guide me, Lady."

The sound of footsteps nearby snapped Euryale out of her prayers and she blinked, peering through the incense smoke. "Who is there?"

"Domina?" came a child's voice. It was Caecus, and he came stumbling through the temple entrance.

Euryale grasped the boy's shoulders and held him at arm's length, grateful for his blindness. "Caecus, didn't Deino tell you to stay inside today? It is dangerous for you to be wandering. What is wrong?"

"It is Deino, Domina! There are terrible noises coming from her room. It sounds like someone is whipping her! Someone must go help her!"

Euryale sucked in her breath. No. Not again. The serpents on her head stiffened, sensing her agitation. "Thank you, Caecus. Go back to your room. And stay there! I will deal with this."

"Yes, Domina. What is that hissing noise?"

"It is the wind in the trees, child. Now go!" Euryale scooted Caecus ahead of her out of the temple. After watching to be sure he was going where he should, Euryale ran to Deino's cell.

Flinging aside the heavy wool door-curtain, Euryale saw what she feared. Deino knelt before a smaller figure of the Lady of the Beasts, her back bare and covered with long, bleeding welts. In the old maidservant's hands was a blood-stained leather whip.

"No. I have told you—" Euryale breathed.

Deino looked up with a chagrined, pained smile, but her weeping eyes held defiance. "It is my Day of Sorrow too, Despoina."

"Not this way! I have told you this is not right." Euryale grasped Deino by the shoulders and lifted her to her feet. Deino winced with pain, and Euryale let her sag against her, embracing her maidservant though careful not to touch her wounds.

"The whip cannot kill me—may I not suffer my guilt as I choose?" Deino gasped.

Through clenched teeth, Euryale said, "You are not responsible for my sister's death. I have never blamed you. It was our Goddess's gift to her."

Deino looked up with a bitter smile. "Are you saying our Lady meant for Medusa to die at the hands of that . . . Perseus?" The name she spit out like a poisonous seed.

"I have always believed so."

"Rather than believe my carelessness?" Deino pulled from her peplum pocket the Eye, the crystal lens. "He stole this from me, even as he charmed Enyo, Porphredo and me. And when we could not see clearly, he stole our sword, Tooth. We were helpless to save her. You cannot deny me my shame."

"Then allow me to deny your means of expressing it. Deino, what would I do without you? You are precious to me beyond words. Can you not see how it hurts me when you hurt your-self?" Euryale took a step back, still holding Deino's shoulders. The two women regarded each other for long moments.

A ghost of a smile appeared on Deino's face. "It was for your feelings that I . . . worshipped when I thought you would not know. But I will try, Despoina—"

"Domina!" Caecus called from beyond the door-curtain. "Come quickly! There is a strange man in the garden!"

"Now what?" Euryale sighed in exasperation. "Deino, quick, wrap my head. It seems Athena will not let me be, even on my holiest of days."

NONVS

Daedalus stood in Euryale's garden, blithely ignoring the scowling, blind gatekeeper and the dog that snarled beside him. He breathed deeply of the storm wind that was gathering the clouds overhead and imagined that the daemons of the air were attuned to his emotions. Daedalus felt a light-headed excitement, such as that felt after the first glass of wine. There was a rightness to it. However mad his guardian genius might seem at times, Daedalus knew he was being guided along the path that would give his soul satisfaction.

He studied the lone statue that stood in the garden, and noted with private pleasure that the young man depicted appeared to be staring back with vague astonishment and horror. As if he know the dark thoughts flowing in my mind.

Presently, an old crone and a veiled woman approached on the garden path. Daedalus pretended not to see them until they came quite near.

"Who are you?" demanded the old crone.

"He says he's got an appointment," said the gatekeeper.

Daedalus looked at the two women as if they had startled him. "Oh. Forgive me. As I was just telling your guardsman here, I believe there has been some mistake. I thought the good praetor had informed you that I would be coming. I am Daedalus, and I have come to give the Domina Euryale more information about my bridge, that she will be funding. Please take me to her and I am sure we can untangle this knot."

"I am Euryale," said the veiled woman. "And Praetor Hispallus told me no such thing."

Daedalus noted Euryale's voice was not that of the elderly woman he expected. And she carried herself like a beautiful woman, or one who believed she was—which, in his experience, meant much the same thing. *Perhaps she is the Scipio's mistress, hidden behind a veil of deceit as well as cloth. Here may be more fuel for my fire.* He suppressed a desire to rip away the veil to see what lay beneath. Instead, he made a disappointed frown and clicked his tongue. "Dear me, I wonder if the praetor is getting forgetful in his old age. Well, no matter. Now that I am here I can give you the necessary—"

"Nor do I think," said Euryale, "it was forgetfulness that stayed the praetor's tongue. I did not say I would fund your bridge, assuming your bridge and his are the same one. I told the praetor I would consider it, but currently I have other plans."

Daedalus affected pained innocence. "Do you doubt the word of a fellow Greek? Would I lie to my own countrywoman? Madame, as strangers in a foreign land, we should trust and help one another." He walked toward Euryale, arms outstretched as if to embrace her.

The veiled woman stepped back and the old crone swiftly placed herself between them. "Have some respect!" the old woman said.

Daedalus gave her a bemused smile. *Do you fear that I will learn how young and tender she truly is?* "Forgive me, I pray you."

"Now I am certain that you have not been sent by the praetor," said Euryale. "I suggest you direct any more questions you have on this matter to him. You have come on a most inauspicious day, Daedalus, and I fear that my time and temper are both short."

"Today is not *nefastus*, Domina. Ah, but you, no doubt, still follow the calendar of our homeland. That is sensible of you. The Roman one is quite hopeless. Our ways are much superior. Especially our art. I was admiring this statue, for example. I hope to adorn my bridge with such fine workmanship. Tell me, which of our great sculptors did—"

"As a matter of fact," Euryale said with strained patience, "that piece is Carthaginian. Now—"

"Carthaginian? Really? I had no idea their artists had been so skilled." Daedalus reached toward the statue.

"Don't you touch him!" Euryale hissed.

Daedalus froze. "Him?"

"The . . . stone is quite delicate. I do not wish it marred. I must ask you to leave. I will inform the praetor when or if I decide to give money for your bridge. Until then, there is nothing for us to discuss. Good afternoon."

"Well! I had expected a . . . friend of the praetor's to be more kind and generous. It would have seem he has chosen a harpy for his companion."

"You are making a grave error," said Euryale darkly.

"Get out," growled the old crone.

The architect drew himself up. "In that case, I wish you good luck and a good day, Domina. It appears you are in need of both." Daedalus turned and walked out of the front gate, hearing it slam shut behind him.

Daedalus smiled. *Such interesting mysteries here. It appears vengeance can be entertaining as well as satisfying to the soul.* The architect turned and ambled down the street, enjoying the way the rain-scented air played wildly with his hair. He heard the rumble of distant thunder and took delight in the dark clouds that roiled across the sky.

Suddenly, a black shape rushed at his face. There came a raucous cry and the rustle of feathered wings. He saw a flash of yellow eyes and the curve of a black beak. Daedalus raised his arm before his face, but it was too late. He felt a sharp claw rake pain across his cheek. He blinked and the black shape was gone. Daedalus spun around and saw a raven flying against the storm wind into the clouds.

He rubbed his arm against his cheek and felt a sting, looked wonderingly at the drops of blood on his arm as he pulled it away. Daedalus sighed. *Just a stupid bird.* He turned back to continue on his way, and stopped. Standing before him was a tall, thin woman whose dark palla rippled in the wind like a storm-tossed sea. The eyes beneath the palla were bright, intense and focused on his face. The sight of her unnerved Daedalus as much as the attack of the raven.

"So," said the woman in a low voice, "you are the one."

"I don't know what you mean," said Daedalus. Deciding he wanted nothing to do with this creature, he started to walk past her. Her bony hand shot out and grabbed his wrist. "Let go of me!" he said, and tried to jerk his arm out of her grasp.

But she held firm. And when she spoke it was with the hollow tone of wind through rock crevasses. "Mors and Nemesis follow you, son of Nyx. Come with me."

"Who are you? Let me be!" Daedalus jumped as the thunder cracked closer.

"You would like to know more about the Domina Euryale, wouldn't you? I can tell you much that would interest you. Come."

Daedalus, still unable to free his arm from her hand, allowed her to pull him down the street. He told himself he might learn something of use from the strange woman, or at least find temporary shelter from the rain that had begun to fall in fat, heavy drops.

Several houses down the slope of the Aventine, the thin woman pulled Daedalus into a rickety shed. As he stumbled inside, he heard the door close hard behind him. A rich scent of herbs, spices, blood and dead things surrounded him. An oil lamp was lit, illuminating walls on which hung dark, drooping shapes. Daedalus did not want to look at them closely. Bits of metal and string and lumps of spent candlewax littered the floor.

The woman stood in the center of the room. Slowly she re-moved her palla, revealing hair bound back with dried snake-skin. "I am Simaetha, of the Marsi," she said.

Daedalus felt an inner voice urge him to caution. "Are you . . . a witch?"

"Yes."

Rain drummed on the wooden roof, nearly masking the anxious thudding of his heart. "You said you had something to tell me."

"What do you know of the Domina Euryale? What do you think she is?"

Daedalus shrugged. "She is a wealthy Greek widow. And I think she may be a mistress of the praetor Hispallus."

Simaetha laughed again. "A dangerous affair that would be indeed. But what of her nature? What sort of woman is she, do you think?"

"You were supposed to give me answers, not questions."

"I want you to believe what I will tell you."

"Well, she is beautiful . . ."

"Yes. A beauty terrible to look upon."

Daedalus snorted. "I wouldn't mind looking."

Simaetha gave him a sardonic smile. "Your curiosity would be the death of you. What did you see in her house?"

"I wasn't in her house. I only saw her garden. And the only thing of interest there was a statue."

"What sort of statue?"

"What do you mean what sort? A young fellow, nude, look-ing surprised. The carving was quite good and very detailed. What of it?"

"Know you how that statue was made?"

"No! What does this have to do with—"

"Everything," said Simaetha, crossing her arms on her chest. "Euryale made the statue herself, from a living man. She is one of the Immortals. She is spawn of the ancient daemons of earth. She is a Gorgon."

Daedalus swallowed. "You're mad." He noticed with discomfort that the witch stood between him and the door.

Simaetha went on as if she had not heard him. "You seek to involve Euryale in an act of vengeance. That would be unwise. Yet there is something of great value we may both get from her."

"All I want from her is money for my bridge!"

Simaetha shook her head knowingly. She pointed a bony finger at him. "Death and vengeance are the food and drink that sustain you. You want power over another. The power of life and death."

Daedalus felt coldness creeping inside him. "How do you know this?"

Simaetha opened her arms and hands in a gesture that included all the paraphernalia in the room. "I have means."

"Oh."

Simaetha began to slowly pace the room. "If you had the power to resurrect one from the grave, could you use it?" Her voice was teasing, seductive.

Daedalus thought of his father, lying six years dead under the villa in Ostia. "Yes. If he could be whole again."

Simaetha inclined her head. "There is a substance that can do this. Euryale has it."

Daedalus looked up sharply, wondering if he dared believe her. "What?"

The witch faced him and crossed her arms again. "Gorgon's blood. A most magical liquid. Given to the living, it is the deadliest of poisons. Give it to the dead and they will rise. So the ancient legends have always said. So my dreams, sent from Hecate, tell me. But are you brave enough, I wonder. Have you the courage to be my Perseus?"

Daedalus stared at her a moment. "You *are* mad. I will not be a lamia to steal blood in the night." He tried to brush past her toward the door.

But Simaetha stepped before him and grabbed his shoulders. "I see, this is my answer. You are a coward. You will deny yourself the sweetest revenge, and deny life to one who deserves it. You prefer your petty schemes to true justice. Is that it?"

Daedalus glared into her eyes, breathing rapidly, his fists clenched. He imagined his father rising from his tomb. He imagined Thessalus pointing a spectral finger at Hispallus before the assembled Senate. He saw with satisfaction the shock and horror on the praetor's face. *True justice.*

Outside, the wind howled and the thunder boomed in a storm that no longer gave Daedalus joy. "What must I do?" he said at last.

DECIMVS

THEY WILL, NO DOUBT, CONSIDER ME A VERY POOR HOST, thought Hispallus. He sat alone in an antechamber whose only illumination was a small bronze lamp in one corner. Dark, heavy wool draperies covered the two doorways, shutting out any light from beyond and muffling the voices of the servants who were shooing the dinner guests out the door. *Completely tactless of me, but how did I know she would arrive so suddenly?* He hoped the after-dinner gifts would mollify the guests somewhat. He wondered what the servants had chosen to give out. *Probably those little silver bowls that have my name stamped on the bottom. The things I do for votes and future favors.*

Hispallus rubbed his sour stomach and chided himself for eating too rapidly the pork in garlic and wine sauce. Perhaps he should not have rushed the dinner, he mused, but he would have been completely unable to give his attention to his guests knowing she was there. The praetor felt a growing impatience. Then the draperies parted and all thought of the meal fled his mind.

She entered. His gaze lingered on her fiery eyes, her sensuous mouth. A life of debauchery was taking its toll—she was thinner, her cheeks were hollow, the rims of her eyes darker. But still she retained the beauty that caused Hispallus to fall in love with her anew each time he saw her.

"Good health and greetings to you, husband."

He sighed and realized he had been holding his breath. "I do not see enough of you, Clodia."

She laughed, and though it was a pleasant laugh, Hispallus thought he heard mockery in it. She did a couple of dancing turns across the room. "Do you mean you have missed me, or do you wish me to remove my clothes?"

She was always a lovely dancer. She is being charming tonight. I wonder why. "Either or both—though the removal of your garments can wait for a bit. These poor old eyes must reaccustom themselves to you gradually. Have the 'shadows' all fled?" The praetor thought the term apt for those idle men who haunted the gates of patricians, hoping to be invited to dinner.

"The sun has set and there is no moon, so the shadows have run into the night, no longer to be seen."

Hispallus smiled and stood. He went to her and took both her hands in his. "You arrived so suddenly I did not have time to give you a proper greeting. Welcome back, my wife." He kissed her, but she did not respond with warmth. The praetor felt familiar hurt returning. Stepping back, he asked, "Why have you come to Rome, Clodia?"

"You never come to Ostia."

"You know why I never come to Ostia."

"You did, once," she said with an artful touch of wistfulness.

"And I still blush at the memory. Your way of life is not for me. So. You come back without warning, sweet as honey. Why?"

"Please do not treat me like an intruder, Gnaeus. This is my home, too, is it not?"

"A fact you rarely choose to acknowledge these days. What has reawakened your memory?"

She looked down. Softly she said, "There have been . . . threats."

"Threats?"

"Notes, letters . . . claiming I will be exposed unless . . . it is someone who knows my secrets. He asks for money."

Hispallus closed his eyes for a moment and felt his stomach grow a little more sour. "I see." *Daedalus wants to torment her too.* He felt a sickening sadness that she had become involved, yet a part of him could not help but think, *It is what she deserves.*

"You don't seem surprised, Gnaeus."

"No. I have received threats also."

"Do you know who is doing this?"

"An ex-slave. Do not worry, Clodia. I am dealing with the matter." *Can I take hope from the fact that you have turned to me in this trouble? If you see me as your saviour, will you return to me?*

"Dealing with it? I remember how you 'deal with' things. Are you ignoring him, hoping he'll go away? Or are you paying him?"

"Clodia, I have said not to worry."

"My very life is in danger and you tell me not to worry."

"You seemed willing to risk death for your beliefs before now. You chose your way of life."

Clodia turned away from him. "When you went away to Hispania . . . all those months . . . what was I to do?"

"As other Roman wives have done; waited with patience. Clodia, you knew this could happen. I could have had your little secret legalized, were you willing to submit to the supervision of the pontifex maximus and limit to five the number of your . . . worshippers. By all the gods, Clodia, aren't five enough?"

"You have never understood, have you? No, Gnaeus. Five are not enough."

Hispallus rubbed his face and turned away from her. "I should divorce you," he said wearily.

"And upon my exile, I would announce that you condoned my behavior, or even encouraged it."

"There speaks Clodia, my loving wife."

There was a pause of frustrated silence. Hispallus did not look at her. It had been an arranged marriage, he reminded himself, and he was much older than she. It was not surprising that she never warmed to him. But he could not stop hoping . . .

Clodia turned and faced him again. "There is no need to fight like this, Gnaeus. The answer is simple if we just look at it."

"Simple?"

"Yes. You know who the criminal is. You should have him killed."

"He will denounce me before the court if he is brought to trial."

"I didn't say he should be tried."

Hispallus stared at her. "You mean to suggest—"

"Surely you can afford to hire some wastrel who would do the job."

"Surely," he agreed, his voice heavy with sarcasm, "and can I afford the blackmail the killer could extort from me? Would I need to kill the killer? Where would it end, Clodia? No. I will not be a party to murder."

"I don't understand you. You would let an ex-slave threaten to destroy us, and with us the reputation of the two greatest families of Rome?"

"You would rather I risked tarnishing their reputations with the taint of murder? Rome has *laws,* woman!"

"But if the laws cannot protect us from abuse, what else can we do? No one of account would miss him. Who would know?"

"He has said that he has alerted friends to watch for his disappearance. It would be known, Clodia. And all our other secrets would become public as well."

His wife stared at him, shaking her head. "What has happened to you, Gnaeus? Where has your courage fled? You were once a soldier. Taking a life did not mean so much to you then. And I do not even suggest that you do the deed yourself."

"There is a great deal of difference between fighting a foreign army for the sake of Rome and the outright murder of a Roman citizen. And that is something you will never understand!"

"An ex-slave . . . a citizen?" Clodia frowned. Then her eyes widened. "Daedalus. Is it Daedalus who is doing this?"

Hispallus sighed, wishing she was not so quick. "Yes. It is he."

"Why? Doesn't he have enough money? A good career?"

"It is revenge he wants. He seems to blame me for his father's death."

Clodia's eyes widened, then she looked down. "That is ridiculous. You had nothing to do with Thessalus's death."

"So I have told him. But he does not seem to believe me."

Clodia touched his arm. "We are in great danger, Gnaeus. He could say terribly things. He knows so much." To the praetor's surprise, his wife put her arms around him. Laying her head on his chest, she said, "Help me, Gnaeus."

Hispallus stroked her hair. "Will you stay?"

She looked up at him, surprised and pensive.

"For a little while, Clodia, will you stay?"

A small smile appeared on her lips. "For a little while. Yes, Gnaeus."

Hispallus held her close and he sighed.

VNDECIMVS

THE GAUZE OF THE VEIL OVER EURYALE'S EYES made the scene before her seem blurred and dreamlike. The weather had become warmer and she chose to sit in the more open atrium to await her guests. The sunlight through the latticed windows cast shadows that crisscrossed the floor, making it appear to be a playing board for a game of "Robbers." *I wonder if this is how my servants see the world, as dim shapes and sinister shadows.*

The slap of sandals on tile alerted her and Euryale looked up. Sevisus trotted in, breathlessly saying, "He's here, Domina! He and Olerus."

Olerus? I suppose he is looking after his interest. This may become awkward. "Thank you, Sevisus. You may—" Her statement was made unnecessary by the entrance of Deino, followed by the stout Olerus and a dark-bearded man Euryale assumed to be the mage Archidemus.

His long, fringed robe and square-cut curly beard reminded Euryale of the winged genii carved on the palace walls of ancient Nimrud. The Chaldean philosopher seemed quite calm and self-assured, compared to the alchemist, who rubbed his hands nervously. Euryale was struck by the fact that Archidemus did not seem disturbed by her veil. His dark eyes expressed patient interest and his face was pleasant to look on. It took Euryale a moment to realize that Deino was speaking.

"The alchemist Olerus again graces us with his presence, and he brings an esteemed associate, the magus Archidemus."

There was strong irony in Deino's tone, and Euryale winced. *I know of your disapproval, Deino. You think these men will try to cheat us, as so many others have. But if there is any chance of aid from them, I cannot help but try.*

"I thank you, Domina Magna," Olerus jumped in, "for this opportunity to consult with you again. As your good servant Sevisus no doubt has told you, I am very close to a solution. There remain only one or two things that I must learn from you."

Despite the experience of many lifetimes, Euryale began to hope again. "What is it you would know?"

"Well, Domina. The sort of transformation I perform depends greatly upon the sort of stone you wish transformed. There is more than one type of rock, as I am sure you are aware. There is rock born of fire, that is hard and glassy. There is rock born of earth, that is many smaller rocks squeezed together. There is rock born of water, and the gods show us it is so by placing impressions of sea creatures upon such stones. And there is rock born of air, that is grey as the cloud and light as a feather. The method of transformation would be different in each case.

"Next, Domina, I must know the shape of the stone you wish transfixed. If it is just a lump, then bestowing life upon it would scarcely be useful. We would require a change in shape as well. However, if it is already in the desired shape, then all is well, but the size and complexity of the creature becomes important. In other words, Domina Euryale, we must see the stat— er, the stone upon which I must do my work."

The statue. What has Sevisus told him? Euryale hesitated, noticing Deino staring meaningfully at her. Euryale glanced up suddenly as she heard Archidemus speak for the first time.

"If one seeks the path to truth," the mage said mildly, "there is no value in obstructing the route. Sometimes even the guides need guidance."

Ah, he is right. If I truly wish an end to this, I should show them what I can. "Very well, Olerus. You may see that which I wish transformed." Euryale stood and walked to the doorway that led to the garden, aware of Deino's dubious, worried stare. Motioning the men behind her to follow, Euryale led the way out into the garden.

She reached the statue ahead of the magi and laid her hand lightly on the stone foot. "Forgive me, Aristo," she whispered, looking up into the handsome face.

It seemed not long ago, though four generations by mortal reckoning, that Aristo had come to her, in her place in the Atlas mountains. A sandstorm had driven him off the regular trade route and Euryale had offered him hospitality.

She remembered his laughter, so hearty it filled the emptiness of her halls and heart. The gifts he gave her—a brooch from Gaul, pressed flowers from Helvatia. He called her his "Oread of the Desert," teased with gentle humor her veil and secretive ways. But when he came to her at night to love her, he treated her like any woman of beauty, worthy of love. She remembered the passionate kisses, the warmth of his skin, the many nights they shared until that one awful night—

A sound beside her startled her, and she looked around. Olerus was chuckling behind one hand. Euryale felt her eyes grow hot. *You obscene pig. Grateful you should be that I wear this veil, or you would soon be standing on a pedestal beside him.*

Olerus suddenly seemed to become aware of Euryale's mood, for he stilled his laughter with a cough. "Ah, yes. A remarkable work of art, Domina."

Euryale looked for Archidemus, and saw him standing behind the statue, examining it intently. Olerus joined him and peered at the stone legs, rubbing them with a pudgy hand. Euryale felt her stomach turn, but said nothing.

"Quite remarkable," Olerus continued. "But I fear I cannot identify the origins of this stone. It is unlike any I've seen. Is the sculptor near enough to speak or write to him, so that I might ask where he got it?"

"No."

"Well, then, I'm afraid I must clip off a small sample so that I may test it. I'll take it from his little toe. He won't even notice—"

"No!" Euryale shrieked and grabbed the alchemist's hands as he started to pull a tiny hammer and chisel from a leather pouch at his waist. "Don't you dare!"

To Euryale's irritation, Olerus sighed and rolled his eyes, then smiled at her as though she were an obstreperous child he must humor. "I know, Domina, it is a shame to mar such a masterful work, even just a little. But," and his tone became more impatient, "if you have any hope of seeing him alive, you'd best allow me to do what I must."

Euryale sighed and released his hands. "Please forgive my outburst, Olerus. It is just that I have prized this statue for so many years. I simply couldn't—"

"Excuse me." Archidemus came up beside her. "Perhaps there are others?" he asked softly.

"Others?" She turned her head quickly in surprise.

"Other . . . works. Carvings in the same sort of stone as this, from which Olerus may take his sample."

"Oh. Yes." Euryale gathered her stola around her and went along the row of bushes behind the statue. She pointed out a cat petrified in a frozen crouching hiss. "Here." She turned and looked beneath another bush. There she found a tiny sparrow that she had once frightened in midflight. Euryale picked it up in both hands. But her grasp was too tight and with a sickening snick she felt the tiny, delicate legs break off in her fingers.

Euryale turned and sadly placed the broken bird into Archidemus's cupped hands. Resting her hands on his, she whispered, "It must stop."

"Yes."

Euryale looked up into the Chaldean's dark eyes, wondering how much he understood. He gazed at her a moment longer, then disengaged his hands and gave the bird to Olerus.

"Here you are. I hope this gives you enough of a sample."

Olerus frowned at the tiny bird legs in his hands. "Well, yes. It is quite delicate work. Are you sure you want me to have this, Domina? You could cement the legs back onto the body—"

"Take it, please," said Euryale.

"And if you hurry," Archidemus suggested, "you may find some shops still open for the materials you need."

Olerus gave the mage a suspicious frown, then turned back to Euryale. "Did your servant happen to mention, Domina, that I am skilled in the making of homunculi? It might be quicker—"

"I do not want a homunculus!" Euryale said tightly. "Thank you. Just do what you must to bring him," she touched the statue's foot, "to life."

Olerus waved his pudgy hands in a calming gesture. "Very well, Domina. Forgive me for trying your patience. I go." He looked at Archidemus. "Well?"

"Go on ahead, Olerus. I have a few more things to say to the Domina. I shall join you later."

The alchemist wrinkled his lips and looked back and forth between the two of them. Then with an explosive, frustrated sigh, he stomped off to the front gate.

"Perhaps I should have been more kind," Euryale murmured, "If he is the one to help me."

"He cannot help you, Domina," said Archidemus.

"No?"

"His art deals with worldly elements, which can provide no balm for a divine curse. And that is the matter we are dealing with here, is it not?" His dark eyes gazed at her, calm and unreadable.

"And if it is?" Euryale felt fear and hope warring within her.

"If the source of the problem is divine, then only those of the divine sphere can aid you."

Disappointment filled her heart and Euryale bowed her head. "For years I have prayed and offered sacrifice to whatever gods and goddesses I felt would hear me, including the very one who cast this curse upon me. And I have received reply from none of them! Were I to believe you, I should have no hope whatsoever."

"Domina, throughout the world many attempt to affect the divine powers through ritual, prayer and sacrifice. Few truly succeed in reaching that which they seek. The divine is set beyond our world. But it is not a judgement of the value of your petition that you are not answered. A child cannot reach the higher shelves of a pantry without a stool to stand on. What we must do, Domina, is extend your reach."

"I do not understand."

"I am a theurge, Domina. My art is to contact the divine sphere through joining with it. In doing so, I could intercede on your behalf, or if need be teach you the art so that you yourself may lay your petition at the feet of the gods."

Euryale studied him a moment, then shook her head. "I have heard so many stories, magus. So many claims to have the right answer. Olerus seems to be earning the reward I have promised. I will not suddenly turn around and deny it him."

"I am not asking you to. I will give you the aid of my art without thought of reward. All I ask is that you allow me to stay with you and show you what I know."

"Why?"

Archidemus smiled. "My philosophy teaches that doing what is right is of more value than any sum of gold. And it is right that one should live according to one's natural place in the universe. If your curse keeps you from living according to your nature, then it is right that I help you and those affected by your curse to return to your natural state. Do you understand this?"

"I . . . am not sure."

Archidemus laughed lightly. "Will you let me stay, to explain it?"

Something in his laughter beguiled Euryale. "Very well, though Deino will think I am being a great fool."

"Then we must show her that the fool's path is often the road to wisdom."

DVODECIMVS

The interior of the taberna vinaria was dim, and smoke from the kitchen fires drifted among the roof beams. *Looks like some part of the Underworld,* thought Daedalus, standing in the doorway. As he entered, the smoke stung his eyes a little and he blinked. The discordant voices and the reek of sour wine brought up vague, terrifying memories. With an effort, Daedalus pushed them out of his thoughts and concentrated on looking for Cnaeus. *Ah. There.* Putting on his best false smile, Daedalus crossed the room to the round-faced, fair-haired young man slouched on a stool in the corner.

At his approach, Cnaeus looked up from his wine cup with bleary eyes. "Salve, Daedalus."

The architect glanced at the empty clay bottles already littering the table. "Going a bit heavy for this time of day, aren't you?"

"Do you know what day it is?"

"How could I ignore it?" Daedalus pulled up a stool and sat. "On the Via Appia I was nearly crushed by the crowd going to watch the Leaping Priests do their dance."

"Mmmm. What else is today?"

Daedalus rubbed his forehead as if to stimulate thought. "Don't the Vestal Virgins hang locks of their hair upon some tree?"

"So they do. For the luck of Rome. And what else?"

Daedalus shrugged. "Tell me."

Cnaeus stared at his wine cup and twirled it in his hands. "It is Matronalia. The holiday of wives and mothers. I have learned that, through some jests of the gods, my mother has come to Rome. I wonder what gift she seeks from my father."

Daedalus smiled to himself. *I'd wager certain letters of mine have something to do with it.*

"Perhaps a new villa, or a hundred new worshippers," Cnaeus went on.

"Don't worry yourself about it. We have other matters to consider."

"Good. I could use a distraction. Your message said you had a proposition for me."

"So I do. Tell me, Cnaeus," Daedalus leaned forward on his elbows and whispered conspiratorially, "do you believe in daemons?"

Cnaeus stared back dully, then grinned. "Of course. Each morning they battle within my head, complaining how I had drunk too much the night before."

"Nay, those are your genii, and what do they know? I meant the great daemons from the old stories; harpies, sirens . . . gorgons."

Cnaeus shrugged and chuckled. "Only on those nights when I *have* drunk too much. Or the woman I am chasing turned out to be unfriendly."

"I'm serious," Daedalus said, irritated.

Cnaeus sighed. "No. Not really."

"What of witches, then?"

"I believe we have already referred to my mother once in this conversation."

Daedalus slapped his arm, exasperated. "You're impossible."

"The Senate said that too, as I recall."

"Cease, I beg you! You know what I meant. Now what of them?"

"Witches?" Cnaeus sighed and shrugged again. "I have heard they exist."

"Well believe it, my friend, for I have met one." And choosing his words carefully, Daedalus told him of his meeting with Simaetha.

"I think your first impression was right," said Cnaeus, rubbing his chin. "The woman is surely mad."

"But what if she is not? If the Greek lady is truly a gorgon, and her blood can do such things, what possibilities there might be!"

"Those are three very great *ifs,* my friend. Besides, there are enough poisons in the world already. For what do we need another?"

"Perhaps the symptoms it causes would make it untraceable. But it is not that feature that interests me. It is the other . . . the raising of the dead."

Cnaeus made a disgusted face. "And have decaying corpses and skeletons staggering about? It would be Lemuria every day."

"No, fool, it's supposed to bring them fully to life! Whole again. Think! What if you could bring the great Africanus back?"

"Well . . . what of it?"

"You would be a hero to Rome by returning its greatest general to life. And he would be grateful for the chance to live again. He would reward you."

Cnaeus frowned and rubbed his chin again. "But people would call it sorcery."

"Not if it is in the service of the state of Rome. We could say you were favored by the gods. You'll be a sacred hero!"

"Hmm. Maybe, if the many *ifs* are true. But tell me, Daedalus, what would you do with this power?"

The architect was silent a moment. "I would bring back my father."

"Ah. You have missed him, haven't you?"

"It's not only that. It's . . . there are things he could say. He could tell people the truth."

"I had not known your father was a philosopher."

Daedalus suppressed the urge to smash a winecup into Cnaeus's face. The boy had not meant it as a wisecrack. *The truth can wait. For now.* Instead he shrugged and said, "If there is the slightest chance that the 'many *ifs,*' as you put it, are true, then I want to take the chance."

"So you are actually going to take some of this woman's blood?"

"No, not just I, Cnaeus. *We* are. I would not dream of leaving you out of this opportunity."

"Me? No, Daedalus, I could not do such a thing."

Daedalus rested his chin on his hand. *The witch said I must do it alone. But I am no Perseus. My inner voice tells me you must help me, Cnaeus. But how do I convince you?* "Neither of us could do it alone, Cnaeus. But together it is possible. The gorgon's servants are all blind, or nearly so. We could not be recognized. The witch has given me the equipment we need. And we need not take much blood . . . two small vials-full is all."

Cnaeus listened, frowning.

Daedalus stared at the table and said softly, "Your family's secrets will not be hidden forever, you know. Even now, rumors circulate. Especially since your father's election. There are those who would love to see a patrician praetor fall."

Cnaeus looked at his hands. "I know."

"Perhaps that is why your mother has returned to Rome. To try to hold back the inevitable."

"Perhaps."

"And is this your gift to her?" Daedalus whispered harshly, banging the table with his fists. "Cowardice and inaction? You would let the gossip hounds bring her and your father down like hunted deer? You have in your hands the chance to save your family and you would fling it into the gutter where you lie? You have the chance to bring the greatest of gifts for Matronalia to your Mother Rome, her glorious past brought to life again, and you would sneer at it!"

Cnaeus stared at him wide-eyed, and he seemed close to tears. "But I—"

"But nothing!" Daedalus grasped the boy's arm. "Will you not take this one chance to redeem yourself? This one chance to save the honor of your family and the glory of Rome?"

"You are sure of this?"

Daedalus stared intently into Cnaeus's eyes. "We will get the gorgon's blood. If it works, no one will notice your family's foibles. They will all be clamoring for you to bring back their exalted dead. We will try it soon. Tonight. And if it does not work, then I promise I will spirit you away from Rome, no worse off."

"And if she is truly a gorgon and we are turned to stone?"

Daedalus shook his head. "We will take precautions. Even Perseus used a mirror. Are you with me, Cnaeus?"

Looking askance, Hispallus the Younger grasped Daedalus's hand. "If I were not so drunk, I would not be agreeing to this."

"In vino veritas," said Daedalus with a smile.

TERTIVS DECIMVS

"**D**O THE MATRONALIA GIFTS PLEASE YOU, CLODIA?" Hispallus watched his wife with concern as she paced back and forth in her chamber. *Already she is restless,* he thought.

Special drapes of gold thread and white wool had been placed over the doorways at her return. Tables and chairs of the finest wood had been brought in, and cleverly wrought lamps of silver and bronze. In the center of the room, on a silk palla the pale rose tint of dawn, lay golden combs, jewel-boxes studded with garnets and emeralds, gold and silver necklaces, earrings and bracelets. Hispallus had saved all these items over the years, to give her when she returned. But now Clodia gave them scarcely a glance as she walked past.

"They are very nice," she said tonelessly and she went to the window. The view was to the west, and Hispallus had no doubts that it was Ostia she longed to see out there.

"Is there something I have forgotten that you would prefer?" Hispallus knew this was a dangerous question but felt compelled to ask. *Why do I do this to myself? Why grasp at straws of hope, knowing they will only be broken?*

"You know what would be the sweetest gift?"

Yes. You have told me. Complete legalization of the cult of Bacchus. "That is not mine alone to give, Clodia." Hispallus imagined himself trying to convince the Senate that the ban against the cult should be repealed. *I long to make a name for myself in the annals of Rome, but not as a laughingstock.*

Clodia slapped her hand against the windowsill. "It has been fifty years since the ban, Gnaeus! Cato and the others who demanded it are dead. Why not try?"

Hispallus shook his head. "Roman men still dislike the thought of our women freely drinking wine. We have enough foreign cults now to watch over. Why add another? What does your life offer you that you cannot find in a way acceptable to Rome?"

Clodia looked at him, her head cocked to one side. "Will you believe me if I tell you? I have found beauty, Gnaeus. A lifting of the spirit. Freedom. Rome would have me worship Duty. To be a patient wife, accepting drudgery and servitude as my rightful lot. My life in Ostia offers me much more. And it has much to offer Rome, if Rome would listen. I have friends there of great knowledge and wisdom—"

"Wisdom!" Hispallus barked a laugh.

"Yes, wisdom! I know men, Gnaeus, who can read the knowledge in the stars. Men who do not give all power to the gods, but who take power in their own hands. Rome would dismiss them as sorcerers, but they know the true way of the world."

Hispallus imagined his wife sitting at the feet of astrologers such as the "Chaldean" who came to his home days before. He imagined her listening raptly to their nonsense, accepting their vile advice. He felt a stab of jealousy and anger. "Neither Rome nor I have need of such 'wisdom.' And were you more sensible, neither would you. You would give up the honor due a good Roman wife for the fleeting pleasures of your cult. Look in any mirror and see what this has done to you!"

Clodia stared at her hands and said nothing.

Hispallus sighed heavily. "I suggest you think on this more. Now I have matters to attend to. Have a pleasant Matronalia." He waited but his wife did not respond or look at him. Hispallus clenched his fists and strode out of the room.

VESPERI

EVENING BIRDS SANG IN THE GARDEN as Euryale placed a few new-budded roses at the feet of the statue. "There is hope, Aristo," she said softly. "I have confided in the Chaldean, and he seems kind and understanding. If the divine powers are willing, you may soon again be living flesh."

She looked up into his unseeing stone eyes. "They have a story here, Aristo, of the love god Cupid and a mortal woman, Psyche. She saw him, though he begged her not to. And they went through many trials, but in time regained each other's love." Euryale's voice trailed away in a whisper. She could not bear the look of horror on Aristo's stone visage for long, it so filled her with guilt.

The nights Aristo had come to her, she had asked him only that there be no light and that he not touch her above the shoulders. One night, at his urging, she allowed him to caress her face, her little ones having been carefully bound beneath her cloth turban. Aristo had exclaimed aloud how beautiful she must be. He began to beg her to let him see her in full light. Euryale had to always answer no.

But the final night, Aristo came to her bedroom earlier than usual, carrying a brightly lit lamp. Euryale was caught unprepared and, to the horror of them both, Aristo was transformed into the statue that now stood in her Roman garden.

"How foolish we both were," Euryale whispered. "But I will make amends, my love. You will see." Euryale caressed one cold stone foot, then she turned and walked the path back to her chambers.

QVARTVS DECIMVS

Y OUNG CNAEUS STOOD TREMBLING BESIDE THE WALL of the Domina Euryale's garden, wishing he were still drunk. *Why am I here?* He thought desperately. *Why don't I leave Daedalus to his mad scheme and run away?* The first-quarter moon cast pale, ghostly light into the alley in which Cnaeus stood. Despite his dark cloak, Cnaeus felt far too conspicuous. To his right, down the alleyway, he thought he saw a shadow moving within a shadow. His heart pounded and his irregular breath seemed loud in his ears. But stare as he might into the darkness, he could see nothing there.

He heard footsteps ahead of him and shrank back against the wall. Out of the shadows Daedalus appeared, carrying a drooping bundle that resembled a lightweight corpse under his arm. Cnaeus knew his chance to escape was past.

"There you are. Are you ready?" Daedalus's whisper sounded too loud in the still night air.

"To be honest, no. Are you?"

"Courage, man! The witch gave me all we need. Here, take this."

Cnaeus was handed a pole with a small bag attached to one end. The bag reeked of henbane and something acrid. "What is this?"

"Don't breathe near the bag! Simaetha said it is to put near the gorgon's face. The fumes will put her to sleep."

Cnaeus held the pole out away from him, wrinkling his nose. "I see. That's why it's on a pole."

"No, the pole is so the snakes on her had cannot reach you to bite you."

"Oh."

"And here is a knife. It's very sharp, so take care."

Cnaeus took the knife, feeling poised between a danger in each hand. "I thought you were going to cut her!"

"Shhh! I will hold the mirror for you, so you need not chance looking at her as you work. And I will hold the bottles to catch the blood."

Cnaeus thought this over and the sheer impossibility of it all nearly overwhelmed him. "Daedalus, can't we—"

"Enough! Let's begin, before we lose our nerve. I'll run over near the gate and hang our friend here—" he hefted the straw dummy he carried—"on the wall to distract the dog. When you hear barking, hop over your wall and I'll meet you by the statue in the garden."

As he heard the architect's running footsteps receding, Cnaeus turned and stared at the wall, trying to gather what courage he could. It would be no easy task to clamber over, holding the knife and the pole. Loud barking came from the south wall.

It's time. His stomach felt as if he had swallowed cold pellets of lead. After a few frustrating moments of trying to figure out how to grasp the wall-top with full hands, Cnaeus tossed the pole and knife over the wall and pulled himself over after them.

He fell with a frighteningly loud crackle onto a pile of dry twigs and hastily felt around for the pole and knife. Tripping over a root, he fell right beside the noisome bag. Grasping it, he sat up, his head reeling. Cnaeus took a few deep breaths which seemed to clear away the dizziness, though he still felt an uncomfortable throbbing in the back of his head. *This is not good. Oh, Daedalus, I should not be here.*

His hand fell on something cold, and from the sharp pain, he knew he had found the knife. *By Pollux, it was not me you were meant to cut,* he chided the knife as he picked it up.

He shook his head and realized he did not know how long he had been sitting. Carefully holding the knife and pole, Cnaeus stood on unsteady legs and went to find the statue in the garden.

He heard voices and people running about. *What if they find Daedalus? What if they find me?* He crouched behind hedges and rose bushes, scuttling forward when he could. He reached a semi-circle of poplar trees and suddenly found himself facing a marble pedestal. Cnaeus looked up.

Towering over him was the statue. It gleamed in the moonlight, arms outstretched, face twisted in an expression of terror. Fear clutched at Cnaeus's insides. *This was one of her victims.* The pose of the statue seemed to be giving him warning.

"What took you so long?" Daedalus hissed at him from the darkness. Cnaeus jumped and felt hands grabbing his tunic and pulling him into the bushes. "Never mind," Daedalus went on, just beside his ear, "the dog's alarm seems to have stirred up the whole household. Just as well we have to wait."

"It's true, isn't it?" Cnaeus said, hearing an edge of hysteria in his voice. "She really is a gorgon. That statue used to be alive! She—"

"Stop it!" Daedalus shook him roughly. "If you didn't believe me before, why did you come along?"

Cnaeus had no answer. He felt as though he were becoming paralyzed with fear. "Are you sure they can't see us?" he whispered at last.

"As I told you, even the ones who have sight have it none too well. Stay still or move silently and they won't notice you."

Cnaeus wished desperately that the ground wouldn't seem to lurch every time he moved. Silently he cursed the fume-bag and the witch who had produced it, and himself for having gone on this lunatic expedition. "What do we do now?"

"We head for the gorgon's sleeping chamber."

"What if she isn't asleep?"

"That's what the bag is for, remember?"

"Oh." Cnaeus clamped his mouth shut and tried to fight down his rising panic.

"The house looks to be of normal design," said Daedalus. "The main bedrooms should be that way. Come on."

Crouching behind him, Cnaeus followed, fear making him stiff and clumsy. They ducked inside a wooden door that was ajar. Daedalus silently closed the door behind them, making the corridor they had entered completely dark.

"Daedalus—"

"Hush!" A tiny candle flame appeared in the darkness, illuminating the architect's worried face. He walked forward to a dark door-curtain and listened. Apparently hearing nothing, Daedalus stepped back and motioned at the doorway. "In there."

After a moment's hesitation, Cnaeus wrestled the curtain aside and stood in the dark room. He dared not move, fearing he might bump into something. He heard the heavy wool curtain fall back in place behind him and felt Daedalus gently push him forward. The faint candlelight showed enough of the room's elegant furnishings to prove that this was indeed the lady's bedroom . . . but the bed was empty.

Suddenly Cnaeus heard women's voices beyond the door-curtain across the room. They spoke Greek, a language Cnaeus had found to be devilishly hard to master, but he understood them well enough.

". . . a prank, Despoina. Foreigner-baiting by some fun-loving Roman citizens, no doubt. You may go back to sleep."

"I still feel uneasy, Deino. My little ones will not stop their restless movement. I doubt they will let me sleep much tonight."

"Shall I fetch some goat's milk for you, Despoina?"

"Yes, thank you, Deino." The curtain across the room moved aside, and light from a hand-held oil lamp spilled into the room. Cnaeus gasped and felt Daedalus tug on his tunic.

"Get ready," Daedalus whispered. "Here's the mirror. Look this way."

Cnaeus snapped his head around and saw the glimmering reflected lamplight in a mirror Daedalus was holding below Cnaeus's right arm. Cnaeus felt his arms begin to shake and his legs begin to weaken as his fear grew stronger.

"Now! Use the bag!"

Cnaeus clenched his teeth and swung the bag into the center of the room. But already dizzy and disoriented from fear, Cnaeus could not help turning as the bag on the pole pulled his arms around behind him. Cnaeus stumbled forward and looked around, just as the gorgon entered the room.

"Don't look at her!" Daedalus warned.

But the warning came too late. The time between heartbeats seemed an age as Cnaeus met the gorgon's startled eyes. A great hissing erupted from the myriad serpents swarming on her head and they stood out stiffly to face him, little green gaping jaws displaying tiny, deadly white fangs. The gorgon's green eyes slowly grew wide and their red rims seemed to glow. Ever so slowly, she began to turn her head, bringing her hands toward her face. Cnaeus tried to move, but his feet felt like lead, and heat like fire was spreading up his legs. His body was filled with an intense tingling, such as that felt when a limb is said to fall asleep. His eyelids would not obey the command to shut, and his arms and hands felt encased in iron bands. The heat spread faster now, through his groin and hips. His abdomen felt hard and heavy. He opened his mouth to moan in despair, but no sound would come out, his lungs no longer moved. His heart gave one final, painful throb before ceasing. His eyes saw the room fade to a milky white and his ears heard their last sounds.

"Forgive me," the gorgon said.

Then all was darkness.

* * *

"Deino!"

"Coming, Despoina." Deino shuffled as fast as she could through the door-hanging. She stopped behind Euryale, seeing the statue in the center of the room. "So. It was an intruder after all."

Euryale's breathing was rapid and shallow, and her little ones writhed in a restless frenzy. "There were two, Deino. I saw another."

"Shall we go search for him?"

"No." Euryale shook her head and buried her face in her hands. "Let him escape."

Deino pursed her lips and shrugged. "As you wish, Despoina. Though, if I may say so, this one has gotten only what he deserved."

Euryale did not reply.

Deino went to the enstoned intruder and examined him. She wrinkled her nose. "What an awful smell. Tcha. A common thief he must be. See here, he carries a knife, and there is a bag to carry his loot away. You need feel no guilt, Despoina. Roman justice would have served him little better."

"They knew, Deino. They knew what I am."

"How can that be, Despoina? If so, they are foolish beyond fools. This one carries no mirror, no shield."

"His companion carried the mirror. I heard him say 'Look in the mirror.' They knew, Deino. What shall we do?"

Deino sighed and shrugged. "As we always do, Despoina. We go on with life and wait. With luck, the other one will have learned his lesson and stay well away from us. Too bad we don't know who he is."

"From what little I saw, he almost resembled that architect we met in the garden."

Deino widened her eyes. "Hmm. Yes, I believe he would be fool enough. Shall I . . . do anything?"

Euryale's arms fell weakly to her sides and she lowered her head. "No. I am not certain enough. We will wait."

"What of this one, then, Despoina? Shall I place him out in the garden with Aristo?"

"No." Euryale gazed at the intruder's face a few moments. "There is something familiar about him. Something in his face I have seen before."

"He seems a common sort of Roman youth to me. And that smell about him! He and Olerus would make a fragrant pair. Regrettably, he is not pretty enough to sell to an art collector."

"Deino . . ."

"Forgive me, Despoina. You are right, there is no need to return to old ways. What do you recommend?"

"Store him in a safe place. If our mages do give us an answer I can restore him as well."

"Knowing our secret, Despoina?"

"If he is the fool you say he is, who will believe him?"

"Hm." Deino nodded.

"Might he have family who will search for him?"

"What man would confess to his family his thievery and his next victim?"

"One from a family of thieves?"

"Then let them come, and we shall give them what they deserve."

Euryale gave an explosive sigh. "I am not the earthly avatar of Nemesis, Deino!" Taking a blanket from the bed, Euryale threw it over her head. "I will be in the Temple, if you need to find me."

"The Goddess will forgive."

"But I do not. Each time this happens, I feel cursed anew."

DAEDALUS RAN UP THE STAIRS OF THE INSULA to his room and slammed the door shut behind him. He leaned back against the door, gasping for breath. His stomach churned inside him. *Did I want him dead? Is that why I brought him into this? Surely the poor fool did not deserve that!* Though he flinched from the thought, part of him knew. *My father was taken from me, so now I have taken the son from the father.*

Simaetha's voice intoned from the darkness, "You pay the price of cowardice, and so shall we all."

Daedalus started, his eyes searching the dark. *The witch! What is she doing here?* "Simaetha?"

"Here." A candle came alight on the small table beside his bedroll. Simaetha stood near it, her shadowed face lined with concern.

"How did you . . . What do you want?"

"You know what I want. But you failed to get it, didn't you?"

"I told you I'd give you the blood tomorrow."

Simaetha shook her head, her expression a mixture of disgust and pity. "You cannot give what you could not get. Even though you have paid a much higher price than was needed."

"What are you talking about?" *She knows. God, how can she know?*

"Your unfortunate accomplice. Do you think you can lie to me, Daedalus? I am not one of Euryale's eyeless slaves. I watched as you sent the poor lad over the wall. And now you return alone and frightened. Do you think that I cannot guess what happened?"

Daedalus swallowed hard and clenched his fists. He took a step into the center of the room. "I didn't know it was going to happen. He made a mistake. I did what I had to do."

"You were to do this alone. Had you done so, all would be well. Now . . ." Simaetha picked up a set of carved wooden knucklebones that lay on the table and tossed them. "The threads of our endeavours are scattered like seeds on the wind. Who knows how they will take root and grow?"

"Don't worry," said Daedalus. He was relieved to see she wasn't angry, yet he found her distant sorrow disturbing. "The Domina doesn't know who was involved. She will not recognized the young Scipio, and she didn't see me."

"Scipio!" The witch whispered, her eyes opening wide. She clutched her palla tighter across her shoulder. "A scepter of stone . . ." she murmured to herself, then stared at Daedalus with burning eyes. "Tell me who he was!"

"The Praetor Hispallus's son. A nobody really. His family forgot him long ago. He won't be missed."

"Won't be missed? Fool! One broken thread can unravel the most complex weaving. I should have seen. Now warnings must be given." Simaetha rubbed her eyes and forehead wearily.

"Should have seen what? Warn whom?" Daedalus did not like the turn her talk was taking. He felt like a fly caught in a giant, invisible web.

"The answer was there, in the dreams and visions Hecate sent me. But I did not understand them well enough. You should have gone alone."

"By Pollux, I am no Perseus, woman, to go hacking away at daemons by myself! I needed help!"

"The gods help those who help themselves. You would have been guided."

"The only god who guides me is Nemesis."

"Ah. So that is why you took the young Scipio along. He is part of your petty vengeance, against Hispallus perhaps?"

Why did I open my mouth? "That is none of your business."

Simaetha crossed the room to him and glared into his eyes. "Do you think you are the only soul in this world? The consequences of your cowardice are very much my business. And the cost will be great to others as well."

"Do you intend to punish me?"

"Justice is not mine to deliver. Your punishment has already begun." Simaetha pulled her palla lower over her face and started toward the door. Daedalus stood aside, but before he moved far, Simaetha caught his arm and gave him a hard smile. "Take heart, little coward. Hecate has promised me we shall all get what we wish. Now, however, the cost will be very dear. Very dead indeed."

A cold draft came in as Simaetha went out the door. For a moment, Daedalus stood, staring after her. *Heh. She only spouts harmless words. She did not even curse me.* He went to his bedroll in the corner and sat, his back against the wall. "Your punishment has already begun." The words echoed in his mind. He drew his knees up to his chest and wrapped his arms around his legs. Staring into the darkness, he tried to keep himself from shaking.

QVINTVS DECIMVS

Hispallus sat in his ivory curule chair and surveyed the crowd of clientes in the atrium. *At least their numbers are back to normal. No embarrassing lack of business today.* As his lictors kept the hopeful petitioners at bay, Hispallus tried to decide which group to give audience to. He recognized one knot of angry men—Ligurians come again with claims that their Roman governor was extorting funds from their merchants. *And I must tell them again that I am still investigating the situation. Their governor is of the Drusi, a family long allied to the Scipiones. These Ligurians do not understand how politically delicate the foreign extortion court can be.*

The praetor scanned more faces and was about to select an envoy who might have been from his old province in Hispania, when he saw a woman at the front of the atrium. Her face was hidden behind the folds of a reddish-brown palla, yet she seemed to command his attention. *Euryale! So—she has chosen to visit me herself!* This gave Hispallus considerable hope, and he ordered his servants to bring her forward. Amid frustrated cries of "We've waited longer!" and other, cruder remarks, Hispallus guided the woman into the tablinum and shut the bronze doors behind him.

"Domina Euryale, this is quite a surprise. I had expected to visit you myself this afternoon."

"More of a surprise than you imagine," said the woman.

The praetor stopped. The voice was not that of the Domina Euryale. She pulled her palla back to reveal a thin face and intense eyes. "Pardon me," said Hispallus, staring. "I seem to have made a mistake." He moved to reopen the doors.

"Yes and no, for I bring you a message concerning the Domina Euryale."

Hispallus frowned, finding it hard to connect this woman with the demure Euryale. This one seemed more like one of his wife's associates. "Did Clodia send you?"

"I know no Clodia," said the woman. "I am Simaetha of the Marsi. I see you have heard of the reputation of my people."

Hispallus, who had unconsciously been making the sign of the fig, unclenched his fist. "Yes, that I have. Now what is your message?"

"You should forget your visit to the Domina Euryale. Never see her again. Much hangs upon this, Magistrate."

"Much hangs upon my visit, woman. Is this the request of Euryale herself?"

Simaetha shook her head. "It is Hecate who bids me speak thus. She who lives in the three worlds has shown me that the lives of her servants are in the balance. You are the weight that shall cause their fortune to fall one way or the other."

Hispallus imagined a merchant's scale with coins falling upon it, and the words of the oracle echoed in his mind. ". . . blood and treachery stains what money buys." And what had it said earlier? "Beware the serpent's eyes." Examining the witch further, Hispallus saw the snake skin entwined in her hair, *and only witches cast the evil eye.*

He gave Simaetha an unfriendly smile. "I see. Well, I am flattered your Lady of Darkness sees me as so important. But you are aware, I am sure, that witchcraft is illegal in Rome. It is written in our Twelve Tables of law. I hope this dire warning of yours did not come to you through means of witchcraft rites while in Rome, else I might have to take action against you. As it is, I suggest you say nothing more, but run along, having done your duty by Hecate. And I will forgive your words and your face and all will be well." Hispallus took her elbow and tried to guide her toward the doors.

"You great fool," Simaetha said in a harsh whisper.

Hispallus narrowed his eyes. "Watch your tongue, woman. If you attempt to curse me—"

"That is unnecessary. You send yourself to your own doom. I need say nothing more."

Hispallus opened one of the bronze doors and the witch, pulling her elbow from his grasp, turned and stalked out. *And this is the sort of person my wife calls wise.*

The praetor followed her, expecting the rude and angry cries of his clients to greet him. Instead, excited murmurs filled the room, and Hispallus noted the eyes of the throng were not on him. All were turned toward the center of the atrium where someone was making his way forward. The petitioners parted to reveal Scipio Aemilianus smiling and nodding, charming the crowd. Hispallus felt suddenly small and grubby. *Younger than I am, and he holds a lesser office. Yet these people respond to him as if he were still the hero, just returned from a defeated Carthage.* The praetor's stomach ached again and he rubbed it absently as Aemilianus approached.

At last Hispallus caught his attention. "Cousin!" Aemilianus exclaimed, arms open wide. They embraced as close relatives ought, and Aemilianus kept a friendly hand on Hispallus's shoulder as he stepped back. "I had feared," the younger Scipio continued, "that I might not get a chance to see you, for these people intimated that you were closeted with . . . an important client."

A few of the clientes laughed and shared knowing looks.

Hispallus shook his head. "It was only a witch-woman from the hills, whom I mistook for someone else." The praetor looked around for Simaetha, but she had gone.

Aemilianus raised an eyebrow. "A witch, eh? Was she seeing you in your capacity as Peregrinus or Decemvir?"

"Neither, cousin. She came to spout nonsense, nothing more."

"Well, my company may not be as interesting as that of a witch, but I would like to speak to you briefly, if I may."

"Certainly. Your company is welcome above all others." Hispallus gestured toward the bronze doors and allowed Aemilianus to precede him through. This time there were no remarks from the petitioners, only a respectful hush. Hispallus asked one of the lictors to bring refreshments, then entered the tablinum.

"I should have you to visit more often," Hispallus said, closing the doors. "My atrium has not been this calm in a long time."

Aemilianus barked a laugh. But as he turned and sat in a wooden chair, his face became serious. "Why were you speaking to a witch, Gnaeus?"

Hispallus frowned. "She came to me with dire portents which I shall pay no attention to. Why do you ask?"

Aemilianus absently studied his hands a moment before speaking. "Our cousin Nasica runs for Consul this year. He worries about his chances of winning."

"I thought his victory was virtually assured."

"Perhaps. But our old enemies, the Claudii, support his opponent. They are very resourceful."

"As are we, Aemilianus. What does this have to do with me?"

"Come, Hispallus. You are the highest ranking Scipio now, even though I am, perhaps, the most visible. What you do in office will affect opinion of our family as a whole. If the Claudii can discredit you, claiming that you consort with low elements such as witches . . . particularly since you are a decemvir, and a guardian of the Roman faith . . ."

"Yes, I see. The witch was trying to warn me away from an important foreign client. Do you think the Claudii might have sent her?"

Aemilianus shrugged. "Who can say? Something you should keep in mind, at any rate."

Hispallus nodded. "Witches and wizards have always been thought enemies of Rome and her gods. It is odd to think that they might be used by Romans against each other."

"Well, they are becoming common enough, here. I know some senators who will not say yea or nay until they have consulted their pet astrologer. My resident philosopher, Panaetius, brought a Chaldean back with him from Babylon. An odd fellow—a stoic. And a theurge, which I presume is some form of the astrology these people all practice. He hopes to find work here in Rome and I'm sure he'll succeed."

A disturbing thought occurred to Hispallus. "If such astrologers could be used for political ends . . . paid to give certain kinds of advice . . . they could have great influence indeed."

Aemilianus frowned. "Are you suggesting we try such a thing?"

"No, no, not us! Far too risky. But what if one of our rival clans were to attempt it? What could we do?"

"Yes," Aemilianus mused. "Something to consider. Indeed. But now I must bring up a more pressing concern. The matter of your wife."

Hispallus rubbed his stomach again. "What of her?"

Aemilianus tilted his head and regarded the praetor carefully. "Her . . . unorthodox practices. It was wise of you to send her to Ostia, out of the public eye. But I understand she has returned to Rome."

"For a while, yes."

"This will, no doubt, cause people to speak of her again, and you know where that may lead. Have you talked to her about submitting her sect to the laws of Rome? Don't look so shocked, Gnaeus. Slaves have big ears and bigger mouths, and I am family, after all."

"Yes, I have spoken to her. She refuses."

"Hmmm." Aemilianus rested his chin on steepled fingers. "You know it is my belief that Rome should retain the old ways . . . particularly in morality and religion. I cannot condone your wife's behaviour. You should have divorced her long ago."

"Yes, I have come to realize that," said Hispallus. "But to divorce her now would only cast more shadows on our family."

"Hmm. You are right, this would not be a good time for that. Well, can you keep her activities discreet for the time being?"

"I am doing what I can."

Aemilianus nodded once, then frowned. "Are you ill, Gnaeus? You seem pale, and you squeeze your toga as a baker kneads dough."

"What? Oh." Hispallus looked at his hand as though he noticed it for the first time. "A minor ache of the stomach, that is all. It comes and goes."

"Hm. You should have a physician look at that. At our age, the gods treat us less kindly, eh? Well, I must be going. I shall, I expect, see you at the senate comitia for that discussion on secret balloting." Aemilianus stood and again placed a hand on Hispallus's shoulder. "Take care, Gnaeus. You have served our family well. I still remember when we went to Carthage together and told them to lay down their arms. It was a glorious moment. May you bring the same honor to us now."

"I will do all I can." *Though it means paying a mad blackmailer for his silence.* "Vale, Scipio." Hispallus watched Aemilianus leave and found himself clutching his toga again. He felt sick. *One more duty today and I will rest. But no witch will keep me from seeing the Domina Euryale.*

SEXTVS DECIMVS

S EVISUS BLINKED IN THE BRIGHT MORNING SUNSHINE as he
stepped into the garden to look for Archidemus. The fresh
scented spring air seemed to banish the leftover fears and anx-
ieties of the night before. Sevisus found the theurge sitting on
a marble bench beneath a peach tree whose pale green leaves
had just begun to bud. Archidemus was staring off at nothing
in particular and did not notice Sevisus standing nearby.

The boy smiled. He was secretly proud that the Domina was
giving the Chaldean a chance, because he had been the one to
bring the mage to her attention and because he simply liked
Archidemus. It was a greater honor that she was allowing Archidemus to stay in her house—she had never had houseguests
during the time Sevisus had worked for her. *She seems to find
this one agreeable, though.* Little Caecus, who loved gossip, had
told Sevisus that Archidemus and Euryale had stayed up very
late last night, speaking in some foreign tongue.

Despite the extra work it made for him, Sevisus hoped Archidemus would stay awhile. It was exciting having nearby a
real scholar to speak to.

Hoping he was not being out of place, Sevisus said, "Good
morning to you, magus."

"Eh? Oh, good morning, Sevisus. I see you weathered the
night little better than I. How fares your Domina?"

"I was hoping you could tell me, magus. I have not seen her
since the middle of the night when we were rushing around

trying to find out why the dog was barking. I heard there was an intruder, but Deino won't tell me anything. All sorts of noises kept me awake later, but I don't know, really, what happened."

Archidemus nodded. "Nor I, exactly. There was an intruder, apparently, but he ran off."

"Was anything stolen?"

Archidemus looked away for a moment. "No, no . . . objects were taken. But your Domina was very upset by the incident. Whatever you may think of her, Sevisus, she is a very kind-hearted woman . . . a most amazing woman." He paused. "I understand now why she so dearly needs my assistance."

Sevisus frowned, wondering what the intrusion might have to do with the Chaldean's powers, or the Domina's stone-into-flesh riddle. He also was not sure of a polite way to ask that might get him an answer. "Then you can help her, magus?"

"I can show her the way to reach the divine power; after that . . . it is out of my hands."

"What must she do, climb Mount Olympus?"

Archidemus laughed. "No, my boy. It is far more simple yet more complex. The divine is not atop a mountain or in the sky, but everywhere and in all of us. It is not her body that must travel, but her mind. Her eyes must learn to see a different world."

Sevisus shook his head. "I don't understand."

Archidemus chuckled gently. "Perhaps someday I may show you, also, Sevisus."

Sevisus grinned. "Thank you, magus. I'd like that." Pausing, he looked down at his sandals. "May I ask you one more thing, magus?"

"You may ask, certainly."

Sevisus took from a pocket in his tunic the scrap of parchment given him by the bookseller. Unfolding it hesitantly, he handed it to Archidemus. "Can you read this? I know it looks like a funny jumble of letters. I've deciphered some of them, but I can't make out the rest."

Archidemus looked over the parchment for a while, then snorted. "It is interesting that you show me this, Sevisus. As far as I can tell, it is an astrological text. See, these symbols here are for the planets Mars and Venus. These symbols show their positions relative to one another and with respect to the sun and moon. The name of the one for whom this horoscope was done, however, seems to be missing. Perhaps fortuitously." He handed the parchment back to Sevisus.

"Why is that, magus?"

"These verses, at the bottom of the scrap, are predictions—oracles, if you will—based on the information at the beginning. And if I read the code correctly, those predictions are dire indeed."

"What do they say?"

"Are you sure you want to know?" Archidemus asked with a grin as he took the parchment. "Mind you, I put little value on knowledge gleaned from the stars in this way. However, the verses read:

"As fresh-plowed soil, your ways are overturned,
Freedom dies where hope and greed have burned.

"A great one rises who will conquer all,
By unsuspected hands this one will fall.

"A mighty city falls from rot and rust,
The tread of tyrants tramples it to dust."

Archidemus handed the paper back to Sevisus. "Quite a collection of ills. Revolution, enslavement, assassination, disease, destruction . . . I'd wager the person who commissioned this reading wasn't pleased. It's no surprise that it was given away for scrap."

"Do you think any of it will happen?"

Archidemus laughed. "Undoubtedly. These verses are so general, they could describe many future events, or past ones.

Men, cities, empires, all rise and fall in their time. Part of the art of being an oracle is wording one's predictions such that one is inevitably right."

"Why isn't the astrologer's name on this? Wouldn't he be proud of being right?"

"Not in Rome."

"No?"

Archidemus closed his eyes and his mouth twitched in an embarrassed smile. "I mean no disrespect to your fair city, Sevisus. But before I came, I was warned by other foreigners who had been here to be cautious in my actions and teachings. Rome can be generous in Her tolerance, so long as you break no law. But let there be the slightest whiff of conspiracy against the Republic, and the forces of Rome will come down on you like the she-wolf that was Her founders' mother. Whoever left his name off this was wise."

Sevisus found this view of Rome interesting and a bit unsettling.

"Where did you get it?" Archidemus asked.

"Joseph the Bookseller gave it to me."

"A Jew? He was wise to get rid of it too, then."

Sevisus was about to ask why, when he heard Deino calling from the house.

"Sevisus! You half-sighted lazykins, come here! There are chores to do and errands to run, another guest comes soon. Make swift your feet, boy!"

Sevisus grinned sheepishly and shrugged at the theurge. "Thank you for your help, sir. I must go now."

Archidemus nodded. "You are welcome. And remember, try not to upset your Domina today, eh? Take good care of her."

"Yes, magus. I will. Thank you." With a bow, Sevisus turned and ran back toward the house. He stuffed the parchment back into his tunic, and wondered which baker Deino would send him to for pastries for the visiting praetor.

Hispallus sat on the silk-cushioned couch in the Domina Euryale's tablinum, feeling oddly vulnerable. His lictors had requested that they be allowed to await him in a nearly wine and pastry shop, rather than on the Domina's grounds. The praetor had easily relented. The farther they were away from this embarrassing business, the more comfortable he felt. Yet, complete calm eluded him. Hispallus looked at the frescoes on the walls; each was a scene of the countryside, with green, rolling hills and small farms and vineyards. The houses depicted were of an ancient style, packed earthen walls with thatched roofs. Simpler ways and simpler times, he thought with a pang of nostalgia, homesick for a way of life he had never known. He remembered how Cato the Elder had said that the only truly noble occupation for a Roman was farming. Even the mighty soldier, returning home from campaigns in foreign lands, should gladly exchange his sword for the harvest scythe.

His reverie was disrupted by the entrance of the Domina Euryale from a side door. She was veiled as before, and dressed in a plain homespun wool palla and stola.

"Please forgive my tardiness, Magistrate," she said as she swiftly crossed the room and sat in a chair opposite him. "My thoughts, of late, have been somewhat distracted."

"There is nothing to forgive, Domina. I was admiring the frescoes on your wall. The artwork is excellent. Very soothing."

"Yes," Euryale replied distantly, "the scenes remind me of my homeland."

"A . . . pleasant place it must be, indeed," Hispallus said, wondering where she might have come from where such an ancient style of house was still built. "I trust you are well."

"What? Oh. Yes, well enough, thank you. And you, Magistrate?"

"The same."

The slave boy Sevisus entered, carrying a small table on which were platters of dried fruit, sweet cakes and cheese, which he set between the Domina and Hispallus. The praetor helped himself to the food, noticing that Euryale did not stir. In fact, he had the unsettling feeling that she was staring at him through her veil. "Is something the matter, Domina?"

"Your face . . ." she said softly.

Hispallus self-consciously rubbed his chin, wondering if his barber had done a sloppy job that morning. He gave an embarrassed laugh. "My face, Domina? What do you find wrong with it?"

"Wrong? Oh, no, no, Magistrate. I am terribly sorry. I meant . . . I have seen someone recently who resembles you. Nothing more."

"Ah, I see." Hispallus thought of his features as being rather ordinary. There might be a hundred men in Rome who looked like him. Sometimes he felt the only items that distinguished him from the rest of the crowd in the Forum were his purple-edged toga, his red leather sandals and the six lictors who proclaimed his name. Hispallus leaned back to recline on the couch, wondering how to broach the main item of business for which he had come. "How fares your 'project,' Domina?"

"I believe it goes well, Magistrate. You are, of course, asking whether I intend to contribute toward the bridge you are sponsoring."

Hispallus inclined his head, trying to appear casual as he held his breath.

"I feel I ought to mention that a young man claiming to be the architect for this bridge came to visit. Quite unexpectedly."

"Oh." Hispallus felt his stomach ache again and he rubbed his toga. *Curse that Daedalus . . .* "I hope he said nothing ill-mannered, Domina. I know he tends sometimes to be . . . overly enthusiastic."

"Presumptuous, I think is a more accurate description. However, I do not hold you responsible for his behavior. And his visit did not alter my decision."

"Yes?"

"I fear," Euryale said, rubbing the arms of her chair with her hands, "that I cannot contribute. There are two people who have promised me an answer; an alchemist, from whom I expect little, and a Chaldean theurge, who I believe may give me what I seek."

Hispallus frowned and sat upright. "A Chaldean? You mean that little Greek fellow you sent to me?"

"What? Oh, no, Magistrate. This is a different one. A philosopher-mage from Nineveh."

Aemilianus was right, they are everywhere, sullying us all with their bogus magic and bad advice. I must do what I can to prevent this "mage" from duping Euryale and interfering with my means of silencing Daedalus. "May I ask, Domina," Hispallus said cautiously, "who sent this mage to you?"

"No one, Magistrate. My slave, Sevisus, mentioned him to me. He was a houseguest of the alchemist Olerus. But of his own he chose to see me. Why do you ask?"

Leaning forward, the praetor said, "I do not wish to alarm you, Domina, but it has come to my attention that there are many of these false wizards entering Rome. They find their way into the homes of the wealthy and powerful, and give whatever advice puts more coin in their pockets."

Hispallus was taken aback as Euryale began to laugh. "Forgive me, Magistrate," she said, "but you sound just like my maidservant, Deino. She would prefer that I never speak to a wizard again."

"Your servant is wise, Domina. Often slaves and servants have useful advice to give. You should listen to her."

"She would be gratified to hear you say that, Magistrate." Then a sigh came from behind the veil. "But this time I cannot. Archidemus is not like the others. He understands my . . . situation. I must give him a chance. I am sure you can find another donor for your bridge, Magistrate."

Hispallus stood, and began to pace behind the couch like a starving lion before the Games. *Another donor. Someone else before whom Daedalus can embarrass me. Oh, that will please him. I can see the cold smirk on his face now, as I beg him for more time.* Hispallus smashed his fist into his palm. "I don't think you appreciate the gravity of the situation, Domina." His voice rose in pitch. "Do you truly believe the positions of the stars can help you bring stone to life? Does this mage have you so charmed that you will give your fortune for the nonsense he will tell you?"

"If you will allow me to explain—"

"No, it is I who should explain something to you, Domina. As praetor peregrinus, and a decemvir, it is my duty to protect Rome from the influence of dangerous, foreign beliefs. And I am hearing too much about these . . . Chaldeans!" *I can't let her turn me away without a denarius. I can't let Daedalus twist the knife further. I won't let some idiot star-gazer get in my way!*

His breathing came rapid and shallow and he grasped the back of the couch as his knees felt oddly weak beneath him. "Domina, I—" There was a sudden stab of pain in his middle and the praetor bent over, clutching his toga to his abdomen.

"Are you all right, Magistrate?"

"I . . . if you please, Domina, direct me to your washroom."

"Of course. Sevisus!"

The boy entered in an instant.

"Please guide the praetor to the washroom, quickly. He is ill."

"Yes, Domina."

Hispallus felt the boy take hold of his elbow. He allowed himself to be led out of the tablinum, fear chasing dark thoughts through his mind. *Could it be poison? Could Daedalus have arranged this, hoping my death would be blamed on Euryale? The witch warned me. What did she know?*

He was guided to a small, title-floored room containing a basin. But attempting to disgorge his stomach's contents brought the praetor no relief. In fact, the pain seemed to be spreading throughout his left side. Desperately afraid, Hispallus called out to Sevisus who stood dutifully beyond the door. "Boy! Fetch me my lictors, who are at Massina's taverna. Bid them come instantly! You will be well rewarded."

"Yes, Magistrate!"

Hispallus heard the slave patter away, and wondered if the boy could be trusted. He felt a sudden urge to flee, to escape, hoping he could find someone to whom the truth could be told before the poison, or whatever it was, took its full toll.

The praetor staggered out of the washroom and saw several doorways. He did not remember which led back to the tablinum. Dizzy and short of breath, Hispallus chose the nearest and flung the door-curtain aside. It was only a storage room, containing a cloth-covered statue. His legs began to give way beneath him. Hispallus pitched forward and clutched at the cloth on the statue as he fell. But his fall knocked the statue off balance and ever so slowly, it seemed, the statue toppled over to shatter into pieces on the stone floor.

Clutching the cloth to his chest and gasping for breath, Hispallus slid to the floor, unable to take his eyes from the statue's debris. He had seen soldiers disemboweled by sword wounds in war, and the shapes of the broken stone of the statue were so very suggestive . . . so like human flesh and organs. The praetor heard movement off to one side, but he did not react to it. He could only feel the pain and stare with wonder at the statue's face; a familiar face; with features like his own.

With a great effort, Hispallus pointed to it and rasped, "That . . . is my son. Why . . ."

And then the pain overwhelmed all his senses. Though he thought he heard the Domina Euryale screaming.

SEPTIMVS DECIMVS

T HE SUNSET WAS A BLOOD-RED SMEAR across the western
sky. Beneath it, the Tiber glowed like liquid fire. Daedalus
approached the Palatine house of Scipio Hispallus, the daemons of his soul singing songs of sweet vengeance. *She will
have turned him down. And he will wring his hands and beg
me let him try again.*

With intense anticipation, he walked up to the great oak
gate. To his surprise, the dusty-togaed "shadows" still lounged
at the gateposts. Normally by now they would have been invited in to dinner or shooed away. They regarded the architect
with sardonic disinterest as he was about to call to the watch-
man for admittance.

"Don't bother," said one idler, "the praetor's out."

"You'll have to wait your turn like the rest of us."

"I had an appointment," Daedalus said.

Laughter erupted around him. "Little good that does you
if he isn't here. The word is he is being entertained by some
rich peregrina and won't be returning until late. But if you're
determined, you can sit and play dice with us while you wait.
Then at least we might profit from your visit."

As the others laughed, Daedalus gave them a disgusted
look and began to walk away. Before he had gone far, however, he felt a tugging on his toga. He turned and saw one of

the "shadows," a thin craven-looking man, standing hopefully behind him. "What is it?" Daedalus snapped.

"Do you truly know the praetor, sir?"

Daedalus half smiled. *A desperate hanger-on, this one.* "Indeed. I am an old friend of his family."

The idler brightened. "Well, then I'm sure there's no harm in mentioning to a friend that I saw, earlier this afternoon, two of his lictors run into his house. Very agitated they seemed, and soon they ran out again with another personage. All three ran off toward the Aventine without a word to anyone."

"I see. Thank you for this news, good . . ."

"Fustis Coccinatus, sir. You may tell him it was I who told you. In fact, I would most appreciate it if you could mention my name to the good praetor. You see, it's concerning the matter of—"

"I will be sure to mention it," said Daedalus, walking quickly away.

"Don't forget!" called the shadow, waving behind him.

But Daedalus had already forgotten the name and the man as his mind spun with worries. *Could the praetor have met the same fate as his son? The gorgon wouldn't dare.* He curled his fingers into his palms and tightened them. *Did she tell the praetor about Cnaeus? No, she did not know him. He pressed his fists to his temples, and grimaced in worry and anger. What, then? Is it a trick? A trap? Does Hispallus know her nature and want to lure me there?*

Daedalus sagged against a wall along the street and breathed deeply of the evening air, trying to clear his mind. *There must be a way to learn what is happening. Mustn't let fear make me mad. He may just be delayed. I mustn't push too hard too soon. Got to think about what to do.*

Daedalus opened his eyes and saw other people on the street give him a wide berth as they passed by him. Women with baskets under their arms hid their faces behind their pallas when he looked at them. "Heh," he sneered and pushed off from the wall. His daemon under control once more, Daedalus walked home to consider what to do.

THE PAIN SWELLED AND EBBED LIKE THE TIDES OF A DARK SEA. At times, Hispallus's awareness seemed to be floating on the surface, then it would plunge again into the depths of pain, seeming to drown. In the floating moments, he remembered hearing anxious voices around him, arms carrying him to a soft surface to lie on. He remembered being given a bitter herb tea to drink, though he spilled most of it down his chest. Now was another floating moment, and he felt a cool hand and soft fabric brush against his arm. He looked up to see the veiled Euryale bending over him.

"Magistrate, can you hear me? Please speak, if you can."

Hispallus still found it difficult to breathe, and when he opened his mouth, the sound that issued from it was not his voice, but a rasping croak. "Poison?" was all he could say.

"Deino! He speaks!"

"That is good, Despoina. What does he say?"

"He wishes to know if he was poisoned." Her veil lightly touched his cheek as she turned her head to face him again. "Magistrate, your physician has been here. He thinks poison is possible. Archidemus says that your ailment is what happens when the spirit is overburdened by too many woes. The body breaks under the strain like a cruelly laden mule."

Who would be poisoning me? Who would want to give me such torment? Old family enemies? Daedalus? How could he arrange it? Through Euryale's astrologer? Cruelly laden. Yes, I have been burdened by woes. If only I could shrug if off like a stubborn mule. Unburden myself. Well, there is one way I may yet do so. I must tell someone the truth before I die. Euryale is kind. She should be told. She should be warned.

Lifting an arm that felt like lead, Hispallus grasped Euryale's sleeve. "Daedalus . . ." he rasped.

"Yes, Magistrate, what of him?"

"The money . . . for blackmail. Daedalus . . . would shame my wife . . . me . . . my family. Money for bridge . . . to keep silent." Hispallus found himself out of breath all too soon.

"Blackmail! That is why you asked me for the donation. You needed a discreet, foreign source."

"Yes . . . Daedalus comes . . . tonight . . . for money."

"I wish it had not taken this for you to tell me your plight, praetor. Of course I will help you. The alchemist has not answered my question, and Archidemus asks little. I can spare the funds, somehow. Fear not, Magistrate. We will see that Daedalus receives what he asks for."

"No . . . I cannot ask you now—" But Hispallus felt cool fingers on his lips to silence him. Then Euryale's hand squeezed his arm.

"It is the very least I can do, Magistrate. Would that I could do more to earn your forgiveness. Here comes your physician. We will leave you in his care. Rest you well."

Forgiveness? What has Euryale done that needs forgiveness? A wave of dull aching passed through him and he closed his eyes to accept his fate. *As Iupiter wills it.*

Intempeste nocte

A PALE GIBBOUS MOON RODE HIGH in the sky as Daedalus approached Euryale's gate, accompanied by his contractor, Nescio. Nescio was strong as a bull, and nearly as easy to anger. *He'll be good in a fight,* thought Daedalus, *if it comes to that.*

Nothing outside the gate betrayed that there was anything amiss within. The street was clear of traffic and all seemed quiet. Daedalus found this more disturbing than the tumult he expected. He announced himself, calling out to the blind gatekeeper within.

"Yes, you are expected. Enter." The gate opened, and the snarling dog was held at bay.

CXVII

"I don't see what worried you," Nescio rumbled softly. "Seems like you hardly need me along."

"Stay with me," Daedalus said, and he stepped inside the gate. He looked around waiting for officers of the aediles to come out from the shadows and arrest him. Instead there were only two of the praetor's lictors standing in the garden beside the gatekeeper, and the old woman servant of the gorgon. She held a torch whose flames were reflected in her small, dark eyes. It gave her an evil, fearsome appearance, enhanced by the ghost of a sardonic smile on her lips. The three of them merely stood and stared at him, saying nothing.

"I am here to see Scipio Hispallus," Daedalus said, uncertain whom to address so speaking to them all. "He expects me."

"The praetor is in private conference now and cannot be disturbed," said the old woman. "But he has told us something of your business and bids us to see that you are well served. Wait here." The old woman turned and walked toward the house, the lictors following her.

"I must speak to the praetor himself!" Daedalus called after them.

"There will be no need," said the old woman.

Daedalus paced a little, looking nervously about him. *He intends to say no again. He thinks to keep himself at a safe distance.* The architect tried to think what the next twist of his knife might be, but the mad daemon within him was oddly silent. The fear of being in this place, where he might be recognized, where perhaps young Cnaeus's ghost lingered still, kept him unsettled and cautious.

Presently, the old woman and the two lictors returned, one lictor carrying a large crate, the other a sack. They stopped three arm-lengths away from Daedalus and the old woman said, "It may please you to know that the Despoina Euryale has chosen to donate money for your bridge. In fact, she is willing to pay for its entire construction, such that you need no longer bother the good praetor with your entreaties."

"What good news, Daedalus!" said Nescio.

The architect felt as though a rug were pulled out from under him. "I . . . could not accept such a generous gift—"

"Don't be a fool!" Nescio shook Daedalus's shoulder. "We can't turn away good money." He looked at the old woman. "We accept your Domina's gracious offer, madam."

Daedalus saw the old woman raise an eyebrow at him, and Nescio staring at him as though he were mad. *Well, perhaps this is a sort of victory. And I have achieved a more fitting vengeance on Hispallus than he will ever know.* "Very well. We—"

The old woman held up her hand. "There is a condition."

"Well, speak it, woman!" said Nescio. "If not unreasonable, I'm sure we'll agree."

"The Despoina wishes that the contents of this box," she said, pointing to the crate, "be given prominent display amid the decoration on your bridge."

Daedalus stared at the box, a chill beginning to walk up his spine.

When the architect did not speak, Nescio said, "What is in the box, madam?"

She shrugged. "Merely a decorative image. Nothing that would offend passers-by, or the authorities."

"Well, it is not unusual for a patron to make such a request. Daedalus? Daedalus?"

"I accept," the architect heard himself say, feeling as though trapped in a nightmare.

"Excellent," the old woman said, with a wicked grin. "This sack contains your first payment, five thousand sesterces."

Daedalus was handed the coin-sack and Nescio was given the crate. After thanks and good-nights were said, they carried their loads toward Nescio's ramshackle hovel near the river. Along the way, the contractor kept up a stream of idiotic and lewd suggestions as to what the Domina's decoration might be. Daedalus concentrated on holding the coin-sack tight against him, to keep the coins from jingling and attracting thieves, or so he told himself.

Upon arriving, Nescio placed the crate on a rough wood table and immediately began to pry open the lid. "Well, let's see what it is our Domina has charged us with. Care to make a wager?"

"No," Daedalus said, softly.

"Here go the wrappings, then. Hmm. It's an ordinary portrait bust. Odd expression on the fellow's face, though. Say, this looks like the young lad you used to go drinking with—"

"Shut up," Daedalus hissed, clenching his fists. "Just shut up!"

DVODEVICESIMVS

IV NON. MART., ANTE MERIDIEM

Sevisus ran down the Vicus Lavernalis, glad to be away from the household for a while. It was becoming impossible to work there. The garden was full of lictors, attendants and the most important clients of the praetor's, inadvertent houseguests of the Domina since the praetor's physician insisted that he not be moved. Deino was worn to a frazzle, and more cross than ever, from dealing with the new guests. Much of the previous afternoon, Sevisus recalled grumpily, he had spent placing support struts around the Domina's precious statue in the garden, just so some drunk or careless person couldn't knock it over. And the new guests were not comfortable with the blindness of the Domina's slaves. Meanwhile, the Domina herself had hidden away in her rooms, not seeing anyone except Deino and Archidemus.

All of this made Sevisus glad to do a chore that wasn't fetching food or hauling wood planks around. A visit to Olerus's house seemed like a holiday. Even the streets seemed to him unusually clear of traffic, after his bustling around the crowded garden.

"Aye, boy, hurry!" called an old woman sweeping in front of one house. "They'll be moving on soon."

Now what did she mean by that? thought Sevisus. *Does she know what household I'm from, and mean our guests?*

As the avenue turned down the hill toward the Circus Maximus, Sevisus slowed as he saw a massive crowd assembled near the north end of the Circus. In the middle of the crowd he saw some movement, bright colors rippling, and he heard the sound of clashing metal. It was not until he was closer that he could see the movement as discreet points of color bobbing up and down in the center of the crowd, and Sevisus knew what was happening.

The Salii! I'd forgotten this is another of their days. Four times in Martius the "Leaping Priests" carry the sacred shields of the legendary King Numa around the city, jumping and dancing in the names of Mars and Quirinus. Crowds gathered wherever they went to watch the sons of noble family dance and sing in the armor of ancient warriors. Later in the day, the Salii go dine at their own feast, said to have the best food in all Rome.

For a moment, Sevisus was tempted to elbow his way through the throng to watch the Salii himself. But after suffering the current conditions of the Domina's household, Sevisus was losing his patience with crowds. *And the Domina is eager to know if Olerus has an answer for her. Well, maybe I'll get a chance to see them later this month.* Looking for a way to get around the mass of people, Sevisus saw a tiny alleyway between a house and a lamp-maker's shop and he scurried into it.

The narrow walls of the passageway he followed made him nervous . . . this was prime thieves territory. But, fortunately, it seemed that the thieves were occupied picking the purses of the priest-watching crowd. The only hostile encounter Sevisus had between the Vicus and the Tiber were with starving dogs and frightened cats.

When Sevisus reached the alchemist's rickety wooden door, he had to knock several times before he heard movement inside. At last the door opened and Olerus's fat, pale face blinked down at him. With a pained smile, he said wearily, "Ah, Sevisus. I feared it would be you. Come in."

The alchemist's home was even darker and more untidy than the last time Sevisus had visited. The books and scrolls were now spilling off the shelves and lay strewn on the floor. Mice nibbled on the remains of dinners days old. The only illumination was a one-wick oil lamp that sat on the wooden table in the center of the room. Bits of grey stone littered the table top, surrounded by various small iron and bronze tools.

"Good morning to you, magus," said Sevisus. "I was beginning to wonder if you'd gone off to see the leaping priests."

Olerus rubbed his face and eyes. "Oh. Are they dancing today? Mmmm. No, Sevisus, those of my calling are more interested in cleansing the daemons from one's spirit, than chasing them from the city with clashing arms and voices."

Sevisus went to the table and bent down to see the bits of stone clearly. One lump seemed to resemble part of a bird.

"Don't touch any of that," said Olerus. He came down to the table and sat heavily on a bench beside it.

"I wasn't going to, magus. This looks like one of the carvings from the Domina's garden."

"It *is* from the Domina's garden. It is a sample of the sort of stone she wanted brought back to life."

"Oh." After a long, uncomfortable pause, Sevisus prompted, "And?"

Olerus looked nervously about him for a few moments. "My dear boy, either your Domina has found the most clever sculptor this world has ever known, or . . ."

"Or?"

With a heavy sigh, Olerus rubbed his face again and stared at a spot between the table and nowhere. "Or she has been witness to a legendary horror, the nature of which I shudder to contemplate."

"What do you mean?" asked Sevisus. He found a stool and sat across the table from the alchemist.

"Take a look at this." Olerus moved bits of the grey stone about with a pair of tiny bronze tweezers that seemed incongruous in his meaty hands. "This stone is like no other I have ever seen. See, this portion is finely layered as if it were stone born of water, yet it is in the shape of flesh. And this bit, of the same color, is porous like stone born of air . . . yet it is in the shape of bone. And this piece is delicate as a frost crystal, in the shape of a feather. These pieces were all parts of a whole, interlocked within the bird. What sculptor would hide such exquisite puzzle-craft where it would never be seen and appreciated?"

Sevisus shrugged, knowing nothing of craftsmen save the outrageous sums they charged for their wares.

"No, boy." Olerus rubbed the side of his nose with a finger. "This is not the work of a sculptor. It is all too apparent that your poor Domina has, at one time, encountered . . . a basilisk."

"A basilisk? What is that, magus?"

Olerus stood and began to pace the room. "It is a serpent, the King of Serpents, in fact. He has a great crest that is his crown and he does not slither on his belly but stands nearly full upright, balanced on his tail. His venom is the deadliest poison, killing not only the one bitten but any who touch the bitten one as well. And his gaze, it is said, kills instantly, burning his victims or turning them to stone."

"Oh. And you think that—"

"Your poor Domina. To have seen her love killed by such a creature. She herself must have been disfigured in some way by the basilisk, which is why she keeps her face hidden. Such a great pity. I'm sure she was beautiful, once."

Sevisus felt uneasy. *The statue in the garden was once alive?* And what of the remains of the shattered statue he had swept up the day the praetor had taken ill? "If you know that is the cause, can you reverse it? Can you help the Domina?"

"Alas, to my great sorrow, no." Olerus flung out his arms to take in the whole room. "All of my books on the subject name ways to kill a basilisk—with mirrors, fire, magic and so forth. But none speak of a remedy. A victim of the basilisk, once dead, remains so. I can do nothing. Neither, I might add, can that pompous philosopher Archidemus. We are all powerless against the might of the basilisk."

"Oh. I see."

"I shall ask no payment, not a denarius, of the Domina. Though should she ever choose to tell me the story of how she came upon the basilisk, I would be a most willing audience. Beyond that . . . " Olerus shrugged his massive shoulders. "Of course, you could always remind her—"

"That you can make a homunculus for her. I will remember."

"You are a good boy, Sevisus. Though I can understand if she declines the offer."

"I suppose I'd better go and tell her what you've learned."

"Yes. And tell her that I will not betray her secret if she wishes it to remain so. And warn her that Archidemus, no mater what he says, can be no more help than I."

"I will tell her, sir." Sevisus went to the door, then looked back to see Olerus staring at the pieces of stone bird and shaking his head. Feeling his world had gone sadly topsy-turvy, Sevisus closed the door behind him and headed home.

VNDEVICESIMVS

MIRRORS OF POLISHED BRONZE SURROUNDED HER, some propped up on tables, some hung on the walls. Euryale sat in the center of the small room, her head bowed, her palla draped loosely over her face and unbound head. "You know the risk you are taking?" she asked.

"Of course," Archidemus replied behind her. "I have seen Aristo, and the Scipio boy, have I not? Why do you think I am using so many mirrors? I may be eccentric, but I am not a fool." He grunted, lifting something heavy. "There, that is the last."

"Perhaps I am the fool," Euryale sighed, "for allowing you to attempt this at all."

"Nothing is gained without risk, Domina. As a teacher, I discovered that the best way to tell if my students were learning was to watch their faces. For what I must teach you, in particular, it is very important that I see your expressions. They will teach me when you are in the proper state of mind for the next step. Do you understand, Domina?"

"Yes, but if we become careless . . ."

"For my sake, let us agree not to. At least, not until the divine powers have revealed to you a cure."

Euryale heard in his voice that he meant it in jest, but she could not find it amusing. "Archidemus—"

"I am ready," he said, still standing behind her. "You may remove your palla."

Euryale shut her eyes and tried to still her trembling. *I am more worried that he. Gods, do not let this go wrong.* She slowly lifted the cloth from her head. She could feel the little serpents stretch themselves, their heads rising, their tongues questing. They shifted to face behind her, toward where Archidemus stood. They seemed curious, but not alarmed, and Euryale let out her breath, relieved.

Once, long ago, in the depths of despair Euryale had tried to cut the serpents off her head with a knife. She had only succeed-ed in removing two. The pain had been as much as if she had cut off a finger. The other snakes attacked her hands—gashing her with their fangs, though their poison could not harm her. And, of course, the two she cut grew back. Since then, Euryale had learned to live with her little ones. They were sensitive to her moods and she, likewise, became sensitive to theirs. If they trusted Archidemus, then perhaps she could too.

Opening her eyes, she raised her head and saw myriad re-flections lift their emerald tresses as well. In front of her, her countenance, golden-hued in the polished bronze, stared back with cautious apprehension. The face of the bearded and dark-robed Archidemus seemed to float over her right shoulder.

"I am a monster," Euryale said softly.

"No," said Archidemus, rapt with awe. "Not at all."

She watched her lips tighten into a thin smile. "You are too kind, magus."

"Am I?" he breathed. "What is a monster, Domina? Some-one who looks different from the rest? All people are different, in their own way. At what point does this difference become monstrous?"

"Not merely looks," Euryale said. "My aspect turns people to stone. It is this horrid power that makes me monstrous."

"Actions, then, can make one a monster. But the lion and the wolf must kill for their sustenance, and they are not 'mon-sters.' Many consider them noble and beautiful beasts. Yet they kill with far more deliberate purpose than you. What harm you have caused has not been by choice, I assume. If we measure by action, then, you are even less a monster than the lion or the wolf. And you are certainly more beautiful."

Euryale closed her eyes and clenched her teeth. His kind words were only needles of pain in her heart. *He does not understand.* "This discussion leads nowhere. Please begin your lesson, Archidemus."

"As you wish, Domina." Archidemus inclined his head and walked over to a small cabinet.

Euryale watched his many reflections as he pulled out various objects from the cabinet's shelves: a brass incense-burner in the shape of an elephant, a papyrus scroll, a clay drinking bowl painted with dolphins. He set these in a row atop the cabinet.

"There are three parts to a theurgical summoning. The words," he said, touching the scroll. "The atmosphere . . ." He touched the incense-burner. "And the mind." He finally touched the bowl. "This last is the most important. The others merely serve to prepare it to receive the divine spirit."

"So I shall be possessed, like a sibyl? I thought I would conjure a god before me, as a witch might conjure up a daemon."

Archidemus laughed. Euryale watched him begin to turn toward her, then catch himself and look in the mirror instead. "No, Domina. There are theurges who claim to have summoned gods in the flesh, but I would not believe them. The divine spirit, I have learned, is spirit only. It takes many forms in this universe, but it is unlikely to pop up as a god fresh from Olympus. Through the eyes of your mind, however, you may see this spirit in whatever guise it deems best to inform you."

"I don't think I understand, magus," said Euryale, keeping her hands close to her face.

"There will be time enough to explain."

Suddenly there came a light rapping on the wooden door. "Domina! Domina!" came Caecus's voice.

Her serpents instantly hissed and whipped around to face the door. Euryale flung the palla over them. "By the gods, I asked not to be disturbed!"

Archidemus went to the door and called through it, "What do you want?"

"A very important man is here to see the Domina!"

"Who?"

Euryale heard Deino shushing Caecus behind the door. "It is the Scipio Aemilianus, Despoina. The censor, and kinsman to Hispallus. He demands to see you. What shall I tell him?"

Archidemus commented wryly. "I suppose even the divine spirits must wait, when you are visited by the most powerful man in Rome."

"Give me time to prepare, Deino," said Euryale. "Pallas Athena," she muttered softly, "could you not spare me, even this once?"

EURYALE SAT AS CALMLY AS SHE COULD, waiting for the censor to speak. Scipio Aemilianus stood staring out of the one window in the tablinum, hands clasped behind his back. Through her veil, Euryale could see that his lined, middle-aged face was handsome, but somehow weary. *He has fought one battle too many,* she thought, *and not only in war.*

At the other end of the room, Scipio Hispallus lay on a couch, looking pale and drained. *As though he has been visited by a lamia,* thought Euryale. Beside the praetor stood his physician, a thin, dour man who refused to speak to anyone in Euryale's household except to give orders concerning the praetor's care. Three young lictors in short tunics stood against one wall, arms crossed on their chests. Beside Euryale stood Deino, composed but wary.

"Please forgive my unannounced interruption of your affairs, Despoina," said Aemilianus in flawless Greek, "but this is a matter of grave importance, requiring swift and discreet investigation."

Does he wish to reassure me by speaking what he believes is my native tongue, or does he imply that he would comprehend anything I might say to Deino? "I am pleased to assist you in whatever I can, Censor. What may I do for you?"

Despite the cordiality, Euryale had no illusions as to what was happening. The praetor's collapse was too sudden not to be regarded with suspicion.

Aemilianus gave a brief smile and sat in the remaining chair. Effortlessly he dominated the room. "I appreciate your gracious cooperation," he said, switching to Latin. Euryale assumed it was for the sake of the lictors. "Hispallus has spoken highly of you. We are not here to accuse you, Domina. But we do wish to ascertain the circumstances surrounding his . . . loss of health. We must know if there is reason for a comitia centurata to be held. Normally the praetor himself would conduct this inquiry but as he is the victim, and not yet fully returned to health, he has asked that I serve in his stead."

Euryale looked over at Hispallus on the couch. He gave only a nod, but she could tell he was listening intently to the proceedings.

"Victim?" said Deino, frowning. "We were given to believe the praetor had merely fallen ill."

"Yes," Euryale added, "Archidemus claimed it was an ailment of the spirit that overwhelmed the praetor's body."

Aemilianus and Hispallus exchanged looks for a moment. "Archidemus. He is the Chaldean who advises you, I take it? We will speak of him later. Though it is possible that it is some disease, our physician can find no signs of sickness upon Hispallus, save his weakness and pallor. Therefore we must allow for the possibility that he was poisoned."

Yes, I feared you would think so, thought Euryale.

"As I have said, I do not accuse your Domina of anything. But there are others in this household whose character and activities are not known to us. For this reason, Domina, I must request that you allow us to search your servants' quarters. May we do this?"

Euryale glanced at Deino, who appeared more indignant than worried. She could think of nothing of the servants' that could betray her. *And it will seem suspicious if I refuse.* "Very well, Censor."

Aemilianus signaled to two of the lictors, who immediately nodded and left. Then he signaled and settled back into this chair. "Now, Domina, I will speak a list of names. I wish to know if you have had dealings with any of these personages: Appius Claudius, Fulvius Nobilior, Aemilius Lepidus, Sulpicius Galba, Licinius Cassus Mucianus, or Junius Brutus Callaicus."

"Some of those names, Censor, I have heard—they are noble and distinguished men. But I have had no personal dealings with any of them."

Aemilianus nodded. "Very well. Let us speak of your servants, then. How many have you, and what is their status?"

"Six, Censor. First is Deino, who is my most trusted servant. She has served my family and myself for all of my life, as her family is kin to mine. She was born in Epirus, as was I.

"Next is Pronus, the gatekeeper, who is a freedman, citizen of Rome."

"Does he live on the grounds?"

"Yes."

"And he is, I understand, completely blind?"

"That is so, Censor."

"How is it that you find him an effective guard if he is blind?"

"His dog has keen eyes and nose, making up for whatever senses Pronus lacks."

"I see. Go on with your list."

"Then there is Emano, the gardener, who does not lice on the grounds, and only visits twice a month."

"And how is his sight?"

"Rather good, I understand, though fading due to age. But his skill and experience more than make up for it.

"Next is our cook. She is a slave, though she may have her freedom whenever she chooses."

"And she chooses to remain a slave?"

"She feels it is the surest position for her, Censor. She is beyond the best years for marriage, and has no male agent to handle her accounts."

"And her sight?"

"Quite poor, Censor, at any but a close distance."

At this, Aemilianus sat up and stared at Euryale. "So. Would it not be possible for someone to tamper with the food unbeknownst to her, or for her to make a mistake?"

Deino gave a snort of disgust.

"That is unlikely, Censor," said Euryale, ignoring Deino. "It is precisely because of her condition that she takes great care in the kitchen. She allows no one in while she is there and she guards her ingredients well."

"But she surely cannot be there all the time, unless she lives in the kitchen."

"She nearly does; her room is right beside it. And were anything to be even slightly out of place, she would notice it."

"Who brings her the ingredients she uses?"

"Sevisus does most of the shopping for us."

"And who is this Sevisus?"

"A very trusted slave, Censor. He is still young, only fourteen years, but I intend to manumit him when he comes of age. He often runs errands in the city, as his eyesight is the best of my servants', though unclear at a distance."

"Therefore Sevisus is the one most likely of your household to have dealings with strangers, yes?"

"I suppose you could say so, but—"

Aemilianus looked over to Hispallus. "Is Sevisus the one who served you before your collapse, cousin?"

"Yes," the praetor rasped, "he was."

I do not like the direction you are heading, thought Euryale.

"Where is this Sevisus now?"

Euryale looked at Deino.

Deino responded, "He is on an errand, but should return shortly."

Aemilianus turned to the remaining lictor and said, "Go keep watch for his return."

The lictor nodded and left the room.

Euryale wanted to pound the arm of her chair with her fist. *No, this is not right.* "I have always trusted Sevisus highly."

"Yes. I'm sure you have, Domina. Can you see how someone might have taken advantage of that trust? Now, have you any other servants?"

"Only Caecus, who is but eight years old and fully blind. He is a slave, and never leaves the household."

"Is he ever permitted near the kitchen?"

"No. For his own safety, Cook would not permit it."

"Very well. Domina, I cannot help but observe that all of your servants are disabled of sight. Could you kindly satisfy my curiosity and tell me why this is so?"

Euryale looked down at her lap. "You may have heard that I am disfigured. I prefer that there be no one nearby who might be disturbed by my appearance. And, perhaps, I feel a sympathy for those who must, like myself, see the world through veiled eyes."

Aemilianus nodded with a rueful smile and seemed about to say something when the two lictors returned.

"We have found nothing of interest, Censor. Except for this." One of them handed Aemilianus a small square of parchment. Euryale thought she could discern writing on it.

Aemilianus frowned. "What is this? It appears to be a random mixture of symbols."

"We know not, Censor. It was in one of the servants' rooms."

Aemilianus held out the scrap toward Euryale and Deino. "Do either of you recognize this?"

Euryale leaned forward and shook her head, unable to make out the letters. Deino paused, pressing her gnarled hand to her chest.

"You, Deino," Aemilianus said. "Have you seen this before?"

The old woman met his eyes for a moment, then looked away.

Euryale placed her hand on Deino's arm. "Deino, if you know something you should tell him. We have every reason to help them."

Softly the old woman said, "As you wish, Domina. Yes, Censor, I have seen it. It belongs to Sevisus."

VICESIMVS

"Indeed?" said Aemilianus, raising his brows. "And do you know if there is a message contained within it?"

Euryale looked from the Censor to Deino, baffled. *What is going on that I do not know?*

Deino straightened and shook her head. "No message that I know of, Censor. It seemed pure gobbledygook to me and I told Sevisus so when he asked me."

"Asked you? So he did not know what it meant?"

"So I would gather, Censor."

Aemilianus rested his chin in his hands. "How did he come by it?"

"He said someone gave it to him."

"Did he say who?"

"No."

Well," Aemilianus said with a cool smile. "I suppose we shall have to ask the boy himself when he returns." He folded the parchment and tucked it into a fold in his toga.

A warm breeze stirred Euryale's veil and she gazed toward the open window. Beyond it lay a view of the Tiber River, glistening as it flowed toward the sea. At that moment she longed to flow with it, to be anywhere else than in this room. Even her barren cave palace in the Atlas Mountains had held more comfort than this tablinum with its chilled miasma of suspicion.

Suddenly she became aware that Aemilianus was speaking to her again.

". . . I am told you have contacted various practitioners of the magical arts, Domina. Might you have encountered a certain witch by the name of . . . what was she called, cousin?"

"Simaetha, I believe," Hispallus said thickly.

Euryale started in surprise. "Simaetha?"

"You have met her then?"

How might they know of her? "Yes, she was one of those I spoke to. But only once, and I did not accept her services. I did not approve of her . . . methods."

Aemilianus gave Hispallus a significant glance, then said, "That is wise of you, Domina. You are aware that witchcraft is illegal in Rome?"

"If all Roman witches are like Simaetha, I can well understand why."

"Oh? Have you a specific reason for your dislike, Domina?"

Euryale shook her head. "I would prefer not to say. It has nothing to do with poisons or the praetor, so I would not consider it relevant to the matter discussed here."

"But it may be," said Hispallus, struggling to prop himself up on his elbow. "Simaetha tried to warn me. She told me not to come here . . . that many lives hung in the balance."

"I have no idea what she could have meant." *Is it possible she knows what I am? How? Might she be connected to that architect and the young Scipio? The strands of this web stretch wider than I thought.*

"You seem disturbed, Domina. May I ask you for your thoughts?"

Euryale turned to Hispallus. "Good Praetor, do you know if your architect Daedalus and Simaetha know each other?"

Hispallus frowned and he looked very worried. "Not that I am aware, Domina. Do you have reason to think so?"

Euryale shook her head. "Just a feeling—"

"Well," said Aemilianus, "I shall have to ask the witch herself, in any case. This Archidemus. What do you know of him, outside of what he has told you?"

Euryale paused. "Very little, actually. He was introduced to me, by the alchemist Olerus, as a Chaldean mage. The rest I have learned from Archidemus."

"Then I suppose we shall have to let this mage speak for himself. Please bring him to us."

With a nod, Euryale sent Deino to fetch Archidemus. She was surprised how quickly they returned. Euryale wondered if he had been waiting nearby. Archidemus seemed quite calm as he stood before the magistrate. *It is his stoic training, no doubt.*

"Greetings, Scipio Aemilianus."

"Greetings, Archidemus. I regret that we did not have a chance to talk much on the return voyage to Rome, but Panaetius has spoken well of you."

They have met? thought Euryale. *What other surprises will this interview bring?*

"I am pleased, Censor. How may I serve you and the noble city of Rome?"

"Tell me, how do you feel about the fact that Rome may make a treaty with the Parthians who have captured your country?"

Archidemus raised his brows in surprise. "I . . . that is a matter for heads of state, Censor. It does not concern me."

Euryale turned to the Censor, wishing she were an ordinary woman so that she might glare at him. *Does he think Archidemus is a spy?*

"Come now, Archidemus. You lost a great deal to the Parthians. It cannot leave you unaffected."

"Indeed. But that is not the fault of Rome. Had I ill will toward the city, I would not have come here to continue my work."

"No? There are many Chaldeans in Rome, some in positions of great influence."

"Many of those 'Chaldeans' are Greeks and Egyptians. They are only called Chaldean for their worship of the heavens and the stars. I feel no kinship with them, nor any need to use their influence."

Aemilianus sat back in his chair and drummed his fingers on the arm. Suddenly the third lictor appeared in the doorway, pushing Sevisus ahead of him.

"Here's the boy, Censor. He'd slipped past me. I found him staring at the statue in the garden."

Why would Sevisus have been doing that? "If you do not mind, I prefer that my servants be treated with more respect."

The lictor gave Euryale an odd look and mumbled an apology. But it disturbed her that he kept a hand firmly on Sevisus's shoulder.

"Of course, Domina," said Aemilianus. He turned to the slave boy. "Do you know who I am, Sevisus?"

The boy looked at Euryale then squinted at the censor a moment. Then he shook his head. "No, sir."

Euryale said, "This is the Censor Scipio Aemilianus."

Sevisus' eyes opened wide.

"He needs to ask you a few questions. You needn't fear. There will be no trouble if you answer truthfully."

"Yes, Domina," Sevisus said softly. He did not look reassured.

"Thank you, Domina," said Aemilianus with a nod. "Now, Sevisus, it was you who served refreshments to the praetor Hispallus on the day of his collapse, was it not?"

Sevisus nodded.

"And were you the only other person to touch the food besides the cook?"

Sevisus nodded again. Then he noticed the praetor on the couch against the wall and the boy turned pale. "But . . . but I didn't . . ."

"What are you implying, Censor?" Deino snapped. "Sevisus is a good boy and a good servant. He would never—"

"I imply nothing." Aemilianus glared at Deino. "I only want answers to my questions. I do not recall asking for your opinion."

Deino glared back in insolent silence.

"Now, Sevisus, with the kind permission of your Domina, we have had all of the servants' quarters searched. In your room we found this." Aemilianus pulled out the scrap of parchment and showed it to Sevisus. "Can you tell me what it means?"

The boy's eyes widened and he drew back a little, then he glanced at Archidemus. "It . . . it's nothing."

Euryale felt a sinking feeling within her. Again she wondered, *What is going on here?* She thought she saw the theurge shake his head ever so slightly at Sevisus.

Aemilianus must have seen it also, for he looked sharply at Archidemus and said, "You may leave."

The theurge opened his mouth to reply, but only inclined his head before turning and striding from the room.

Sevisus watched him go, his eyes seeming to plead for him to return. Euryale felt an impulse to run and embrace the boy, but instead she sat as if tied to her chair.

"You know, boy, I can have this translated by the scholars in my household. So I will know the truth eventually. And I will know if you have lied. Believe me, I would much rather hear the truth from you now. If it is nothing, as you say, then you have nothing to fear, do you?"

Sevisus stared at the floor.

"Tell him, Sevisus," Euryale encouraged, impatient to know the answer herself.

The boy looked at her sadly, then said, "It is a star-casting, a reading of the stars' positions in the sky—"

"Ah, an astrology text, you mean. I am familiar with the concept. For whom is it a reading?"

"I don't know."

"But you know something of its contents?"

Sevisus again stared at the floor and said softly, "It is a list of predictions."

"What sort of events are foretold?"

Sevisus replied almost inaudibly, "Revolution, assassination, the downfall of a great city."

Hispallus sat up and stared aghast at the boy. Silence hung heavy in the room for a moment. "Did you hear, Aemilianus?" Hispallus rasped.

Euryale felt as though her heart had stopped. *Gods, what now?*

Aemilianus held up a hand toward Hispallus. "Peace, cousin." He tapped the chair arm before asking, "Is that city meant to mean Rome?"

"I don't know! Archidemus said it could mean any great city, any time in the past or future."

"Archidemus? Did he cast this?"

"No! It was given to me."

"To give to Archidemus?"

"No!" Sevisus clenched his fists and stamped his foot.

Aemilianus sighed. "Who gave it to you?"

Sevisus bit his lip and looked as though about to cry. "It was Joseph . . . Joseph the Bookseller."

Aemilianus raised his brows.

"A Jew," one of the lictors said, and snickered.

Aemilianus gave the lictor a sardonic glance and said to Sevisus, "Is this the same Joseph who works a bookstall near the Forum? Then be at peace, Sevisus, for I know the man. I have bought quite a few books from him in years past and I have fond memories of the hours I spent in his company. But tell me how he came to give this to you."

Sevisus stood a bit straighter, a hopeful light in his eyes. "I . . . I often go by his stand, when I am running errands for the Domina. I like to see what books he has. Sometimes he will let me look through one or two. I hope someday to buy one. Anyway, some days ago, as I was looking, he gave me the scrap, knowing I like to read, saying he had no use for it. That's all."

"But you showed it to Archidemus."

"First I showed it to Deino, but she thought it was nonsense. Then I went to our library and tried to translate it myself. But I couldn't. So then I showed it to Archidemus and he was able to read it for me."

Aemilianus folded the parchment and seemed to laugh to himself. "I see. And Archidemus no doubt told you that his reading might upset someone such as me? Well, I think I shall keep this, if you do not mind."

Sevisus shrugged. "Keep it, Magistrate, if you wish."

Aemilianus nodded to him with a smile, then turned to Euryale. "I think, Domina, we have imposed upon your household quite enough for today. I thank you and ask only one more imposition—that I might be left alone to speak privately with Hispallus. Otherwise, I ask you to please continue your normal activities, and take no more notice of us." He stood and went to the couch where Hispallus lay.

Euryale felt her breath go out of her in a great sigh. *None of her household were to be accused . . . yet. But much danger remains. If the praetor learns the truth about me . . . and about his son . . .* She motioned for Deino and Sevisus to join her and she stood to leave. Deino patted Sevisus on the shoulder and said a few kind words before they followed.

VICESIMVS PRIMUS

I DO NOT LIKE THIS, thought Hispallus as he watched Euryale and her servants leave the tablinum. *There is more here than meets the eye, but what and where to seek it?* He shifted on his couch and propped up his head on his arm to face the censor. "Well, what do you think, cousin?"

Aemilianus rested his fists on his hips and sighed heavily. "It is difficult to say. There is no reason to suspect any of these people of plotting your death. There is no solid evidence of a conspiracy. Yet there are tantalizing hints, clues, possibilities." He shook his head. "I have no idea what it all means."

Hispallus nodded and rubbed his eyes with one hand. "Simaetha. That astrological oracle. Might the ancient fears be justified, Aemilianus? Is sorcery the next enemy Rome must face?"

Aemilianus snorted. "From the few of these magi I have met or heard of, I would say we have little to fear. They are rife with such professional jealousy that you couldn't get two of them to work together, let alone enough for a grand conspiracy. And that witch Simaetha tried to save your life, remember."

"From guilt, perhaps. Wanting to save her skin while she could. Perhaps the plans went awry—"

"Such speculation without facts is useless, cousin. And, I suspect, bad for your health."

Hispallus looked up at the censor and stabbed a finger at him. "What of those astrological verses, then? Is that mere speculation? I would like to find the man who paid for those to be written."

"Seeking oracular wisdom is no crime, Hispallus. Even Rome must do so on occasion. That is why we have the Sibylline Oracles that you decemviri consult."

"Those are meant to provide remedies when Rome faces a crisis. Such as when the oracles advised that the Idean Mother Goddess be brought to Rome to assure us victory over a foreign invader. These astrological verses give no remedy. Any potential conspirator could see them as a sign from the gods that their plot would succeed."

"Perhaps," said Aemilianus, rubbing his chin. "But finding any source of evil intent here may be difficult. I cannot ascribe any guilt to the boy Sevisus. He is an unwitting dupe at most, and seems too bright for that. The old woman is not exactly cooperative, but she is proud and protective of her Domina. The theurge, however . . ."

"Yes, he is the logical link to any conspiracy."

"I meant merely that is the loosest thread in this web. Who knows what outside ties he might have."

"So. What do you recommend we do, cousin?"

"First, I will order your physicians to have you moved home soon. Tomorrow, if he feels you can bear the short journey. There may be no direct danger lingering here, but let us not take chances, eh? Next, there are others I must speak to. I will try to find this Simaetha and see what she knows. Also, Hispallus, you must reveal to me the identity of your blackmailer. It is natural to assume he may have some role in all this."

Hispallus felt a cold, gnawing ache inside. "Aemilianus . . . if he learns I have betrayed him . . . "

"But he need not know, if I am careful. I have connections all over Rome. I daresay I can invent a reason to speak to just about anyone. Clearly it is a risk that must be taken if he endangers your life. And whatever improprieties committed by your family he may know of, surely the accusation of attempted poisoning would weigh far more heavily in the minds of the Roman people. They would be in sympathy with you against him."

Hispallus sighed. His chest hurt from the effort of speaking and he was losing breath again. "It is Daedalus, the son of my old slave, Thessalus. I think . . . he blames me for Thessalus's death. That is why . . . " Hispallus's voice caught and he coughed.

"Enough, cousin." Aemilianus laid a hand on his shoulder. "You need tell me no more. I will see to it. You must rest now. Your physician already has cause enough to chide me."

"Vale, Scipio," Hispallus rasped with an ironic smile.

"And you." Aemilianus grasped Hispallus's forearm a moment, then departed.

With a groan, Hispallus lay back on the couch feeling a sickness of spirit worse than that of his body. *Here I am, weak and helpless, watching my celebrated kinsman do my duties for my sake. Bad enough that I am jealous of his acclaim. Now I must be grateful, too. Will I die, leaving nothing of note except a slight controversy surrounding my demise? All glory to Aemilianus, none for poor old Hispallus. I cannot even defend my own person from danger, let alone defend Rome as is my duty. Those meddling wizards and witches! There is a danger Rome should be warned of. If only I had my health . . .*

Hispallus drifted into a gentle half-sleep, watching the dust motes dance in the shaft of warm sunlight that slanted down from the window. Though he could hear the movements of others in the house around him, in this room there was peace and stillness and he felt quite alone.

The spot of sunlight crept bit by bit across the mosaic-tiled floor, illuminating a scene of a shepherd using a staff to drive a serpent away from his sheep. A crimson gleam sparked off the bit of glass that was the serpent's eye.

"Beware, Hispallus, beware the serpent's eyes," the voice of the white owl in the sacrificial fire ran again through his mind.

"Two faces has a coin and two has Janus. Blood and treachery stain what money buys." *I had forgotten that oracle! Now, does it offer a remedy or a threat? Who or what is the serpent? What is the meaning in the symbol of its eyes? Have I already encountered the danger it warned against, or is there worse to come?*

The sound of footsteps interrupted his train of thought and he looked up to see Sevisus approaching. The boy did not look him in the eye and his steps were hesitant.

"Come, lad. I do not bite. What is your business?"

"The Domina sent me to ask if you have everything you require. Is all well, Magistrate?"

"Reasonably well, all considered. If you are asking if I wish you to bring me refreshment, forgive me if I decline for now."

Sevisus looked at the floor and wrung his hands.

For a moment, the boy reminded the praetor of his son Cnaeus—the way he was not many years ago, before he drifted into the dark life of the tabernas. "Oh, bother. It was a poor joke. I apologize. Aemilianus thinks you are blameless and I believe him, so let that be the end of it."

Not looking up, Sevisus very softly said, "Thank you." He turned to go.

"Wait," said Hispallus. "Come here."

Sevisus obeyed, but still approached the praetor's couch with caution.

"Tell me, boy, your Domina thinks highly of Archidemus, doesn't she?"

Sevisus nodded.

"And you think well of him, also, don't you?"

"I think he is very wise, Magistrate."

"Well, I am in a situation where I could use some wisdom. Perhaps I may benefit from his. Bring him to me. I would speak with him."

A hopeful look came into the slave boy's eyes and he ran from the room. *If he knew the real reason I asked,* Hispallus thought, *he would not be so pleased and eager.*

Before long, the door opened again, and Sevisus entered followed by the Chaldean Archidemus.

"Ah, greetings again, Archidemus. I am sorry to ask more of your time, but I fear my cousin may have been unfair in casting aspersions upon you. I wished to have the chance to speak with you myself."

Archidemus bowed his head graciously. "Whatever I may do to ease the praetor's mind, I am pleased to do."

"Excellent. Both the good Domina and her servant here speak well of your learning and wisdom, and there are some matters on which I should like to hear your opinion."

"As you wish, Magistrate. On what would you bid me speak?"

Ah, why not? Let us see what he says to this. "I wish to know, wise Archidemus, what the meaning may be of a serpent, and the serpent's eyes."

The Chaldean's bearded face became wary. "It may mean many things, Magistrate, depending upon the context. What leads you to ask?"

"Well, I noticed that the Domina has many snakes depicted in this house. And not long ago I received a warning to beware a serpent's eyes." *Ah, he reacts to that, I see. How interesting.*

"From whence came this warning, Magistrate?"

Hispallus smiled thinly. "It is best that I not say. So. What do you think it means?"

Archidemus sighed and began to slowly pace the room. "To many, the serpent is a symbol of earth, upon which the snake moves, or the underworld, into which the snake digs its burrow. Because it sheds its skin, the serpent may represent rebirth or immortality." At this, Archidemus stopped and seemed lost in thought a moment before going on. "Its sinuous movements suggest the waves of the deep, and therefore deep wisdom and mysteries. Despite its shape, the serpent is often associated with the female essence and women." Again Archidemus stopped and mused, stroking the curls of his beard.

"This is all very interesting," Hispallus said with impatience, "but I have also heard the snake is a harbinger of evil. And what of its eyes?"

"Yes, yes, there are those who argue that the snake symbolizes weakness of spirit, or the soul seduced by the material. But this is not universal, and I do not know how it would apply to you and your warning."

Hispallus thought with irony, *I can think of a number of ways such qualities apply to me or those in my life.* "Go on."

Archidemus smiled to himself. "The Domina Euryale has told me how in the temple in her homeland of Epirus they would keep tamed snakes in a pit. If the snakes refused to eat, if signified there would be a poor harvest that year." He looked at Hispallus. "I don't suppose you were being warned of crop failure, do you think?"

"Somehow I doubt it. It was a more . . . personal message." Hispallus noticed though, glancing around him, that the images of serpents were linked with those of plants and farming. And Euryale once told him her goddess was connected with the earth.

"Ah. Well, the Eye, to the Egyptians, is symbolic of the light of knowledge, the intelligence of Man. It is also accorded great power, as in the 'evil eye,' so feared by some here in Rome that they wear amulets against it." Archidemus chuckled to himself as if at a private joke. "The eye symbol combined with the serpent could indicate intelligence combined with hidden knowledge—"

"As in witchcraft or wizardry?"

"Perhaps."

"So I am warned to beware of witches and wizards, eh?" Hispallus did not bother to keep the irony from his voice.

"It could be interpreted so. There are many charlatans who use tricks and flattery to gain money and favor."

"Present company excepted, of course."

Archidemus gave a thin smile. "I am glad you are so generous as to give me the benefit of the doubt. To continue, the serpent's eyes can also be said to have great power to heal or to harm, to bring illness or death. The basilisk, for example, may kill instantly with its glance, turning its victims . . ." Archidemus stopped and his eyes were wary again for a moment.

"—to stone." Hispallus finished. "Yes, I have heard such fables. So the warning may apply to how I have been struck down with illness, as if with a serpent's poison." Something else nagged at Hispallus's mind . . . the memory of the statue he toppled, falling . . .

Waving the thought away, he said, "Well, as you see, I am interested in learning more about my fate. So perhaps your skills may help me, Archidemus. I want you to foretell my future. Shall I live or die? What is to become of me?"

The Chaldean frowned. "From what I can see, and what your physician has said, you are on the mend and should have no fear of dying."

"Ah, but he has also said that if I become too excited or leave my bed too soon, the gods may strike me down again and not give me the chance to arise. He claims he has seen it happen."

"Such is possible."

"So, shall I give you the date of my birth, that you may consult the stars?"

Archidemus shook his head. "Though many of my countrymen are astrologers, I do not foretell futures from the heavens."

"Well, whatever method you choose, then; sheep's livers, eagle's flight, chicken droppings, read what you must. It matters little to me."

"Do you not, in this city, have augurs whose duty it is to reach such things?"

"The augurs," Hispallus said gravely, "serve the state of Rome, and their readings are for the good of Rome, not any one man. It would be sacrilegious to ask such a thing of them."

"Please pardon my misunderstanding, Magistrate. But could it not be said that because of your position, your interests reflect those of Rome?"

"*Republica sum?* You flatter me. But at the moment my only interest in Rome is reclining on this blasted couch. Why do you hesitate, magus? I'd think you would be eager to show me your great mystical skill."

Archidemus pursed his lips and narrowed his eyes. "To prophesy for a powerful man is dangerous business, Magistrate. If one is not flattering enough in one's prognostication, one is accused of treachery. If one flatters too much, one is called a liar."

"And if one chooses to ignore my wishes, I can have one shown to the Esquiline Gate by nightfall. Now what say you?" *Ah, that troubles him. Clearly he wishes to stay with the Domina. Perhaps they share more between them than philosophy, eh?* Hispallus realized there might be a more sinister reason for the Chaldean wishing to remain, as well. *Unfinished business, perhaps?*

"If you will accept what occurs, Magistrate, as merely what the divine powers wish to show us, then I will make efforts on your behalf."

After taking a moment to puzzle out this statement, Hispallus replied, "Of course, Archidemus. You are but a mouthpiece for the will of the gods." *And if I believe this, may Iupiter change me into a mule.*

"In a manner of speaking, Magistrate," Archidemus said with a slight bow. "Sevisus, here is the chance I promised you to learn some of my art. I need your help. Please bring a bench from the dining room, and a lamp, and a metal bowl filled with water."

Happily, Sevisus brought the items required, sloshing water out of the bronze bowl he carried in one hand.

"Very good," said Archidemus. "Set the bench here, in the center. We must align its ends from east to west. Place the bowl at the east end, and the lamp at the west. Now, Sevisus, you will give your greatest help. I require a medium. And as you are, I presume, an innocent boy, you would do admirably. Will you do this?"

Sevisus nodded, but his face showed traces of fear.

Yes, Sevisus, you may have reason to fear, thought Hispallus. *I have heard stories of what wizards do to young boys in the name of their "art." Be wary, indeed.* Hispallus briefly wondered if what Archidemus was about to perform qualified as witchcraft, and would be, therefore, illegal. But it was too important that he learn more of the mage. He would justify it later, if need be.

"Now, Sevisus," said the Chaldean, "please lie upon the bench, on your stomach if you please, with your head at the east end over the bowl."

The boy did as he was bid, and Archidemus placed some sticks of incense in the lamp and lit them. The tang of sandalwood and cinnamon soon filled the air. Hispallus found it rather pleasant and soothing. Sevisus sneezed.

"You must take deep breaths," Archidemus counseled.

"It makes me dizzy."

"That is the point. Your mind must be freed from its moorings to join with the spirit of the divine."

"My soul isn't going to leave my body, is it?"

"No, Sevisus. Fear not. You will remain where you are. Now, calm yourself, breathe deeply, and look upon the surface of the water in the bowl. What do you see?"

"My face."

"Very good. Keep watching. Try to not see your face as you look. The divine shall place images on the water for you to see, if your mind is ready. Breathe deeply. And watch."

Archidemus then began to walk slowly around the bench making deep, sonorous sounds somewhere between singing and chanting.

Hispallus thought he heard the names of various gods, Roman and foreign, in the chant: Serapis, Thoth and Hermes among them. The voice and the incense together had a relaxing effect on the praetor, and he lay back on the couch, feeling the pain in his chest and limbs ease. *If I learn nothing more, at least I may thank the magus for this.*

"Do you see anything now?" Archidemus asked quietly.

"No, magus. Only . . . fuzzy shapes."

"Very well," and the Chaldean continued his chant.

Some minutes later, Sevisus gasped and said, "I see something! But it wavers . . ."

"Breathe deeply and calm yourself. What do you see?"

"It is . . . a procession. There is a throne carried by four men, who are crowned with olive branches. In front of the throne walks a man, a priest I think, who is swinging a censer. On the throne sits someone . . . a man, wearing a basket on his head and there is a dog at his feet. They have stopped and are looking at me. They beckon me to follow."

Hispallus found that by some trick of the mind, he was able to imagine quite easily what Sevisus was describing. When he closed his eyes, the scene became as clear as though he saw it with eyes open.

"Very good," Archidemus said. "Follow them, Sevisus, with your eyes. Tell me where they go."

"They . . . they're going down a street in Rome. I think it's the Via Appia. But it's deserted, empty. We're going out a gate, the Porta Capena, I guess. Now we've come to a fork in the road. The throne-bearers stop and look back at me . . . they're pointing down the Via Appia at a stone building."

From what Hispallus imagined in his mind's eyes, he knew very well what they were pointing at, and his insides went cold. Along the Via Appia, past where the Via Latina split from it, lay the Tombs of the Scipios; the final resting place of all his family. "So," he said, barely above a whisper, "I am to die."

"Wait!" said Sevisus, "they are turning. Now they point down the other road . . . but it isn't the Via Latina anymore. It leads back to the Forum. There is a great crowd there, and you, Magistrate, stand above them. The crowd is turning into ravens . . . and you are scattering them with your voice. The ravens call your name, "Hispallus! Hispallus!" Now . . . oh, it's too much to describe!"

But description was not necessary, for the praetor also saw and heard how the cries of the ravens echoed into the skies as if down many long corridors. And down each, he saw someone seated, inscribing his name; old men with shaven heads scribbling elaborate letters with quills on parchment, men with odd lenses perched on their noses sitting at bizarre contraptions that tapped letters onto paper, a small woman with dark hair who stared at letters of light moving across the glowing face of an odd-shaped box . . .

The echoes grew fainter and Sevisus spoke. "Now it's just the procession again. They point to each way, and now they turn their backs to me and they're moving on. But they aren't going down either of the streets, they're going between them . . . They're fading away. I can't see them anymore."

And the images faded from Hispallus's mind as well. He opened his eyes and realized he was afraid. *I saw the images as if before my eyes. This mage has power. If he is a threat, there is danger indeed.* He looked questioningly at Archidemus.

The Chaldean seemed very calm and satisfied. He went to Sevisus and patted the boy on the shoulder, then picked up the lamp and snuffed out the burning incense. "You did very well, Sevisus."

"So," demanded Hispallus, "what is the meaning of this vision?"

"Eh? Oh, I thought it was clear. You must choose your own path, Magistrate. If you continue the straightest and easiest way, it leads to emptiness, oblivion. Since I recall it is Roman custom to build tombs along roads, then it may indicate death as well, though not imminent. But there is another way, one which involves government, and power over many people. What this indicates exactly, I cannot say. Your own mind must answer this. Whatever it would be, it would cause your name to be heard far and wide."

"I see. And that is all you can tell me?"

Archidemus turned and glared at him. "Magistrate, we are fortunate that the divine power has deigned to show you this much. Consider yourself well served. More so for being offered a choice of paths while you still have the opportunity to choose. I have done as you bid me. Now I must return to my work. Good evening and good health to you, Praetor. Come, Sevisus." And the Chaldean strode from the room.

With an apologetic glance at Hispallus, the boy picked up the bench and the bowl and clumped out of the room behind the mage.

For a moment, Hispallus felt as though he had been abandoned by his guide in a strange and dangerous land. Then he felt his insides sour with anger. *So the mage teases me with confusing visions, then tells me to rest content! He has skill, that is clear. If he wants to influence my actions through his visions, what is he trying to make me do? It is as though he knows my desire for recognition and was playing to it. Says I have power over many people . . . does he seek to use it? I will not let him.*

Hispallus rolled over on the couch and faced the blank, white plaster of the wall. *But to do nothing . . .* He saw again before his mind the road to emptiness and death. The praetor tossed onto his back and faced the ceiling. *How can I still strive for fame, yet thwart the machinations of these magi?* And suddenly there it was. Like a flower blossoming in his mind, the praetor realized what he could do. *Yes. I will show you what power I have, Chaldean. And if I succeed, a grateful Rome will indeed cause my name to be echoed down the corridors of time.* "Marcus!" he called, as loudly as he could.

Within moments, his physician and his secretary came rushing in. "What is it, Magistrate? Are you in pain?"

"No. In fact, I feel better than I have in a long while. Bring me a wax tablet and stylus."

"Magistrate," said the physician, "you must not excite yourself. You must rest, particularly if you are to be moved home tomorrow. You are not yet well enough—"

"The business of Rome does not wait upon the frail, mortal husk of one man, physician. There are laws to be written. And if there is a chance that I haven't much time left in this world, shouldn't you allow me to do what work I can while I am here?"

"Of course, Lord," said Marcus, and he ran out to do his bidding."

The physician stood by the couch, shaking his head, his face disapproving.

"What, good physician? Would you deny an old soldier his last battle?"

"If it need not be his last, and the battle hastens his end, yes."

Hispallus patted the physician's arm. "Fear not. I have had a vision from the gods. So long as the fires of purpose burn within me, I shall not fall." *I have chosen my road, Archidemus. But it will not lead where you and your kind direct. No, not at all.*

VICESIMVS SECUNDVS

Nescio watched the Tiber flow by below him, light from the setting sun glinting off its ripples like floating bits of gold. *Like the gold you have brought us, Tibernus. And more gold to come, if Fortuna stays with us.*

He had spent the day at the slave market, looking at what men were available for work. Also he had asked around for sculptors and stonemasons who were quick and cheap. Daedalus had asked to meet him here, near the Porta Trigemina on the east bank of the Tiber, to learn of his progress.

Naturally, I'll tell him that I have chosen the best men, at appropriate value. But I will take whoever I can, providing they're cheap enough. The difference will fatten my own coffers. It doesn't matter whether the bridge is well built. The authorities won't let it stand more than a day, once they see it. Hah! I almost wish I could be here when the bridge is unveiled and they see the riotous Bacchanalia on the northern face, and the slaughtering of Greeks depicted on the south. Nothing like those plans the Senate saw. But by then I will have long left Daedalus to meet whatever fate he's made for himself. I'll be in Brindisium, basking in my villa, surrounded by lovely Hircini girls . . .

"Pleasant thoughts, Nescio?" Daedalus said close beside him.

Nescio jumped and turned around. "Ah, Daedalus! Yes, I was just thinking about our bridge. How grand it will be!"

"Mmm." Daedalus looked out over the river, his face very serious. "This is where it will be, Nescio. We will build it here."

"What, right here?" Nescio frowned and rubbed his chin. "The riverbed here is not as solid as it is farther north. And the water is deeper. IF we build across Tiber Island—"

Daedalus slapped the low stone wall in front of him. "There are already bridges across Tiber Island! And here, our bridge will serve the Via Ostiensis. A fine, ironic touch, don't you think?"

This revenge business is driving the boy mad. Well, I guess it doesn't matter, so long as I get my share. Nescio clapped a hand on the architect's shoulder. "It will be magnificent, Daedalus."

"Hmmm." Daedalus jammed his hands into his short toga and frowned at the river.

"What is wrong with you?" Nescio asked. "Ever since we got the Domina's money, you've been acting like a bad loser at dice."

Daedalus leaned his elbows on the wall and rested his chin on his arms. "It is not enough," he said softly.

"What isn't enough? You mean the money? The old woman said the Domina would give us more when we needed it."

"I don't mean the money."

"Then what, Daedalus?"

The architect sighed. "It was too easy."

"Too easy? We've both worked very hard for this—"

"Not for us! For Hispallus. He only has to get a little sick and that . . . creature gives him whatever he asks. They have been very clever, Nescio. He thinks he has me tame as a sheep."

Nescio felt fear creep in his belly. *I was right. He's mad as a Greek prophet.* "Daedalus," he said with soft warning, "you will have your bridge. You have the money. You've had and will have your vengeance—"

"It isn't enough, I say! He has not suffered enough!"

"Daedalus, we've been lucky. It's worked . . . so far. By Pollux, don't ruin things now, man!"

Nescio found his advice rewarded with a sneer. "Of course you don't care," said Daedalus, "you only want the money. Honor means nothing to you, does it?"

"Of course it does! But what good is honor if your last glimpse of it is from the heights of the Tarpeian Rock? Don't push the praetor too far, Daedalus, I beg you."

"Just one step more . . . one more twist of the knife . . . "

"No! Daedalus, have you gone mad? Pull the reins in on your daemons, man!" Nescio gripped the architect's shoulders and gently shook him. "Come, let's be sensible. Let's go down to a taberna and let a river of wine wash this sourness out of you."

Daedalus's face turned red and contorted in rage. He grabbed Nescio's wrists and tried to pull his hands off his shoulders. Suddenly his eyes focused on something behind the contractor's right shoulder. His expression changed to suspicion.

Nescio turned around and saw a young man with the self-important bearing of a lictor approach them.

"Salve! Is one of you the architect called Daedalus?"

"I am," Daedalus growled. "What do you want?"

"I bring you greetings from Censor Scipio Aemilianus. He wished to inform you that, because of the illness of Praetor Cornelius Scipio, he has become overseer for your project."

Nescio and Daedalus exchanged a worried glance.

"This is a private bridge," Nescio said. "We do not need a government overseer."

"Well," said the lictor casually, "this land is owned by Rome, and the roads your bridge will serve were built by Rome. Therefore, the Senate must have some say, though I doubt they will appoint a whole commission for this as they would for a public work. Don't worry," the lictor added with a wink, "Aemilianus doesn't tend to get too involved with these things. He'll leave you to work in your own way. But he would like you to appear before him tomorrow morning, just to give him some of the details. That way if the Senate should ask any questions, he can pretend he knows what you're doing."

"Well," Daedalus said dryly, "I don't see how I can refuse."

"Good. He thought you'd understand. Until tomorrow morning, then." The lictor spun smartly on his heel and walked back the way he came.

"Hmmm," said Nescio. "Now what?"

"I don't like it. Scipios stick together like well-mortared bricks. Yet, it may give me the opportunity I hoped for."

"Daedalus . . ."

"It will be just a little thing, Nescio. Never fear."

INTEMPESTE NOCTE

Shafts of moonlight spread into the hovel through cracks high in the wall. By this light alone, Simaetha packed her few possessions into a leather sack.

What is there to wait for? she thought with weariness and a little anger. *Hecate, you have said I would get what I wish, but all has gone wrong. Daedalus didn't listen, neither did the praetor. Now he lies ill and the Censor Aemilianus has summoned me. What would he accuse me of, I wonder? Forgive your servant, Hecate, but I will not stay to find out. The gorgon is beyond my reach now, no doubt, alerted to caution by Daedalus's failure. No point to my remaining. I'm going home.*

Even at midnight, the city of Rome was not silent. In the distance she could hear the barking of dogs and some Salii going home from their feast, drunkenly singing the Carmen Saliare. Simaetha doubted anyone would notice her departure.

She cinched tight the leather thongs of the sack and wrapped her palla tightly around her shoulders. Without regrets, she took a last glance around the single room, then picked up the sack and went to the door.

Suddenly, before her hand reached the door handle, the door banged open. A great, cold gust of wind blew in, stinging her face and hands with blowing leaves and sand. Something large and white came at her and she raised her arms, dropping the sack. She heard a shriek and something beat her about the face until she staggered, gasping, back into the center of the room. Abruptly, the wind and the beating ceased, and Simaetha lowered her arms.

On the floor between her and the door sat a huge, white owl, staring at her with eyes black as onyx. Simaetha swallowed hard, her fists clenched with anger and fear.

"Hecate," she whispered hoarsely at the owl, "why do you abuse me thus?"

The owl made no reply.

"Mother of the Night, let me pass!"

"Ou! Ou!" cried the owl, raising its wings threateningly.

To Simaetha, it sounded like a Greek negation. "Not? I am not to leave? Have mercy, Mistress. Have I not done all your dreams have bid of me? I came to Rome in your name and all the help I have offered has been rejected or undone. What more can I do? Have I not been your good servant?"

"Ouk oun?" the owl seemed to say.

"'Therefore . . . ' Therefore what, Hecate? Am I to serve you also by remaining? By possibly giving up my life? To serve you is a crime in Rome, Mistress. Send me anywhere you wish, but do not force me to remain! Where shall I go for you?"

"Oudamou," said the owl.

"'Nowhere'?" Simaetha whispered. "Something yet remains for me to do here, nai?"

The owl blinked and ruffled its feathers.

Simaetha stared at the creature a long time, feeling her heart pounding within her. Her inner daemon screamed at her to flee. But Simaetha would not defy the gods. "Then be it as you will, Mistress. I shall remain."

The owl bobbed its head once, turned and flew out through the doorway, into the moonlight. Simaetha walked slowly to the door and shut it, noting as she did so that the owl sat in the nearest tree, watching her. The witch turned and leaned her back against the rough, rotting wood of the door. Closing her eyes, she let out her breath in long, gasping sobs.

VICESIMVS TERTIVS

EURYALE WATCHED the last of the lictors and clientes leave through the gate, their cries of "Vale, bona Domina!" echoing down the street.

"Vale, indeed, and good riddance," grumbled Deino standing beside her. Euryale looked at the part of the garden her guests had occupied and could not help but agree. The ground was torn up by the passage of many feet, branches were broken, a deep path had been worn to the latrine. *Emano will be devastated when he sees this. He's so meticulous in his care of the garden.*

"Cook nearly baked her arms off to see that they were all served," said Deino.

Euryale took the hint. "By all means, give her two days' holiday. She has earned the rest. Everyone may rest today. The gods know we have been through enough."

"They will bless you for your graciousness, Despoina." Deino nodded to her and returned to the house.

Euryale turned and walked along the garden path, surveying the damage. *It is not as bad as it might have been.* She came to the statue, still shored up with planks of wood. She looked him over carefully, almost caressing him as she ran her fingers lightly over his legs and feet. She noted there were no scars or broken areas. She stepped back with a deep sigh. *Definitely, it could have been worse.*

"I told them it was the praetor's favorite statue," Sevisus said behind her. "That made them respect it."

Euryale started in surprise, and turned to regard the boy. He was squinting up at the statue, his head tilted to one side.

"That was clever of you, Sevisus. Thank you."

Very softly, the boy said, "He was alive once, wasn't he?"

Euryale pulled her palla closer around her. "I . . . don't know what you mean."

Sevisus looked at the ground. "Olerus told me. He said you met a basilisk who turned that one to stone and made you have to wear a veil. That is why you want to turn stone to flesh. To bring him back."

Euryale held very still a moment. *A basilisk. Not quite the truth, but it is a convenient explanation, if he believes it.* "Yes, Sevisus. He is right. But you must tell no one else. Do you understand?"

"Yes, Domina. Domina?" He gazed up at her, worried questioning in his eyes.

"Hmmm?"

"What of . . . the statue that the praetor broke. I swept up the pieces. It looked just like the bird Olerus took apart. Was the statue once alive too?"

Euryale felt her heart sink. *Oh Goddess help me, what do I say?* "No, Sevisus. That was just a statue." *Forgive me.*

Sevisus' hands nervously toyed with one another. "As you say, Domina." He sighed.

After an uncomfortable silence, Euryale said, "Did Deino tell you that you may have today as a holiday? You are free from chores. Do whatever you wish."

With a nod, the boy replied, "Thank you, Domina." But he did not move.

"Was there something else you wanted to tell me?"

Sevisus looked at her again, blinking. "Olerus also said that Archidemus couldn't help you."

"I think Olerus has his own reasons for saying that, Sevisus."

"Oh. Do you trust Archidemus, Domina?"

"Yes. I trust him."

"Good. I do too."

"Then let us hear no more such talk, Sevisus. Be off and enjoy your holiday."

"Yes, Domina." With a little smile, he turned and ran off toward the gate.

Euryale laid her hand upon the foot of the statue in the garden. "I think the worst aspect of Athena's curse, Aristo, is the curtain of lies and half-truths I must weave about myself. But I am not Arachne, to boast of my weavings. I would make a most reluctant spider."

WAITING IN THE VAST ATRIUM of the Censor Scipio Aemilianus, Daedalus did his best to appear nonchalant. The ruse failed him quickly. He noted the huge, colonnaded hall was filled with the most important men in Rome, as well as emissaries from everywhere in the known world. The architect felt small and ignorable.

Tucking the "approved" plans for his bridge under one arm, Daedalus ducked into a side passage between one row of fluted marble columns and the wall of the atrium, where it was not as crowded. For diversion, he studied the architectural design of the hall. He thought the Corinthian columns too massive, the false peristyle around the second story too ornate. Looking along the wall, he saw small shrines on which lay deer and antelope horns and the tusks of wild boar. Daedalus had heard that hunting was one of Aemilianus's greatest passions. *If he is also a hunter of men, then I may be in more danger than I thought.*

Interspersed between the hunting trophies were trophies of a different sort: silver and sculpture from conquered Greece. *Yes,* thought Daedalus coldly, *such admirers of Greek culture you Scipios are—when you can use your plunder to ornament your houses.*

As he continued looking around, he noticed movement at the far end of the gallery. There stood a tall, thin woman in a dark palla. She stared at him a moment, then quickly glanced away. *Simaetha! What is she doing here?* The witch stepped into the shadows between two columns, pulling her palla around her.

So. She chooses not to recognize me. Does she come to bear witness against me, as punishment for my failure with the gorgon? Well, let her try. I will tell the censor vile tales of her witchcraft and we shall see which one of us is believed.

Someone shouted over the rumble of voices in the atrium and quickly the crowd hushed to hear what was said.

"Daedalus!" came a stern announcement. "Is the architect Daedalus present?"

"I am here!" Daedalus shouted back. Holding the rolls of papyri in both hands, he plunged through the throng, enjoying how the noblemen indignantly made way for him. He was directed to the lictor who had made the announcement.

With a bland expression, the lictor said, "The censor asks for you. This way." Daedalus was guided to a set of bronze doors, not unlike those outside Hispallus's tablinum. But the room beyond the doors was different indeed.

The tablinum of Scipio Aemilianus was nearly as large as the atrium, though not quite as crowded. The long walls were painted with scenes of great cities and places the censor had, no doubt, seen. Daedalus found it odd that there was no mural commemorating the destruction of Carthage. In fact, there were no battle scenes at all. *Has this Scipio grown soft, I wonder?*

In the center of the room sat Aemilianus, engaged in animated conversation with two other men. He seemed youthful to Daedalus, despite his greying short hair and lined face. The chair Aemilianus sat upon was ordinary, but he looked as magisterial upon it as if it were the ivory curule. He had been the youngest man ever made Consul, Daedalus reminded himself. And the aura of that title remained with him still, though now he was only censor.

Daedalus rustled his papyri nervously. He had not felt intimidated by Hispallus at all. *But this man . . .* Waiting for

Aemilianus to notice him, Daedalus felt like a servant again. At last the Censor finished his conversation and glanced in the architect's direction.

"Greetings, Daedalus," said Aemilianus with an easy smile. With a wave of his hand, the censor beckoned him forward.

"Magistrate," Daedalus replied, approaching the chair.

"I thank you for taking time from your busy schedule to stop by, Daedalus. I will try to make this quick as I can. I understand that construction is a tedious process, though I am better known for the razing of cities than the building of them." This produced an appreciative chuckle from those nearby.

Does he think to frighten me by mentioning past might? "This makes you an . . . interesting choice for overseer for my bridge, my Lord."

"Well, the gods do love to fling us into unaccustomed roles, don't they? Those who would be the builders of temples of marble may find themselves destroyers of the temple of the soul." Aemilianus gave Daedalus a knowing look.

Now what is that supposed to mean? Daedalus paused, uncertain how to reply.

A man with the long hair and beard indicative of a scholar smiled and murmured appreciatively at the censor's words.

"But enough of philosophy," Aemilianus went on. "I am acting in my kinsman Hispallus's stead, as I believe you know. Because of his illness."

"Please give him my best wishes for the improvement of his health."

"Of course. I am touched that you show such concern."

"Naturally I am concerned," Daedalus said. "If he should die," he held out his arms in an exaggerated shrug, "I would have no bridge." Daedalus felt gratified by the few chuckles this elicited from nearby listeners.

"Ah," said Aemilianus, wryly wagging a finger at the architect, "but I hear you've another source for your funds."

"That is not important. It is more important that the good praetor live to see the completion of our project. It is to be a tribute to Hispallus and his family. I often dream of the day when the bridge will be unveiled and I may see the wonder in the praetor's eyes. That shall be my best reward, Censor."

Aemilianus regarded him for long moments, and Daedalus began to feel uncomfortable. *He heard the double meaning in my words. Has Hispallus told him? The censor seemed surprised that I wished the praetor well.*

"Your words . . . say much of you, Daedalus," Aemilianus said at last. "Are those papers you carry the plans for the bridge?"

"Yes, Magistrate." Daedalus handed to him the rolls of papyrus.

Aemilianus spread open the rolls on his lap. "Yes, these appear to be the same as Piso described. But I do not see how the scenes in these friezes particularly honor my cousin's family."

"They honor his sensibilities, Magistrate, in the choice of scenes he wished depicted."

"Hmmm. Have you made any changes to the design that are not shown here?"

"Only one addition. There will be a bust of Hispallus's son worked into it."

"Young Cnaeus? I was not aware he had particularly distinguished himself."

Daedalus felt an unexpected flash of anger. "I have been friend to him. Besides," he added with a shrug, "it was the wish of the Domina who is providing the funds."

Aemilianus raised an eyebrow, then dismissed this with a nod. He rolled up the plans and handed them to a lictor. "Thank you, Daedalus. We shall keep these drawings with our records."

"No!" Panic rose within the architect. If the progress of the bridge was checked against the drawings, discrepancies would become obvious too soon.

"I beg your pardon," said Aemilianus mildly, "but this is normal procedure. You don't mean that these are the only copies, do you?"

"Yes. The only ones. I didn't think others would be needed."

"I see." Aemilianus rubbed his chin. Then his face brightened. "Well, I can have my excellent draftsman make a copy and return the original plans to you. That way, you needn't worry if your originals are lost or damaged. How does that sound?"

Curses on the man. I cannot reasonably refuse. With a thin smile, Daedalus replied, "That will be fine, Censor. Thank you."

"Good! Now I should let you return to your work. I know you must have much to do in the way of preparation. We will speak again soon, I assure you. I have great interest in your project and will be watching your progress closely."

Daedalus felt the daemon rage within him and he fought to appear outwardly calm. *Cursed be whatever god set this jackal of a magistrate on me! My vengeance is nothing without the bridge. I can't let this happen. Not without a price. Now, now I must do it! The last twist of the knife . . .*

"If you please," Daedalus said tightly. "I would like you to pass a message on to Praetor Hispallus for me."

"If I can."

"Tell him . . . tell him 'The score is even, but the race is not yet won. The father loses, as once had lost the son.'"

Aemilianus shifted forward in his chair and narrowed his eyes. "What does this mean, Daedalus?"

"The praetor will understand." *Or he won't, but it will haunt him all the same.*

"I see." The censor sat back, regarding Daedalus gravely. "Very well. I will tell him."

"My thanks, Magistrate." Daedalus bowed his head, then strode out of the tablinum, sensing more eyes upon him than when he had entered. As he passed through the atrium, Daedalus saw Simaetha being led into the tablinum, still refusing to meet his eyes. *It no longer mattered. There is much yet to be done.*

VICESIMVS QVARTVS

I WONDER WHAT DAEDALUS TOLD HIM, thought Simaetha, as she was led into the censor's tablinum. *Did he give evidence that I am a witch?* She had rested a little during the night, and her mind felt distracted, like a wandering orphan. When she came to the censor's chair she scarcely looked at him and only murmured greetings.

"Welcome, Simaetha," Aemilianus said warmly. He motioned to his lictors and the nearby clientes were herded back, leaving some open space on the floor surrounding them. Simaetha noticed this with a distant twinge of fear. *Hecate, guide thy servant.*

"I thought we should have some privacy," Aemilianus continued. "That is, what little a man of my place may be allowed."

"What do you want of me, Magistrate?"

"I? I ask nothing of you, Simaetha. Instead I wish to offer you my gratitude. And that of my family."

"What?" Simaetha blinked, surprised.

"For your timely warning to my cousin, the praetor peregrinus. Oh, I agree, Hispallus was a fool for not heeding you, but his folly only proved the wisdom of your warning. I only wish that my cousin had had the equal wisdom to believe you."

"Oh."

"Your people, the Marsi, have always been good allies of Rome. Your knowledge and courage are widely known and respected. Your kindness toward Scipio Hispallus is only further proof of this."

Simaetha thought it wise to say nothing in response. *Better that he believe a lie that I have not spoken.* She nodded her head once in silent acknowledgment.

"Now, Simaetha, please tell me by what agency you received the warning you gave Hispallus. If from a man, pray tell us his name so that we may thank and reward him too. If from a god, tell us which one so that we may make proper sacrifices."

Ah, here is how he seeks to entrap me. "I learned it through a dream, Magistrate."

"A dream? Shall I lay wreaths at the Temple of Morpheus then? or Aesculapius? or, perhaps, Apollo?"

"Place them where you will, Magistrate. I have already given sacrifice for my dreams, and I expect I will sacrifice even more in future."

"And at whose feet do you lay your offerings? Tell me that I may do likewise."

"She whom I serve asks more of me than you should rightfully give, so ask no more. You could not serve her."

"If she required acts inimical to Rome, then indeed I could not. But surely your goddess is not one of those foul sort, such as Cybele or Hecate, is she?"

Simaetha sighed. *And here it is. Shall I lie for thy sake, Hecate?* "My goddess is of the earth and hidden things. I have heard it is wise not to dig deeply into that which the gods have hidden."

Aemilianus sighed in return and leaned back in his chair. "You disappoint me, Simaetha. I have only offered to repay one who has helped my family. Which does not mean I will overlook you." Aemilianus motioned to a lictor who handed Simaetha a small bag of coins. "Should you again become aware of danger toward my cousin, myself or any of my family, you are welcome to tell me. I assure you I will listen better than Hispallus."

Simaetha looked at the small leather bag in her hand. "The only danger to you and your kin comes from pride and sense of power. For your salvation, look not to the gods but to yourselves." Then she turned and walked out of the tablinum, ignoring the murmurs at her back.

He thinks I have accepted his bribe. But others have seen me take this bag of gold, and should I be apprehended for anything, I will claim he has paid me for witchcraft. It might not save my life, but it would make my prosecution cost him dear.

But for what have you spared me this much, Hecate? Just tell me thy purpose in remaining here and I will rest content.

Post meridiem

THE MIRRORS ON THE WALL SPUN CRAZILY AROUND EURYALE and her stomach felt as though her myriad little serpents writhed there instead of on her head. Reaching for a leather sack, she promptly relieved her stomach of the latest of Archidemus's experimental concoctions.

"You didn't chant the words," the Chaldean gently chided behind her.

"I cannot say the words when I am too ill to concentrate!" Euryale rested her flushed face in her hands. "Must I become sick in order to face the gods?"

"No. Certainly I do not wish that." Archidemus rested a hand on her shoulder.

Euryale stiffened beneath his touch. "Careful . . ." she breathed. The theurge removed his hand and stepped away. Euryale immediately missed the warmth of his touch. "Is there not . . . some other way?"

"What would you have?"

"Sevisus said he saw visions in a bowl of water, and you only had him breathe incense."

"Hydromancy is best with a virgin youth as a medium. You have told me that, despite your appearance, you are not young. As for the other . . ."

Euryale felt her cheeks flush. "No, I am not that, either. So I am unsuitable. Are there no others?"

"To become a haruspex, one must study for years under an Etruscan master. However, I do not think the reading of sheep's livers, lightning or prodigies would give you the answer you seek."

"Most likely not," Euryale said, amused.

"Or you might lock yourself away in a sulphurous cave and become a bride of Apollo—a sibyl. But somehow I think this would give you more problems than it would solve."

"Indeed."

"Or you could try to gain wisdom by staring at a precious stone, watching the shoulder blade of a sheep cracking in a fire, throwing dirt into the wind, or watching someone's twitches and sneezes—"

Euryale laughed. "Really, Archidemus!"

"I assure you, these methods have all been used at one time or another. With varying success, I should add."

The gentle, ironic tone the theurge used did not make it easy for Euryale to stop her laughter. Her earlier discomfort was fading and she realized that, whatever else happened, she was grateful for Archidemus's good-humored, understanding companionship. *It is worth it, even with the sickness . . . I think.* "So, I must endure your potions, nai?" She coyly smiled from beneath her palla at one of the mage's reflections.

His reflections all smiled ruefully back at her. "I promise I will find one that does not make you ill. Your constitution is different from that of mortals such as I. It may take awhile to discover what will work for you. I think I will consult with Deino on this. Perhaps she may have some ideas. Ah, here she is now."

"Despoina?"

"You may enter, Deino. I believe we are finished for today. Are we not, Archidemus?"

"Yes, Euryale. We should let your poor stomach rest."

"A letter has arrived for you, Despoina. From the East," the old woman added knowingly.

"Stheno!" Euryale cried joyfully. "Bring it here, Deino." She sat up, beaming at Deino's reflection, and held out her hand.

The old woman shuffled over and placed in Euryale's hand a packed of oiled parchment that had clearly gone through many trials in its journey. The corners were all bent and wrinkled, and dark cracks marred the surface. The wax seal, embossed with the image of a serpent, was, however, unbroken. This spoke highly of the trader who brought it, though no doubt the sender had chosen and bribed him well to begin with.

"May I speak with you a moment, Deino?" said Archidemus.

Euryale watched in the mirror, as Deino looked from the theurge to her and back. "Go on with him, Deino. He needs your help. I will share the letter with you later."

The old woman's reflection bobbed her head and she and Archidemus walked away. For a moment, the room felt much lonelier. Then, eagerly, Euryale broke the seal on the package and unrolled the letter she found within.

To my dearest sister, and blessed Deino, greetings and many embraces of joy.

It was with much regret that I read of your abandoning our palace in Mauritania, but I understand. The memories of that place are sad and deep. I understand that your opportunities may be better in the great city of Rome, but the dangers! Do be careful, dear sister. I hear the Romans are more suspicious of outsiders than many.

You know how I feel about your search for an answer to our problem. If you feel it gives you purpose, than so be it, but I fear you will find no success. Most of the practicing wizards I have encountered were cheats and charlatans who knew better how to manipulate the minds of their patrons than the elements of the universe. I hope you have allowed Deino to advise you. She always seems to have a level head with regards to these things.

Frankly, I think you should forget your young Carthaginian, and look to the future. There are so many men, my dear, and we have so much time! As I recall he was a handsome and ardent fellow, but rather foolish, don't you think? Ah, well, you must decide for yourself what you must do.

As for myself, I believe I have found a paradise here in Sindhuh, the land your Romans call India. The people in the village where I live have quite taken me to their hearts. They have not yet decided which goddess I am the avatar of (I have been called Durga, Bhairavi, Rudrani, and Nagini) and they find this a good excuse for occasional battles between their priestly factions. In the meantime, I have been given my own temple and my own treasure to hoard—just in case I am one of those daemons who likes that sort of thing. I also have my own holiday, twice a year, where I may walk the streets of the town completely uncovered. Any who dare look upon me get precisely what they deserve and the priests think none the worse of me for it. They give me the most luscious blind dancing boys for my pleasures, and the food is a delight to the eye and tongue. Flies in this unwashed place are abundant, so my little ones do not lack for sustenance either.

Really, Euryale, I wish you could forget your quest and join me here. You would soon to love it as I do. Nowhere have we known the freedom to live among mortals as I do here. If you should ever become discouraged or have trouble in Rome, please say you'll come to me. You can be one avatar and I'll be another, which will either thoroughly confuse the priests, or help them resolve some of their squabbles. It doesn't matter. Come to India when you can. I long to see you. It has been so many years and I do miss your sweet temper. Who else can we truly confine in but each other? Do take good care of yourself. You always were the sentimental one, and I ache to think of the hurts you may suffer in your search. Write me and tell me all that is happening to you, though I would prefer to see your lovely face more than anything else. May the Goddess guide you and keep you always!

Your loving sister,
STHENO

(Porphredo and Enyo send their love as well and send fond embraces to Deino . . . they want me to say the warm weather here is a balm for aged bones, but the dampness is not. Don't listen to them. Come and bring Deino too).

Oh, if only I could, Stheno, Euryale thought. *You always were the strong one. How I miss you. But I cannot leave Rome until Aristo is restored, or there is no hope left.*

VICESIMVS QVINTVS

B Y THE FLICKERING FLAME OF HIS BEDSIDE LAMP, Hispallus
read again the note sent to him from Aemilianus:

> ... The witch Simaetha I cannot puzzle out. Either
> she is a poor madwoman beset by nightmares, or she
> believes strongly in the cause of our enemies and will not
> speak against them. At any rate, I do not think she will
> be bribed. It is, I suppose, possible that her warning came
> from divine inspiration. I heard stories in Greece about
> how those so inspired are often ill-used by their divine
> master and can appear mad. But, as you and I know, it is
> our duty to be cautious before we accept such things. I fear
> for Rome, should an oracle settle here, more for the sort of
> crowd she would attract than the truths she might utter.
>
> The architect Daedalus, on the other hand, is a
> more tangible danger. He seems to have some further
> mischief in mind, regarding the design of the friezes on
> the bridge. I believe I may have figuratively cast some
> pebbles into his millworks and frustrated whatever
> plans he had, but I remain concerned. "The score is
> even, but the race is not yet run. The father loses as once
> had lost the son." He claimed you would understand
> its meaning. As I recall, you mentioned that Daedalus
> held you responsible for his father's death. This brings
> to mind an ominous interpretation of the message. I

would look after your errant offspring, were I you, and make sure he is well.

I must finish this and return to my own duties which have sat long neglected. If Piso were not such a friend of our family I am sure I would have received censure by now. Take care, cousin. Guard your health and your son.

Aemilianus

With a sigh, Hispallus set the papyrus note on the bedside table. He rubbed his eyes wearily. *I have sent my lictors to search the tabernas for Cnaeus, but who can say if he will be found?* The sight of the shattered statue of his son filled his mind again. *And was that another omen? To signify . . .* The praetor shuddered and pulled his wool blanket higher around him.

I am doing all I can. Hispallus picked up the wax tablet and thin, wooden stylus from the floor, and continued to work on his notes as he waited for his wife to come in. He softened a word here and there with a forefinger to write in something more appropriate or stronger. *The trouble with creating restrictions to annoy and curb the power of wizards is that they are from so many diverse places. I could offend the Greeks, the Persians, and valuable allies such as the Marsi, all in one stroke. I must be careful. These things must be done delicately . . . .*

He heard movement at the curtained bedroom entrance and saw Clodia enter in a swirl of silken stola. "Don't let a censor see you in that," Hispallus jokingly chided. "Wearing eastern fabrics instead of good Roman wool marks you as a decadent hedonist for certain."

Clodia smiled and came forward, planting a fond kiss on the praetor's balding pate. "It has been too long since you sent for me to come to your bed, Gnaeus. But your physician bade me tell you I am not to stay long or to overexcite you. You are not well enough, he says."

"Mmm. Much as I would love to prove him wrong, that is not why I called you to me, Clodia."

Clodia sat back on her heels. "No?"

"No." Hispallus set the wax tablet and stylus on the floor. He sighed and propped himself up on one elbow, trying to hold his wife's gaze with his own. "Clodia, I have a very important question to ask. And I want the truth. Much is at stake in this."

"Of course, Gnaeus. Ask."

"What truly happened to Thessalus, Daedalus's father?"

Clodia looked away. "He died of a sudden fever. You—"

"The *truth,* I said!"

His wife stood, frowning, and turned away, twisting her fingers together. "What would you have me say? Why do you press me thus?"

"Daedalus has sent me another love-note." Hispallus read to her the message from Aemilianus's letter.

She turned and stared at him. "What does this mean? What sort of threat is this?"

"I am not sure. But I am having my lictors search for Cnaeus. I pray that he will be found alive and well."

"My son . . ." Clodia hissed and clenched her fists. "What has Daedalus done to my son?"

"I do not know that anything has been done to our son. But it would help to know what Daedalus thinks happened to his father . . . just in case. Please, Clodia—" Hispallus reached out his left hand to her and lightly grasped her wrist. "—tell me what you know."

His wife backed away from him, out of his grasp. She shook her head. "You would not understand."

"Understand? What is there to understand? Just tell me!"

With a sob, Clodia ran to the near wall and slapped the palm of her hand against the plaster. "You should have killed him while you had the chance! Now he will ruin everything!"

Hispallus glanced momentarily at the curtained doorway, wondering if any servants listened there. Dread of another sort slowly grew within him, like a hand closing slowly around his heart. The praetor pulled back the blankets and carefully got out of bed. He walked over to Clodia and placed his hands on her shaking shoulders.

"Tell me," he whispered.

Clodia looked up at him, tears running down her cheeks. Her eyes held contempt, but also fear. "You always let things go, past the point of repair. You'll ignore any problem until it's gone too far. My rites . . . Cnaeus's drinking . . . this black-mail—"

"Stop this!" Hispallus growled and squeezed her shoulders hard. "Stop changing the subject and tell me about Thessalus."

He could feel her steeling herself beneath his hands. Swallowing hard, she glared at him defiantly. "It was Liberalia," she breathed. "Thessalus died . . . in the temple."

No. Oh, gods, no. "It was one of your rituals. It was one of your damned rituals, wasn't it? Wasn't it?!" He slammed her up against the wall, his hands pinning her arms hard against the plaster.

"Yes!" she wailed, struggling feebly against him.

Though an inner voice urged him to have pity, Hispallus was deafened to it by cold, seething rage. He clenched his teeth and growled close to her ear, "Tell me everything."

Between gasps and sobs, Clodia said, "One of the priests of my sect . . . an astrologer, declared that to best dedicate the grounds of our temple we ought to have a sacrifice . . . to spill the wine of the body. Some offered a bull from their estates, some offered a sow. But the priest said the offering should be more precious . . . a human life, like in the ancient days of the Etruscans."

Astrologers again. Gods, how I will make them pay. "And?"

"Once that was decided, our choice of victim was clear. Who would be better to bless the stone of our temple with his blood than the man whose sweat and toil had built it? Our priest read the stars and said our choice was appropriate."

"Yes," hissed Hispallus. "And how convenient, to dispose of one who knew the whereabouts of your temple."

Clodia nodded, sniffling.

"How was it done?"

"I lured Thessalus into the cellar temple, telling him there would be a party in his honor. He was reluctant, but with soft words and kisses I was able to coax him down. We dressed him in a white and gold toga and placed a crown of grape leaves on his head. We gave him sweet, drugged wine and spiced meats, and he began to join our joyous mood. We sang songs praising him and we danced for him, telling him how our god was pleased with his work. When he had had enough of the wine, he danced and sang with us and seemed a very happy soul.

"As it came close to midnight, we began to dedicate our song to Bacchus, and we played our pipes and citharas and tambourines louder and louder. Our singing became the cries of ecstasy. We each pulled out a knife and slashed at Thessalus as he danced." His wife's face grew enraptured as she described the scene and Hispallus had to look away, sickened. "Clodia . . ." he moaned.

"No, my husband. You wanted to know all. At first, Thessalus scarcely noticed his blood running in rivulets down his toga. Then as our knives struck deeper, his eyes opened in wonder and he began to scream. We covered his screams with the clashing of cymbals and our own cries to Bacchus for blessing. With his blood on our feet and the hems of our garments, we danced around the entire temple and so it was consecrated."

Hispallus tightened his grip on her shoulders until she gasped in pain, but Clodia continued her tale. *As though she seeks to punish me. But for what? Because I dared to ask?*

"We rejoiced at the successful consecration and freely loved one another on the blood-smeared temple floor. The priest gave the death-blow to Thessalus and offered the liver as final sacrifice. The temple was a place of sweet joy until morning."

Hispallus's lips curled back in disgust. *So this is why the law against Bacchanalia was passed. The shade of old Cato must be howling in Hades.* He looked at Clodia, no longer recognizing her as a woman he loved. "You . . ."

Clodia glared back at him in defiant joy. "And here is what you will never understand, my husband. The consecration was an act of the most religious piety. We shared the god's sacred gifts that are his blessings to our world. Thessalus's death was not the slaughter you think. It was ennobled. It was beautiful."

Hispallus abruptly let go of her shoulders, not wanting to touch her, not wanting to be near her. "Get out," he whispered.

Clodia rubbed her arms. "What will you do with me?"

"Out! Get back to your temple and pray to your blood-splattered god for mercy because I have none any longer!"

Without another word, Clodia turned and walked out of the room. Hispallus stood very still for some moments. Then he walked back to his bed and stamped hard on the wax tablet on the floor. Picking it up, he smoothed out the footprint and all other impressions on the soft wax to begin anew. *They will pay . . .*

VICESIMVS SEXTVS

Daedalus strode along the Via Labicana, between the Viminal and Esquiline hills, ignoring the enticements of the *lupes* with their painted faces and artfully displayed ankles. He paid no mind to the cries of the begging children around him, or the suspicious stares of men from dark doorways. Daedalus thought only about the meeting toward which he was heading, and how best to make his demands to the one he would meet.

The bridge would have to be built as fast as possible. Faster, perhaps, than any stone bridge had been built before. The sculptures would have to be carved separately, in a secret location, so that they could be assembled on the friezes all at once. Some of the sculptures shown on the false plans given to the censor should be carved as well, and placed near the building site to reassure the overseer. It could be done. But more money would be needed.

And I have a sure source for the money now, he thought. *Should there be any balking, I know which arm to twist. The Domina Euryale surely does not want her secret known, nor the fate of the praetor's son. So long as I am more careful than poor Cnaeus . . .*

Daedalus knew it was a very risky game he was about to play. It was one thing to blackmail a slow-witted old patrician. But a gorgon . . . a horror out of legend! To Daedalus's surprise, his inner daemon relished the greater danger, and the excitement grew within him the closer he came to his adversary.

That witch Simaetha dared call me a coward. Hah. I am simply not a fool. Her plan had no chance of success. Mine, however, cannot fail. I may drain this creature yet . . . of money, if not blood.

He knew better than to try to meet with the gorgon, especially in her own home. Instead, he would meet her old servingwoman, Deino, in the disreputable marketplace in the Subura district. It was a well-crowded public area. *I should be safe enough.*

Ahead he saw the marketplace and his sandals slapped harder on the paving stones. He scanned the crowd for a glimpse of the old crone, but the square was full of people, many of them elderly women with pallas pulled low over their faces. Slowly he moved among them, wrinkling his nose by the snack vendors' carts where stale wheat cakes soaked in vinegared wine were sold. The pavement of the square was occupied by hopeful sellers as well, mostly poor craftsmen from surrounding farms. Daedalus nearly knocked over a row of plain earthenware pots as he maneuvered around a clot of shoppers. The curses of the pot-seller faded behind him as he spotted Deino.

Besides a blacksmith's stall she stood, resolute and firm as if she too had been turned to stone. Only the crafty glitter in her eyes told Daedalus she was alive, and quite aware of his presence.

Well, I shall see if I can bend her a bit. With a stride meant to display confidence, Daedalus walked up to her. "I see you received my message. I had worried when I couldn't find you in this crowd."

The old woman said nothing, but she nodded once, her hard eyes watching him intently.

Daedalus paused a moment. *What is it about her that is so unnerving? She's just someone's dried up old grandmother.* "Did you tell your Domina you were meeting me here?"

"I do not bother the Despoina with trivialities."

Her tone nettled him. "Good. But perhaps you will think it less trivial when you hear what I have to say."

Again the old woman did not reply.

Daedalus snorted a sigh. "Very well. If you choose not to be polite, I will be blunt. I need more money for the bridge. A great deal more."

Deino nodded again, and the hint of a cynical smile appeared on her thin lips. "I thought it would be that."

"Well? When can I have it?"

Deino raised her chin. "How much do you want?"

"One million sesterces."

Deino's eyes narrowed but her smile remained. "That is impossible."

"Is it? I believe your Domina has many more resources than she cares to admit. Certainly she would not want it asked how she came by her treasure, would she?"

Deino's smile disappeared and she blinked slowly. To Daedalus she resembled nothing so much as a basking lizard. "What do you think?" she asked. "That we have the keys to the Capitoline treasure room?"

"I think, old woman, that your Domina will find for me the million sesterces. Or else I will let the world know what kind of monster she is, and what happened to the praetor's son."

At the word "monster," Deino sucked the air through clenched teeth and her eyes became small and hard as flint. Very softly she said, "Will you, now?"

Daedalus felt as though he had suddenly stirred up an angry cobra. *But it's too late to take back any words. What do I have to fear from her, so long as I avoid her lady?* "I will. You may wager your withered cheeks on it. So. When will you have the money?"

"It will take some time to make arrangements. Twelve days."

"Four."

"Impossible. Eight at the earliest."

Daedalus thought on this. *In twelve days was the festival of Liberalia. Eight years, to the day, since his father died. If I get the additional money on the Ides, I can have the foundations of the bridge begun on Liberalia. It would be fitting to begin the final vengeance on the anniversary of his death.* "Very well. Eight. And you will meet me here in this same place—"

"Just a moment, young man. Do you think I am such a fool as to carry such a sum of money openly through this place? Thieves could snatch it from me. You might even hire them to do so, so that you could again demand the money and drive us to poverty."

"I'll not come to your Domina's house. I am not such a fool either!"

"The money will be given to a third party, then. Someone we both trust."

Why is she so intimidating? She should be bending to my demands, not making them herself. "Leave it at the Tabernum Romanum, then."

"Tchah! Another den of thieves."

"I'll not take it in any deserted place where your Domina might surprise me."

"If my Despoina so frightens you, perhaps you would feel safer surrounded by mirrors. There is a shop of mirrors on the Street of the Etruscans that is run by a merchant with an honorable reputation. Ask around for yourself, if you wish. We will leave the money with him."

"Neither you nor your Domina shall be present in the shop when I come for the money."

"I promise you neither of us will be there. Come in the afternoon, the money will be dropped off in the morning."

"I will be there precisely at mid-day, no later."

Deino inclined her head. "So be it. Eight days hence at the shop of mirrors." The old woman turned and walked away, dignified, through the crowd.

Again I feel as though she wears the triumph though I am the victor, Daedalus thought. *No matter. I will ask about the trustworthiness of this merchant. If he is honorable, as the crone said, then all should be well.*

"NOTHING," EURYALE SAID, her tongue dry from chanting strange, foreign words. "I feel nothing. Except that I am getting a headache from the concentration." She sighed heavily. "I fear, good Archidemus, that your methods simply do not work for me."

Archidemus shook his head, rubbing the end of his long, curly beard. "It is a mystery. Deino said these herbs would not harm you. At least you are no longer sickened by the mixture. But why aren't the mind-releasing ingredients having an effect?"

Euryale frowned, watching her delicate brows knit in the reflection in front of her. "Perhaps we have been forgetting something important, Archidemus. Isn't it true that most substances that cause delirium are, in fact, poisonous?"

"When given in too large an amount, or in combination with the wrong things, yes. Why do you ask, Euryale?" His face in the mirror grew worried. "Surely you aren't suggesting that I—"

Euryale laughed, the movements of her head disturbing the serpents that lay calm and contented on her head and shoulders. They raised their little heads, blinking and flicking their tongues. "No, no, my friend, I suggest nothing. I only meant that I am immune to poisons. It is one of the 'blessings' conferred upon me along with my immortality and my little ones. That being so, it is not surprising that my mind is not released by your potions."

"Ah. Yes, we should have thought of that." Archidemus looked sadly away from the mirror

Euryale gazed at herself in the bronze mirror and her mood became serious once more. "It would seem I am doomed to remain as I am. And Aristo must remain as he is."

Archidemus looked back at her reflection. Then, his face taking on an expression of resolve, he approached her from behind and rested a hand on her shoulder. "Perhaps it is not meant for you to change your condition, sweet Euryale, but to learn to appreciate it. It might not be the curse that it seems." He stepped beside her. Then he stepped in front of her until she was staring at his sandaled feet and the fringed hem of his robe. "Archidemus . . . " she warned. His hand reached down and approached her face. "The little ones, Archidemus, beware!"

"You know," he said as his hand came within inches of her, "I think your little ones rather like me."

To Euryale's surprise, the little ones indeed did not respond to her fear and coil to strike. Instead, glancing aside, she saw the green serpents stretch out to meet his hand. Their scarlet tongues flickered and they seemed to greet him with curiosity, not anger. The Chaldean moved his hand closer and the snakes glided along his fingers, sensing, questing. They curled up against the warmth of his skin, rubbed against him like affectionate kittens. Archidemus brought his hand even closer and caressed Euryale's cheek with his fingers. Euryale gasped and shut her eyes firmly. *If I can keep my eyes closed . . .* The feel of his touch was so sweet it was nearly painful. *It has been so long.*

His other hand touched her and she felt his warm palms brush across her forehead and brows. His fingers traced her nose and cheeks. Euryale felt her lips part and she firmly clasped her hands in her lap, tensing for fear she might sob.

Archidemus's hands came to rest beneath her chin and he lifted her face. "Look at me, Euryale," he whispered.

"*No.*"

"You need not fear. I shall not turn to stone."

"You fool. You will!" Tears began to well in her eyes.

"Your little ones know it is not so. Look at me."

Euryale felt the serpents resting calmly against his hands and her cheeks. "If . . . I lose you . . ." She felt a deep pang inside, realizing she could not bear to see him turned to stone. His companionship had meant so much, and her friends were so few. She raised her hand and ran her fingers along the edge of his palm. Fat tears began to roll down her face.

"You will not lose me, Euryale. I would stay by your side forever, if you would let me."

This so surprised Euryale that her eyes blinked open. Through her wavering tears, she saw Archidemus's warm brown eyes gazing back in pure admiration. He smiled and his face seemed to glow with joy.

Euryale opened her eyes wider and gasped. "How . . ."

"With love, Euryale. And the absence of fear. How do you think your maid Deino survives? It is not from her half-blindness, for she sees you quite clearly when close. No, Euryale, she loves you and fears you not and this keeps her from harm. As my love for you does, Euryale."

"Oh. Oh, no." For a moment there was nothing in the world but his hands on her cheek and his face before her. Time slowed in its inexorable march. Part of her rejoiced at his words, but on the heels of her joy came fear and guilt. *Aristo . . . if he had loved me . . . and if I still love him, what must I tell Archidemus?*

"This is not possible." Euryale shook her head and looked away. "Aristo loved me, yet it helped him not at all."

"Did you let him see you as I do now?"

"No." Memories came of nights she had lain naked upon her bed, except for the tight turban that bound her little ones, waiting in the dark to hear Aristo's footfall in the stone hallways of the palace in Mauritania. The dim echo of the sweet anticipation she had felt came back to her. *Will Archidemus be hurt if I speak of Aristo? He asks as though he will not mind.* "In daylight I was always veiled. He came to my bed only in darkness. And when I let him touch me, I made certain that my little ones were always bound and hidden."

"And did he know your nature as I do?"

"He knew I was different. That I had felt the hand of the gods in a way that kept me apart. I dared not tell him my true nature."

"Hmm. Yet one day he finally saw you."

"Yes. He must not have believed my warnings, for one night when he came to me, he secretly brought a lamp. And as soon as he beheld me in full light . . . it happened." She saw again in her memory Aristo's handsome face shifting from surprise to awe to shock, and freezing in solid stone before he quite reached a scream of horror. The screams that had been heard that night were her own.

"So you see, Euryale, he could not truly love you for what you are. You did not permit it. And his fear at suddenly learning your true aspect doomed him."

Euryale stared up at the theurge, and her heart became heavy as lead. "Then his fate is even more my fault." She looked away and buried her face in her hands. "I am a monster."

"No, Euryale. You could not know that twist in Athena's curse. You must not blame yourself."

"How can you possibly love me, knowing what I am?"

"How could anyone not love you, knowing who and what you are? A woman who is kind-hearted and gentle. A woman who is beautiful and will be so eternally. A woman with the wisdom and knowledge gained by centuries of experience. How could I not love you?"

Euryale's emotions swirled and surged like an incoming tide, threatening to drown her. *Could I not return Archidemus's feelings? But it would be murder to not bring Aristo back if I can. What have I felt for him all of these years? I have longed for him, yes. But is it not duty that has driven my heart? Duty and guilt . . . what sort of love is that?*

Archidemus went on, "If you will, Euryale, let us leave suspicious Rome, and I will go with you to anywhere in the world you wish. To your home in Greece, or to the farthest ends of the east, even to your sister in India. Take me to your heart and I will love you for all the years left in my life, few though they may seem to you. Leave Aristo to your memory, and devote yourself to your own future, not the past."

Oh, do not tempt me so. Euryale shook her head. "To leave Aristo as he is, his body a stone tomb . . . I could not possibly do so unless you tell me there is no hope whatever. As for leaving Rome, Aristo in his current state is very delicate. Once broken . . . " She could not finish. *Have I given Archidemus an impossible dilemma? Would he lie and tell me there is no hope, so that he might have me? Will he refuse to help me further out of jealousy?* She looked up at the theurge, trying to see the thoughts behind his eyes. "I thank you, Archidemus. I will treasure you always as a dear friend. If you are still willing to help me, I beg you to do so. Apply your love for me in this way and I shall be eternally grateful. But I will not abandon Aristo."

Archidemus stepped back and bowed his head. "In truth, I expected this. It makes you the more beautiful in my sight that your love is not easily transferred from one to another. I will gladly help you, Domina, until you no longer wish my service. And I shall keep the desires of my heart to myself."

Euryale sighed with relief and regret. *He is indeed a good man.* In hopes of easing his spirit, she said, "You have said, Archidemus, that you are a Stoic. Yet is it not taught among those of The Porch that love, while a natural desire of man, is without merit and not to be sought?"

Archidemus looked up with a rueful smile. "So it is said. Yet while the logic of the mind may appreciate one teaching, it can be overwhelmed in battle when the body and spirit believe differently. I will return to my studies, Domina, and see if there is any way I may help you further." With a small bow, Archidemus walked out of the room without another glance at her.

VICESIMVS SEPTIMVS

"Two days, Magistrate?" said Marcus anxiously. "I do not think it can be done."

Hispallus glared up at him from his bed. "Are you telling me how the business of Rome should be conducted? My edict is ready for approval by the Senate. I charged you to arrange for their assembly on the soonest available day. Tomorrow would be too soon, I grant you. But on a matter thisurgent, the Nones should be acceptable."

Marcus rubbed his chin and frowned. "Many senators will be hard to reach. Consul Laenas is out of the city—"

"Then assemble those you can! It will be worse later. The festivals of Equirria and Anna Perenna come soon. And Aprilis is filled up with Games. I want this edict passed before Liberalia."

"Please pardon me, my Lord. I do not mean to tell you your own business. But this is a major declaration you are proposing. The senators will tell me that you should call a *contiones* first . . . discuss it with the other Scipiones and Cornelii."

Hispallus narrowed his eyes. *And you would like to avoid a lot of last-minute work.* "You may tell them that when they hear my declaration, they will understand its urgency." *And I cannot risk Aemilianus talking me out of this. This edict is too important to me.*

Marcus made half-gestures with his hands, seeming uncomfortable. "They will also remind me that the date of assembly must be announced twenty-four days in advance, and must be posted throughout Rome for the people to see."

Hispallus sighed and leaned back onto his pillows, his hands clasped behind his head. "Marcus," he began in a deceptively conversational tone, "you have served as my freedman secretary for several years. During those years you have given me no cause for complaint, and you have become like a friend to me. But I can have you dismissed, you know."

Marcus smiled ruefully and bowed. "My Lord. I will do as you wish. But—"

"But what?" Hispallus groaned.

"Your physician, my Lord. He has asked all of us who serve you to tend you with utmost care. He is concerned that you do not overexert yourself. He has reminded us that, Iupiter forbid, should you die and it is deemed a poisoning, all of us in the household could be put to death for failing to protect you."

"Such a kind man," Hispallus said dryly, "to make threats on my behalf. I am more likely to die from frustration than from exertion. If you must, tell the senators that they must come to hear the divine inspiration of a dying man . . . perhaps that will attract their ghoulish attention. I'll talk to the physician myself. Be off now."

"If my Lord—"

"Marcus, shut up and go."

"Yes, my Lord. At once."

DEINO HURRIED DOWN THE STREET OF THE ETRUSCANS, trying not to trip over the uneven paving stones. She was breathless and her legs ached terribly by the time she reached the shop of mirrors. Clutching her disheveled palla to her chest, she paused near the doorway in the shade of a pillar to catch her breath. She squinted her eyes and regarded the shop front thoughtfully. *Now, if it is as I remember it . . .* Gathering her breath and her wits, Deino decorously rearranged her palla and stepped through the doorway.

"Good madam Deino!" the proprietor, a hirsute man with well-muscled arms, called out upon seeing her. "Does your Domina require yet another mirror?"

Deino feigned mild offense. "My Despoina is an admirer of your fine wares, good merchant."

"As well as her own fine looks, I gather."

"My Despoina is very beautiful."

"Yes, I'm sure. Well, how may I serve your lovely lady today?"

"Two things. One a small favor."

"For such a good customer? Anything."

"We need to make a valuable delivery. Because of the nature of the transaction, it must be done discreetly, through a trusted third person. You are known to be reliable."

The mirror seller placed a hand on his chest and bowed slightly. "It honors me that you think so. If it does not take me away from my shop duties, I am happy to be of assistance."

"I don't think that it should," Deino said, looking around. Mirrors of polished bronze and silver hung on the walls, some with their reflective surfaces facing the wall to display the intricate designs on their backs. At one corner of the shop was a curtained doorway.

"If you will pardon an impertinent question from a curious old woman, good merchant, could you tell me what lies beyond that wall? Do you make your home here as well?"

"Why, no, madam. My business is better than that. I have a house on the Oppius Mons, where I live with my family. That room back there I use to store merchandise."

"I see." Deino went to the doorway and pulled aside the curtain. This revealed a short, narrow hallway, with a door along one side. "Excellent," Deino mused.

"Madam?"

"Pardon me. This would be a good place for keeping the item that is changing hands. Customers will not see it, yet the young man will find it easily."

"If it is valuable, I could lock the item in the storeroom."

"No need, I think. This should serve." Deino let the curtain fall back in place.

"And the other request, madam? You said there were two."

"Yes. Do you remember that mineral you showed me the last time I was here?"

"The mica from Gaul, you mean?"

"Yes. You were thinking of making mirrors from it."

The shopkeeper shrugged. "It proved too brittle, too fragile. And I cannot find the right backing for it."

"Did you try smoking the back with soot from a candle flame?"

"I did. It was still too transparent."

"But when the light is right, it serves as a good mirror. You showed me."

"Yes," the shopkeeper sighed, "it can be. But the light must be just right. And whatever is behind the mica must be dark. It is too much trouble."

"Ah, but sir, these interesting qualities are precisely why I want a mirror of this mineral."

"Well . . . perhaps a small one would be possible."

"Oh, no. It must be large. And I would like to have use of your storeroom for its display so that the mirror need not be moved. And I need it in eight days."

The mirror merchant rubbed his chin. "This is beginning to sound complicated."

"I will pay you twice what your shop earns in a week."

The shopkeeper's eyes widened. "Well. You have my attention, madam."

"Here is what I wish . . ."

VICESIMVS OCTAVVS

THE MORNING WAS BRIGHT AND CLEAR and the trees of the garden were garbed in leafy togas of yellow-green. Sevisus walked through the garden, his early chores completed. He noticed that the damage done by the praetor's "guests" had been nearly erased. The groundsman, Emano, had come and after nearly fainting, had gotten right to work. Now, as if they had waited for the strangers to leave, the rosebushes were finally starting to bud.

Sevisus caught sight of Archidemus sitting on a marble bench beside a tall poplar, and the boy ambled over to him. "Good morning, magus."

"Eh?" Archidemus looked up, his face tired and sad. "Oh. Good morning to you, Sevisus, and good health."

"I should say the same to you, magus? Is all well?"

Archidemus sighed. "I wish I could say yes, Sevisus, but it is not. Everything I try to help your Domina fails me. I fear I shall be of no use to her at all." The theurge closed his eyes and leaned back against the poplar.

Just as Olerus said, whispered a part of Sevisus's mind. *No. He's just discouraged. He'll find a way. He's got to.* He kicked a pebble into some bushes, then squatted on his heels before the theurge. "I've been reading a lot in the library. I actually found a scroll that mentions basilisks, but I don't think it would help much. It just talked about how it was so deadly, and how even touching something that touched one would kill you. Everything about them is deadly, their venom, their skin, their blood, their glance, everything!"

"What are you blathering about, boy?" Archidemus said distractedly.

Sevisus stopped a moment, stung. Archidemus had never been cross with him before. *Maybe I shouldn't talk about it so loud.* In a loud whisper, Sevisus said, "You know . . . basilisks . . . like the one that hurt the Domina and made the statue over there out of a live man."

Archidemus opened one eye. "Where did you get this tale, Sevisus?"

"Olerus told me. And when I asked her, the Domina said it was true."

The theurge raised an eyebrow. "She did, did she?"

Sevisus nodded. "I promised to keep her secret. So did Olerus. But since you already know, I can talk to you, can't I?"

With an ironic smile, Archidemus said, "Of course you may, Sevisus. But please do not mention it to anyone else." He frowned. "What else did Olerus tell you?"

Sevisus shrugged and picked at the rocks on the path between his feet. "Not much. He thought you wouldn't be able to help the Domina, but he's wrong, isn't he?"

Archidemus sighed and looked away. "It may be that Olerus has more wisdom than he knows."

"What do you mean?"

"Nothing, Sevisus. Never mind. So, you were speaking of basilisks."

"Oh. Yes. The scroll said their blood was so poisonous that if you stuck one with a spear, the poison would creep up the spear and into your hand and kill you."

Archidemus chuckled. "That sounds like a flight of fancy, lad."

"The scroll said so! Why would anyone make that up?"

The theurge shrugged. "I don't know. Nonetheless, many legendary creatures are said to have poisonous blood; centaurs, hydras, gor . . ." Suddenly the mage's eyes opened wider and he stared into space for long moments.

"Magus? What is it?"

A faint smile appeared on Archidemus's face. "Sevisus, did you not tell me once that the building over there is where your Domina houses her ancestral gods?"

"Yes, magus."

Archidemus stood. "Let us go see it."

Sevisus jumped up, alarmed. "Oh, no! No one but she is allowed to enter it. Don't go in. She'll sell me to another master!"

Archidemus walked up to him and placed a hand on his shoulder. Softly he said, "My boy, you have given me what may be the answer to your Domina's sorrows. If things are as I think, and all is successful, your Domina will do naught but thank you."

Sevisus clenched his fists. "But if it isn't . . . But if—"

"If we are discovered, I will claim all is my fault, and that you are blameless. I will see that you are not punished, I promise."

"You are sure this will help her?"

"No. But it is the only hope I have left."

Sevisus thought for long moments, trying to gather his courage. Then he nodded. "Very well."

"If we are quick and quiet about this, you need not fear. Let us go."

So Sevisus led the mage to the earthen-walled hut in the garden, and with great anxiety crossed the threshold into the dark interior. "There's nothing in here. It's empty."

"Not quite. Over there, in that corner."

Sevisus squinted and saw a squat, grey shape in the shadows.

Archidemus went ahead of him. "Yes, this is what I hoped for. Now if only my other assumption holds true . . ."

"What are you talking about?" Fear gnawed at Sevisus's stomach.

"Come help me with this."

Sevisus glanced once over his shoulder to the bright, beckoning spring morning outside. Then, with a sigh, he shuffled over to where Archidemus kneeled. As his eyes adjusted to the dim light, and as he drew near enough, the shape of the grey object became clear. With horror he viewed the statue of a woman with snakes in her hands and snakes in her hair and a snake around her middle. The stone leopards on either side of her seemed to snarl at him threateningly out of the darkness.

"*That's* her family god? Ick!"

"It is not wise to disparage another's gods, Sevisus. And this Goddess is one of the most venerable in the world. She has been worshipped in one form or another since the most ancient of times, long before your gods came to Olympus. She is the Earth, Life and the growth of all things."

Sevisus heard the respect in his voice and wondered if Archidemus worshipped her also.

"Now," the theurge said conspiratorially, "help me move this."

"But that's sacrilege!"

"Yes. But necessary."

"But you just said not to—"

"Sevisus! Do you wish the Domina's Goddess to see you refusing to help her?"

"I don't want to touch it!"

Archidemus sighed and bent tiredly over his knee. "It is only a carved lump of stone, Sevisus. This was not even once alive. The Goddess it represents does not live here, but in the heart of one who worships her. I ask you, for the sake of your Domina, for the sake of our friendship, however you may value it, please help me."

Sevisus swallowed hard and looked at the statue. *Just a carved lump of stone. I once thought the statue in the garden was too.* With a sigh of resignation, Sevisus said, "What must I do?"

"Grasp hold of one side. We must tip it forward so I may look at the back."

Sevisus closed his eyes and carefully wrapped his arms around the stone. He let Archidemus pull the statue forward and Sevisus bore the weight a few moments, straining.

"It's not in the back," Archidemus said.

"What isn't?" Sevisus grunted.

"What I'm looking for." Archidemus eased the statue back onto its base. "One moment."

"What?"

"Move the statue this way. Lift it off the base entirely."

"I don't think I'm strong enough."

"I will help you, and we will set it on the ground."

This struck Sevisus as being greater sacrilege, but he felt already committed to the act. He took one side of the statue and Archidemus took the other. Grunting, they lifted and carefully set the statue on the earth floor of the hut."

"Yes!" Archidemus exclaimed. "Here it is."

Despite his fears, Sevisus looked at what the theurge was pointing out. There was a dark rectangular hole in the stone base, directly beneath where the statue stood. Archidemus reached into the hole with both hands and reverently pulled out a golden jar. "It is here," he whispered.

"What is it?" Sevisus whispered back.

"A relic."

"Oh." Sevisus swallowed hard. In Roman families, it was customary to preserve mementos of one's ancestors in the shrine of one's Lares familiares. Usually it was a lock of hair, or a wax death-mask. Whatever was in the golden jar, it was a very private, holy thing, and Sevisus prayed to the Goddess, as well as Iupiter, Minerva and Mars, that he and Archidemus not be cursed for what they were doing.

Archidemus pulled a small vial from his waist-pouch. He took the lid off the golden jar and dipped the little vial into it. Despite himself, Sevisus leaned closer to look. But all he could see was a reddish-brown dust on the vial as Archidemus pulled it out again. Gently, Archidemus brushed the excess dust back into the jar and replaced the lid. The vial went swiftly back into his pouch, and the golden jar back in the hole. Archidemus motioned for Sevisus to pick up the statue again and, with difficulty, they raised it back onto the platform.

"There!" Archidemus dusted off his hands very carefully and stood back. Lifting his hands, palm upwards, the theurge intoned, "We thank you, Goddess, for your gift to your servant, and to those who love her." Turning to Sevisus, his eyes shone as he said, "Let us leave now. Swiftly!"

Sevisus took a last look at the Goddess and bowed to her, also thanking her in his heart. *For the Domina. Please don't curse us.*

"Sevisus! Come!"

He hurried to the entrance and stepped out, looking around for Archidemus. But the theurge was already far down the garden path, walking with long, bouncing strides.

INTEMPESTE NOCTE

THE FULL MOON SHONE WITHOUT MERCY on the ghastly burial ground of the Esquiline hill. The wind moaned through the bare skeletons of trees, who perhaps were late to bear leaves because of what lay around them. The torn-up earth was littered with the bones of slaves and the very poor, dug out of their shallow graves by wild animals. The cold night air was fulsome with the stench of mould and rotting things.

"Why have you brought me here, Hecate?" asked Simaetha, pulling her palla tighter around her shoulders. "This is a place of death." She had not slept or eaten much in the past three days, and she felt light-headed, floating, as though she were one of the spirits that haunted here.

The owl on the barren tree beside her said nothing, staring implacably at the grisly scene around her.

"Am I to summon a shade to speak to us, as others are doing?" Among the trees, Simaetha could see people moving; women in black stolas, their hair unbound, searching among the graves for bones and peculiar herbs.

"Ou ou!" said the owl.

"Not that, then. I await your direction, Mistress." Simaetha crouched beside the tree and ran her hand over the ground before her. A long, pale finger-bone came to the surface. Simaetha picked the bone up and examined it. "To whom did this belong?" she murmured.

Hearing footsteps behind her, Simaetha stood and turned around. In the moonlight, she recognized the dark, curly hair, the young face just a bit too angular to be handsome.

"I'm not disturbing your business, am I?" Daedalus said sarcastically.

Simaetha frowned. "What do you want here?"

Daedalus took a jaunty step forward. "I followed you."

"Why?"

"I want to know what you told the censor."

Simaetha tilted her head to one side. "I told him nothing."

"You expect me to believe that?"

In her altered state of mind, she thought Daedalus appeared different. The pale moonlight on his skin was the color of the finger-bone she held. His eyes were dark pits in which daemons hid. His stance was no longer cock-sure, but subtly rigid, like a stick-man in the hands of a master puppeteer. The pout of his lips was not sardonic, but pleading. "I do not know what you will believe, little coward."

"Don't call me that! I'm not a coward! Your plan to bleed the gorgon was stupid, that's all."

"What would you know of wisdom, Son of Nyx?"

"What does that mean?"

"Nyx is primeval Chaos, She who was before all things came to be. You surely do her work."

Daedalus sneered. "If I served anyone, it would be Nemesis."

Simaetha shook her head and pointed the finger-bone at him. "The daemon who rides you is Fear; fear of pain, fear of loneliness, fear of death."

"I fear nothing!" Daedalus shouted.

"Precisely."

The laughter of nearby scavenging witches startled them both for a moment. When Simaetha looked back at the architect, his fists were clenched but his face showed confusion.

"I must have been right the first time," he said. "You are mad. I will achieve through my own methods what your crazy scheme would not. Through blackmail I will drain the gorgon of gold. After that, why should I not ask her for her blood? It's so simple."

A cloud passed across the moon, darkening Daedalus's face. Simaetha gasped. *Now I understand, Hecate.*

"What's wrong?" growled the architect.

Simaetha gave him a grim smile. "I finally realized why my goddess guided me to this place. It was not for my sake, but yours."

"Heh. What does your goddess think I should see in a bone-yard?"

"She asks another difficult task of me." *Am I doomed to be another Cassandra? I could tell him . . . but I shall have pity on myself and the world and not say. He would do as he wished anyhow.*

"Well?"

"Ou ou!" said the owl in the tree behind her.

So I must say something. "What does this place mean to you?"

Daedalus kicked at the dirt in front of him and part of a skull rolled away down the hill. "Death. Stupidity. Pointlessness. All these poor slaves"—he stretched out his arms—"they worked hard all their lives and what did it get them? Their bones are gnawed by wolves, while their masters lie in grand tombs on the Via Appia. If there is a god of justice, he doesn't rule here."

"I think," Simaetha said, "you see all that my goddess intended."

"Oh, did I? Well, thank her for me. Thank her for nothing."

"I shall."

"But I still don't have the answer from you that I came for. What did you tell the Censor Aemilianus?"

Simaetha threw back her head and laughed, the peals of her laughter deepening the silence around them. "He is the least of the dangers that threaten you, Son of Nyx, as am I. You will not have to face either of us again."

"Oh? And what is the greatest danger to me?"

"Yourself."

"Tcha!" Daedalus kicked a clod of dirt toward Simaetha. "Mad. I shouldn't have bothered." Hands thrust in his tunic pockets, he turned and trudged away down the hill.

A cold, noisome gust of wind blew after him, flapping and flinging Simaetha's palla around her. "Is this the last service you ask of me, Mistress?"

"Ou," said the owl.

Simaetha hung her head and walked back to the path that led to the Sacra Via and her hovel on the Aventine.

VICESIMVS NONVS

"YOU HEARD ME CORRECTLY," said Hispallus as he stood staring out of his bedroom window. "I asked for my toga pulla." Across the vale that was the heart of Rome, he saw the Temple of Jupiter Capitolinus gleaming in the golden-rose light of dawn. *There*, he thought. *There I shall save Rome from its foolishness and give my name to history.*

"Yes, Lord." The slave left quickly and soon returned, bearing a garment deep maroon in color.

As the slave properly draped the toga over the praetor's shoulders. Hispallus had to admit to his misgivings. *I might fail to convince them. What then? Do I give my name only to a marble plaque on the Via Appia?* The fluttering of his stomach became worse and he took a deep breath. *I must not think like this or all my courage will flee. This garment may help gain me sympathy.*

The toga pulla was worn on occasions of mourning or to announce some great calamity. Hispallus had done nothing to dispel rumors that he might be near death. The words of a man thought to be dying would carry the weight of divine inspiration. *They may think that by wearing this toga I mourn for myself. What will they think when I tell them that I mourn for Rome?*

AFTER A LIGHT BREAKFAST OF WHEAT GRUEL, dried fruit, cheese and bread, Hispallus set out in his litter. The praetor had grown very tired of spending most of his time reclining, and during the trip across the city he could not find one comfortable position on the pillows. His mind found no comfort as well. His spirits were similar to that just before a battle, highly alert and aware, but there was no promise of satisfying physical action to come. The battle he now faced would be waged with words, and he had far less confidence in his skill in oratory than in the strength of his sword arm.

Hispallus groaned as he descended from his litter, and his lictors rushed to help him. *Should I feel embarrassed for my public lack of vigour, or will this help my cause as well?* At the top of the stairs to the Temple, and around him in the forecourt, citizens and senators stared at him with concern and wonder. He nodded to them gravely and began to ascend the Temple steps, his lictors by his side, carrying a long, wooden staff to lean on for support. He wondered which god to invoke for aid in his oratory. *Minerva for inspiration? Iupiter for the command of authority? No, though this is not his temple, it should be Mars. I fight for the defense of my name, my family and Rome. Could he withhold his aid from such a noble cause?*

At the top of the stairs, he met another possible obstacle to his plans—the augur. Hispallus had hoped that Aemilianus could do the auspices, but he had been advised that it would have appeared too partisan. The augur had the power to disband an assembly simply by claiming the gods disapproved. Looking at the dark-cowled augur, Hispallus didn't recognize him. At least Aemilianus found someone unbiased.

Hispallus cleared his throat. "Well, have the gods given their sign?"

The augur bowed, solemn-faced. "I measured the *templum* of my gazing in the northwest portion of the sky. As I watched, a hawk flew by, pursing a flock of ravens."

"Is this . . . favourable?"

"It is, Lord."

"Good. My thanks to you—"

"However," the augur went on, frowning, "there was one other occurrence that I think you should be aware of."

"Oh?" *Spare me. I need no more omens now.*

"Just before my time of gazing was at an end, a white owl flew near me and flung down a stick that it carried in its beak. It loudly hooted at me, then flew away to the south."

There were whispers and murmurs around the praetor, speculations on what it might mean. *Not the owl again,* thought Hispallus. *I have not even yet divined the meaning of her first oracle. The owl is a bird of Athena, Minerva, Hecate . . . witchcraft! That mage Archidemus hinted as much. Naturally the forces of the Night would disapprove of what I am about to do. No matter. I'll not let them stop me.*

Hispallus gave the augur the best smile he could manage. "Why, good augur, this omen is even better. It is Roman custom that, before a battle, spears are thrown across the enemy's border. Now Minerva herself appears to fling down the symbolic spear, as if to say 'let the battle begin!'"

While the augur pondered this, Hispallus heard enough approving noises around him that he felt secure in taking the initiative. He turned and entered the great Temple doors, exuding confidence that the gods had given their permission. To his relief, the senators followed.

The wide central aisle of the Temple had been furnished with tiers of benches set up by the high priests of Jupiter Capitolinus. The benches were set in a semi-circle, whose open end faced the doors. Three hundred senators served Rome but this day scarcely one hundred disgruntled men filed onto the benches. Due to the suddenness of the assembly, no doubt. Again, Hispallus wondered if the situation put circumstances in his favor. It felt vaguely shady to him to have his advocate's instincts arise on an occasion of such importance. *But no. I need all the skills I have. A thief may be a hero if his talents save Rome.*

The consul Calpurnius Piso sat in the central bend of the semi-circle, on his curule chair. His expression was brooding and uncertain. *At least it is not anger.* Behind the consul, the enormous statue of Jupiter Capitolinus loomed over the gathering. Hispallus had very deliberately chosen this most venerated of temples for his oration. He hoped it would impress upon the Senate the importance of what he had to say.

Aemilianus swiftly walked past Hispallus with scarcely a nod of greeting, and sat on a bench near to Piso's right hand. He leaned to whisper something to the consul. Piso nodded and cleared his throat. The massive doors behind them were closed with a deep rumble and boom. Almost all eyes turned to Hispallus, and he leaned more heavily on his staff to hide his unease.

Piso spoke. "With the approval of the gods, this session has been called by Cornelius Scipio, for a matter he considers most grave and worthy of our attention. Therefore, let him come forward and speak."

With great dignity, unassisted by his lictors, Hispallus walked to the middle of the semi-circle of men. "Patres conscripti," he began, "you may be blessed in the sight of the gods for your willingness to unselfishly serve Rome in these unfortunate times." He noted a few sardonic frowns among the senators' faces, and some men whispered to their neighbors. A few senators had brought their young sons, as was common at senatorial assemblies. A couple of the boys giggled behind their hands until their fathers shushed them.

"As you may have heard," Hispallus continued, "I have been gravely ill, and my physicians even now are concerned for my life."

Hispallus overheard a senator to his right mutter, "He doesn't seem so ill to me." The praetor paused and coughed heavily.

A lictor approached Hispallus and asked if he needed aid, but the praetor waved him away. "I beg your pardon, gentlemen. As I was saying, I have been ill. Yet during this time of illness, I have learned of a danger to Rome—a danger so great that I must rise from my sickbed and request your immediate advice.

"As a praetor peregrinus, it is my duty to suggest remedies for the ills that beset Rome, much like the physicians who attend to me. Therefore let me speak to you of this disease that now threatens the body of Rome, and hear me as the physician who seeks to remedy it. And though the cure may sound harsh, it is often so with the worst of ailments."

Hispallus paused and coughed again, this time from genuine need. It had been a long time since he had delivered oratory, and his illness had taken much of his wind from him.

"So it shall be—must be—today as I tell you of the pernicious danger that threatens us. As praetor peregrinus, it falls among my duties to watch over those foreigners who live in Rome. Most of these peregrini are honest people; Acheans in the service of their government . . .

(*Never mind that they are, in fact, hostages,* thought Hispallus.)

". . . scholars from the East who come to learn of our ways, merchants and labourers from our allied states in Latium, Gauls who come to offer us trade and tribute. Yet among these good folk, like stowaways aboard an honest ship, there come those who do not wish Rome well, and would be agents of her downfall."

The faces of the senators blinked or nodded with impatience. The consul Piso said, "It has always been so, Scipio. It is ever a Roman's duty to be vigilant against foreign threats. But I presume you have something more specific in mind."

I have not yet captured their interest, Hispallus thought worriedly. "Indeed, my Lords, Calpurnius Piso speaks truly. Rome has often, in her past, had to cleanse herself of the evil that threatens to invade her. I do not speak, my Lords, of armies or spies who seek to conquer Rome by force of arms. I speak of those who would take hostage our very minds, or souls! I speak of the evil of foreign gods, of foreign wizardry!"

Instant hubbub filled the temple. The little boys stared at Hispallus wide-eyed. The praetor overheard one senator mutter, "I think his mind has been taken hostage by his disease."

"You scoff," said Hispallus, pointing at the muttering senator. "But as I have said, Rome has faced this danger before. Seventy-three years ago, the man who held my office decreed all books on foreign cults be burned and all new rites and magics suppressed. Fifty years ago, the curule aedile Albinus brought witches to trial. Now it is time again to show that Rome will not tolerate the abuse of its laws, its citizens and its gods."

"One moment!" called out a voice from among the senators. Hispallus turned and saw a narrow-faced man stand up—it was Sulpicius Galba, long an enemy of the Scipiones. "I find it interesting that the praetor mentions the expulsion of the Bacchanites. You have all heard the rumors, I believe, that this man's own wife is involved in such a cult. Perhaps Hispallus would like to speak to us on that!"

The murmurs and mutterings grew louder and there came cries of "Yes, tell us!" Hispallus felt his insides tighten, yet he had expected this objection. He was ready.

Hispallus walked over to Galba and fixed him with a sad stare, leaning heavily on the staff. "Ah, yes. My wife. Painful as the subject is to me, I am glad you have mentioned her. Her case is indeed relevant. My Clodia has confessed to me that she was compelled to commit acts totally contrary to the behaviour of a good Roman wife and matron. And the man who influenced her is precisely the sort that I must warn you of today.

"I speak of those who call themselves 'Chaldeans.'" Hispallus said the word as if it were the vilest curse possible to utter. "Those who worship the stars as gods, and claim to see the future in the movement of the heavens or flickerings in a bowl of water. These men do not allow the gods to steer the course of Roman history. Instead, these magi of the East whisper in the ears of powerful citizens, urging them to do this or that, for the stars say it must be so. Had Clodia confessed this to me years ago, I might have saved her from the terrible life she has been leading. But it is too late for her. In shame, she has exiled herself, and will never come to Rome again. But it may not be too late for other good Roman wives and citizens! Let us do away with this pestilence of soothsayers, before the sickness becomes madness and the madness turns to death!"

Angry talk both for and against him broke out among the senators. Hispallus leaned upon his staff to catch his breath, and gather his wits. *This does not go as well as I'd hoped.*

The consul Piso clapped his hands for silence, and the hubbub subsided. "This is all very interesting, Scipio. But is strikes me that your cause against these 'Chaldeans' is a personal one."

"Personal?" said Hispallus. "Yes, my Lords, it is personal. But does an ordinary citizen not have the right to address a court for wrongs done against his person? And might not this wrong have implications for other citizens as well? Is one not more aware of crime when he hears victims complain of their plight? My experiences, gentlemen, are a warning to all of Rome, and it would be wise to heed this warning while we can. My own illness, if illness it be and not poisoning, may be the result of not heeding such a warning."

There were gasps among the assembly, and the word "poisoning!" was heard softly exclaimed here and there as if in a valley with many echoes.

Ah, now I have their attention.

"This is a serious supposition," said Piso, rubbing his chin.

"Indeed. Allow me to explain. Not long ago, I requested a favor from a foreign client, a Greek noblewoman. But she was undecided as to whether to render me this service. She also was being counseled by one of these very same Chaldean mages. On the day that I was to visit her to learn of her decision, I was visited by a witch. Some of you were there and saw the witch. She had come to warn me of some unspecific danger if I was to see the Greek domina again. Thinking her a nuisance, I paid no heed to this witch and I went to the lady's home anyway. It was during that very visit to the Greek domina, after partaking of her food and hearing her denial of my request, that I collapsed in great pain and in great fear of my life."

The hubbub began anew and Hispallus saw concern on many senators' faces. Conspiracy and poisoning were dangers nearly every patrician feared. The praetor gained a little hope. *I may yet win.*

"Now," Hispallus quickly went on, "before you think my suspicions groundless, I would ask Scipio Aemilianus to speak. He has investigated this matter and can tell more." Hispallus gestured to Aemilianus. The room quieted and all eyes turned to the illustrious censor.

Aemilianus shifted uncomfortably on his bench. "I am uncertain as to what you would have me say, Hispallus. It is true, senators, that I have looked into the incident of which he speaks. The domina he speaks of has also sought the counsel of other witches and magicians, before this Chaldean. There appears to be some strange connection between this Greek woman, the Chaldean, the witch who gave Hispallus warning, and one other who means to do the praetor harm. Nonetheless, I cannot outright declare it a conspiracy, for there is no proof."

"No proof?" Hispallus asked mildly. "Tell me, Aemilianus, did you not find at this house an interesting scrap of papyrus?"

Aemilianus frowned a little. "I did, yes."

"Will you please tell the good senators here what was written upon it?"

Aemilianus sighed with resignation. "It was written in a strange code of many languages and astrological symbols. When my scholars translated it, the main body of the message turned out to be three prophetic verses. One verse seemed to suggest the overturning of the current state, the next suggested the assassination of an important personage, the third . . . the downfall of a great city."

Senators now stood on their benches, crying, "Who did this? Arrest him! Treachery!"

Hispallus raised his arms and shouted over the din, "You see how these Chaldean astrologers write of disaster and destruction—words to incite despair in our citizens!"

Aemilianus held up his hands for silence. "We cannot arrest the one who wrote the message. We do not know who he is. And we do not know that the verses refer to Rome."

"These mages are not fools," Hispallus said. "They will not let their intentions be discovered easily."

"Cornelius Scipio, I would speak!" called a voice.

"Yes? What have you to tell us, Drusus Livius?"

The white-haired senator stood. "It is true, what Hispallus is saying. My wife consulted a soothsayer to choose the most suitable marriage partner for our daughter. The soothsayer ran off with our daughter himself, and now we will have no grandchildren to honor us. Listen to Scipio. He speaks the truth!"

As the senator sat, Hispallus's heart filled with joy. "If others have such a tale, let them speak out as well!"

"I have had an astrologer advising me these past two years, and he has served me well in matters of the sale and purchase of land."

"And have no calamities befallen you these past two years?"

Crassus frowned. "I had a baby son die of the fever, but what of—"

"Would it not have been better to be warned of your son's death than told the best time to sell your villa?"

"Scipio, let me speak!" called yet another voice. A young senator stood and said, "Just this past week, I sought advice on where to borrow for the purchase of a villa. One of these 'Chaldeans' told me whom to see, and it turned out to be a disreputable usurer. I was lucky to escape with what fortune I have intact!"

Hispallus nodded. "I have met that very Chaldean myself. A potential menace indeed. You see, my Lords, how these fortune-tellers feed upon the body politic of Rome like the vultures sent by Zeus to feed upon the liver of Prometheus?"

"Throw them out!" called the white-haired senator.

Hispallus pointed toward him. "There, my Lords, there speaks wisdom! There is a man who remembers the moral days of Cato and Africanus! Let there be a cleansing! The gods would ask no less!"

Acclamations erupted from some of the senators, and heads were nodding vigorously among the doubting frowns.

Piso slapped his hand on the curule chair and called "Silence!" As the Temple quieted, he continued, "I think we can agree, Cornelius Scipio, that your complaints have some merit, and that this matter deserves a hearing before a *comitia centurata*."

Hispallus allowed his alarm to show on his face and, leaning heavily on his staff, he approached the consul's chair. "My Lord Consul, I fear we should not wait for a comitia. May I speak of one more concern?"

"Very well."

Turning to face the rest of the assembly, Hispallus said, "My Lords, in ten days comes the festival of Liberalia. That night is a favorite for dark cults to gather, and for dark deeds to be done. My own wife confessed to . . . unspeakable things, that her wizard compelled her to do on Liberalia. I tremble to think what damage might be done as more Romans, befuddled with wine, are led by the nose by conspiring wizards. I did not heed the warning given me, and I nearly died for my heedlessness. I may lose my life yet for it. But do not let Rome die with me. Free our City of the foul treachery that would lead us to decadence and ruin. Expel these Chaldeans before it's too late!"

Hispallus ran out of breath once more and began to cough and wheeze. No laughter broke the silence in the Temple this time. His lictors ran to him, gently taking his arms, and guided him to an open space on a bench.

For a moment the only sounds were Piso's fingers drumming on the arm of his curule chair, and the shifting of togas on the wooden benches. "Well," he said finally, "what is the Senate's wish?"

"Listen to him!" the old senator called out again. "The gods speak through his voice. Throw the wizards out! Any who stay, throw them off the Rock!"

Amidst the mixed grumbling and assent Aemilianus's voice carried. "My Lord Piso, let us speak sensibly. It is a serious thing to propose execution for one's beliefs. Some of these so-called soothsayers are also philosophers, or pious people who mean no harm to Rome."

"And how would we weed them out from the others?" asked Piso.

"We could not," said Aemilianus. "But we can be fair. Give them the ten days until Liberalia to leave the city. Any who are still here at midnight on that day can, at that time, be arrested in the midst of their troublemaking. All honest magi will have left by then. Is that acceptable?"

"Cornelius Scipio, what say you?"

Hispallus sat up and looked at Aemilianus. *Must you always steal my thunder?*

"Let me add," continued Aemilianus, "that the only name on this decree be that of Praetor Hispallus. If any wizards seek to cast curses for their discomfort, let them be directed at the one man who is willing to risk his life and health for the sake of Rome."

Piso raised an eyebrow to Hispallus.

And must I always owe you gratitude? Hispallus bowed his head. "I am honored to do this service for Rome. Let it be on my head."

The murmuring among the senators was now filled with awe and respect.

Amid the noise, Piso said, "Very well. Cornelius Scipio has stated his desires. Let there be a vote among us. Let those who sit to my right indicate those in favor of this decree. Those upon my left vote against it. What shall be your judgment?"

Hispallus saw before him a flurry of white and purple togas as the senators chose their position. Beyond them he saw Aemilianus nod to him, but not move to either side. His expression seemed to say to Hispallus "I hope you know what you are doing."

At last all the senators were settled, and although not all sat to the consul's right hand, Hispallus saw that he had clearly achieved victory.

"Let it then be so decreed," said Piso. "Within ten days, beginning at midnight tonight, all Chaldeans, wizards, witches, followers of forbidden cults, and those who unlawfully consort with same, are to leave the city of Rome. Any of those found within its confines after ten days shall be stripped of citizenship, if Roman, and executed. Aemilianus, see that placards proclaiming this decree are placed with prominence in the common areas of the city."

"Yes, Lord Consul."

The senators stood to depart for baths and other business, many thanking or congratulating Hispallus on their way out. The praetor did not feel like a victor, but he was satisfied, and he nodded and smiled weakly to the senators as they passed. The young boys walked by him wide-eyed, saying nothing.

As the last senator said his "vales," Hispallus closed his eyes and sighed. To no lictor in particular he said softly, "Take me home."

TRICESIMVS

E URYALE PULLED HER PALLA TIGHTLY AROUND HER as she
allowed Deino to guide her down the Street of the Etruscans. *Cursed be the magistrate who decreed that foreign women
may not ride upon a litter in Rome. This is too hazardous.* "Is
it far, Deino?"

"No, Despoina. Just a little farther."

"I wish the streets were not so crowded."

"Do not worry, Despoina. The Romans have too many other things on their minds to pay much attention to us."

"Including the praetor's edict."

"Nai, that too."

"If I did not trust you, Deino, I would think we had both
lost our senses. We should be at home, preparing our household in case we, too, have to leave, along with the wizards.
Archidemus tells me his final potion is ready, and I should
make a last attempt as soon as possible."

"You may do so this afternoon, Despoina. I promise this
trip will not take long."

Deino had Euryale stop for a moment beside a crossroads
shrine, and checked the sundial that stood there. "I believe we
will be there in time, Despoina."

"In time for what, Deino? What does time have to do with
this present? And why couldn't you find me a present you

could bring home, rather than . . . oh, I'm sorry. You are the dearest person to me, and here I am questioning your gift. Forgive me."

"I understand, Despoina. I am sorry to inconvenience you so. But come. It is just up ahead."

"Ah, that must be the shop where you and Archidemus purchased the mirrors for my study."

"Quite right, Despoina."

"Deino, you're not giving me another mirror, are you? I have so many already."

"This is a magic mirror, Despoina. It was specially made for you. Wait until you see it."

Euryale tried to hold onto her patience as Deino led her up a tiny, narrow alley, and down another, kicking chickens and cats out of their path and avoiding the puddles of filth. "Why are we going this way, Deino?"

"Privacy, Despoina. We enter a back way so that no one knows you are there."

"But the mirror merchant—"

"He knows we will be using this storeroom this morning and will not disturb us. I have seen to it. Here we are."

They stopped at a large, wooden door beside which stood two burly men. They nodded to Deino and she wished them good health.

"Who are these men, Deino?"

"They are laborers who will stand guard out here while we are inside. If you like your present, I will make arrangements with them to bring it home. If you do not, they will take it elsewhere, or destroy it."

"I see."

Deino pushed the door open. Euryale went before her, nodding greetings to the laborers, who bowed to her as she passed. She stepped into a room that was nearly bare and without light except for two oil lamps burning on either side of a curtain to her left. She heard Deino shut the door and come up behind her. "Well, Deino, where is this magical mirror? Is this it, behind the curtain?"

"Don't look at it yet, Despoina! I must first be sure everything is safe." She hurried across the dusty room and, putting the lens before her eye, put her eye to the chinkhole in the wall.

"What is this silliness, Deino?"

"I want to be sure no one is in the store by the merchant. Because I want you to take off your palla when you look in the mirror."

"Deino . . ."

"Otherwise how will you tell if it is a good mirror or not? Ah, I think we will have our chance soon . . ."

DAEDALUS ENTERED THE MIRROR SHOP, pleased that were no other customers and passers-by outside. *All the thieves have gone to the horse races to pick purses. No one will notice me carrying a treasure home.*

The mirror merchant sat in a corner, polishing a piece of bronze. Daedalus cleared his throat and the merchant looked up. "Ah, are you Daedalus?"

"I am."

The merchant stood and walked over. "Yes, you match the description. Your package is in here, sir." The merchant went to the curtain at the back of the store and pulled it aside.

Immediately cautious, Daedalus peered past the curtain. He saw a short, dark corridor at the end of which a bulging sack sat on a stool. "Are there no doors or windows in there?"

"Only the storeroom door, sir, and it is currently obstructed. You'll have to leave by the front."

"Just as well." *It is all so easy.* Daedalus straightened up and marched into the corridor, humming to himself.

"Now, Despoina!" In one flowing gesture, Deino flung Euryale's palla aside and pulled the curtain down. Behind it lay a large, rectangular mirror, framed in gold.

Euryale stepped closer to examine it. The surface was not totally smooth, like polished metal. It seemed to have ripples, as if one were seeing one's reflection in clear, deep water. Euryale thought its unique qualities softened the angular planes of her face, and for a moment she imagined herself a normal woman beholding herself in a garden pond.

Suddenly there was a shifting of light and shadow within, or behind, the mirror. "Deino?" she whispered. She swallowed hard. In the next moment, her green serpents, frenzied, came boiling out of their wrappings and hissed at the mirror. Euryale's eyes grew wide and turned from green to scarlet. She felt flickers of heat racing up and down her body. Try as she might, she could not pull her eyes away. *So this is what those who fear me see!* She stood trembling as her serpents writhed on her head and her eyes glowed with scarlet light. "Deino! Help me!"

"Oh, I am so sorry, Despoina!" Deino peered into the mirror, then threw Euryale's palla over the furious snakes. She pulled Euryale aside and gathered her in her arms. "I did not know the mirror would distress you so. I will have it destroyed. Come away, there now. Calm yourself, Despoina."

Euryale still trembled. "I almost feared I would turn myself to stone, Deino. It is . . . so horrible!"

"I am so sorry, Despoina. I was hoping you would see the beauty in yourself that others see."

"It was not Archidemus who magicked this mirror, was it?"

"No, Despoina. It was the mirror merchant. That is the last time we trust an amateur, nai? Here, let me redo your wrappings and we will go home."

"Yes, Deino." Euryale clutched the ends of her palla to her chest, feeling sick and despairing. "You wanted me to see my beauty, but all I could see was a monstrosity."

"Think no more of it, Despoina. There, your wrappings will hold. Come away, now." Deino led Euryale back out the door and said to the laborers. "It does not suit us. Remove it and take it to the place I told you. I will meet you there to pay you your balance."

The workmen nodded and went into the storeroom. Euryale huddled beneath Deino's arm as they hurried down the alley. Hearing movement behind them, Euryale looked back over her shoulder. The laborers were emerging from the storeroom, carrying a heavy, angular bundle in dark cloth. "What will they do with it, Deino?"

"It will be given to someone else, Despoina. Think no more of it. It cannot harm you any longer."

TRICESIMVS PRIMVS

N ESCIO SAT IN THE APARTMENT OF DAEDALUS, waiting impatiently for the architect to return.

The fool. He should be back with the money by now. Where could he be? Maybe he bragged out loud about how he tricked a rich woman out of her gold, and an enterprising thief had taken it from him. I would have. Maybe Daedalus sits in a high-class taberna, surrounded by the best courtesans he could buy, and they are having a laugh on poor, stupid Nescio who sits and waits for nothing.

Nescio pounded the table beside him with his fist. "Where could he be?" he growled. Noticing a set of wooden knuckle bones on the table, he idly scooped them up and tossed them. They came up Vultures. "Heh. Are you trying to tell me something, Fortuna? Maybe Daedalus has left Rome with the money, and the aediles are coming to put me in jail, eh?"

There came the sound of footsteps on the stairs, and the scraping of something heavy along the landing just beyond the door. For a moment, Nescio entertained the thought of leaping out the window to save himself from arrest. Then he snorted. *It is only Daedalus, who has been drinking and has finally dragged himself and his moneybags home. There was a fumbling at the lock, and Nescio bounded to the door and flung it open.* "Daedalus, you pig—" But he stopped and stared in surprise.

Equally surprised was the old woman blinking in the doorway, and the two burly men beside her.

"What do you want, hag? This is not your . . . Wait, aren't you the servant of the Domina Euryale?"

"I am," the old woman replied, either offended or cautious, Nescio couldn't tell which. "And you are that contractor who works with Daedalus."

She is the one who gave us the money before. I'd better be polite. "My deepest apologies, madam. Yes, I'm Daedalus's . . . associate. I suppose you decided to bring the money here. That was very wise of you."

"Money? No. We bring no money. We have brought something else." She gestured to the two men, who wrestled a large, heavy cloth-covered bundle through the door.

Nescio, frowning, stood aside to let them pass. "What is that?"

"A special commission."

Nescio scratched his head and closed the door behind them. "Commission? He said nothing about any commission. Let's see it."

At a nod from the old woman, one of the workmen pulled off the cloth. Nescio stared. It was a statue of Daedalus, perfect in every detail. But the pose was odd; the architect was crouching slightly, his head turned to one side. His arms looked as it they were reaching for something, and his expression was that of one overwhelmed by surprise. *Hah. He probably wanted to put himself in the Bacchanite scene, probably reaching for someone's wife.* "Looks like it was sculpted by the same fellow who did the bust you gave us."

"It is the work of the same artist, yes."

"It's a funny pose, though."

The old woman shrugged. "That is how it turned out."

"Well, I won't pay you for it."

"It has already been paid for."

"Heh. I hope Daedalus didn't spend too much on it."

"He paid quite dearly for it, I assure you."

Nescio grimaced. "How like him. Have you seen him lately?"

The old woman shook her head. "Not a word. We'll not take any more of your time. I must return to my Despoina. Good health to you, Nescio." She and the two men left quickly, leaving Nescio alone with the new statue.

"You treacherous, vain little peacock!" Nescio growled. "You say you are going to get more money for us and the bridge, and you spend it on a ridiculous statue! It was probably my share you spent too. Well Nescio will not be your fool any longer. I am to Brindisium with what I have left. As for you . . ." Nescio kicked the statue over. One arm and the nose broke off. "So sorry, Daedalus. It was an accident. But you only needed the statue for one day's joke, didn't you?"

Nescio spat on the statue, then he turned and thundered out the door.

"ARE YOU SURE YOU STILL WISH TO ENDURE THE CEREMONY?" asked Archidemus. The room of mirrors was dark, and to Euryale the many reflections of his face were pale, dim moons in a starless sky. Though he sat close beside her, he rarely looked at her.

"I must," said Euryale, quiet but determined. "My experience today with the magic mirror has only made me more resolute. Besides that, for your safety, I do not want you to remain in Rome any longer than you must. Undoubtedly the aediles will come seeking you here."

"Yes. I feel as though the praetor's edict was aimed at me, though I cannot think what I have done to offend him so."

"Nor I. But the Romans are often suspicious of foreigners, particularly those claiming magical powers. You must have impressed him too well. If all goes right, I want you to leave tonight. Leave as soon as I am safely out of the divine influence."

"Domina, there are four days remaining to me."

"And I want you to use them to be as far away as possible when the final day comes. If the guards choose to demonstrate their patriotic zeal, they might arrest a day or two early."

Archidemus smiled a little. "I am touched by your concern," he said wistfully. "I would rather stay, but if you feel I will be of no further use to you then I shall do as you bid."

Oh, I have hurt him. He thinks I wish to be rid of him. "Please believe that I ask this only from concern for you. I would have liked you to stay also." She reached out and laid her hand on his. Archidemus at last looked at her, his eyes filled with gratitude and hope. This time it was Euryale who had to look away. "Where will you go, Archidemus?"

The theurge sighed and stood. "Alexandria, I think. It is one place where wizards are still appreciated. If I cannot start a school there, at least my skills will not be wasted there."

"Your skills have not been wasted here."

"Well. It is time to put that to the test. Are you ready?"

"Yes," Euryale said with more sadness than she expected. "Let us begin."

"You have fasted this past day?"

"I have not eaten since the last sunset."

"Or your little ones?"

"Nor they."

"Good." Archidemus took up a vial of oil and, pouring a small amount into his hand, he lightly anointed Euryale's forehead, nose, cheeks and chin.

This may be the last time he touches my face. Euryale steeled herself to keep tears from filling her eyes. *This is not the sorrow I want the gods to see.*

Archidemus took long, new-flowering vines that had been picked from the garden that morning and gently wound them around Euryale's head, interweaving them around the little serpents, who didn't seem to mind. Then he pressed a laurel branch into her right hand. He placed tiny rolls of papyri, on which had been written magical symbols, on Euryale's feet. Then he stepped back and said, "Begin your recitation."

Euryale closed her eyes and began her now-familiar chants. They consisted of prayers to the gods of many places and times. Though there was one goddess she hoped most to see, any divine spirit might be asked to be intermediary. Interspersed between the prayers were phrases that seemed to be nonsense. Yet Archidemus had said that they held power, in the way their sound transformed the orientation of the mind and made it receptive to the influence of the divine.

She smelled cinnamon and sandalwood, and she knew that Archidemus was heating spiced water upon the brazier across the room. She let the heady scents lift her awareness, rather than distract it.

A metal cup was placed in her hands, and she heard him say, "Drink."

Euryale obeyed, finding the taste powerfully different from the draughts the theurge had given her before, but in no way she could describe. Archidemus placed a bowl of steaming water at Euryale's feet, then took the cup and poured what drops remained into the bowl. A great gout of steam hissed up from the bowl, bearing the scent of wine and something more animal.

Archidemus returned to the brazier and poured oil upon the embers. The fire grew high and bright. Euryale's eyes began to water from the brightness of the flames and the steam at her feet. She began to chant anew, and heard Archidemus join in with moans and sighs and hisses that set her teeth on edge and made her skin shudder.

As Euryale stared at the fire, she saw it spread, flowing like water out of the brazier. The flames rushed toward her and surrounded her. For a moment, she was afraid. *Is it real? Will I burn?* She felt unable to move, as if iron bands had clamped around her. Yet she was not discomfited by the sensation. She felt only partially connected to her body; merely a mind with eyes attached to a pounding heart and gasping lungs. The resonance of her chanting and the theurge's noises caused her ears to ring with ethereal, vibrant tones. A voice pitched higher than any human voice seemed to be calling her name. "Euryale, Euryale . . ."

Suddenly, the fire rushed in on her, filling her with energy and light, but not consuming her. The view of the room wavered and dimmed, becoming only white and golden shimmerings. Her chanting stopped, yet still she heard the high, sweet ringing, and beneath it a choir of voices so pure that they could only come from the throats of gods. Again her name was called, "Euryale . . . Euryale . . ."

"I am here!" she tried with all her heart to say. She was not certain that her mouth obeyed. She felt completely without physical form . . . a spirit suspended in fire and beauty.

"Welcome," the chorus responded, many voices blending as one. "We greet you, and are pleased that you come among us." The voices took shape, faces, bodies and flowing fabric that drifted in and out of visibility. Finally one form became more solid than the others, a nude young girl, pale and slim, bearing a tall hunting bow.

The girl sank to one knee and said, "We know why you seek us. We cannot give you the answer you hope for."

Another form drifted into visibility, a voluptuous woman with thick, brown hair, carrying stalks of wheat. She said, "The one who cursed you will not undo her work. It is a great injustice, for it is not you but us that she truly wished to punish. She is of thought and air and the creations of men's hands. We are of nature and earth . . . that which cannot be controlled by Man. She mistrusts and fears us, and takes her revenge through you."

"What shall I do?" said Euryale.

A more familiar form coalesced from a pearly fire, a woman flanked by hunting dogs, with serpents instead of hair. "Medusa!" cried Euryale.

KARA DALKEY

"Sweet greetings, sister. May patience guide you, for you will have sore need of it."

Euryale's joy became tempered with worry. "What do you mean?"

"It is your doom, and Stheno's to remain as you are, forever bound to the earth, forever in the image of the Goddess—She of the Thousand Names, whom we love. But we ask you not to let this be your defeat. The power of the Goddess, of all of us—" she held out her arms to include the other visions—"is fading as that of the one who cursed you grows. In time, few will worship the vessel from which all life springs. Instead they shall wreak their own destructive works upon it. You can do little, yet do all you can to prevent us fading entirely from the mind of Man. Protect our domain. Do not give the one who cursed you complete victory."

"I will. But is there nothing I can do for Aristo? And for other innocents who suffer for Athena's curse?"

The images looked down, then moved aside. The young girl said, "Here comes one who can answer."

Another woman appeared, with dark eyes and hair, wearing a white shroud belted with a snake. On one shoulder sat a small, brown owl. "We are not permitted to tell you what you wish to know. But seek my servant, with whom you have spoken before. She knows the answer. It lies within you and she has seen this. Go to her, and reward her well."

"Thank you. I will."

"We have told you all we may, and even now we weaken," said Medusa. "Keep you well, and continue your service to our Goddess. It may do little, and yet it may keep us all from destruction. Be of good spirit. Our love and hope is with you."

One by one, the visions stepped back, Medusa last. There was so much Euryale wished to say to her, yet her sister's parting expression said that all was known, forgiven, expected and shared.

Then her image blended with the others, each image overlapping the one behind it, until together they formed one Image that was all of them. This was a wide-hipped, deep-breasted woman in a short tunic, who held snakes in her muscular hands and wore serpents in her hair. Then this vision faded completely into the surrounding opalescent fire. The fire in Euryale's mind dimmed and her head dropped to her chest.

Completely spent of energy, Euryale slumped toward the floor. But strong arms grasped her and lifted her up. She felt herself carried for a little way, then set down upon a soft surface that she knew to be her own bed.

She felt a light caress on her cheek, then heard the slap of sandals quickly receding. With the clarity remaining from her visit with the gods, she knew it was the last time she would hear Archidemus's footsteps on her floor.

TRICESIMVS SECVNDVS

S IMAETHA SAT ON THE ONLY CHAIR IN HER HOVEL, watching the door. The world seemed extraordinarily quiet, not even the usual dog barks or birdsongs. She thought she heard in the far distance a crowd shouting, "Mammurius! Mammurius!" but she did not know what it meant.

She nibbled on a dry crust of bread that had been sprinkled with the last of her crystallized honey. Had she not managed to catch the attention of a baker's delivery boy the day before, she would have had only honey to eat. The white owl avatar had not allowed her another excursion since her midnight walk to the Esquiline. Since then she had been a prisoner of duty.

Now she waited, a dagger at her elbow on the table, for the aediles to come and take her away. It seemed certain. But the one thing her skills could not do for her was tell her own future. *Whatever happens, may it be what you ask, Hecate.*

There came a knocking at the door and Simaetha stiffened. Slowly, she grasped the dagger and took it onto her lap, hiding it in a fold in her stola. "Enter."

Slowly the rotting door creaked open and Simaetha clutched the dagger tighter. But instead of the armored men she expected, there stood on her threshold a veiled woman and her elderly maidservant. "Simaetha? May we speak to you?"

For a moment, Simaetha was too stunned to speak. But she knew. *It was for this meeting I stayed.* She cleared her throat.

"Yes, Domina Euryale. I will speak with you." *Have you come to make a statue of me for your goddess? If you know that I know your secret and that I once schemed against you . . .*

Cautiously they entered, the old woman first. Euryale gently shut the door behind her, as if it were the most fragile glass.

"Why do you seek me?" asked Simaetha, standing.

The old woman suddenly flung an arm out before her lady. "Beware, Despoina! She has a knife!"

Simaetha looked at the dagger as if seeing it for the first time and wondering how it got there. *Against an immortal gorgon, this is useless.* The witch dropped the dagger on the table. "Forgive me, Domina, I intended no threat. I have been awaiting the city guard to arrest me for my defiance of the edict."

"You still have three days, Simaetha."

"But my goddess has bid me stay, I know not for how long. I think perhaps for this meeting. What is it you wish?"

"I have come for that which you offered the first time we met. I have been told by divine spirits that you indeed are the one with the answer. You can tell me how I may turn stone to flesh."

Simaetha felt her jaw drop open. She felt something shaking inside her. Suddenly she began to laugh, loudly and uncontrollably.

The old woman wrinkled her nose. "She laughs at us, Despoina. I told you you had been ill advised. Let us go, before—"

"No," said Euryale firmly. "Simaetha, forgive me if my request seems laughable to you now, but I am serious. I am bidden to give you anything you wish that it is within my power to give. The gods said that the answer lies within me. They say you know the answer to this riddle. Please tell me, Simaetha."

Her laughter calmed down to a giggle. *Anything I wish. Yet there is only one thing I wish, and my effort to get that failed. Would she simply give it to me if I asked? And what is the answer that she wants? It lies within her* . . . Simaetha felt her knees weaken as she understood. Her face stretched into a hysterical grin and she held out both arms. Unable to contain herself, Simaetha erupted again in laughter.

"It is no use," muttered the old woman. "She is mad."

"No! No!" Simaetha gasped. "It is the gods who are mad, Domina. They laugh at us from their domain, even as I laugh now at their handiwork. Yes, I know the answer, and it lies within you."

"Well?" Deino growled.

"It is . . . your blood!" Simaetha shouted amid new spouts of laughter. "Gorgon's blood! Deadliest poison to the living, yet the nectar of resurrection to the dead. Bathe one you have made stone in your blood and he will live again." Simaetha sat heavily on the chair, clutching her middle which ached from laughter.

She heard the old woman say, "Faugh! This is foolishness."

"No, Deino, I believe her. It is the sort of cruel jest Athena would play. I have carried the answer with me all along, yet I dismissed those stories about gorgon's blood as myth. Perseus's slander. I thank you, Simaetha, for showing me the truth. Now what will you have of me?"

The witch fought to keep from laughing again. "Why, that self-same thing, Domina. Your blood. I wish some of your blood, that I may use it for healing among my people."

To the old woman's apparent horror, Euryale said, "Very well. You have earned it, though I cannot spare you much." The veiled woman held out her arm and drew back the sleeve of her stola.

Simaetha gaped a moment, not believing her success. Hastily, she rummaged through her belongings, finally finding a little glass bottle with a stopper. Euryale came forward and took the dagger from the table. With a quick swipe, Euryale made a shallow cut on her arm. Simaetha held the bottle beneath the cut to catch the precious red droplets. It did not take long for the bottle to fill.

As Euryale pulled her arm back, her old maidservant rushed forward and wrapped part of her palla around the cut and held it. Simaetha reverently put the stopper in the bottle and sealed it with soft candle wax.

"Now I suggest you leave Rome, Simaetha. Find a land more accepting of your beliefs. Archidemus, the theurge who served me, has gone to Alexandria. He said it is a place that welcomes wizards and scholars of the arcane. I think you could find a place there."

Simaetha shook her head. "I thank you for your kindness, Domina. But if my goddess allows me, I would return home to the hills of the Marsi."

"May your goddess grant you this wish, then."

"Will you help me see if it is so? Will you do me one last favor, Domina? As you go outside, please tell me if there is a big white owl in the tree?"

"An owl?"

The old woman tsked. "Foolish one. The white owl is the avatar of Athena, not Hecate."

Simaetha frowned. "You are wrong."

"Well, some animals, like people, serve more than one god," said Euryale. "Let us see if it is there." Removing the old woman's hand from her arm, Euryale went to the door and opened it. "No, Simaetha, there is no owl."

Simaetha signed deeply. *Blessings to you, Hecate. I will build a shrine to you when I am home.* "Then I am gone. Good fortune to you, Domina Euryale." Grabbing up her leather sack, the witch dashed past the veiled gorgon out the door. Simaetha's feet felt light and the dust of the street smelled fresh and welcome as she headed for the Capena Gate and home.

"I hope she gets home all right," said Euryale, watching the witch depart. She felt a lingering sadness at seeing the effect of the praetor's edict. She felt somehow responsible for it. And she felt regret that Archidemus had not stayed to say farewell. There had been only a terse, respectful note left on her pillow to mention that he had left last night. *And may he find a home as well.*

"I hope your faith in her knowledge is justified," said Deino. "Silly woman. So concerned about an owl . . . oh."

"What is it, Deino?" Asked Euryale, turning.

"There is an owl. Up there. Large and white, like she said.

Euryale peered through her veil, and saw it on the lowest branches of the nearest tree. The owl looked back with cold eyes. *I have more pity than you credit to me,* said a voice inside Euryale's mind. Then the owl stretched out its great wings and flew away.

TRICESIMVS TERTIVS

T HE NIGHT FELT EERIE as Sevisus traipsed through the
garden after Deino, carrying the heavy water jar. Perhaps
it was because he knew that he was going to be part of a magic
spell to bring the statue back to life. They carried no lamps,
walking only by the light of the waning moon that had just
risen. Every tree's shadow seemed to hide ghosts or daemons
and Sevisus started with each chirp of a nearby cricket. *I wish
Archidemus was still here.* Sevisus stumbled over a twig.

"Careful, there," said Deino.

Sevisus walked more cautiously, staying well behind Deino
and the gruesome load she carried. *It's only pig's blood in her
jar,* Sevisus chided himself. *Yet she carries it as if it was filled
with precious jewels and gold. I guess to the Domina it is precious, if it's going to wake up the statue.* It occurred to him to
wonder where Euryale was.

"Deino, isn't the Domina going to join us to watch?"

"Hush, boy! The Despoina is . . . ill tonight and cannot
watch. She will speak to him later."

Doesn't make sense, thought Sevisus. *Even if ill, she'd want
to try and get up to see him come back to life, wouldn't she?*
"Deino, wouldn't she want us to wait until she's well enough
to watch?"

"And what if she does not recover in three days? We cannot carry a fragile statue out of Rome without the possibility of harm to it. Enough of your questions. Hurry along, now."

"Yes, ma'am." They had learned that day that the praetor's edict applied to Euryale's household. Sevisus thought it terribly unfair. *We're not witches or wizards, just because my Domina talked with them.*

Sevisus and Deino walked into the small, private bath in the back of the house. The water had been drained, and now the statue that had been in the garden lay incongruously in the sunken tiled basin. With much relief, Sevisus set down his jar of water and stared at the statue.

"Here," said Deino, handing him a wide horsehair brush. "Help me coat him with the blood. As much of him as you can, especially the head, hands and feet. Be very careful to get none on yourself. If you do, wash it off in the water right away. Now hurry, before it dries."

Deino took the lid off her jar and Sevisus dipped the brush in, nearly gagging on the heavy smell of blood. Together he and Deino worked quickly. Sevisus tried to think of the blood as just red paint whenever his stomach began to rebel. But now and then he was forced to go to the doorway and take deep breaths of fresh air. Before long the jar was empty.

"It is done," Deino said at last, stepping back. They both stared at the statue awhile. In the moonlight streaming through the window, the statue was a ghastly sight. They waited. Nothing happened.

"Maybe we were supposed to say some magic words or something," Sevisus said tentatively.

"Faugh. Muttering nonsense over him wouldn't help. To Hades with this. I'm going to get a lamp. Wait here."

Sevisus started to protest, but Deino had gone before he could say a word. He didn't want to be alone with a blood-covered statue that might come to life at any moment. He sat by the wall, drawing his knees up to his chest, and waited, shivering.

Deino came back sooner than he expected, a welcome flame of golden light flickering above the lamp she held. "Any change?"

Sevisus didn't want to admit he hadn't been watching closely. "None that I can see."

Deino's face twisted into an ugly grimace of anger and hate. "Damned be that witch Simaetha! I will have her sought out and strangled for this! Such waste! I told the Despoina it would be no use! Her precious blood wasted . . ."

Pig's blood isn't cheap, but it's not precious, thought Sevisus, confused. *Wait . . . her blood?* He turned and looked back at the statue, aghast. "You said it was pig's blood, Deino."

"Oh? Nai, our Despoina has been oblivious as a pig at the slaughterhouse, to obey Simaetha's directions so willingly. I am sorry I lied to you, Sevisus. We have to lie to so many people. For what little good it does us."

So much blood from one person. No wonder she is ill. "Is . . . is the Domina going to die, Deino?"

"No. Though I think she would like to, that is one mercy Athena will not grant her. She cannot die."

This surprised Sevisus more. *She cannot die?* Then he thought he saw a flicker of movement on the statue's face. "Deino, the lamp! Bring it here!"

Deino came forward, the light of the lamp turning the moonlit black of the blood to bright crimson. The man's shoulders twitched and he slumped in the bath, no longer rigid. His eyelids fluttered, then suddenly opened. Bewildered, the man stared at Deino and Sevisus. He looked slowly around the room. Then his gaze lowered to his body, and he screamed.

"The water, Sevisus," Deino shouted, "quickly!"

Sevisus ran to the water jar and knocked the lid off. Raising it high over his head, he carried it to the bath and dumped the water over the man. The man screamed again and wrapped his arms around himself, cowering down in the bath.

Deino threw a towel at him. "Stop your noise, Aristo. You live again, at greater cost than you know. Dry yourself."

Worry, fear and confusion warred on Aristo's face.

"It's all right, sir," Sevisus said.

Still shaking, Aristo stood and clumsily toweled himself, looking in wonder at the blood.

"It isn't yours," snapped Deino.

"How—" Aristo rasped, then coughed.

How long has it been since he has spoken? thought Sevisus.

"All will be answered soon enough. Here is a fresh tunica for you." Deino handed the garment to Sevisus.

Sevisus cautiously gave the tunic to Aristo and helped him put it on. Aristo seemed still unable to believe where he was or that he lived. He moved slowly and his eyes were very wide. He kept pressing his hands against the flesh of his arms and chest as if reassuring himself that he was no longer stone.

Sevisus thought, *He is as handsome as an actor. No wonder the Domina likes him. But why does he behave so strangely, as if everything in the room might bite him? Oh, of course.* "There's no basilisk here, sir. That was a long time ago. You're safe now."

"What?" said Aristo.

"Sevisus," snapped Deino, "go to the kitchen and bring us some bread, wine and cheese. We must see that Aristo is well cared for before he speaks to the Despoina."

Aristo's head shot up to stare aghast at Deino. "No," he said, backing out of the bath. "Not her. No. No. No!" He continued stepping back until his shoulders struck the wall behind him.

Sevisus waited, unsure if he should stay to help calm the man.

"Don't be a child, Aristo," said Deino. "It was your own mistake that put you in this mess. The Despoina has always been careful, and will be more so now, after what it has cost her to save you."

But Aristo stayed against the wall, hugging himself and shaking his head. "No. I didn't mean to . . . I didn't know she was a monster. Please don't make me look at her again. Spare me, Deino!"

"Monster?" Sevisus exclaimed, upset that Aristo should insult Euryale. "It's not her fault that a basilisk looked at her!"

"Sevisus! To the kitchen!"

Sevisus unwillingly left the room, but listened to them as long as he dared.

"You ungrateful wretch," Deino was saying. "She gave you shelter and her love. At great cost she redeems your foolishness, and this is how you thank her?"

"I didn't know!" Aristo wailed. "I thought she was just a shy beauty. She seemed so kind. How was I to know she had snakes for hair and a daemon's eyes?"

Sevisus felt his heart stop within him. He had read enough to know what Aristo was describing. The mirrors. The Domina's veil. *I should have guessed. It wasn't a basilisk at all.* He headed toward the kitchen, not wanting to hear any more. He felt hurt inside, but not for himself or Aristo. *She's not a monster, whatever she looks like. She's not. Archidemus knew. He loves her. She's not a monster!* Tears filled his eyes as he fled into the darkness.

To Euryale, the waiting seemed forever. She was awake and aware, lying on her bed, but felt unbelievably weak. Her little ones lay drooped on her pillow and shoulders. Her arms lay heavily at her sides. A screen of heavy wool completely encircled the bed. She could only stare at the plain plaster ceiling and wait.

Presently, she heard voices approaching. One she knew to be Deino's and the other . . . with a sweet pang of past familiarity she knew it to be Aristo's.

"There, you see?" said Deino, entering the room. "She is covered. You will be safe."

"She will not move from her cover?" His voice held a breathy tone of fear.

"Fool! She would not have given so much to make you live, had she wanted you stone. Speak to her! She is your love!"

Euryale heard Deino's sandals angrily slapping away. There were long moments of silence. "Aristo?"

"Euryale. Deino . . . tells me that I owe you thanks. Therefore I thank you . . . for restoring me."

"You are more than welcome, my love."

She heard him gasp, or sob. "I . . . I'm sorry that I . . . looked at you. I . . . didn't know."

"I understand, Aristo. I forgive you. And I owe you an apology. I should have told you my secret sooner. This problem could have been avoided."

There were moments of silence. "What . . . will you do with me now?"

"You may do whatever you wish, my love. I must leave this place soon, but you are welcome to come with us. We could start anew in another place."

"Where are we? This is not where I . . ."

"No, Aristo, it is not. We are in Rome."

"Rome! By Tanith, I must flee. If I am caught here—"

"Do not fear, Aristo. Calm yourself. The Punic wars are over. You have been a long time in stone. The Romans will not harm you now."

"The War is over? How long was I in stone?"

"Seventy years, my love."

"Seventy . . . !" He ended with a choking cough. "All my family . . . all I knew . . . it is all dead and gone!"

"Yes, Aristo, I fear it is so. It has taken me this long to discover how to restore you. I am so very sorry. Please forgive me."

"Forgive you! You wait till all I loved is dust and then ask my forgiveness?"

"I had no choice, my love. I did not learn of the means to free you until this very day. There was nothing I could do!"

Euryale heard him sigh heavily. "Very well. Tell me . . . who won?"

"Who won . . . oh."

"Does the son of Hannibal rule in Rome now?"

Very softly, Euryale said, "No, my love. Carthage lost."

There was silence again, and then Euryale heard bitter laughter. "So. The gods play cruel jokes, indeed. The beauty I loved turned out to be a daemon of legend. I am restored to life again only after all that was my life is gone."

"We can start again, my love. You can have a new life—"

"Euryale, don't you understand? How can I . . . After what I went through . . . you don't understand how awful it was."

"I will be more careful now. And the sage who helped me restore you said that if you look on me with love, and without fear, you will not turn to stone. He has proved it."

Again bitter laughter echoed in the room. "Can a daemon be so naïve? Can't you see that it can never be the same between us? After the pain . . . How could I not fear you? How can I love someone who could kill me with a glance? Who could love you, knowing what you are? Please, Euryale, I beg you, if you still care for me then let me go. I will tell no one your secret. For the sake of the love I once had for the woman I thought you were, I promise you that. But please let me go!"

Euryale felt a great emptiness spread inside her. Hope was drained from her, as well as blood. "If that is what you wish." Then, with dread, she asked. "Where will you go?"

"Home. To Carthage. At least I can return to familiar surroundings, even if my country is defeated and the people are strangers to me."

Euryale ached for what she must tell him. *If I do not, he will only hear it in less kindly fashion elsewhere.* "Oh, my love, listen and try to understand. Carthage is no more. Rome sacked the city and razed her to the ground seven years ago. You cannot go home, it is not there. I am so very sorry, Aristo."

There was a very long silence. "Gone?" She heard him sob and her ache deepened. "My family, the city . . . all gone?"

"Yes," she whispered.

"Gods!" he cried. "Why didn't you leave me dead?"

Euryale closed her eyes, and her own tears flowed. "I loved you."

"What am I to live for now? Revenge?"

"Please, my love, I owe you a thousand apologies. If there is anything I can do for you to ease your heart, tell me and it will be done."

She heard him try to control his weeping. "Very well. I ask you then, if there is any pity left in you, tell me who ordered Carthage destroyed."

Euryale could answer this truthfully. "Cato the Censor. And he is long dead."

"Then who is the commander who saw it done? Am I robbed of his life too?"

To this, Euryale wished not to reply, though she knew the answer. It was the very same Scipio Aemilianus, who spoke to her at the praetor's illness. He seemed a fair man. And it is said that he wept to see the ruins of his army had made of Carthage. "The war is over, Aristo. Let there be no more killing."

"So. You give me not even this mercy. Have you become a monster in spirit as well as form? Well, as long as I am in Rome, I will seek this commander. I'll wager he was given an unforgettable triumph. His name must be known to every Roman. I will find him."

"Aristo, don't . . ."

"Please! Say nothing more. The woman I once loved . . . the woman I thought you were . . . I must think of her as dead, along with everything else I once cared for. You may as well think of me as dead, also. My spirit has died. The rest of me will surely follow it soon."

Euryale heard his footsteps leaving. "Aristo! May the divine powers keep you well, and stay your vengeful hand."

She heard him pause in the doorway. But he said nothing, and his footsteps continued away down the corridor.

She sighed and closed her eyes. *I have loosed another Daedalus into the world.* She heard Archidemus's voice in her mind, asking "What is a monster, Euryale?" *By appearance, deed or intent, my friend, it would seem I am. And I have made my lover one as well.*

Her heart felt numbed beyond breaking. By strength of will, she reached up to the table beside the bed, on which lay the knife used to bleed her. Grasping the knife, she poised it, point down, above her chest. "If you have more pity that I credit to you, Athena, will you grant my death? May I join my sister in Elysium, and trouble this world no more?"

"Domina?" Sevisus whispered just outside her bedcurtain.

Euryale started. "Not now, Sevisus."

"Domina, please. I have been listening. I hid in the doorway. I couldn't help it. He is wrong, Domina. Don't listen to him. You aren't a monster. And it's not true that no one could love you. Archidemus does, and so do Deino and I! Don't die, Domina. No one I've served has been as nice as you. I don't care what you look like."

"You are a good boy, Sevisus. Shall I free you? Would you like that?"

"Well, freedom is something I hope for. But even then I'd like to serve you as a freedman. Please, Domina. Let me stay with you. Don't desert us!"

With sad realization, Euryale said, "I don't want to leave you or Deino, either, Sevisus." Tears rolled down her cheeks. *What is a monster? Is it just one way others may think of you? And if some think you a monster and some do not, who is right? Do I believe those who think the worst of me, or the best? If I agree with those who say I am a monster, then I become one. If I agree with those who do not . . . then perhaps there can be hope.*

Euryale let her arm drop over the bedside and the knife clattered onto the floor. A warm hand reached under the bedcurtain and grasped her hand, holding it tightly. With a gasp of painful joy, she squeezed it in return.

TRICESIMVS QVARTVS

"IT WAS KIND OF YOU TO ASK ME TO JOIN YOU," Hispallus said to Scipio Aemilianus as they strolled atop the Servian wall near its western terminus. Their lictors followed at the base of the wall, giving the two magistrates some measure of privacy. "My physician is recommending light exercise these days. Yet I am surprised to find you at work inspecting the walls. I would think you would be celebrating the feast day of Minerva on the Aventine."

"Ah, is it her day today? No wonder I see so many school-boys at large this morning. Well, she is no particular guardian of mine. Although . . . perhaps I should pay one of her temples a visit this afternoon." Aemilianus paused and lowered his voice. "In fact, Hispallus, I needed to walk to soothe myself. There was a rather upsetting incident this morning."

"Yes?"

"During my salutatio, a man approached me and said he was a historian who wanted to write about my destruction of Carthage. I politely declined, telling him that my friend Polybius had already written one for me. Suddenly the man pulled out a knife and declared himself 'the ghost of the Glory of Carthage' and he attempted to stab me."

"Indeed? I trust you were not harmed?"

"Me? No. My lictors caught him before his knife touched me. But as they dragged him away, he managed to wrestle his knife-hand free and stab himself. His last words were, 'Fear not for me, I have been dead seventy years.'"

"How strange. It is disturbing when the gods choose to make men mad."

"Yes. The more so when their madness makes an odd sort of sense. You know, I still fight the battle of Carthage in my dreams many nights. I wonder when that war will end."

So . . . your laurels do not rest as easy on your head as I had thought. Hispallus found this both reassuring and disturbing.

"Anyway," Aemilianus went on, "I have better news to give. I have spoken with Scipio Nasica, and he has only glowing words for you. Apparently your ousting of the wizards and philosophers has been popular beyond expectation. Nasica believes the good will you bring to our name should make his election this summer a certainty."

Hispallus drew himself up, very pleased. "That is good news. And I have more to join it. My freedman Marcus told me today that the blackmailer Daedalus has apparently absconded from Rome with the funds that Domina Euryale gave him."

"You call that good news?"

"It is better than his remaining to torment me and threaten our good name. Apparently his associates have fled also, so I need not fear reprisals. I had Daedalus's apartment searched, just in case. The only thing there was a broken statue of himself."

Aemilianus snorted. "Wanted to cast himself in stone for posterity, did he? What was done with the statue?"

"Nothing yet. I'm thinking of having it repaired and putting it in my garden, as a constant reminder to caution."

They reached the end of the wall at the east bank of the Tiber. To their right, the river was divided the boat-hull shaped island, connected by small wooden bridges to either bank. To the left, the Tiber flowed past the great open cattle and vegetable markets.

"You know," said Aemilianus, leaning his elbows on the wall balustrade, "it is a shame, in a way, that your bridge was never built. One thing your edict has shown is that when many people must pass through Rome's gates, more bridges are needed."

"Well, I, for one, am not sorry. Considering your suspicions, that was one monument to my name best left unbuilt."

"Still," Aemilianus mused, staring out at Tiber Island, "we ought to have a new bridge. Perhaps I should commission one, when I am in a position to do so. The 'Pons Aemilianus.' What do you think?"

"It sounds excellent, cousin. But as for me, I believe I will stay away from public works from now on. I—"

He was interrupted by shouts from below. "Magistrate! Praetor! Hispallus!"

Hispallus looked over the edge, frowning. "Ho, what's the noise?"

"There is an altercation at the Jugurthine Gate, sir. Your presence has been called for, since it was known you were nearby."

"Can't the gatekeeper handle the matter?"

"It is not he who calls for you, Magistrate. There is a woman there who claims she is known to you. The Domina Euryale. She begs your assistance."

"What's this?" said Aemilianus. "What trouble is that woman mixed up with now?"

"I believe I ought to find out," said Hispallus. "Bring the litter," he ordered his lictors. "I'll go straightway."

"If you don't mind, I'll follow," said Aemilianus. "I could use a diversion."

"Certainly."

As they neared the gate, it was difficult for the litter-bearers to press through the crowd, despite the shoving of the lictor and the cries of "Make way!" Hispallus signaled for the bearers to let him down, and he shoved through the crowd on foot, closely followed by Aemilianus. Upon reaching the gate itself,

Hispallus saw the gatekeeper, a swarthy man in tarnished armor, standing defiantly before an old woman. Hispallus recognized her as Euryale's maidservant Deino. Near Deino stood Sevisus, with some household items strapped to his back, looking frightened. Behind the boy was a long, elegant litter beside which stood six Bithynian bearers. Behind the litter stretched a long rope, onto which held the heavily laden blind members of Euryale's household.

Hispallus strode up to the gatekeeper. "What's the matter here?"

"Ah, my Lord—"

"Thank you for coming, Magistrate," both the gatekeeper and Deino began at once.

Hispallus held up his hands. "One at a time, please."

"My Lord," the gatekeeper out-shouted the scowling Deino, "this woman's lady has broken the law. She is a foreigner and yet rides in a litter through the streets of Rome!"

"Magistrate," said Deino, in the tones of an exasperated mother, "my Despoina is very ill. She cannot walk. She must ride in a litter, or not move at all."

"I am sorry to hear this, Deino," said Hispallus. He looked at the litter and through its translucent curtains saw a recumbent woman's form. The image of a funerary procession came to his mind, and he quickly shook away the sad thought. *I wonder if she fell ill as I did. Was my edict too late to save her from her wizard's machinations?*

"My Lord," said the gatekeeper, "I might have let them pass for that reason, but see . . ." He let a scroll unroll from his hand. "Her name is on the list of those subject to your decree. Therefore she is already a criminal and I thought it best to detain her."

"She is?" Hispallus grabbed the scroll from the gatekeeper and stared at it.

"It is two days after Liberalia," Aemilianus reminded him. "If she is on the list, then she is in violation of your edict."

"Her name is here!" said Hispallus. "Who wrote this list? Marcus?"

His freedman secretary shrugged. "It was at her home you became ill, sir. And we knew she consorted and encouraged the sort of wizards you wanted to expelled. I assumed—"

"Magistrate," said Deino, "has my Despoina not been so ill, we would have left before Liberalia. We had no intention of breaking the law."

Hispallus turned to the gatekeeper. "Have you other reasons for detaining her?"

"We would not pay him a big enough bribe," Deino sniffed.

Hispallus noticed a pile of packages and various valuable items by the wall. *So. Some are making unexpected profits from my edict. I suppose the threatened foreigners haven't complained too loudly, until now.*

The gatekeeper looked insulted. "This hag lies, my Lord. Her lady violates the law and should be punished. What say you?"

Hispallus gazed at the litter and remembered as he had lain frightened and sick in her house, her warm voice, and her modest, gentle manner. And how she tried to spare him Daedalus's wrath by paying for the bridge.

Aemilianus leaned toward Hispallus and said, "If you make one exception . . ."

"—then I shall be deemed judicious," Hispallus finished. "The Domina is ill and has lawful reason to leave in whatever manner possible. Let her and her household pass the gate in peace."

Deino bowed. "Thank you, Magistrate." Sevisus jumped up and down as much as his load would let him, grinning. There came a few cheers from the crowd.

The gatekeeper wrinkled his nose, but gave the order to his men to let the group pass. Hispallus watched Euryale's household troop beneath the gate, heading down the road that would take them to Ostia and the sea. He was reminded of

Sevisus's vision of a procession, but that one had been heading toward tombs. He turned to his lictors. "Send fresh horses and mules after them for her servants. And send them with extra cloaks, and filled winebags. And if they need a ship, see that they get the finest available in Ostia. Go!"

Hispallus looked at Aemilianus, who gave him a surprised, approving nod. Hispallus smiled and turned back to his lictors, raising his arms. "Am I not judicious?"

"Slave, praetor," they cried.

EPILOGVS

Archidemus stood on the rooftop of his house in Alexandria and gazed up at the brilliant night sky. The stars here blazed nearly as bright as they did over his Chaldean homeland, but he read in them no portents to bring joy or concern.

He looked out over the vast city of Alexandria, known as "the crown of all cities," second in size only to Rome itself. To the north, on the island of Pharos, stood the great lighthouse known throughout the world. To the west was the Serapeum, the great library that drew scholars from every civilized land. *Sevisus would have loved to see that,* thought Archidemus.

He briefly considered whether he should write to Euryale, to tell her he was well and safe, and to ask if the gods had aided her. *But if she has received the answer she sought, then her love will be alive and with her once more. She will have no wish to hear from me. She might even have left Rome by now, for who knows where.*

Archidemus sighed and looked to the east. There, beyond the city wall, lay the necropolis; a city of tombs through which scholars of a darker nature combed for the ingredients necessary for their practice. *At least this is one place where wizardry finds a welcome home.*

Trying to shake memories from his mind, Archidemus considered taking a trip upriver to see the famous sights of Egypt: the temple of the Apis bull at Memphis, the pyramids at Giza, the singing statue of Memnon, the great temples of Karnak and Luxor. Perhaps there he might learn of ancient ways to enhance his art—

"Archidemus! Archidemus!" called a boy climbing the stairwell onto the roof. It was Amset, the new apprentice. The boy's Greek was shaky and his Latin was worse, but he had seemed bright enough and eager to learn.

"What is it, Amset?"

"A woman come to see you, Magus. She say something about her children."

Archidemus sighed and looked back out over the city. Until he had the chance to start his school, he was forced into the role of common fortune-teller, or dispenser of minor medicines. The problem with a city of wizards and philosophers was that there was a great deal more competition for the spiritual drachma. "Tell her to come back tomorrow, Amset."

"No, no, Magus! She say you want to see her. Her children do not strike you . . . or something."

"What? Come here, Amset."

The boy appeared at his elbow, and Archidemus looked down at him sternly. "Now, repeat, very carefully, exactly what the woman said."

The boy looked aside, searching his memory. "Uh . . . she say . . . she say . . . "

"I said," came a woman's warm voice from the top of the stairwell, "that my little ones have missed you."

Archidemus turned and saw across the rood a veiled woman shining like a divine spirit in the starlight. "Euryale," he whispered, and he smiled.

ABOUT THE AUTHOR

Kara Dalkey was born in 1953 in Los Angeles, California. She studied Anthropology at UCLA, and fashion design and merchandising at, appropriately, the Fashion Institute of Design & Merchandising. She has written fifteen novels and a dozen short stories, all fantasy, historical fantasy or science fiction. Her specialty is stories set in Heian-era Japan (700-1100 A.D.). Dalkey's most recent publications have been *Water,* a trilogy of Young Adult novels she describes as "the Atlantis and Arthurian myths mixed in a blender." Her most recent short stories have appeared in the *Firebirds* anthologies and *Tales of the Slayer II.* Her current project is an alternate history/fantasy set in early California. Kara now lives in the Seattle area, land of coffee lovers, writers, musicians and other creative eccentrics, where she feels right at home. Her current hobby is learning the basics of boating and navigation in order to explore the Puget Sound by boat.

ABOUT JUNO BOOKS

Juno publishes fantasy featuring strong female characters in richly-imagined contexts. Adventurous quests, dark secrets, light humor, deep desires, high imagination, supernatural stories, paranormal plots, mystery, metaphysics, magic, myth . . . our heroines might be swept into another world, live in the future, or display their "kickassitude" in an alternative "now." Juno Books offer a variety of fantasy and its fiction seeks to go beyond the ordinary and take the reader with them.

Launched in November 2006, Juno titles are distributed nationally by Diamond Distributors (www.diamondbookdistributors.com). Four books were released in 2006, another 24 are being published in 2007. Paula Guran serves as the editorial director of the line.

Juno Books takes its name from the ancient Roman goddess who was queen of the gods and female counterpart to her husband/brother Jupiter. Juno was the daughter of Saturn, sister to Jupiter, Neptune, and Pluto, and Jupiter's consort. Juventas, Mars, and Vulcan were her children. Juno was closely identified with the Greek goddess Hera and connected to all aspects of women's lives—fertility, pregnancy and childbirth, and especially marriage. Individualized, Juno was a female inner force, a female principle of life. Each man had his *genius,* every woman her *juno.* Just as with the male's *genius*, a woman's *juno* enlivened the spirit and enhanced her sexuality.

Juno is often portrayed wearing a diadem and veil and holding a scepter. The peacock was sacred to Juno. The Juno Books logo is a stylized peacock feather.

The Juno Web site is www.juno-books.com. We hope you drop by and learn more about our books!

Collins
**Language
Revolution!**
This Time
You'll Remember

French
Grammar Buster

Tony Buzan
and **Sophie Gavrois**

First published 2010
by Collins an imprint of

HarperCollins Publishers
77-85 Fulham Palace Road
London
W6 8JB

www.collinslanguage.com

10 9 8 7 6 5 4 3 2 1 0

ISBN 978-0-00-730306-9

A catalogue record for this book is available
from the British Library

Edited by Huw Jones

Design by Q2AMedia & Anthony Smith

Typeset by Davidson Publishing Solutions, Glasgow

Printed in India by Gopsons Papers Ltd

Contents

How to use this book

Contents

How to use this book

You may know your vocabulary off by heart, but vocabulary without grammar is just about as useful as a car without wheels or a bird without wings! Learn how to really kick your French into action with the **French Grammar Buster**.

Set out in an easy-to-follow format, we've divided the book into 28 colourful units, each clearly explaining a separate grammar point. As we don't use any confusing or complicated jargon, you'll soon find that learning these basic principles is simple and will not only dramatically improve your written and spoken French but will increase your confidence when approaching grammar in the future. Crosswords, word searches, anagrams and Mind Maps make learning grammar fun while Tony Buzan's tried and tested memory techniques will mean you'll always remember what you've learnt. If you don't believe us, then all you have to do is try out our mental gymnastics exercises to put your new found skills to the test – you'll be surprised by just how fast you progress! Any unfamiliar terms will be explained in the glossary (if you see a G after a word, it is referring you to the glossary for further information) and a handy pocket-sized verb wheel means you'll be grammar-perfect at home and away. The answers are all at the back of the book for easy reference.

How it works
We've based this book on the principles of ASSOCIATION, IMAGINATION and MIND-MAPPING. We use this method because *we remember best when we associate what we learn with something we already know*.

Mind Maps®
Mind Maps are one of the best thinking tools available. Some Mind Maps are already drawn for you to help you visualise and retain new information but the best Mind Maps are those you make yourself. Feel free to add new branches to the Mind Maps in the book as you increase your vocabulary, or make a new Mind Map with words important to you.

To make a Mind Map® follow these simple steps:

Step one: Take a blank piece of paper and some coloured pens. Turn the page to landscape format, to make a wide rectangle. In the middle, draw an image of what your Mind Map is about: for example, if it is about food, draw something delicious.

Step two: Next draw branches coming out in all directions from your central image, one for each main group of words.

Step three: Connect second-level branches to the first, and third-level branches to those. Make your branches curves rather than straight lines and use colours and images throughout.

Go to **www.collinslanguage.com/revolution** to find out more about Mind Mapping.

Repeat and Succeed!

Learning a foreign language means first understanding, then learning and finally remembering. Revision is therefore essential.

> The specific formula for fixing information in your long-term memory is:
> - **1st repetition** – an hour or so after first learning it
> - **2nd repetition** – a day later
> - **3rd repetition** – a week later
> - **4th repetition** – a month later
> - **5th repetition** – six months later

Rest and Learn Best

You will find it easier to retain information if you *take regular breaks between study periods*. During breaks your brain will naturally and spontaneously integrate what it has learnt.

Your brain finds it easier to remember more from the start and end of study periods than from the middle. Regular breaks cut the amount of time in the middle of study sessions.

You are now ready to get to grips with grammar!

We hope you have fun!

How to name people, animals and things

In this unit you'll find out that French naming words have genders.

Naming words have genders

Naming words for people, animals, objects and ideas are called **nouns** (G). Nouns are either **feminine** (G) or **masculine** (G) in French. You'll find the **gender** (G) given in a dictionary, but below there are some hints to help you work out the gender for yourself. There is some logic to it – at least for people and animals!

People
In French, most nouns that refer to people, people's jobs or status have the same gender as the person they refer to.

masculine/male
homme *om* man
garçon *gar-soñ* boy
prince *prañs* prince

feminine/female
femme *fam* woman
fille *fee-yuh* girl
princesse *prañ-sess* princess

Some 'people' words have only one gender, no matter who you are talking about:

always masculine
bébé *bay-bay* baby boy or girl

always feminine
personne *pehr-son* male or female person
vedette *vuh-det* film star, celebrity

Animals
In French, as in English, there is often both a female and a male word for animals (e.g. stallion and mare) but the neutral word, which can be used for both (e.g. horse) will <u>also</u> always be either masculine or feminine in French – there's no pattern to these, and it doesn't change depending on the sex of the animal it describes. You just have to learn them.

always masculine

crocodile *kro-ko-deel* crocodile
chimpanzé *shañ-pahñ-zay*
chimpanzee
These are always masculine –
even if you are talking about a
female crocodile or chimpanzee.

always feminine

tortue *tor-tew* tortoise
girafe *zhee-raf* giraffe
souris *soo-ree* mouse
These are always feminine –
even if you are talking about a
male tortoise, giraffe or mouse.

Tony's Tip

To make it easy and fun to remember which nouns are masculine, pick a well-known French male figure and associate him with every masculine noun. Do the same with the feminine and it will be easy to decide whether to put le or la in front of the French noun. Let's say you've chosen Napoleon as your masculine figure and Brigitte Bardot as your feminine figure. For crocodile imagine Napoleon riding a crocodile and for souris imagine Brigitte Bardot with a mouse on her shoulder!

To sum up

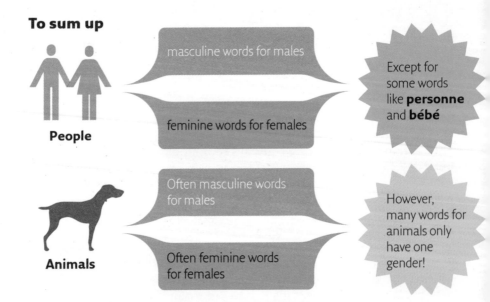

People

masculine words for males

feminine words for females

Except for some words like **personne** and **bébé**

Animals

Often masculine words for males

Often feminine words for females

However, many words for animals only have one gender!

Things

Objects that you can see and touch like 'table' or 'house', and even abstract things like 'beauty', 'history' or 'decision' have a gender too. This has nothing to do with male and female in that case.

French dictionaries indicate the gender of nouns. There are also some rules to help:

always masculine
- words ending in –oir, –ou, –al and –isme e.g. tiroir (drawer), genou (knee), alpinisme (mountaineering)
- days, months and seasons e.g. lundi (Monday)
- names of languages, e.g. le français (French)
- many English words that the French have borrowed, e.g. le tennis

always feminine
- words ending in –tion e.g. information
- words ending in –tude e.g. attitude
- words ending in –ure e.g. voiture
- words ending in –tte, –ppe e.g. carotte, nappe (tablecloth)

You'll remember them by practising, memorising and hearing them a lot.

Mental gymnastics 1

Here is a list of French words which are very similar to English.
Try to guess their gender with the help of the explanations above.

1	accusation	8	prince	15	bungalow
2	colonel	9	octobre	16	maman
3	architecture	10	journal	17	commandant
4	action	11	admiration	18	décembre
5	badminton	12	papa	19	carotte
6	diva	13	question	20	attitude
7	administration	14	culture		

How to turn a masculine word into a feminine one and vice versa

Sometimes the masculine and the feminine words are very different, like **homme** and **femme**. However, in many instances you can turn the masculine word you find in the dictionary into a feminine one by changing the ending. There are three main patterns:

1 Add an **–e** to make the masculine word into a feminine word:

> **étudiant** *ay-tew-dee-ahñ* male student
> **étudiante** *ay-tew-dee-ahñt* female student
> **ami** *a-mee* male friend
> **amie** *a-mee* female friend

2 When the word already ends with an **–e** you can often leave it as it is. Just use the feminine equivalent of 'a' or 'the' (see the next section).

3 If neither of the above applies, follow the patterns below:

masculine/male	feminine/female	
–f e.g. veuf	–ve e.g. veuve	widower/widow
–eur e.g. vendeur	–euse e.g. vendeuse	sales assistant
–teur e.g. acteur	–trice e.g. actrice	actor/actress
–on/ien e.g. espion, comédien	–onne/ienne e.g. espionne, comédienne	spy, actor/actress
–er e.g. infirmier	–ère e.g. infirmière	nurse
–e e.g. prince	–esse e.g. princesse	prince/princess

Changing genders sometimes changes the pronunciation too

There is no pronunciation change for words ending with a vowel, like **ami**. When the word ends with a consonant, it's simple:

- don't pronounce it for the masculine: e.g. **étudiant** *ay-tew-dee-ahñ* (no '*t*' sound on the end)
- do pronounce it for the feminine, when you have added an **–e**: e.g. **étudiante** *ay-tew-dee-ahñt*

How to say 'the'

The French words for 'the' are: **le** (masculine), **la** (feminine), and **l'** (both masculine and feminine).

masculine/male	**feminine/female**
le prince the prince	**la princesse** the princess
le garçon the boy	**la fille** the girl
l'ami the male friend	**l'amie** the female friend
l'étudiant the male student	**l'étudiante** the female student

masculine 'the'

le

feminine 'the'

la

'the' for words beginning with a vowel (except for 'y') or 'h'

l'

Mental gymnastics 2

Put the right 'the' before each word. Some have been done for you.

1	**le** lait	9	...... épicier
2	**la** bière	10	...... chocolat
3	...... bouteille	11	...... fils
4	**l'**inspecteur	12	...... musicienne
5	...... croissant	13	...... tartine
6	...... pression	14	...... hôtel
7	...... confiture	15	...... bébé
8	...... personne	16	...... nappe

How to say 'a'

The French words for 'a' are: **un** (masculine) and **une** (feminine)

masculine 'a' **un**   feminine 'a' **une**

Mental gymnastics 3

Solve the anagrams to find some words from this unit preceded by **le**, **la**, **l'**, **un** or **une**.

1   NEU MEFEM   ....
2   TL'DIÉUNTA   ....
3   NUE EAMI   ....
4   AL NOSPENER   ....
5   NU NOGRAÇ   ....
6   AL RUVITOE   ....

Mental gymnastics 4

Fill in the missing letters to find some more words from this unit preceded by **le, la, l'**, **un** or **une**. A little hint: they're all vowels!

1   .....n   h.....mm.....
2   .....n.....   f.....ll.....
3   l.....   s.....   .....r.....s
4   .....n.....   q.....   .....st.....   ..... n
5   .....n   .....nf.....rm.....   .....r
6   .....n.....   v.....nd.....   .....s.....

How to make things plural

2

In this unit you'll find out how to make French nouns plural (**G**).

Singular and plural

Generally, you make a **singular** (**G**) noun into a plural by adding an **–s** at the end as in English.

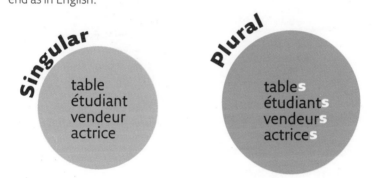

Singular

table
étudiant
vendeur
actrice

Plural

table**s**
étudiant**s**
vendeur**s**
actrice**s**

When there is already an **–s**, **–x** or **–z** at the end, the spelling doesn't change in the plural.

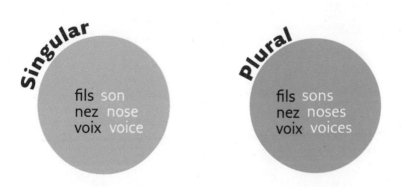

Singular

fils son
nez nose
voix voice

Plural

fils sons
nez noses
voix voices

When speaking do not worry too much about plurals, as French people don't usually pronounce the plural final −s, −x or −z. Like in English, words are sometimes said as if linked together, e.g. 'bed and breakfast' is usually pronounced *bed'n'breakfast*, as if it were a single, long word. When a French word ends with a consonant and is followed with a vowel (a, e, i, o, u) or an 'h', they are often said linked together, e.g. **artistes associés** is pronounced *arteest-zassossyay*.

Sometimes, like in English, some plurals are a bit irregular, e.g. tooth/teeth and child/children.

Some add an −**x**

Singular

Ending in:
- **eau** *château* castle
- **eu** *jeu* game
and some in
−**ou** *bijou* jewel

château**x** castles
jeu**x** games
bijou**x** jewels

Plural

Mental gymnastics 1

Guess the plural form of the following words.
**accusation · château · nez · tableau · vendeur · question
princesse · chanteuse · époux · musicien · girafe · genou**

−s	−x	no change
....	....	....
....	....	....
....	....	
....		
....		
....		
....		

How to say the plural 'the'

The French word for the plural 'the' is: **les** (both masculine and feminine, in the plural).

les princes the princes
les garçons the boys
les amis the male friends
les étudiants the male students

les princesses the princesses
les filles the girls
les amies the female friends
les étudiantes the female students

'the' for all plural words: **les**

Mental gymnastics 2

Solve these anagrams to find some nouns from Units 1 and 2 in the plural, starting with **les**.

1   ELS NUVEDRES   ....
2   SEL XIVO   ....
3   ELS MEHOSM   ....
4   SEL HUTEXACÂ   ....
5   ELS SIAM   ....
6   SLE RIFIMENSIR   ....

Mental gymnastics 3

Fill in the missing letters to find some nouns from Units 1 and 2 in the plural.

1   le.....   .....a.....o..... .....e.....
2   .....e.....   ....o.....o.....i.....e .....
3   .... s   .....é.....é.....
4   .....e.....   .....a..... .....o..... .....
5   .....es   .....e..... .....o..... .....e.....
6   le..... é.....u.....ia..... ....

How to say *I, you, he, she, it, we* and *they*

3

I, you, he, she, it, we and they

In English, I, you, he, she, it, we and they can help us understand what – or who – a sentence is about. When this is the case, they are called the **subject** (G). For example, in the sentence 'They visited some old friends on Sunday', 'they' is the subject of the sentence.

In this unit, you'll learn the French equivalents of I, you, he, she, we, and they (when these words are the subject), and how to use them.

I, he, she and it
Here are the equivalents of I, he, she and it.

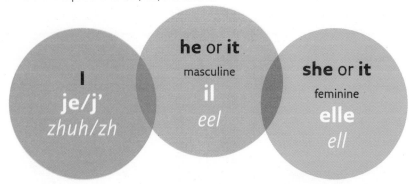

I
je/j'
zhuh/zh

he or **it**
masculine
il
eel

she or **it**
feminine
elle
ell

He, she or it?
As you saw in Unit 1, French nouns referring to people, animals, objects and ideas have a gender. Now this is important when you have to choose between **il** and **elle**.

Let's take an example: 'a table' is **une table** in French. It's a **feminine** word. In English, to describe the table you would use 'it': e.g. 'it is rectangular', 'it is expensive'. In French, you'll need to use the **feminine** equivalent of 'it': **elle**. **Elle** est rectangulaire. **Elle** est chère.

To sum up, **il** means both 'he' and 'it'. You use **il** (rather than **elle**) to mean 'it' when the thing you're talking about is a **masculine** word in French.

Elle means both 'she' and 'it'. You use **elle** (rather than **il**) to mean 'it' when the thing you're talking about is a **feminine** word in French.

Two yous

There are two words for 'you' in French. Here is how you choose which one to use:

Tu   for people you know very well, your friends and family and when you're talking to only one person.

Vous for when you need to be formal (with one or more people) or when you're talking to two or more people.

If you're not sure which one to use, a person's age can be helpful to decide whether to use **tu** or **vous**. Use **vous** to speak to an older person, and **tu** to a child. Usually use **vous** to speak to any adults you don't know. You could receive the invitation to be less formal from a French speaker with the question **On se tutoie?** 'Shall we call each other **tu**?'

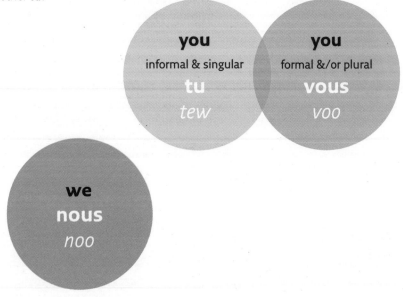

you
informal & singular
tu
tew

you
formal &/or plural
vous
voo

we
nous
noo

They: masculine or feminine?

This is quite similar to **il** and **elle**. When you have several nouns referring to people, animals, objects and ideas that are **masculine** you should use **ils** to talk about them.

les fruits *(masc.)*   **Ils** sont bons.   They are good.

When you have several nouns referring to people, animals, objects and ideas that are **feminine** you should use **elles** to talk about them.

les pizzas *(fem.)*   **Elles** sont bonnes.   They are good.

What about when there is a mixture of masculine and feminine nouns? **Masculine** is always the winner in grammar, so you would use **ils** to talk about them.

les fruits et les pizzas
Ils sont bons.
They are good.

they
feminines only
elles
ell

they
ils
eel

Easy pronunciation for **il**, **ils, elle** & **elles**: **il** and **ils** are pronounced the same way (*eel*), and **elle** and **elles** too (*ell*). For **ils** and **elles**, you'll hear a 'zz' sound when they are followed by a word starting with a vowel or an 'h', e.g. **ils ont** *eelz ohñ* (they have).

Mental gymnastics 1

Take two minutes to memorise as many words on this page as you can. Read Tony's Tips on the next page and apply them to your memorisation.

How many words can you now remember without looking back?

If you remember by looking at things, write the words on a new piece of paper. Using different colours may help you pick out whole words or parts of words.

If you remember better with sounds, **link** the words and their gender to **a rhythm or a melody** (a jingle or a rap); record yourself and listen regularly.

You could also **link each word with sounds**:

je sounds like the middle part of trea**su**re
nous sounds like ca**noe**
tu sounds like s**tew** or s**tew**ard
vous sounds like rendez-**vous** (or vava**voo**m)
il and **ils** sound like **eel**
elle and elles sound like **belle**

If you remember better when doing something, perform an action while memorising, e.g. write the words on cards and move the cards around. Doodle or play with a stress ball. You could write or draw the words with their sounds. For example: **il** written by the body of an eel or the word **nous** in a canoe.

Mental gymnastics 2

Solve the anagrams to find the French equivalents of I, you (formal), you (informal), he, she, we, they (masculine) and they (feminine).

1	LLEES	....	5	EJ	....
2	OSUN	....	6	LELE	....
3	LI	....	7	SIL	....
4	UT	....	8	UVSO	....

Mental gymnastics 3

Find all the French equivalents of I, you (formal), you (informal), he, she, we, they (m) and they (f) in this puzzle.

```
J  I  E  T  I  E
T  V  L  O  U  S
N  E  L  L  E  S
O  N  U  S  J  E
U  V  O  L  E  L
S  L  I  L  S  L
E  V  O  U  S  E
```

Mental gymnastics 4

Reorder the pairs of letters so that you can see the French equivalents of I, you (formal), you (informal), he, she, we, they (m) and they (f). Some pairs are given in the empty grid to help you out.

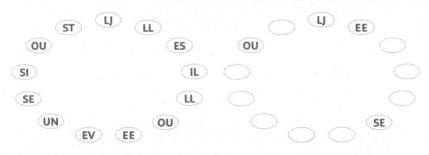

Mental gymnastics 5

Which word (**je**, **tu**, **il**, **elle**, **nous**, **vous**, **ils**, **elles**) would you choose in the following situations?

1   To speak to the French president ....
2   To talk about your friends and yourself ....
3   To speak to your French friends' child ....
4   To speak to your French friends' children ....
5   To talk about your car (une voiture) ....
6   To speak to your daughters ....
7   To speak to the French shop assistant
    you're meeting for the first time ....
8   To talk about your French friends' parents ....
9   To talk about your new mobile phone
    (un portable) ....
10 To talk about your parents-in-law ....
11 To talk about your nieces ....
12 To talk about yourself ....

How to say
am, *is* and *are*

A verb (**G**) is a word that describes what something or someone is or does. Its **basic form**, the one you find in a dictionary, is **être** (to be).

I am
je suis
zhuh swee

you are
informal & singular
tu es
tew eh

we are
nous
sommes
noo som

you are
formal &/or plural
vous êtes
vooz eht

he or **it is**
il est
eel eh

she or **it is**
elle est
ell eh

they are
ils sont
eel ssoñ

they are
female or feminine only
elles sont
ell ssoñ

In Unit 3, you learnt how to remember new words by associating their sounds with familiar words. Here are some new sound combinations to help you memorise the words in this unit.

je suis I am a trea**su**re full of **swee**ts.
nous sommes At the ca**noe**? We are awe**some**!
tu es A secret agent is given his new cover:
you are a **stew**ard who is going aw**ay**.
vous êtes you are at a rendez-**vous** which is secr**et**.
il est the **eel** is on displ**ay**.
elle est The b**elle** is in a pl**ay**.
ils sont they are the **eels' son**s
elles sont The b**elles** are near the statue of Nel**son**.

You could write or draw the words with an expression, e.g. I am married:

Useful expressions with être

être amoureux(-euse): to be in love   **être fatigué(e)**: to be tired
être bien: to be comfortable   **être endormi(e)**: to be asleep
être en retard: to be late   **être obligé(e) (de)**: to have to

Sometimes you cannot use the verb **être** where you would use the verb 'to be' in English, e.g. to say that you are hungry or thirsty. In these cases, French uses 'to have'. We'll look at these expressions in Unit 7.

Mental gymnastics 1

Take two minutes to memorise as many words on the previous page as you can. Use the tips above and your own memory techniques.

How many words can you now recall without looking back·at the previous page?

Try to recall them again in **two hours**, in **one day** and in **one week**. The more you repeat them, the longer you will remember them.

Mental gymnastics 2

1 Vous ....
2 Je ....
3 .... es
4 elle ....
5 ils ....
6 .... est
7 nous ......
8 il ....
9 tu ....
10 ...... sont

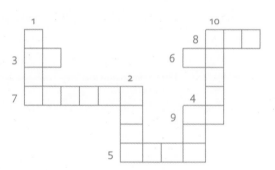

Mental gymnastics 3

These words are missing their vowels. Rewrite them inserting the missing letters. Watch out for accents.

1   LLS SNT ....
2   VS TS ....
3   L ST ....
4   J SS ....
5   NS SMMS ....

Mental gymnastics 4

The words from the last exercise are hidden in the following questions.
Rearrange the letters in each question to form two pairs of words.
All the letters must be used up. The first one has been started for you.

1	MUST SEN SUMO OSE	...........tu es...........	....
2	LITTLE SEES LONS	....	....
3	LIJELE SETESUS	....	....
4	STÊVE TONSIL OSUS	....	....

Mental gymnastics 5

What do these phrases mean in English?

1 Il est amoureux. ....
2 Nous sommes en retard. ....
3 Ils sont fatigués. ....
4 Elle est endormie. ....
5 Je suis obligé! ....
6 Vous êtes bien? ....
7 Elles sont en retard. ....

Mental gymnastics 6

Try writing these in French.

1 I am tired. ....
2 We're in love. ....
3 She has to. ....
4 They are asleep. ....
5 He's comfortable. ....
6 You are late (informal singular). ....

How to talk about your nationality

You learnt how to say 'I am' in Unit 4. Now let's use it to describe your nationality.

Very similar to English

américain
ah-may-ree-kañ
American

canadien
ka-na-dyañ
Canadian

italien
ee-tah-liañ
Italian

suisse
sweess
Swiss

australien
os-trah-lyañ
Australian

Not so similar to English

britannique
bree-tah-neek
British

espagnol
es-pa-nyol
Spanish

français
frahñ-sseh
French

Quite similar to English

belge
belzh
Belgian

anglais
ahñ-gleh
English

chinois
shee-nwa
Chinese

néo-zélandais
nay-oh-zay-lahñ-deh
New Zealander

Quite different from English

allemand
ah-luh-mahñ
German

écossais
ay-ko-sseh
Scottish

gallois
gah-lwa
Welsh

irlandais
eer-lahñ-deh
Irish

Spot the differences and patterns: look at these mini-conversations and try to work out the differences and the patterns in the use of nationality words in French.

C'est une voiture italienne?

Oui, c'est une voiture italienne.

C'est un vin italien?

Oui, c'est un vin italien.

Vous êtes française?

Oui, je suis française.

Vous êtes français?

Oui, je suis français.

Vous êtes espagnole?

Oui, je suis espagnole.

Vous êtes espagnol?

Oui, je suis espagnol.

C'est une montre suisse?

Oui, c'est une montre suisse.

C'est du fromage suisse?

Oui, c'est du fromage suisse.

What have you spotted? Differences? Patterns?

1 There is a feminine form for nationality words, which is different (most of the time) from the masculine one.
This form is used to describe people (**je suis française** – I am French), animals and things (**C'est une voiture italienne** – It's an Italian car).

2 The nationality word goes after the word it is describing
(**C'est une montre suisse** – It's a Swiss watch).

3 Nationality words do not start with a capital letter in French.

Now spot the patterns for creating the feminine form:

belge *belzh*	**belge** *belzh*
britannique *bree-tah-neek*	**britannique** *bree-tah-neek*
suisse *sweess*	**suisse** *sweess*
écossais *ay-ko-sseh*	**écossaise** *ay-ko-sseh**z***
français *frahñ-sseh*	**française** *frahñ-sseh**z***
anglais *ahñ-gleh*	**anglaise** *ahñ-gleh**z***
irlandais *eer-lahñ-deh*	**irlandaise** *eer-lahñ-deh**z***
néo-zélandais *nay-oh-zay-lahñ-deh*	**néo-zélandaise** *nay-oh-zay-lahñdeh**z***
gallois *ga-lwah*	**galloise** *ga-lwah**z***
américain *a-may-ree-kañ*	**américaine** *a-may-ree-**ken***
allemand *a-luh-mahñ*	**allemande** *a-luh-mahñ**d***
espagnol *es-pa-nyol*	**espagnole** *es-pa-nyol*
canadien *ka-na-dyañ*	**canadienne** *ka-na-dy**en***
australien *os-tra-lyañ*	**australienne** *os-tra-ly**en***
italien *ee-ta-lyañ*	**italienne** *ee-ta-ly**en***
indien *añ-dyañ*	**indienne** *añ-dy**en***

What have you spotted? Differences? Patterns?

1 To change the masculine nationality words **ending with an -e** into feminine words, **don't change anything**.

   belge (m)   **belge** (f)   Belgian

2 To change the masculine nationality words **ending with a consonant** (s, n, d, l) into feminine words, just **add an -e**.

   français (m)   **française** (f)   French

3 To change the masculine nationality words **ending with -ien** into feminine words, just **add an -ne**.

   italien (m)   **italienne** (f)   Italian

4 The pronunciation changes between the masculine and the feminine forms for some words:

   • words ending with an −s/−se:
     - in the **masculine** form you don't pronounce the final 's'.
     - in the **feminine** form you pronounce it 'z'.

   • words ending with the consonants −d/−de and −t/−te:
     - in the **masculine** form you don't pronounce the final letter.
     - in the **feminine** form you do pronounce it.

   • words ending with −ien /−ienne:
     - in the masculine form you pronounce the ending as 'yañ'. You don't really pronounce the 'n' sound: it is as if you were pinching your nose to say 'yan'
     - in the feminine form you pronounce it 'yen'.

Now spot the differences and patterns for the plural forms

belges *belzh*	**belges** *belzh*
britanniques *bree-tah-neek*	**britanniques** *bree-tah-neek*
suisses *sweess*	**suisses** *sweess*
écossais *ay-ko-sseh*	**écossaises** *ay-ko-sseh**z**
français *frahñ-sseh*	**françaises** *frahñ-sseh**z**
anglais *ahñ-gleh*	**anglaises** *ahñ-gleh**z**
irlandais *eer-lahñ-deh*	**irlandaises** *eer-lahñ-deh**z**
néo-zélandais *nay-oh-zay-lahñ-deh*	**néo-zélandaises** *nay-oh-zay-lahñdeh**z**
gallois *ga-lwah*	**galloises** *ga-lwah**z**
américains *a-may-ree-kañ*	**américaines** *a-may-ree-**ken**
allemands *a-luh-mahñ*	**allemandes** *a-luh-mahñ**d**
espagnols *es-pa-nyol*	**espagnoles** *es-pa-nyol*
canadiens *ka-na-dyañ*	**canadiennes** *ka-na-dy**en**
australiens *os-tra-lyañ*	**australiennes** *os-tra-ly**en**
italiens *ee-ta-lyañ*	**italiennes** *ee-ta-ly**en**
indiens *añ-dyañ*	**indiennes** *añ-dy**en**

To make the nationality words ending with an **-e** or with a consonant plural, just add an **-s**.

belges (m)   **belges** (f)   *Belgian*

To make the nationality words ending with an **-s** plural, don't change anything.

français (m)   *French*

The pronunciation is unchanged, even with an extra **-s**.

To sum up:

masculine form found in the dictionary

feminine form: add **-e** or **-ne** or no change

Nationality words

masculine plural form: add **-s**

feminine & plural form: add **-es** or **-nes** or just **-s**

Mental gymnastics 1

Match the celebrities with the appropriate nationality words.

1	Antonio Banderas	a	américain
2	Donatella Versace	b	galloise
3	Catherine Zeta-Jones	c	écossais
4	Cate Blanchett	d	italien
5	Ewan McGregor	e	australienne
6	Bill Clinton	f	américaine
7	Britney Spears	g	italienne
8	Leonardo Da Vinci	h	australien
9	Russell Crowe	i	écossaise
10	KT Tunstall	j	espagnol

Mental gymnastics 2

Here are fragments of messages in French. You are asked to say whether a woman, a man or both wrote it. Sometimes, more than one answer is possible.

1	je suis indienne	5	nous sommes écossais
2	je suis espagnol	6	je suis belge
3	nous sommes belges	7	je suis anglaise
4	je suis chinois	8	nous sommes allemandes

Mental gymnastics 3

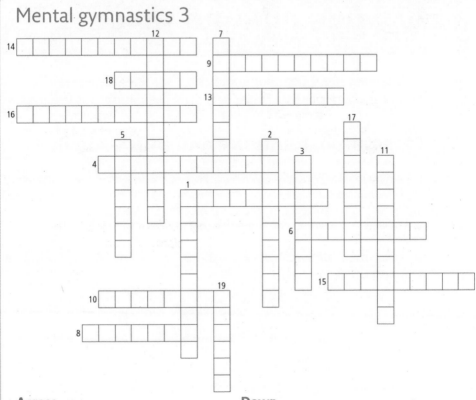

Across

1. Elle est ... (Allemagne)
4. Ils sont ... (Pakistan – pakistanais)
6. Il est ... (Écosse)
8. Le chianti est un vin ... (Italie)
9. Il est ... (Australie)
10. Il est ... (France)
13. Jennifer est ... (Angleterre)
14. Katja est ... (Finlande)
15. Ils sont ... (Côte d'Ivoire – ivoirien)
16. Elle est ... (Colombie – colombien)
18. Tintin est ... (Belgique)

Down

1. Nous sommes ... (États-Unis d'Amérique) (male)
2. Elles sont ... (Espagne)
3. Elle est ... (Inde)
5. Ils sont ... (Pays de Galles)
7. C'est un acteur ... (Canada)
11. Il est ... (Grande-Bretagne)
12. Nous sommes ... (Irlande) (feminine)
17. Elle est ... (Chine)
19. Il est ... (Suisse)

How to say *my, your, his, her, our* and *their*

In this unit, we'll be talking about masculine, feminine and plural again – this time for words indicating possession.

Masculine, feminine and plural again

As you saw in Unit 1, nouns which refer to people, animals, objects and ideas are either masculine or feminine. In Unit 5, you learnt that nationality words also need to have the same gender as the people or thing we are talking about. It is the same for the French equivalents of my, your, his, her, our and their.

When you talk about a **male** or a **masculine** thing, you choose the **masculine** equivalent of 'my': **mon**.

mon père my father   **mon château** my castle

When you talk about a **female** or a **feminine** thing, you choose the **feminine** equivalent of 'my': **ma**.

ma mère my mother   **ma maison** my house

When you talk about several **males**, **females** or **masculine** things, you choose the **plural** equivalent of 'my': **mes**.

mes parents my parents   **mes châteaux** my castles
mes maisons my houses

This is the same for the equivalents of 'your', and 'his/her'.

It is simpler for 'our', 'your' (plural or formal) and 'their', because the masculine and feminine forms are the same.

mon *moñ*   my

ton *toñ*   your
(informal, singular)

son *soñ*   his/her

notre *no-truh*   our

votre *vo-truh*   your
(formal, plural)

leur *luhr*   their

ma *ma*   my

ta *ta*   your
(informal, singular)

sa *sa*   his/her

notre *no-truh*   our

votre *vo-truh*   your
(formal, plural)

leur *luhr*   their

mes *may*   my

tes *tay*   your
(informal, singular)

ses *say*   his/her

nos *no*   our

vos *vo*   your
(formal, plural)

leurs *luhr*   their

No distinction for his and her

As you can see from the diagram, there is no distinction between **his** and **her** in French. You just use **son** if the word is masculine, **sa** if the word is feminine and **ses** if the word is plural. It's usually clear from the context whether the speaker is referring to a male or a female.

son père his/her father   **son château** his/her castle
sa mère his/her mother   **sa maison** his/her house

ses parents his/her parents
ses châteaux his/her castles
ses maisons his/her houses

'mon', 'ton', 'son' for some feminine words

For some feminine words, you have to use **mon** (my), **ton** (your, informal and singular) or **son** (his/her). For example, for those **beginning** with a **vowel** (a, e, i, o, u).

mon amie (f) my (girl)friend   **son école** (f) his/her school

Mental gymnastics 1

Find all the French equivalents of my, your, your, his/her, our and their in this grid. There ar 14 words in total.

```
M  E  V  T  E  N  O  S
O  M  A  V  N  R  L  E
T  O  S  O  T  E  S  U
E  T  E  T  U  S  R  S
M  O  N  R  R  O  T  V
O  N  L  E  U  N  U  A
S  L  S  A  R  M  E  S
S  E  V  N  L  T  R  E
E  N  A  L  U  E  A  N
S  N  O  R  T  O  U  S
V  A  E  T  S  L  O  R
V  O  S  N  R  T  T  O
O  N  S  R  T  E  A  S
R  L  E  U  R  S  L  U
```

Mental gymnastics 2

Match the French and English equivalents. You can check in the previous units whether the words are masculine or feminine.

1	mon amie	a	his baby
2	sa table	b	their table
3	son bébé	c	our friends
4	notre château	d	your baby
5	ton bébé	e	their castles
6	leur table	f	my friend
7	nos amis	g	her table
8	leurs châteaux	h	our castle

Mental gymnastics 3

Complete the sentences, using the words below. Go back to previous pages to check genders when in doubt. Some answers have already been given.

fils · **ami** · **parents** · ~~**mère**~~ · **question** · **parents** · **pizzas** ·**sandwich**
maman · **boissons** · **maison** · ~~**amis**~~ · **parents** · **père** · **château**

1   Voilà <u>nos amis</u> (our friends)
2   C'est <u>sa mère</u> (his mother)
3   C'est ....? (your (formal) son)
4   Voilà .... (their house)
5   C'est .... (my father)
6   Ce sont ....? (your (informal, singular) parents)
7   .... est intéressante. (your (formal, singular) question)
8   .... sont italiens. (her parents)
9   Voilà .... (your (formal, plural) pizzas)
10   C'est .... (my mummy)
11   C'est .... ? (your (informal, singular) sandwich)
12   .... sont français. (my parents)
13   Voilà .... (their drinks)
14   C'est .... (her castle)
15   C'est .... Paul! (our friend)

How to say what you have

'Have' is a verb. Its **basic form** – the one you find in a dictionary – is **avoir** (to have).

I have
j'ai
zheh

you have
informal & singular
tu as
tew ah

we have
nous avons
nooz ah-voñ

you have
formal &/or plural
vous avez
vooz ah-vay

he or **it has**
il a
eel ah

she or **it has**
elle a
ell ah

they have
ils ont
eel zoñ

they have
females or feminine only
elles ont
ell zoñ

Sometimes you cannot say things in the same way as you would in English, e.g. to say how old people are. In French, people 'have years': they say J'ai 25 ans – literally 'I have 25 years' – for 'I'm 25'. Look in the **useful expressions with 'avoir'** for more examples.

How to remember them?
You could write or draw the words with an expression, e.g. I have a car:

Useful expressions with 'avoir'

avoir faim: to be hungry (literally: to have hunger)
avoir soif: to be thirsty (literally: to have thirst)
avoir 35 ans: to be 35 (years old)
avoir froid: to be cold
avoir chaud: to be hot
avoir sommeil: to feel sleepy
il y a: there is/there are

Mental gymnastics 1

Take two minutes to memorise as many words on the previous page as you can. Use the tips above and your own memory techniques.

How many words can you now recall without looking back at the previous page?

Try to recall them again in **two hours**, in **one day** and in **one week**. The more you repeat them, the longer you will remember them.

Mental gymnastics 2

Fill in this criss-cross grid with the different forms of **avoir**.

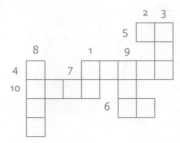

1	tu ...	6	... as
2	il ...	7	nous ...
3	... ont (masculine)	8	vous ...
4	elle ...	9	elles ...
5	j'...	10	... avez

Mental gymnastics 3

Complete the words with their missing consonants.

1   OU AO ....
2   U A ....
3   I O ....
4   EE A ....
5   OU AE ....

Mental gymnastics 4

Match the pictures with the French words.

1   J'ai soif.
2   J'ai faim.
3   J'ai sommeil.
4   J'ai chaud.
5   J'ai froid.

Mental gymnastics 5

Let's sort out **avoir** and **être**! Cross out the word you think is wrong.

1	Je/J'	suis/ai	fatigué.
2	Elle	est/a	faim.
3	Nous	sommes/avons	en retard.
4	Il	est/a	amoureux.
5	Vous	êtes/avez	18 ans?
6	Tu	es/as	sommeil?
7	Ils	sont/ont	endormis.
8	Elles	sont/ont	froid.

How to describe someone or something

In this unit, you'll learn how to talk about the appearance, colour and character of people and objects.

Describing words

In Unit 5, you learnt how to talk about someone's nationality. You might also want to describe their appearance (e.g. tall, pretty), the colour of their eyes and their character (e.g. nice, shy). These describing words are called **adjectives** (G).

Regular adjectives
Most French adjectives follow the same patterns as the adjectives for nationality that you saw in Unit 5. They become **masculine** or **feminine**, and **singular** or **plural**, just like the people or the things they are describing:

il est intelligent   elle est intelligent**e**
ils sont intelligent**s**   elles sont intelligent**es**

To make the **feminine** and **plural** forms, most adjectives follow the same patterns as the adjectives for nationality did in Unit 5:

masculine form: as found in the dictionary

Regular describing words

feminine form: add **-e** or **-ne** but don't change if word ends with **-e**

masculine and feminine **plural forms**: add **-s**, but if word ends with **-s**, **-z** or **-x**, don't change

As you learnt in Unit 2, the **-s** of the plural is not usually pronounced. So don't worry about it when speaking! You might hear a 'z' sound when some adjectives are followed by words starting with a vowel or an 'h', like **des grands artistes** *day grahñz arteest* 'great artists' or **des beaux hotels** *day bohz otel* 'nice hotels'.

Changing letters before the -e

For some adjectives with particular endings, the change to feminine requires more than adding an **-e**. Some letters before the **-e** change as well. For example, those ending with **-eux** such as **joyeux** (merry, happy) have a **feminine** form ending in **-euse, joyeuse**.

Some of the patterns go like this:

-oux → -ousse	e.g. **roux → rousse**	ginger
-anc → -anche	e.g. **blanc → blanche**	white
-eau → -elle	e.g. **beau → belle**	beautiful
-el → -elle	e.g. **naturel → naturelle**	natural
-er → -ère	e.g. **cher → chère**	expensive
-f → -ve	e.g. **créatif → créative**	creative

A very different feminine form

Some the feminine forms simply don't follow the usual patterns. These ones you just have to memorise. Here are some useful ones:

doux	**douce**	soft, sweet, mild, gentle
faux	**fausse**	false, wrong (answer)
favori	**favorite**	favourite
fou	**folle**	mad, crazy
frais	**fraîche**	fresh, chilly, cool
gentil	**gentille**	nice, kind
gros	**grosse**	big, large, fat
long	**longue**	long
nul	**nulle**	useless
sec	**sèche**	dry, dried
vieux	**vieille**	old

Two forms for masculine

Some adjectives have **two masculine forms** depending on the word that follows them. If the words that follow the adjective begin with a vowel (a, e, i, o, u) or an 'h', you use the second form. Here are some very useful ones:

beau/bel • nouveau/nouvel • vieux/vieil

Ce château est beau. This castle is beautiful.
C'est un bel appartement. This is a nice flat.

French word order

As you now know, French adjectives go after the word or words they are describing, except for these ones:

beau handsome, good-looking **bon** good
court short **grand** tall, big, long, great
gros big, large **haut** high
jeune young **joli** pretty
long long **mauvais** bad, poor
meilleur better **nouveau** new
petit small, little **premier** first
vieux old
Bonnes vacances! Enjoy your holidays!
Bon appétit! Enjoy your meal!
C'est un petit château. It's a small castle.

Mental gymnastics 1

Put these jumbled phrases in the correct order.

1 château/un/joli ....
2 verte/une/maison ....
3 étage/premier/le ....
4 jolie/une/cité ....
5 grande/française/ville/une ....

Mind Map it! Complete the following Mind Map to remember everything you've learnt about adjectives.

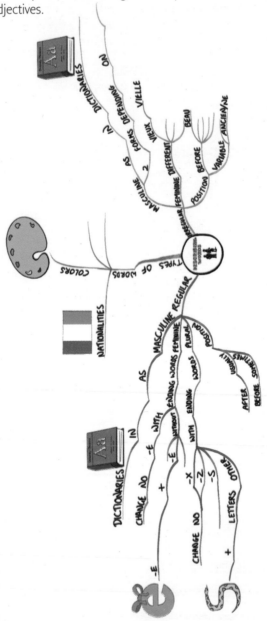

Mental gymnastics 2

The best man at a wedding has made a list of prompts for his speech, but his notes have got mixed up. Which adjectives can he use to describe the groom, the bride or both of them?

intelligents · belle · joviale · impatient · élégant · différente · tolérants · brillant · patiente · intéressants · galant · grands · adorables · créative · charmant · observatrice · sociables

Groom	Bride	Both

Mental gymnastics 3

How would you say these phrases in French?

1   a brief story   ....
2   a round suitcase   ....
3   a grey mouse   ....
4   a strange man   ....
5   a lovely (adorable) baby   ....
6   a pretty actress   ....

Mental gymnastics 4

In each clue the basic form is given. Should the spelling stay the same, or does it need to be changed?

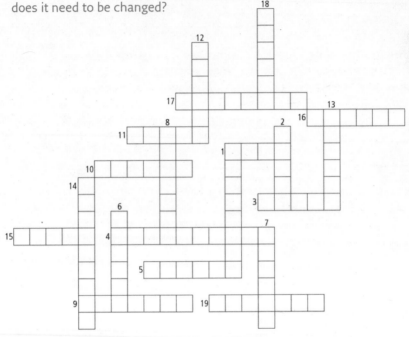

Across

1 ... Albert (cher)
3 Vincent est ... (jeune)
4 Ed est ... (australien)
5 C'est une ... valise. (gros)
9 C'est une ... femme. (vieux)
10 ... anniversaire! (Joyeux)
11 C'est un ... homme. (brave)
15 La table est ... (rond)
16 C'est une femme ... (blond)
17 C'est la ... maison. (premier)
19 Ma femme est ... (absent)

Down

1 Wei (*female*) est ... (chinoise)
2 C'est une ... absence. (bref)
6 C'est une valise ... (carré)
7 C'est mon ... appartement. (nouveau)
8 Jacques est ... (amusant)
12 Cette histoire est ... (court)
13 C'est une ... table. (long)
14 Sophie est ... (inventif)
18 Claire est ... (petit)

How to say *this, that, these* and *those*

There are three main uses of 'this' and 'that' in English; you'll find the French equivalents for each in this unit.

In a phrase such as 'I want that table', 'that' is linked to 'table', whereas in the sentences 'I want that' and 'that's impossible', 'that' is on its own - whatever it's referring to is not named. In French these two situations require a different word for 'that'.

'This' and 'that' on their own

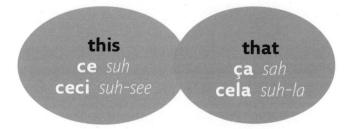

this
ce *suh*
ceci *suh-see*

that
ça *sah*
cela *suh-la*

Ce and **ça** are used most often out of the four. **Ceci** and **cela** are the slightly more formal alternatives. **Ceci** is not often used.

Ce and **être** are a pair: **ce** is usually used with the verb **être** (see Unit 4). **Ce** becomes **c'** when it is followed by **est**:

C'est impossible. That's impossible.
Ce n'est pas mon ami. This is not my friend.

The distinction between 'this' and 'that' is not clear-cut in French. Generally speaking, **ce** and **ceci** mean 'this', whereas **ça** and **cela** mean 'that '. However, **ce** often more closely translates as 'that' or 'it', particularly when it is followed by 'est', for example:

C'est dangereux.   It's/That's dangerous.

Similarly **ça** can mean 'this', 'that' or 'it':

Je veux ça. I want that.   **Ça marche!** It/this works!

Instead of trying to translate these words precisely, observe how they're used when you hear or read them – you'll gradually get the feel for when to use them by 'thinking in French'.

Mental gymnastics 1

Here are some useful phrases - but do they need ce, ça or c'?

1	.... est compris.	This is included.
2	.... va?	How are you?
3	Comme ....?	Like that?
4	.... n'est pas juste!	That's not fair!
5	Pourquoi ....?	Why is that?
6	.... n'est pas vrai!	That's not true!
7	.... est loin?	Is it far?
8	.... est du vol!	That is a rip-off!

'This', 'that', 'these', 'those' linked to other words

Sometimes in English, you use 'this', that', 'those' and 'these' to talk about specific named things or people: e.g. 'I want that table', 'these tourists are Spanish'. In these cases, 'that' is linked to 'table', and 'these' to 'tourists'.

In this case, French makes no distinction between 'this' and 'that' – the same word is used for both.

However, as usual there are **masculine, feminine, singular** and **plural** forms because they are referring to a masculine or feminine and singular or plural word.

ce crocodile that crocodile
ce château this castle
ces crocodiles those crocodiles
ces châteaux these castles

cette tortue that tortoise
cette maison this house
ces tortues those tortoises
ces maisons these houses

There are actually **two** masculine **singular forms**: **ce** (again) and **cet**.
Cet is only used before words beginning with a vowel (a, e, i, o, u) or an 'h'.

cet hôtel this hotel   cet infirmier this (male) nurse

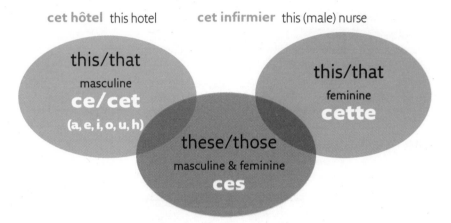

Mental gymnastics 2

Cross out the incorrect word in the following sentences. Check in
the previous units if you cannot remember a word's gender.

1   C'est **cet/ce** hôtel!
2   **Cet/Cette** question est intéressante.
3   **Cette/Ce** personne est canadienne.
4   **Ce/Ces** crocodile est féroce.
5   **Cet/Ces** problèmes sont difficiles.
6   **Cette/Ces** vendeuses sont anglaises.
7   **Ce/Cet** bébé est beau.
8   **Ce/Cet** homme est grand.

'This one', 'that one', 'these ones', 'those ones'

Finally, in English, 'this', 'that', those' and 'these' are used to say 'I'd like this one' and 'these ones are superb!'

Once again, there are different forms:

Je voudrais **celui-ci**.	I'd like this one. (masculine)
Je voudrais **celle-ci**.	I'd like this one. (feminine)
Je voudrais **celui-là**.	I'd like that one. (masculine)
Je voudrais **celle-là**.	I'd like that one. (feminine)

Ceux-ci sont superbes!	These ones are superb! (masculine or mixed)
Celles-ci sont superbes!	These ones are superb! (feminine)

Ceux-là sont superbes!	Those ones are superb! (masculine or mixed)
Celles-là sont superbes!	Those ones are superb! (feminine)

Masculine 'this one' – singular	**celui-ci**
Masculine 'that one' – singular	**celui-là**

Feminine 'this one' – singular	**celle-ci**
Feminine 'that one' – singular	**celle-là**

Masculine (or a mix of masculine and feminine) 'these ones' – plural	**ceux-ci**
Masculine (or a mix of masculine and feminine) 'those ones' – plural	**ceux-là**

Feminine 'these ones' – plural	**celles-ci**
Feminine 'those ones' – plural	**celles-là**

Mental gymnastics 3

Which one would you choose in the following situations? Celui-ci/là, celle-ci/là, ceux-ci/là or celles-ci/là? The first one has been done for you.

In a department store, when referring to:

1	shoes, **les chaussures**	Je voudrais	..celles-ci/là....
2	pullovers, **les pulls**	Je voudrais	....
3	coat, **le manteau**	Je voudrais	....
4	skirt, **la jupe**	Je voudrais	....
5	socks, les **chaussettes**	Je voudrais	....
6	computer, **l'ordinateur**	Je voudrais	....
7	chair, **la chaise**	Je voudrais	....
8	fruits, **les fruits**	Je voudrais	....

Mental gymnastics 4

Choose the correct option for each of the ten sentences.

1　I prefer this one (about a car; une voiture). **Je préfère ...**
　　a　ce
　　b　ceux-ci
　　c　celle-ci

2　This competition is difficult. **... compétition est difficile.**
　　a　Cette
　　b　Celle-ci
　　c　Cet

3　I work in this hotel. **Je travaille dans ... hôtel.**
　　a　celui-ci
　　b　ces
　　c　cet

4   I'll take those ones (about some shoes).   **Je prends ...**
   a   ceux-là
   b   celles-là
   c   ces

5   These jewels are beautiful! **... bijoux sont beaux!**
   a   Ces
   b   Ceux-ci
   c   Ça

6   I don't like that. **Je n'aime pas ...**
   a   ce
   b   ça
   c   celui-ci

7   These ones are French (speaking about cheeses). **... sont français.**
   a   Ces
   b   Ceux-ci
   c   Celles-ci

8   This is not difficult! **... n'est pas difficile!**
   a   Celui-ci
   b   Ça
   c   Ce

9   I can't do that! **Je ne peux pas faire ...!**
   a   ça
   b   ce
   c   celui-ci

10   This is unbelievable! **... est incroyable!**
   a   Celui-ci
   b   Ça
   c   C'

How to talk about the present: regular verbs

He eats spaghetti

When you are doing something now or if you do something regularly you might say '**I write** every day', '**he eats** spaghetti', '**they listen** to music'. This is called the **present tense** (G). It's not in the past or the future – it's in the present, it's now.

In French, the present tense works the same as in English – you need 'I', 'you', 'he' or another **subject** (G) and then the **verb** (G).

Endings and types of verb

French verbs need you to add endings. Choosing an ending depends on **two** things:

- whether you are talking about 'I', 'you' or 'he'. For example, **j'aime** (I like) but **tu aimes** (you like)
- what type of verb you're using

There are three types of **regular verbs** (G) in French:
- the **-ER** type
- the **-IR** type
- the **-RE** type

These types are determined by the last two letters of the **infinitive** (G). This is the form of the verb that begins with 'to' in English. So **habiter** (to live) is an **-ER** verb, **finir** (to finish) is an **-IR** verb, and **attendre** (to wait) is an **-RE** verb. When you look a verb up in a dictionary, what you are given is the infinitive – the 'to' form.

A verb is known as 'regular' if the different parts of the verb follow a predictable, set pattern. Each of the three types above follows a slightly different regular pattern.

Using the correct ending

To create the correct form of the verb in French, first take off the ending that you have found in the dictionary:

habiter → habit

finir → fin

attendre → attend

er

ir

re

Then add the endings to the bit you are left with. But which ending do you need?

Each **je, tu, il/elle, nous, vous, ils/elles** calls for a specific ending. For example for **-ER** verbs, the ending for **je** is **-e**

j'habit + e = j'habite   I live

and the ending for **tu** is **-es**

tu habites   you live

Supposing you wanted to say 'I live in London':
you take **je** + **habiter** → take off the **-er** bit → add the ending for **je** (**-e**):
habite → finally combine the subject and the verb: **je** → **j' + habite**

j'habite à Londres. I live in London.

Let's look more closely at each of these verb types.

the -ER type

Almost 90% of all French verbs fall into the **-ER** category. Here are the endings for the **-ER** type:

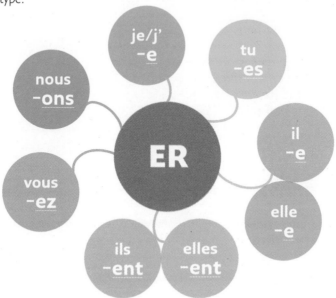

Did you notice? The endings for **nous** and **vous** are the same as those for **avoir** (see Unit 7). Those for **ils** and **elles** have **-nt** in common. The good news is that this is also the case for the **-IR** and **-RE** verbs!

Here are some useful **-ER** verbs:

ador**er**	to adore (something/ someone)	habit**er**	to live
		jou**er**	to play
aim**er**	to like (something)	march**er**	to walk
	to love (someone)	par**ler**	to speak
cherch**er**	to look for	regard**er**	to watch
donn**er**	to give	travaill**er**	to work
écout**er**	to listen to	trouv**er**	to find
étudi**er**	to study		

Tony's Tip

Great news! The verb endings may all look different on paper, but when you speak, the verbs for **je**, **tu**, **il**, **elle**, **ils** and **elles** sound the same.

For example:

j'habite *zh-ah-beet*		I live
tu habites *tew ah-beet*		you live
il/elle habite *eel/ell ah-beet*		(s)he lives
ils/elles habitent *eelz/ellz-ah-beet*		they live

Mental gymnastics 1

Take two minutes to memorise as many words on the previous page as you can. Use the tips above and your own memory techniques.

How many endings can you now recall without looking back?

Try to recall them again in **two hours**, in **one day** and in **one week**. The more you repeat them, the longer you will remember them.

Mental gymnastics 2

Join the two halves of each -ER verb together to complete the verbs and add the correct subject (**je**, **tu**, **nous**, **vous** or **ils**).

-ent   -llez   -hent   -tons   -ns   -nes   -rdez   -me

1	.... parlo-..........		5	.... ai-..........
2	.... rega-..........		6	.... habit-..........
3	.... écou-..........		7	.... travai-..........
4	.... don-..........		8	.... marc-..........

the -IR type

A relatively small number of French verbs belong to the **-IR** category. Useful ones include **finir** (to finish) and **choisir** (to choose).

Some indicate physical changes, e.g. **grossir** (to put on weight), **maigrir** (to lose weight), **vieillir** (to grow old). Here are the endings for the regular **-IR** verbs:

As with the **-ER** verbs, the endings look different on paper, but when you speak, the verbs for **je**, **tu**, **il** and **elle** sound the same.

For example:

je choisis *zhuh shwah-zee*   I choose
tu choisis *tew shwah-zee*   you choose
il/elle choisit *eel/ell shwah-zee* (s)he chooses

Here are some useful –**IR** verbs:

chois**ir**	to choose	réag**ir**	to react
fin**ir**	to finish, to end	réfléch**ir**	to think
grand**ir**	to grow tall	rempl**ir**	to fill in (e.g. a form)
gross**ir**	to put on weight	réuss**ir**	to succeed
maigr**ir**	to lose weight	vieill**ir**	to grow old

Mental gymnastics 3

Take two minutes to memorise as many words on the previous page as you can. Use the tips above and your own memory techniques.

How many endings can you now recall without looking back at the previous page?

Try to recall them again in **two hours**, in **one day** and in **one week**. The more you repeat them, the longer you will remember them.

Mental gymnastics 4

Complete the subjects and verbs with their missing consonants.

Verbs to look for in different forms:

finir · grandir · grossir · réfléchir · remplir · rougir · vieillir · finir

1	OU ÉÉIO	5	I OI ....
2	U OUI	6	I EIE ....
3	EE AI	7	OU IIE ....
4	E II	8	E IEII ....

The -RE type

The **-RE** type is a small but important category. It includes useful verbs such as **répondre** (to reply, to answer), **vendre** (to sell), **attendre** (to wait for). Here are the endings for the regular **-RE** verbs:

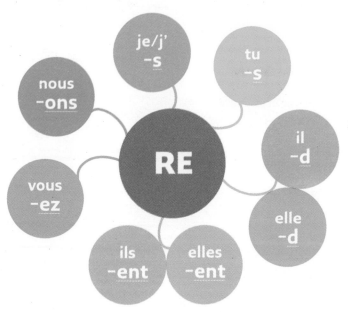

Nothing for il and elle

You don't add anything for **il** and **elle**: you just keep the final letter 'd' once you have removed the '-re' bit: répondre → répond → il/elle répond

Tony's Tip

As with the **-ER** and **-IR** verbs, the endings may look different on paper, but when you speak, the verbs for **je**, **tu**, **il** and **elle** sound the same.

For example:

j'attends *zh-ah-tahñ* I wait
tu attends *tew ah-tahñ* you wait
il/elle attend *eel/ell ah-tahñ* (s)he waits

Here are some very useful **-RE** verbs:

attend**re**   to wait for
descend**re**   to go down (stairs, hill, etc.)
entend**re**   to hear
perd**re**   to lose

rend**re**   to give back, to hand in
rend**re** visite à   to visit (someone)
répond**re**   to reply, to answer
vend**re**   to sell

Now, now, now!

There is another way of talking about something you are doing **now** in English – 'I am walking', 'he is running', 'they are talking'. In French, you can just use the normal present tense for this.
For example 'I work and 'I am working' are both **je travaille**. 'He eats' and 'he is eating' are **il mange**. Simple!

Mental gymnastics 5

Take two minutes to memorise as many words on the previous page as you can.

Try to recall them again in **two hours**, in **one day** and in **one week**. The more you repeat them, the longer you will remember them.

Mental gymnastics 6

Add the correct subject (**je**, **tu**, **il/elle**, **nous**, **vous** or **ils**) to the front of each of these verbs.

1   .... réponds
2   .... vendent
3   .... attendons
4   .... descend

5   .... entends
6   .... perdez
7   .... vendent
8   .... rend

Mental gymnastics 7

Complete the crossword using regular verbs with their appropriate endings.

Across
1   Je ... (réfléchir)
3   Tu ... à son e-mail? (répondre)
6   Vous ... anglais? (parler)
7   Vous ... (attendre)
9   Michelle ... Paris! (adorer)
11 Tu ... à Nice? (travailler)
12 Je ... (descendre)
13 Ils ... leur maison. (vendre)
16 Ils ... dans les Alpes. (marcher)
17 Mes parents ... dans une
    pharmacie. (travailler)
19 Tes enfants ... (grandir)

Down
2   Je .... français. (parler)
4   Nous ... à deux heures. (finir)
5   Nous ... du jazz. (écouter)
7   Nous ... beaucoup Toronto.
    (aimer)
8   Vous ... le formulaire. (remplir)
10 Nous ... toujours nos clés.
    (perdre)
14 Tu ... à Londres? (habiter)
15 Paul ... les pizzas. (aimer)
18 Maman ... (vieillir)

How to talk about the present: irregular verbs

11

There are a large number of **verbs** (G) in French that do not follow the rules for **regular verbs** (G) as explained in Unit 10. These **irregular verbs** (G) are generally the most common ones, so it's important that you try to learn how they work.

In the verb wheel that accompanies this book, you will find lots of irregular verbs with the present tense endings nearest the rim of the wheel. Look at the wheel as you progress through this unit, and we will try to find patterns to help you remember these slightly more difficult verbs.

Finding the root
As with regular verbs, to create the correct form of the verb in French, first take off the ending that you have found in the dictionary:

prendre → prend

 **re**

Then add the endings to the bit you are left with. Each **je, tu, il/elle, nous, vous, ils/elles** calls for a specific ending.

For example for **prendre**, the ending for **je** is **-s**:
je prend + s = **je** prends   I take

and the ending for **tu** is **-s**:
tu prends   you take

Endings and changing forms
What's different about irregular verbs is that they can also have form changes, like **être** and **avoir** (see Units 4 and 7). This is also true of **prendre**: let's go back to this verb.

The form of **prendre** you need for **nous** and **vous** is **pren** rather than not **prend**:

pren + **nous** ending → **pren-ons** → **nous** prenons 'we take'

Patterns of endings

nous, vous, ils and elles
The **nous** and the **vous** endings are often similar from one verb to another: -ons and -ez, e.g. **nous** prenons 'we take', **nous** faisons 'we make/do', **vous** prenez 'you take' or **vous** pouvez 'you can'. There are some exceptions, but they are quite rare.

The ils and elles endings often involve -nt, e.g. **ils** font 'they make/they do', or **ils** vont 'they go'. When you say or hear these verbs, the -nt is usually silent.

Je and tu, il and elle
In irregular verbs, je and tu often share the same ending: either -s or -x Remember, there's no **t** ending for je and tu.

Il and elle end in -d or -t.

Patterns of forms

Je, tu, il and elle often share the same or a similar form, which is sometimes very different from the basic form of the verb. **Je** vais 'I go' and **tu** vas look quite different from **aller** 'to go'.

Nous and vous often have the same form too. For example, in **nous** prenons 'we take' and **vous** prenez 'you take', only the endings are different.

Irregular -ir, -re and -oir

Irregular verbs usually end in -ir, -re or -oir. There are three different patterns among them:

1   Je, tu, il, elle, nous, vous, ils and elles share the **same form**,
    but not the same endings. Have a look at ouvrir on the verb wheel.
2   Je, tu, il and elle share the **same form** but not the same endings and
    nous, vous, ils and elles share **another form** but not the same endings.
    Have a look at écrire and savoir on the verb wheel.
3   Je, tu, il and elle share the **same form** but not the same endings.
    Nous and vous share **another form** but not the same endings,
    and ils and elles have **another form**. Have a look at recevoir, venir
    and vouloir on the verb wheel.

However, it is difficult to predict which group a verb belongs to just by looking at it!
Check them on the verb wheel first (or in a dictionary) and memorise them as you
need them. They're usually worth the effort as many of them are used very often.

How to remember your verbs

If you learn well by hearing, you could invent some poems or lyrics of your own.
Which English word(s) do the French verbs and forms sound like? Or you can make
your own associations. The crazier and more personal, the better you'll remember!

You could also write or record a personal profile using the irregular verbs:
je fais du tennis, je fais du piano, je fais des gâteaux, etc.

Tony's Tip

Little and often: you could set yourself a goal of learning (say) two irregular verbs
a day or a week.

Commuting wheel: use the verb wheel anywhere to learn them: e.g. on the bus,
during your lunch break or in the park.

Remember 'no pain, no gain': learning the irregulars can seem a bit boring,
but knowing them will get you beyond the basic set sentences and will enable you
to say things you want to say for yourself in French.

Mental gymnastics 1

Join the halves together to complete the irregular verbs and add the correct subject (**je**, **tu**, **il/elle**, **nous**, **vous** or **ils/elles**).

-nais -tes -ut -lez -lent -vons -it -nent

1 .... pe-.........
2 .... sa-.........
3 .... veu-.........
4 .... con-.........
5 .... do-.........
6 .... al-.........
7 .... pren-.........
8 .... fai-.........

Mental gymnastics 2

Complete the subjects and verbs with their missing vowels.

Words to look for in different forms:

faire • prendre • pouvoir • vouloir • devoir • venir • savoir • connaître

1 NS PRNNS ....
2 VS PVZ ....
3 LLS DVNT ....
4 T FS ....
5 J CNNS ....
6 LL VT ....
7 L ST ....
8 LS VNNNT ....

Mental gymnastics 3

Solve these anagrams to find some more irregular verbs.

1   UOSN NEVOSD   ....
2   EJ SIFA   ....
3   LIS VUNETEP   ....
4   LI NITEV   ....
5   SOVU SNAZONICES   ....
6   USON LOSOVUN   ....
7   LELES TOFN   ....
8   UT ISSA   ....

Mental gymnastics 4

What do these sentences mean in English?

1   Je fais du foot.   ....
2   Elle sait faire des gâteaux.   ....
3   Nous prenons le train.   ....
4   Ils veulent visiter le château.   ....
5   Vous faites du sport?   ....
6   Tu connais Bordeaux?   ....
7   Il va au cinéma.   ....
8   Ils viennent ce soir.   ....

Mental gymnastics 5

Complete the crossword using irregular verbs with their appropriate endings.

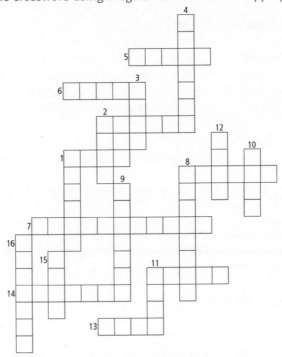

Across

1 Il ... (savoir)!
2 Vous ... du sport? (faire)
5 Tu ... de Lyon? (venir)
6 Elle ... des photos. (prendre)
7 Nous ... cette artiste. (connaître)
8 Vous ... venir? (pouvoir)
11 Vous ... de Paris? (venir)
13 Elles ... un gâteau (faire)
14 Ils ... venir. (vouloir)

Down

1 Nous ... (savoir)
2 Tu ... un gâteau? (faire)
3 Je ... travailler. (devoir)
4 Je ... bien Paul. (connaître)
8 Ils ... le train (prendre)
9 Ils ... parler anglais. (devoir)
10 Elle ... faire du volley. (vouloir)
11 Elles ... au cinéma. (aller)
12 Je ... venir! (vouloir)
15 Je ... venir? (pouvoir)
16 Nous ... venir. (pouvoir)

How to talk about your daily routine: reflexive verbs

The reflexive family

Do it yourself

Some of the **regular** (G) and **irregular** (G) verbs can sometimes become **reflexive** (G), which means that the action is directed back to the person doing it – just as your 'reflection' is directed back to you in a mirror.

In English, reflexive verbs look like this:
I washed myself
He hurt himself
The baby can't feed himself
Help yourself!

They are more common in French than in English. In French you don't just say 'I brush my teeth' you say 'I brush me my teeth'. You also say 'I wake myself' and 'I get myself ready'.

Reflexive French

In French, you add a reflexive bit, like in English you add 'myself'. You add it before the reflexive verb.

For example:

Je **me** **lave** les dents	I brush (me) my teeth
Je **me** **réveille**	I wake myself

There is one for each **je**, **tu**, **il/elle**, **nous**, **vous**, **ils/elles**. They look like this:

me *muh*	myself
te *tuh*	yourself (singular and informal)
se *suh*	himself/herself/itself
nous (no change) *noo*	ourselves
vous (no change) *voo*	yourself (formal)/yourselves
se *suh*	themselves

What to do with the reflexive bit

This is when you may think you are starting to speak like a child proud of his or her independence: 'Look mum – I can wash myself! I can dress myself!'

You put the reflexive bit just after **je**, **tu**, **il/elle**, **nous**, **vous** or **ils/elles**, and then follow it with the verb.
The order of words differs from English: it's like saying 'I myself wash'.

Je me **lave**	I wash myself
tu te **laves**	you wash yourself
il/elle se **lave**	he/she washes himself/herself
nous nous **lavons**	we wash ourselves
vous vous **lavez**	you wash yourself/yourselves
ils/elles se **lavent**	they wash themselves

When looking up a reflexive verb in a dictionary, look for the word itself, not for the reflexive bit. So if you were looking up se coucher, you'd look under 'c' instead of 's'. You'll find out that a verb can be used as a reflexive with this little indication: (**se**), which is the basic form of the reflexive bits in the dictionary.

Some useful reflexives for talking about your routine:

(se) réveiller	to wake up	**(s')habiller**	to get dressed
(se) lever	to get up	**(se) préparer**	to get ready
(se) laver	to wash	**(se) dépêcher**	to hurry up
(se) doucher	to have a shower	**(se) déshabiller**	to get undressed
(se) maquiller	to put on make up	**(se) raser**	to shave

Some useful reflexives to talk about accidents and injuries:

(se) casser	to break
(se) couper	to cut yourself
(se) brûler	to burn yourself
(se) faire mal	to hurt yourself
(se) piquer	to get stung, to prick yourself
(se) tordre	to twist (e.g. your ankle)

A reflexive nuance

In French, there are a lot of verbs that have two nuances: one in which the action is applied to 'myself', 'yourself', 'himself', etc.; another where the action is applied to someone or something else.

Let's take some examples. In French, **réveiller** means 'to wake' as in 'to be woken by something/someone', **laver** means 'to wash (something/someone)', **demander** means 'to ask'. They are members of the regular –**ER** family of verbs, and to use them to speak in the present tense you just follow the steps explained in Unit 10. Here they are with and without the reflexive nuance.

Le coq réveille Paul tous les matins.
The cockerel wakes Paul up every morning.
BUT
Je me réveille tous les matins à six heures.
I wake up every morning at six.

Je lave la voiture.
I wash the car.
BUT
Je me lave.
I wash (myself).

Je demande à Hélène: « Tu viens avec nous ? ».
I ask Hélène: 'Are you coming with us?'.
BUT
Je me demande pourquoi.
I wonder why. (I ask myself why)

Every time the action is turned back to **je**, a **me** appears. It's the reflexive bit for **je**.

Mental gymnastics 1

Match the pictures with the sentences.

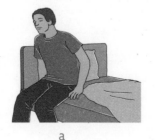

a

b

c

d

e

f

1 Elle se maquille.
2 Je me dépêche.
3 Il se rase.
4 Elles se préparent.
5 Nous nous habillons.
6 Tu te couches?
7 Ils se réveillent.
8 Vous vous levez?

g

h

Mental gymnastics 2

Rearrange the words in each question to make a reflexive verb.

1   coupe – se – elle ....
2   se – dépêchent – ils ....
3   t' – tu – habilles ....
4   vous – maquillez – vous ....
5   me – couche – je ....
6   nous – préparons – nous ....

Mental gymnastics 3

Sort out this mixture of reflexive verbs and reflexives bits and join these words to the appropriate subject (**je**, **tu**, **nous**, **vous** or **elles**).

maquille – elles – tu – nous – me – je – vous – nous – réveillent – fais mal – dépêchons – vous – lavez – se – te

1   ....
2   ....
3   ....
4   ....
5   ....

How to use don't and aren't

Don't and aren't

In English, to make something **negative (G)**, you add 'not', 'don't' or 'doesn't'.

I am French → I am **not** French
I work → I **don't** work
Jacques has children → Jacques **doesn't** have any children

Ne/n' and pas

In French, you use **ne** and **pas**, and you put the verb in the middle.

I am **not** French	Je **ne** suis **pas** français
I **don't** work	Je **ne** travaille **pas**
Jacques **doesn't** live in Lille	Jacques **n'**habite **pas** à Lille.

Ne becomes **n'** when the word that follows starts with a vowel (a, e, i, o, u) or an 'h'.

Jacques **doesn't** live in Lille   Jacques **n'**habite **pas** à Lille

When it comes to making a negative, just wrap **ne** and **pas** around the verb. You can't recreate 'do' with **faire** here – thinking in French will be more helpful than trying to translate directly from English.

In informal conversations, French speakers often drop the **ne**, so watch out for the **pas**! For example, you might hear J'aime pas ça! instead of Je **n'**aime pas ça! (I don't like that!).

Mental gymnastics 1

Rearrange the words in each question to make a negative sentence.

1   pas – parle – elle – français – ne ....
2   pas – notre – nous – vendons – maison – ne ....
     ....
3   joue – pas – je – ne ....
4   le – il – prend – train – pas – ne ....
5   se – pas – lèvent – ils – ne ....
6   pas – tu – travailles – ne ....
7   mariée – êtes – n' – vous – pas? ....
8   ne – pas – italien – parle – je ....

Don't have/'de'
When you're talking about things you don't have, you use **de** or **d'** just before the thing you don't have or do, or to mean **any**.

I **don't** have a castle.	je n'ai pas **de** château.
She **doesn't** have any children.	Elle n'a pas **d'**enfants.
He **doesn't** sell cars.	Il ne vend pas **de** voitures.

Mental gymnastics 2

Complete these sentences with the missing vowels (a, e, i, o, u).

1   ....ll .... n.... v.... ....nt p....s.   She's not coming.
2   N.... ....s n.... tr...v.... ....ll....ns p....s.   We don't work.
3   ....ls n'....nt p....s d.... v.... ....t...r.....   They don't have a car.
4   ....l n'....c.... ....t.... p....s d....   He doesn't listen to
      m....s....q.... .....   any music.
5   J.... n.... f.... ....s p....s d.... sp....rt.   I don't do any sport.
6   T.... n'....s p....s d.... cl....?   Don't you have a key?

What about the reflexives with 'ne' and 'pas'?

Remember the verbs used for describing your daily routine from Unit 12, such as **se laver** (Je me lave 'I wash')? How do you combine a negative and a reflexive?

Ne and pas wrap around the pair. Here is the sequence:

1 Je, tu, il/elle, nous, vous, ils/elles, or any noun
2 ne
3 me, te, se, nous, vous, se
4 verb
5 pas

Je **ne** me lave **pas**. *zhuh nuh muh lav pa*   I don't wash.
Il **ne** se rase **pas**. *eel nuh suh raz pa*   He doesn't shave.

Tony's Tip

You could write or record some information about yourself that you might want to say during a holiday in a French-speaking country. You could talk about things you don't have, activities you don't do (always useful if you have to decline an unwelcome invitation!) and who or what you are not, e.g. **je n'ai pas mon sac! je ne fais pas de rugby, merci; je ne suis pas anglais**.

Mental gymnastics 3

The interpreter has got it all wrong! Change these sentences to make them negative.

1   Elle est américaine. ....
2   Ils ont faim. ....
3   Nous avons des enfants. ....
4   Je me lève à 5 heures 30. ....
5   Il se prépare. ....
6   Elles préparent une pizza. ....
7   Il attend à la gare. ....
8   Paul se dépêche. ....

How to ask questions

In French, there are a variety of ways of forming a question.

Oui ou non?

In French, there are **three** ways you can choose from to ask a question if the answer is likely to begin with 'yes' or 'no':

1. Use intonation
The simplest way is this: don't make any changes to a normal sentence, like 'Tu habites à New York.' – just add a **?** and raise your voice at the end when you say it.

Tu habites à New York?   Do you live in New York?

Il travaille en Grande-Bretagne?   Does he work in the UK?

Vous êtes australien?   Are you Australian?

Elle est fatiguée?   Is she tired?

2. The 'is it that' way
This way, you don't make any changes to a normal sentence but you add the equivalent of the phrase 'is it that' to the front of it: **est-ce que ...**

Est-ce que ✚ tu habites à New York?
Est-ce qu' ✚ il travaille en Grande-Bretagne?
Est-ce que ✚ vous êtes australien?
Est-ce qu' ✚ elle est fatiguée?

Did you notice that there were two examples where the **que** became **qu'**? This happens when the next word begins with a vowel.

3. The 'changing the word order' way
This is the most formal-sounding way. For this method, you put the verb first:
tu habites → **habites-tu**

Habites-tu à New York?   **Êtes-vous** australien?
Travaille-t-il en Grande-Bretagne?   **Est-elle** fatiguée?

When the verb ends with a vowel and the next word also begins with a vowel or an 'h', French adds an extra '**t**' to make it easier to say (as in the second example above).

There is no rule as to when you should use each of the above options – just choose the way you prefer!

How do I say 'do' in French questions?

The easy answer is: you don't. Questions are made in English using the verb 'to do', but French questions are formed in a different way, as we saw above. Only translate 'do' as '**faire**' if you have a question about what people are making or doing, e.g. **Faites-vous du sport?** Do you play sports?

Mental gymnastics 1

The first time you meet some French people they might have some questions about you and vice versa. Let's practise by turning these sentences into questions. Try all three ways.

1   Vous êtes anglais(e).   ....
2   Vous habitez à Londres.   ....
3   Vous êtes étudiant(e).   ....
4   Vous travaillez.   ....
5   Vous êtes en vacances.   ....
6   Vous voulez boire quelque chose.   ....
7   Vous restez une semaine.   ....
8   Vous parlez anglais.   ....

Mental gymnastics 2

Guess the questions that would prompt each of these responses.

1   Oui, je viens de Paris. ....
2   Non, nous n'avons pas d'enfants. ....
3   Oui, J'habite à Sydney. ....
4   Oui, j'aime cette musique. ....
5   Non, je ne joue pas au tennis. ....
6   Oui, je travaille à Manchester. ....

Any other questions?

The options on the previous page are for yes/no questions. But how would you form a question that requires a more complex answer? You need to learn the question words:

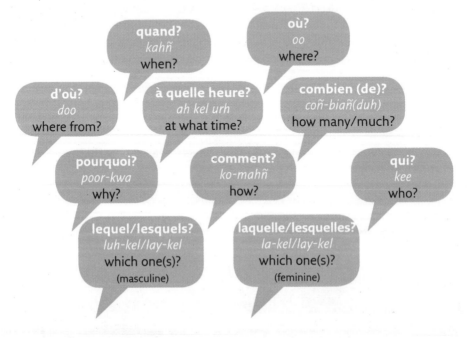

How to make questions with the question words

As with questions with a yes/no answer, there are three ways of making a question with these words:

1 The **raising your voice** + **question word (usually) at the end** way

Where do you work?   Tu travailles **où**?

2 The **question word** + **'is it that'** way

Where do you work   Où est-ce que tu travailles?

3 The **question word** + **changing the word order** way (the most formal)

Where do you work?   tu travailles → **travailles-tu** → **Où** travailles-tu?

Mental gymnastics 3

Solve these anagrams to find the question words.

1   uropuqio ....
2   daqnu   ....
3   steucqee ....
4   luqele   ....
5   nocibem   ....
6   suqeslle   ....
7   uqi   ....
8   ùd'o   ....

Mental gymnastics 4

Rearrange the words to make a question.

1   français – est – vous – ce – parlez – que? ....
2   elle – d' – est – où? ....
3   comment – est – fais – ce – tu – que? ....

....

4   nous – ce – faisons – qu' – que – est? ....
5   vas – est – que – tu – ce – où? ....
6   ne – il – est – pourquoi – vient – ce – pas – qu'? ....

....

7   allez – où – vous? ....
8   ça – combien – coûte? ....

What about 'what'?

In French, there are two ways to ask 'what' questions:

1 When you want to ask about what someone is doing, as in:

'What are you doing?' 'What are you waiting for?' 'What is this?'

you use the question word **que**. There are two ways to use it:

• **Que + 'is it that' way:**
Qu'est-ce que tu fais?   What are you doing?/What do you do?

• **Que + changing the word order:**
Que fais-tu?   What are you doing/What do you do?

Just choose the way you prefer!

2 But if you are asking for a specific answer, you use **quel** (which) instead of **que**.

Quel est votre nom?   What is your name?
Quelle est votre nationalité?   What is your nationality?
Quelle couleur est-ce? or **C'est quelle couleur?**   What colour is this?
Quelles chaussures préférez-vous? Which shoes do you prefer?
Quels jeux préfères-tu? Which games do you prefer?

Did you notice? There are four different forms of **quel** (**quel**, **quelle**, **quels**, **quelles**) depending on whether the next word is masculine or feminine, plural or singular.

Mental gymnastics 5

Match the questions with their answers.

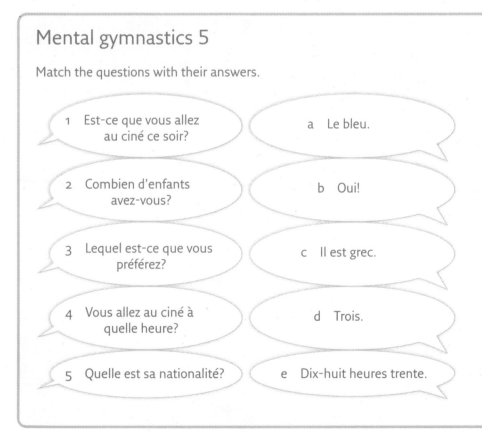

1   Est-ce que vous allez au ciné ce soir?

a   Le bleu.

2   Combien d'enfants avez-vous?

b   Oui!

3   Lequel est-ce que vous préférez?

c   Il est grec.

4   Vous allez au ciné à quelle heure?

d   Trois.

5   Quelle est sa nationalité?

e   Dix-huit heures trente.

Mind Map it! Complete the questions Mind Map or do your own, with colours and – **Pourquoi pas?** – some examples.

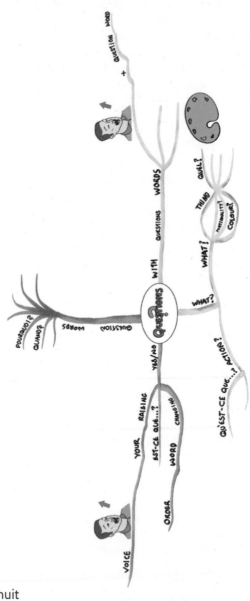

How to talk about abilities and preferences

In this unit, you'll learn how to say I like, I don't like, I can, I can't, and other ways of expressing abilities and preferences. These phrases may all sound rather different in English, but in French they are all formed by following exactly the same rule.

I like doing, know how to do and can do

In French, you always use the same structure to say:

I like doing **j'aime faire**   I want to do **Je veux faire**
I know how to do **Je sais faire**   I can do **je peux faire**
I have to do **je dois faire**

No 'to', no 'ing'
Use this structure instead:

person or animal (subject) + taste or ability verb in the appropriate form + infinitive form of the verb (as found in the dictionary)

Now you know the rule you can also apply it to these words: **détester** (to hate), **préférer** (to prefer), **espérer** (to hope), **penser** (to think).

I like going to the cinema.   j'aime aller au cinéma.
Olivier knows how to cook.   **Olivier** sait cuisiner.
She hates dancing.   **Elle** déteste dancer.
We have to go.   **Nous** devons partir.

Saying what you cannot do

Follow the same rule for negative sentences:

They cannot come.
You don't know how to swim.

Ils ne peuvent pas venir.
Tu ne sais pas nager.

Tony's Tip

You could write or record a personal profile so that you can talk about yourself when you are on holiday in a French-speaking country, e.g. **je n'aime pas faire du shopping, j'adore faire du piano, je ne sais pas cuisiner.**

Mental gymnastics 1

1   I can come tonight. ....
2   She knows how to make pizzas. ....
3   We want to take the train. ....
4   He wants to live in France. ....
5   You (formal) can work in Great Britain. ....
6   They know how to play the piano. ....
7   They don't want to ski. ....
8   He has to go to Paris. ....

Mental gymnastics 2

The interpreter has got it all wrong again! Change these sentences to make them negative.

1   Je dois être à l'aéroport à deux heures.   ....
2   Nicolas veut venir.   ....
3   Nous pouvons prendre des photos.   ....
4   Vous devez faire le ménage.   ....
5   Elles veulent prendre le bus.   ....
6   Mes parents aiment faire du shopping.   ....
7   Ces enfants peuvent regarder la télé.   ....
8   Tu peux venir?   ....

Mental gymnastics 3

Rearrange the words in each question to make a sentence.

1   ne – peut – elle – venir – pas
     ....

2   veulent – travailler – ils
     ....

3   parler – savons – français – nous
     ....

4   peut – Jérémy – attendre – pas – ne
     ....

5   à – finir – voulons – cinq – nous – heures
     ....

6   ne – elle – marcher – pas – doit
     ....

7   pas – le – n' – faire – aime – je –ménage
     ....

8   adorent – photos – elles – des – prendre
     ....

How to say *some* and *any*

In this unit, you'll learn some equivalents of 'some' and 'any'.

No difference between 'some' and 'any'

In French, there is no difference between 'some' and 'any' – they are both dealt with in the same way. However, there are two different equivalents for these words: deciding which one to use depends on the situation.

'some' and 'any' things

Situation one is when 'some' or 'any' are connected to a thing or a food item, e.g. 'I'd like **some salad**' or 'Do you have **any apples**?' Once again, the equivalent words for 'some' in French involve **masculine**, **feminine** and **plural**. You have to choose the **some/any** equivalents according to the gender of the word they are connected to. **Dude Lades** is a memory aid to help you memorise **du**, **de la**, **de l'** and **des**, which all mean either 'any' or 'some'.

I want some salad.	**Je veux <u>de la</u> salade.**
Do you have any apples?	**Avez-vous <u>des</u> pommes?**
We have some money.	**Nous avons <u>de l'</u>argent.**
I'd like some bread.	**Je voudrais <u>du</u> pain.**

du before **masculine** words

de la before **feminine** words

equivalents of **some/any** + thing or food item

de l' before **singular** words starting with a vowel or an 'h'

des before **plural** words

Talking about playing music and sport

The **Dude Lades** equivalents are also used a lot when speaking about sport and music activities with either **faire** (sports and music) or **jouer** (only for music).

faire only
faire du foot to play football
faire du golf to play golf
faire de l'équitation to go horse riding
faire de la natation to swim

faire or **jouer**
faire du piano to play the piano
faire de la clarinette to play the clarinet
jouer du violon to play the violin
jouer de la trompette to play the trumpet

Mental gymnastics 1

Put the words below in the appropriate column.

vin · tomates · carottes · gratin · limonade · coca · café · aubergines glace · bière · tarte · gâteau · pizza · champagne

du	de la	des
....	....	....
....	....	....
....	....	....
....	....	
....	....	
....		

Situation two is when 'some' or 'any' are on their own in a sentence, e.g. 'I want **some**!' or 'I don't have **any**'. In those examples **some** and **any** are not connected to any word: they are on their own. In this situation, the equivalent is just **en**.

I want some! **j'en veux!**   I don't have any. **je n'en ai pas.**

French equivalents of **some/any** on their own ➡ **en**

You'll find some more information on **en** in Unit 23.

Listen out for people using these forms and write down or record what they say to refer back to later as a review. Hearing real language is definitely the best way to learn and **to remember** what you have learnt!

Mental gymnastics 2

Which equivalent (**du**, **de la**, **de l'**, **des**, **de**, **d'** or **en**) would you choose when you want to say:

1   **Some** sauce, please! (sauce) ....
2   **Some** shallots (échalottes) ....
3   **Any** wine? (vin) ....
4   I play tennis (tennis) ....
5   We don't have **any**. (argent) ....
6   They don't have **a** car. (voiture) ....
7   Would you like **some pizza**? (pizza) ....
8   Do you sell **any bread**? (pain) ....
9   I have **some** money. (argent) ....
10 The girls play basketball. (faire ... basket) ....

Mental gymnastics 3

Rearrange the words in each question to make a sentence.

1   prend – de – Sébastien – bière – la
2   sport – fais – du – je
3   guitare – de – fait – la – Michel
4   Louise – des – vend – pizzas
5   les – veulent – gâteaux – enfants – des
6   mes – font – golf – parents – du
7   aime – natation – de – j' – faire – la
8   vous – prenez – gâteau – ne – de – pas?

How to use *y*

In this unit, you'll learn how to use the important one-letter word **y**.

Y's a stand-in

You might have noticed the **y** in **il y a** (there is/are) in Unit 7, or heard French speakers say **J'y vais!** (I'm going!) **Y** is one of those stand-in words you'll learn more about in Unit 23. It can be translated in a number of ways, but it is always used as a way to prevent having to repeat yourself. Let's look at some of its uses:

Y means there

Y often means 'there'. It's a really useful word when you don't want to repeat a whole location phrase. Here are a couple of examples:

- 'Est-ce que vous allez **chez Carine**?'   'Are you going **to Carine's house**?'
- 'Oui, nous **y** allons.'   'Yes, we're going (**there**)'.
La clé est **sur la table**.   The key is **on the table**.
Non, elle n'**y** est pas!   No, it's not **there**!

Where does *y* go?

Y usually goes before the verb, e.g. **j'y vais** (I'm going there), **j'y retourne** (I'm going back there) and **j'y habite** (I live there). In commands and instructions, **y** goes after the verb: **Allons-y!** Let's go (there)!

Mental gymnastics 1

Rearrange the words in each question to make a sentence which includes **y**.

1   allons – nous – y   ....
2   retourne – pas – y – n' – je   ....
3   est-ce – vous – que – habitez – y?   ....
4   Carine – passe – ses – y – vacances   ....
5   habitent – mes – y – parents   ....

How to say *in*, *to* & *at* about locations

18

In this unit, you'll learn some equivalents of 'in', 'to' and 'at' when referring to locations.

In, to and at

In French there is no difference between **in**, **to** and **at**, but you need to watch out for:

- whether the word that follows is feminine, plural or masculine
- the <u>type</u> of place you are referring to
- whether or not movement is involved.

In/to for feminine countries and regions

Even countries are either **feminine** or **masculine** in French. Many are feminine, and they are easy to spot:

feminine countries & continents → end with an **-e** in/to → **en**

I am <u>in</u> England/in Europe/in Africa.
Je suis en Angleterre/en Europe/en Afrique.

I am going <u>to</u> England/in Europe/in Africa.
Je vais en Angleterre/en Europe/en Afrique.

We are i<u>n</u> Ethiopia.   **Nous sommes en Éthiopie.**
We are going <u>to</u> Ethiopia.   **Nous allons en Éthiopie.**

Some countries end with **-e**, but are masculine:

le Mexique   le Mozambique   le Cambodge (Cambodia)   **le Zaïre**

En is also used before certain masculine countries starting with a vowel, to make them easier to say: **en Israël**, **en Angola**.

In/to for masculine countries
Masculine countries are also easy to spot:

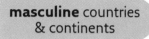 

masculine countries & continents → ending with any vowel except for -e or with a consonant → in/to → **au**

I am in Canada.	**Je suis au Canada.**
I am going to Canada.	**Je vais au Canada.**
We are in Japan.	**Nous sommes au Japon.**
We are going to Japan.	**Nous allons au Japon.**

In/to for countries with a plural name
Some countries and regions have a plural name, like in English. Notice how **les** becomes **aux** when you're talking about being in or going to one of these places; it's the same whether they are masculine or feminine:

The United States/I am in the United States.
Les États-Unis (m pl):
Je suis <u>aux</u> États-Unis.

The West Indies/We are going to the West Indies.
Les Antilles (f pl):
Nous allons aux Antilles.

at/to for other places

Now let's think about other types of location, such as shops and local facilities, and physical locations like mountains or beaches.

au before
masculine locations

à la before
feminine locations

equivalents of **at/to** + places

à l'
before **singular**
locations starting with
a vowel or an 'h'

aux
before **plural**
locations

I am going to the bakery.	**Je vais à la boulangerie.**
We are going to the cinema.	**Nous allons au cinéma.**
We are at the post office.	**Nous sommes à la poste.**
We are going to the mountains.	**Nous allons à la montagne.**
I am going to the hospital.	**Je vais à l'hôpital.**
She's going to the Olympic games.	**Elle va aux Jeux olympiques.**

Mental gymnastics 1

Solve the puzzles and find some more places with the in/to equivalents.

1	.... l.... ph....rm....c....	to the chemist's
2	....n A.... .... e	in/to Australia
3	... . J....p....n	in/to Japan
4	... . p....rc	in/to the park
5	.... R....m....	in/to Rome
6	... . c....n....m....	in/to the cinema

Mental gymnastics 2

Complete the sentences by using one of the words from the list.

boulangerie · **toilettes** · **Pérou** (m) · **Espagne** (f) · **école** · **musée**

1   J'habite au ...   .
2   Je vais en ...   .
3   Ils sont dans le ...   .
4   Nous allons à la ...   .
5   Elles sont à l'...   ....
6   Il est aux ...   .

In/to for cities and islands

I am in Melbourne.   **Je suis à Melbourne.**
I am going to Moscow.   **Je vais à Moscou.**

We are in Cuba/Mauritius/Reunion.
Nous sommes à Cuba/l'île Maurice/l'île de la Réunion.

There are a small number of masculine cities such as the port of **Le Havre** and **Le Mans**, famous for its racing circuit. The first part of their name changes like masculine countries:

Je vais au Havre.   I'm going to Le Havre.
Ils habitent au Mans.   They live in Le Mans.

in/inside for any places other than countries

For buildings, vehicles, and anything a person can go into.

places ➡ in/inside ➡ **dans le/le/l'/les**

I am in the bakery.	**Je suis dans la boulangerie.**
I am in(side) the cinema.	**Je suis dans le cinéma.**
We are in the car.	**Nous sommes dans la voiture.**

Mental gymnastics 3

Put the words below in the appropriate column.

Chine · Pérou · Manchester · Nigeria · Antilles · Hawaï · Mexique Paris · Brésil · Écosse · Delhi · France · Bretagne · États-Unis

à	en	au	aux
....	....	....	....
....	....	....	....
....	....	....	
....	....	....	

Mental gymnastics 4

Choose the right equivalent for 'in', 'to' or 'at'.

1   I'm going to Portugal.   ....
2   I'm in Portland.   ....
3   We're at the restaurant.   ....
4   They're in the Caribbean.   ....
5   She's going to church. (église)   ....
6   Chris lives in Nice.   ....
7   Émilie works in Great Britain. (Grande-Bretagne) ....
8   Are you in the café?   ....

Mind Map it! Complete the locations Mind Map.

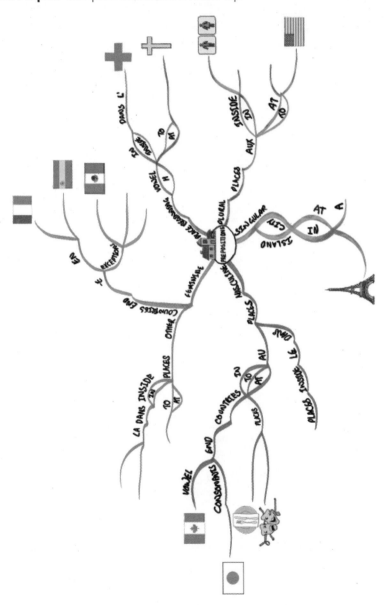

How to use *il faut*

In this unit, you'll learn the different uses of **il faut**.

Six letters for strong ideas

You might have come across il faut and wondered what it meant or how to use it. You'll find it in the dictionary under its **infinitive (G)** form falloir, and faut is the form for the present tense. This four-letter **verb (G)** is always used with il. In this case il means 'it'. Il faut has a strong meaning and can compel people to do things, as it literally means **it is necessary/mandatory to (have)**. It's used a lot in administrative French, notices and signs, instructions, and also in recipes.

Il faut can be translated into natural-sounding English using **need**, **must**, or **should**.

Need: shopping lists, and recipes
Il faut can mean **people/one/you need**, as in 'You need flour, eggs and milk to make pancakes'. It can also mean **we need** – the context will help you understand who the speaker is referring to.

For lists of items you need, just add the names of the items afterwards. Here's how:

il faut **+** name of item(s) **= You/we need + thing**

Il faut **des champignons, des oignons, et des œufs.**
You need (some) mushrooms, (some) onions and (some) eggs.

Chéri, pour demain matin, il faut **du lait, et du beurre.**
Darling, we need milk and butter for tomorrow morning.

I've got to have it!

You can slightly alter the **need** meaning to say **I really need ...** or **I've got to have ...**: just add me (pronounced *muh)* for **I**.

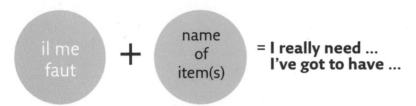

il me faut + name of item(s) = I really need ...
I've got to have ...

me for **I**; te for **you** (informal); lui for **he/she**; nous for **we**; vous for **you** (plural and informal); leur for **they**.

Il me faut **ma valise ce soir!** (at the airport)
I've got to have my suitcase tonight!

Il nous faut **les clés.**
We really need the keys.

Using il faut in the negative

Il faut can also be translated by 'people/one must/should' and il ne faut pas by 'people/one mustn't (or shouldn't)'. To use il faut in this way, just add the action one should or shouldn't do using the **infinitive** form of the verb.

il faut + infinitive = you must/should do ...

Il faut **faire le ménage avant votre départ**. (the holiday apartment landlord)
You must do the housework/clean up before you leave.

Il ne faut pas fumer ici. (a waiter speaking to a customer)
You shouldn't smoke in here./Smoking is not allowed in here.

Mental gymnastics 1

Rearrange the words in each question to make a sentence including **il faut**.

1   ce – venir – il – soir – faut ....!
2   faire – faut – du – il – sport ....
3   le – prendre – faut – bus – il ....
4   des – faut – fruits – manger – légumes – des – il – et ....
    ....
5   lait – œufs – des – faut – du – il – et ....
6   me – faut – sac – mon – il ....!

Mental gymnastics 2

How would you say in French:

1   We really need some milk.
2   You shouldn't smoke. (fumer)
3   I really need vitamins. (des vitamines)
4   You need (some) tomatoes, (some) tuna and (some) mayonnaise.
    (tomates – thon – mayonnaise)
5   You should choose. (choisir)
6   You must practise. (pratiquer)
7   We've got to have our luggage. (bagages)
8   One must try. (essayer)

How to give commands and instructions

20

In this unit, you'll learn how to give commands and instructions.

Just action!

In English, to give an order, you usually just use the **verb** (G): **Come! Eat! Call** me! **Come** in! No 'you' – you get straight to the point. French does the same: you use only the verb to give an order. For example:

Eat! **Mange!**   Listen! **Écoute!**

However, the examples above are for when you are talking to just one person. If you want to tell more than one person to do something you use a different form of the verb. Let's look at the different forms:

Single person, informal command
In Units 10, 11 and 12, you learnt how to use verbs in the **present tense** (G). To give commands or instructions to one person you know well, a person whom you call **tu**, you'll need to remember the **tu** form of the present tense. Let's take an example: **Take your keys**.

1 Use your verb wheel to find the **tu** form of **prendre** in the present tense
   → **tu prends**
2 Drop the **tu** in **tu prends** → prends
3 **Prends tes clés.**
   Take your keys.

Another example: **Come!**
1 **Tu** form of **venir** in the present tense → **tu viens**
2 Drop the **tu** in **tu viens** → viens
3 **Viens!**
   Come!

Single person, drop the -s, -ER and go!

The only exception to this pattern is for the **-ER** family and **aller**. In this case, you also drop the **-s** at the end of the verb. Let's take an example: 'Speak English, please!'

1 **Tu** form of **parler** in the present tense → tu parles
2 Drop the **tu** <u>and the</u> –s in **tu parles** → parle
3 **Parle anglais, s'il te plaît!**
  Speak English, please!

You don't need to think about the **-s** when you speak, as most of the time no one will hear the difference.

More than one person or polite commands

To give commands or instructions to more than one person or to a person whom you call **vous**, you'll need to remember the **vous** form of the present tense. Let's take some examples: 'Take your keys'.

1 **Vous** form of **prendre** in the present tense → vous prenez
2 Drop the **vous** in **vous prenez** → prenez
3 **Prenez vos clés.**
  Take your keys.

'Come!'

1 **Vous** form of **venir** in the present tense → vous venez
2 Drop the **vous** in **vous venez** → venez
3 **Venez!**
  Come!

'Speak English please!'

1 **Vous** form of **parler** in the present tense → vous parlez
2 Drop the **vous** in **vous parlez** → parlez
3 **Parlez anglais, s'il vous plaît!**
  Speak English, please!

Let's do it

In English, you use **let's + verb** to suggest or request things in a group:
'Let's go to the restaurant!'

In French, you use the nous form of the **verb** in the **present tense** (without **nous**).

1   Nous form of aller in the present tense → nous allons
2   Drop the nous in **nous allons** → allons
3   Allons au restaurant!
    Let's go to the restaurant!

nous

Mental gymnastics 1

You and your friends are bored. Here are some activities you could do. Let's be positive and turn these into 'let's' sentences!

1   aller au cinéma ....
2   jouer aux cartes ....
3   faire du shopping ....
4   rendre visite à des amis ....
5   visiter un musée ....
6   prendre un verre au café ....

Be! Have! Know!

These three verbs have special patterns for commands and instructions in French.

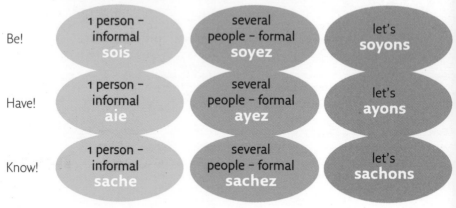

	1 person – informal	several people – formal	let's
Be!	**sois**	**soyez**	**soyons**
Have!	**aie**	**ayez**	**ayons**
Know!	**sache**	**sachez**	**sachons**

Vouloir 'to want' also has an irregular command form. It's mainly used in the **vous** form **veuillez**. It can be used to make polite requests: **Veuillez** nous excuser. **Please** forgive/excuse us.

Mental gymnastics 2

Solve the puzzles and find the commands or instructions for the following: vendre • être • aller • regarder • prendre • écouter.

1 GEERARD! ....
2 ZOCUTÉE! ....
3 NEEZDV! ....
4 YOZES! ....
5 AV! ....
6 NRDPES! ....

Don't do it!

In English, you use **do not** or **don't** to make negative commands or instructions. **Don't come!** (informal)

In French, you use: **ne** + verb in the present tense (without **tu**, **vous** or **nous**)

1 Tu form of **venir** in the present tense → tu viens
2 Drop the tu in **tu viens** → viens
3 Add ne and pas
4 Ne viens pas! Don't come!

Mental gymnastics 3

Rearrange the words to make a negative command or instruction.

1 pas – ne – venez ....
2 de – pas – gâteau – ne – faites ....
3 retard – soyez – pas – ne – en ....
4 le – ne – pas – train – prenez ....
5 vous – ne – pas – faites – mal ....
6 partez – ne – pas ! ....

Reflexive commands and instructions

To give commands or instructions with reflexives, use the **verb** + **reflexive bit** afterwards:
dépêche-toi! hurry! (informally)
Notice how the reflexive bit has changed from **te** to **toi** when it follows the command. We'll look at this in more detail in Unit 23.

To give negative commands or instructions with these verbs, use **ne + reflexive bit + verb + pas**.
Ne te dépêche pas! Don't hurry! (informally)

Mental gymnastics 4

How would you say these phrases in French?

1 Get up! (to one person, informal) ....
2 Wake up! (to a group of people) ....
3 Don't cut yourself! (to one person, informal) ....
4 Let's hurry! ....
5 Don't hurt yourself! (polite form) ....

Mental gymnastics 5

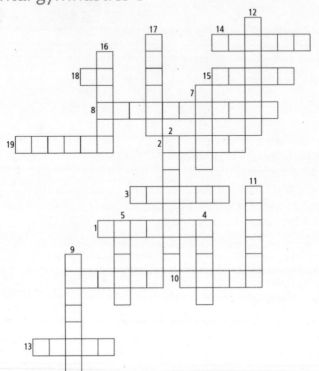

Across

1 Let's go out! (sortir)
2 ... un peu! (manger – to one child)
3 ... vos verbes! (savoir – to a group)
6 Come in! (entrer – to someone you don't know)
8 Let's phone your parents! (téléphoner)
10 ... demain. (venir – to an older neighbour whom you don't know well)
13 ... ton travail! (finir – to a teenager)
14 ..., s'il te plaît! (chanter – to your best friend)
15 ... la vérité. (dire – to a group)
18 ... en France. (aller – to your friend)
19 Let's drink! (boire)

Down

2 Let's walk! (marcher)
4 ... patients. (être – ask a group to be patient)
5 ... la porte! (ouvrir – to your brother)
7 ... ! (donner – to one person)
9 Let's sell our house! (vendre)
11 ... la première à droite. (prendre – to your boss)
12 Let's go! (partir)
16 ... une exception! (faire – to your boss again)
17 ... les clés! (donner – to a group)

How to say *mine, yours, his, hers, ours* and *theirs*

In this unit, you'll learn how to say 'mine', 'yours', 'his', 'hers', 'ours' and 'theirs'.

Genders genders

In English, if something belongs to you, you say it is 'mine'. If it belongs to her, you say it is 'hers'. If it belongs to both of us, it is 'ours' and so on. In French, this works in exactly the same way but with one added element – you must also look at the gender of the 'thing' that one's got (e.g. an object, animal, person or idea).

For example, 'a car' is **une voiture**. If you want to say that that one individual car is 'mine' you'll need the **feminine singular form** of **mine**: **la mienne**. If you have several cars and you want to say they are <u>all</u> 'mine', you'll have to choose the **feminine plural form** of **mine**: **les miennes**.

Let's look at this more closely:

Mine, yours, theirs, menu
On the next page are the options for saying who something belongs to. Choose according to the gender of what you are speaking about.

Mental gymnastics 1

Fill in the missing letters to find some of the equivalents of mine, yours, his/hers, ours and theirs.

1 l....　m....　....nn....　　4 l....s　s....　....nn....s
2 l....　v....tr....　　　　　5 l....　t....　....n
3 l....　l....　....r　　　　　6 l....s　n....tr....s

Mental gymnastics 2

Solve the puzzles and find some of the equivalents of mine, yours, his/hers, ours and theirs.

1 TE ÔLERN　　..
2 LE SULERS　　...
3 NI LEEM　　..
4 SE LENINA　　..
5 TÔ RESVLES　　...
6 NE ITESSL　　...

Mental gymnastics 3

Which equivalent of mine, yours, his/hers, ours and theirs would you choose when speaking about:

1 une maison – hers　　..
2 un château – theirs　　...
3 des pizzas – ours　　..
4 des enfants – mine　　...
5 une fille – yours (informal)　　......................................
6 une voiture – yours (formal)　　....................................

How to compare people, things and actions

22

In this unit, you'll learn how to make comparisons.

More or less spacious than
In English, there are two ways to compare things. Either you add **-er** at the end of an **adjective** (G), e.g. young → young**er**, or you just use 'more', e.g. spacious → more spacious. Which of these two you use generally depends on the length of the word.

More is plus
In French, you use **plus** followed by the adjective to make a comparison. The structure works like this:

Je suis plus grand que Claude. I'm **taller than** Claude. (male speaking)
Elle est plus grande qu'Emmanuel. She's **taller than** Emmanuel.
Tu joues plus vite que Florian. You play **faster than** Florian.

Here's a variation for when you're comparing how many <u>things</u> you have.

J'ai plus de bijoux que Frédérique. I have **more** jewels **than** Frédérique.
Elle a plus d'amis que Claire. She's got **more** friends **than** Claire.

Less is moins
To say something is 'less expensive' or 'less fast' you use the word 'moins'

Je suis moins **grand** que **Claude.** I'm **less tall than** Claude. (male speaking)
Elle est moins **grande** qu'**Emmanuel.** She's **less tall than** Emmanuel.
Tu joues moins **vite** que **Florian.** You play **less fast than** Florian.

Here's a variation for when you're comparing how many things you have.

J'ai moins de **bijoux** que **Frédérique.** I have **fewer** jewels **than** Frédérique.
Elle a moins d'**amis** que **Claire.** She's got **fewer** friends **than** Claire.

Aussi, autant

In English, to say that two things are equally tall, equally good, equally expensive, you say they are 'as ... as'. To say this in French, you use **aussi ... que** for adjectives and **autant de/d'**... for things.

Here's the structure for when you're comparing things and how things are done.

Je suis aussi **grand** que **Claude.** I'm **as tall as** Claude. (male speaking)
Elle est aussi **grande** qu'**Emmanuel.** She's **as tall as** Emmanuel.
Tu joues aussi **vite** que **Florian.** You play **as fast as** Florian.

Here's a variation for when you're comparing how many things you have.

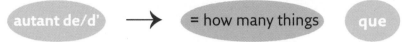

J'ai autant de **bijoux** que **Frédérique.** I have **as many** jewels **as** Frédérique.
Elle a autant d'**amis** que **Claire.** She's got **as many** friends **as** Claire.

Mental gymnastics 1

Look at the sign in brackets (+, - or =) and say what's missing:

plus/plus de/plus d'
moins/moins de
aussi/autant de/que/qu'

1   Les éléphants d'Afrique sont .... féroces que les éléphants d'Asie. (+)
2   Les enfants d'Annie ont .... jeux que vous. (=)
3   Mon frère est .... grand .... moi. (+)
4   Mes parents font .... voyages maintenant (-).
5   Votre sœur est .... sympathique .... vous! (=)
6   Ah! Tu as .... bagages .... ta mère! (-)
7   Votre mari a .... humour .... le mien! (+)
8   Mon fils a .... patience .... moi! (=)

Mental gymnastics 2

Which French word or phrase would you choose for the English word in bold?

1   He speaks **as** fluently as her now.
    a. plus   b. autant   c. aussi
2   You have **as much** talent as our brother!
    a. aussi   b. autant de   c. moins de
3   I feel **more** confident now.
    a. plus   b. moins   c. aussi
4   They had **less** trouble than us!
    a. plus de   b. moins de   c. autant de
5   She has **more** power than the prince.
    a. moins   b. plus de   c. plus
6   You have **as many** shoes as a shoe shop!
    a. aussi   b. plus de   c. autant de

Irregular comparisons

As in English, some comparison words don't follow the regular pattern,
e.g. **good** becomes **better** (rather than 'gooder')

bon(ne) good	becomes	**meilleur(e)** better
bien well	becomes	**mieux** better
mauvais(e) bad	becomes	**pire** or **plus mauvais** worse
petit small	becomes	**moindre** or **plus petit** smaller, lesser

---

Mental gymnastics 3

Solve the anagrams, then match the adjectives on the right with their comparison forms on the left.

1 RINOMED .... a. USIVAMA ....
2 UXIME .... b. TEPIT ....
3 RIEP .... c. NOB ....
4 ILULEREM .... d. NIBE ....

The most and the least

In French, to say the most or the least you use **plus** and **moins** again, except this time you put **le**, **la** or **les** in front, e.g. **la plus haute tour** 'the highest (most high) tower'. You now know the masculine, feminine and plural French pattern. So use **le** for masculine words, **la** for feminine ones and **les** for all plural words.

le plus beau village   the most beautiful village
la plus grande ville   the biggest city
les plus beaux villages   the most beautiful villages

Use the same irregulars you learnt on the previous page to say 'the best', 'the worst' etc., e.g.
les meilleurs restaurants 'the best restaurants'.

Mental gymnastics 4

Rearrange the words in each question to make a sentence that includes a comparison.

1   plus – que – est – il – Christophe – sympa ....

2   avez – clients – autant – nous – de – vous – que ....
     ....

3   ont – d' – que – vous – moins – argent – ils ....

4   es – grand – que – Carine – aussi – tu ....

5   cuisine – Nathalie – mieux ....

6   melons – meilleurs – sont – ces ....

7   meilleur – le – c' – gâteau – est ....

8   vieux – je – le – plus – suis ....

Mental gymnastics 5

How would you say in French:

1   We have fewer holidays. (vacances)
     ....

2   This cheese is better. (fromage)
     ....

3   I have as many problems.
     ....

4   The children are taller.
     ....

5   Florence has more humour.
     ....

6   They work less.
     ....

7   French wines are the best. (vins)
     ....

8   This shirt is the least expensive. (chemise – chère)
     ....

How to say *me, you, him, her, it, us* and *them*

In this unit, you'll learn the various ways of saying 'me', 'you', 'him', 'her', 'it', 'us' and 'them', as well as how and when to use 'them'.

Me, me, me

In **English**, there are some little words, which **stand in** for names of people, things or animals. Let's call them **short stand-ins**, as they are usually quite short words: me, you, him, her, it, us, and them. We use them when we don't want to repeat a **noun** (**G**) over and over.

For example, the following paragraph is very repetitive:

I want some **shoes**. I want the **shoes** to be green and comfy;
I have seen the **shoes** in a shop in town.

Instead, you can just say: I want some **shoes**. I want **them** to be green and comfy; I have seen **them** in a shop in town. 'Them' stands in for **shoes** and avoids repetition.

This is the corresponding set of these short stand-ins in English: 'me', 'you', 'him', 'her', 'it', 'us' and 'them'.

In French, however, there is more than one set depending on which word comes before the stand-in. Before deciding which one to use you need to understand the **verb buddy system**. Let's look at it:

Verbs and their buddy
In English, many **verbs** have some kind of buddy, such as **at**, **up**, **down**, **away**. These buddies are quite important, as they make the meaning of the words change. For example, **look** has different meanings in **look up**, **look away**, or **look at**.

This is also the case in French: many verbs have buddies. These are often à or de. They do not always change the meaning of the words, as in English. However, without them, the verbs would sound as wrong as 'I speak Jamie' instead of 'I speak **to** Jamie'.

Dictionaries will tell you if a verb has a buddy and how the meaning changes. Here are some useful French verbs and their buddies:

Buddy 'à'
Communication and travelling verbs often have à as their buddy.

aller à	to go **to**
demander à	to ask (someone)
donner à	to give (someone)
parler à	to speak **to**
réfléchir à	to think about something
répondre à	to answer (someone)
retourner à	to return **to**
téléphoner à	to phone (someone)

Buddy 'de'

avoir besoin de	to need (something or someone)
avoir envie de	to feel like something/to want someone
avoir peur de	to be afraid of someone or something
être amoureux de	to be in love with
dépendre de	to depend on
rêver de	to dream of
se souvenir de	to remember someone or something

Stand-in and buddy
In French, the buddy helps you to choose the right stand-in.

Here are some examples using 'him':

• **situation 1: No buddy**
  The equivalent of 'him' when the verb has no buddy is **le/l'**:
  She hates **Paul**. She hates **him**.   **Elle déteste Paul. Elle le déteste.**

- **situation 2: buddy 'à'**
  The equivalent of 'him' when the verb has **à** as a buddy is **lui**:
  She is speaking to **François**.   She is speaking to **him**.
  Elle parle à François.   **Elle lui parle.**

- **situation 3: buddy 'de'**
  The equivalent of 'him' when the verb has **de** as a buddy is **lui**:
  She is in love with **François**.   She is in love with **him**.
  Elle est amoureuse de François.   **Elle est amoureuse** de lui.

- **situation 4: on its own**
  The equivalent of 'him' when used on its own is **lui**:
  Him? I hate him.   **Lui? Je le déteste.**

Weird word order and disappearing buddy

As you can see, you need to think in another way when using the stand-ins,
because the order of words is different from English.
Elle lui parle is literally 'She (to) him speaks'

Did you notice? Buddy **à** disappears when a stand-in is used:
Elle lui parle → No **à** any more

me, you, him, her, us, and them in every situation!

On the next pages, you'll find the sets of French stand-ins.

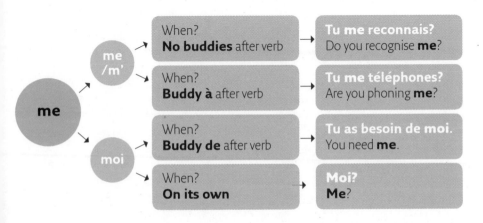

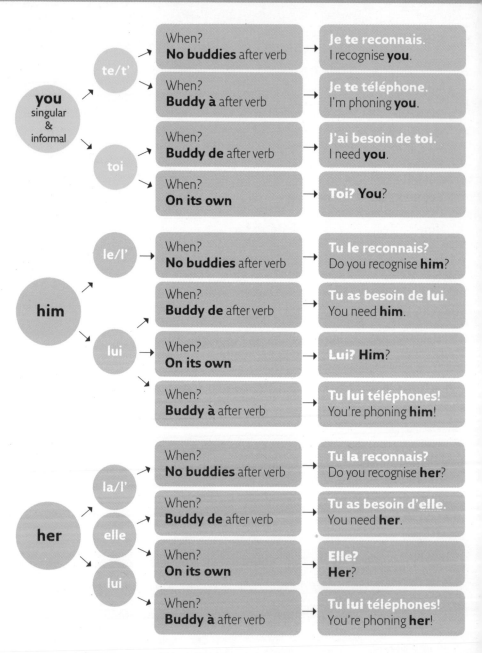

you
singular & informal

te/t'

When?
No buddies after verb → **Je te reconnais.** I recognise **you**.

When?
Buddy à after verb → **Je te téléphone.** I'm phoning **you**.

toi

When?
Buddy de after verb → **J'ai besoin de toi.** I need **you**.

When?
On its own → **Toi? You**?

him

le/l'

When?
No buddies after verb → **Tu le reconnais?** Do you recognise **him**?

lui

When?
Buddy de after verb → **Tu as besoin de lui.** You need **him**.

When?
On its own → **Lui? Him**?

When?
Buddy à after verb → **Tu lui téléphones!** You're phoning **him**!

her

la/l'

When?
No buddies after verb → **Tu la reconnais?** Do you recognise **her**?

elle

When?
Buddy de after verb → **Tu as besoin d'elle.** You need **her**.

When?
On its own → **Elle? Her**?

lui

When?
Buddy à after verb → **Tu lui téléphones!** You're phoning **her**!

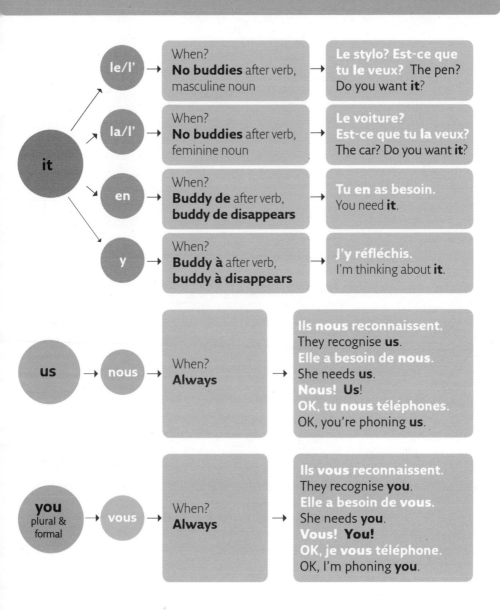

it

le/l' → When?
No buddies after verb, masculine noun → Le stylo? Est-ce que tu **le** veux? The pen? Do you want **it**?

la/l' → When?
No buddies after verb, feminine noun → Le voiture? Est-ce que tu **la** veux? The car? Do you want **it**?

en → When?
Buddy de after verb, **buddy de disappears** → Tu **en** as besoin. You need **it**.

y → When?
Buddy à after verb, **buddy à disappears** → J'**y** réfléchis. I'm thinking about **it**.

us → **nous** → When?
Always → Ils **nous** reconnaissent. They recognise **us**. Elle a besoin de **nous**. She needs **us**. **Nous! Us**! OK, tu **nous** téléphones. OK, you're phoning **us**.

you
plural & formal → **vous** → When?
Always → Ils **vous** reconnaissent. They recognise **you**. Elle a besoin de **vous**. She needs **you**. **Vous! You!** OK, je **vous** téléphone. OK, I'm phoning **you**.

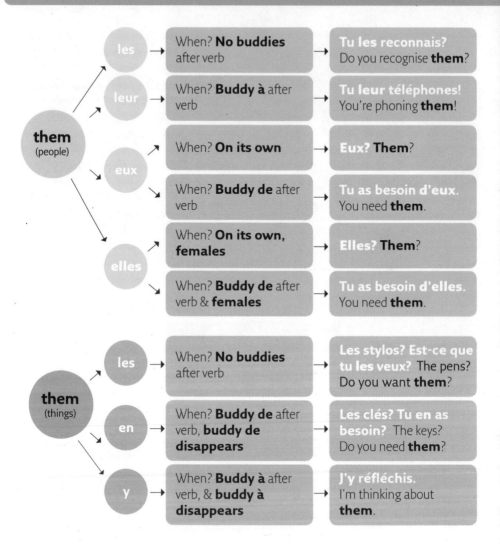

them (people)

	When? **No buddies** after verb	Tu **les** reconnais? Do you recognise **them**?
les		
leur	When? **Buddy à** after verb	Tu **leur** téléphones! You're phoning **them**!
eux	When? **On its own**	**Eux? Them?**
	When? **Buddy de** after verb	Tu as besoin d'**eux**. You need **them**.
elles	When? **On its own, females**	**Elles? Them?**
	When? **Buddy de** after verb & **females**	Tu as besoin d'**elles**. You need **them**.

them (things)

les	When? **No buddies** after verb	Les stylos? Est-ce que tu **les** veux? The pens? Do you want **them**?
en	When? **Buddy de** after verb, **buddy de disappears**	Les clés? Tu **en** as besoin? The keys? Do you need **them**?
y	When? **Buddy à** after verb, & **buddy à disappears**	J'**y** réfléchis. I'm thinking about **them**.

Not before me

For **negative** (**G**) sentences, here's where the **ne** and **pas** fit in:
For <u>no</u> buddies and <u>disappearing</u> buddies situations:

ne + stand-in word + verb + pas

Je ne le connais pas. I don't know him.   **Je ne les veux pas.** I don't want them.

For the other situations:

ne + **verb** + pas + **little buddy** + **stand-in word**

Je ne **dépends** pas **d'eux.**   I don't depend on them.
Il ne **rêve** pas **d'elle.**   He doesn't dream of her.

Stand-in words, commands and instructions

To give commands or instructions with stand-in words, the **verb** is followed by the relevant **stand-in word**:

verb + stand-in word: moi, toi, lui, le/la, nous, vous, leur/les

Phone me!   **Téléphone-moi!**
Please give **us** the key.   **Donnez-nous la clé, s'il vous plaît.**

To give negative commands or instructions with stand-in words, use
ne + **stand-in word** + **verb** + pas.

Do not lose it! (formally)   **Ne la perdez pas!** (speaking about a key, une clé)
Do not wait for us! (informally)   **Ne nous attends pas!**

Mental gymnastics 1

Rearrange the jumbled-up words to make sentences that include stand-ins.

1	les – connais – je	....
2	prend – la – elle	....
3	nous – adorons – les	....
4	veut – il – en	....
5	besoin – elles – ai – d' – j'	....
6	ne – vous – me – pas – connaissez	....
7	lui – ils – téléphonent	....
8	t' – attend – elle – ne – pas	....

Mental gymnastics 2

Which stand-in word would you use to replace the words in bold?

1   Je prends **la robe**.   ....
2   J'attends **Marie**.   ....
3   Elle veut **les chaussures**.   ....
4   Il veut **le ballon**.   ....
5   Nous avons besoin **des clés**. ....
6   Je demande à **Isabelle**.   ....

Mental gymnastics 3

What does that mean in English? Translate the following sentences, which all contain stand-ins. Sometimes more than one correct answer is possible!

1   Je lui réponds.   ....
2   Elle rêve de toi.   ....
3   Ils en ont besoin.   ....
4   Il y réfléchit.   ....
5   Nous lui demandons.   ....
6   Vous avez peur d'eux? ....

Mental gymnastics 4

How would you say in French:

1   They are phoning me.   ....
2   I'm in love with you. (informal) ....
3   She's speaking to him.   ....
4   They need me!   ....
5   You? We don't know you! (formal) ....
6   I want it! (speaking about a diamond: un diamant)

....

Mind Map it! Complete this Mind Map or do your own for the French equivalents of me, you, him, her, it, us and them.

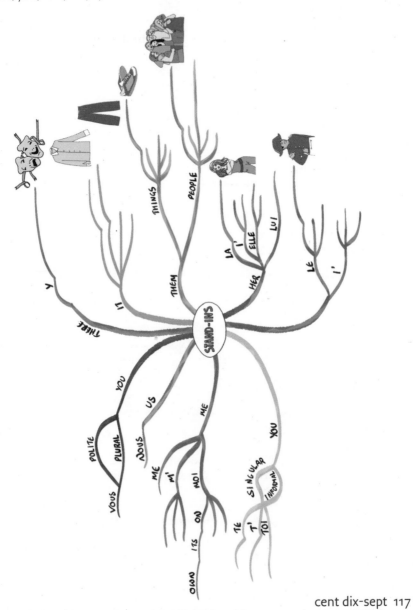

How to talk about what happened 24

So, what happened?

In English, you could talk about the past this way:
'I **spoke** to Mary' and 'We **visited** a castle' or also this way: 'I **have eaten**' and 'I **have been** to Paris'. In French these are both expressed in the same way, using the **perfect tense** (**G**).

Avoir and the past
You need two words to make the perfect tense:
- the verb **avoir** (have – see Unit 7 or the verb wheel if you have forgotten it)
- a 'past part'.

The **subject** (**G**) is followed by the correct form of **avoir** + the past part.

I **spoke** to Marie	**J'ai parlé à Marie**
We **visited** a castle	**Nous avons visité un château**
I **have eaten**	**J'ai mangé**

The word order goes like this:

person, animal or thing — present tense form of **avoir** — 'past part' form of verb

Past parts
In English, past parts are forms of the verbs such as **written**, **spoken,** or **worked**, as in 'I **have written** a letter'. How are past parts made up in French? Most verbs have a past part ending specific to their family:

- the **-ER** family's ending is **-é** *ay*
- the **-IR** family's ending is **-i** *ee*
- the **-RE** family's ending is **-u** *ew*

As with the present tense, you just:

1   take the ending off the **infinitive** (**G**), e.g. for **parler**,
     the **-er** bit → **parl-**

 **er**

2   add the 'past part' ending → **parl**-é → **parlé** and that's it,
     you have a past part in French!

Mental gymnastics 1

Join the halves together to complete the past parts.

-mé -du -si -ni -du -dié -si -vé -du -lé -chi -du

1 par–............	4 ren–............	7 étu–............	10 per–............
2 réus–............	5 ai–............	8 atten–............	11 choi–............
3 ven–............	6 fi–............	9 réflé–............	12 trou–............

What you didn't do

To talk about what you didn't do, just surround **avoir** with the two fellows **ne/n'**
and **pas**.

I did not speak to Marie.   **Je n'ai pas parlé à Marie.**
We didn't visit a castle.   **Nous n'avons pas visité de château.**

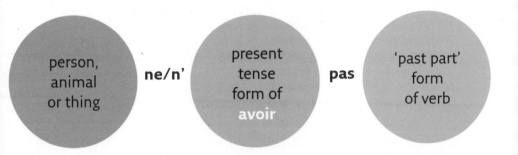

person, animal or thing   **ne/n'**   present tense form of **avoir**   **pas**   'past part' form of verb

Mental gymnastics 2

Solve these puzzles to find some past tense sentences.

1   J'.... .... v....nd.... m.... m.... ....s.... .....
    I sold my house.
2   M....n b....b.... .... gr....ss.....
    My baby put on weight.
3   N.... ....s ....v....ns r....fl....ch.....
    We thought (about it).
4   ....v....z – v.... ....s ....tt....nd....?
    Did you wait?
5   T.... m....r.... n'.... p....s t....l....ph....n.....
    Your mother didn't phone.
6   ....ls ....nt tr....v.... ....ll.....
    They worked.
7   V.... ....s ....v...z ch.... ....s....?
    Did you choose?
8   T.... n'.... .... p....s r....g....rd.... l.... t....l....?
    Didn't you watch TV?

Some like it better with être
Most verbs make their past with **avoir**, however some verbs make it with
être (to be). We first met this verb in Unit 4.

The verbs that go with **être** are:

naître (to be born) and **mourir** (to die)
venir (to come) and **aller** (to go)
entrer (to enter/get in) and **sortir** (to go out)
partir (to leave/to go) and **rester** (to stay)
monter (to go up(stairs)), **descendre** (to go down(stairs)) and **tomber** (to fall down)
arriver (to arrive)/**rentrer** (to come home)/**retourner** (to return)

In an **ascending** and then **descending** 'life' sequence:

Ascending:
naître (né) – **aller** (allé) – **venir** (venu) – **entrer** (entré)– **sortir** (sorti)
partir (parti) – **monter** (monté) – **arriver** (arrivé) (top)

Descending:
rentrer (rentré) – **retourner** (retourné) – **rester** (resté) –
descendre (descendu) – **tomber** (tombé) – **mourir** (mort)

I went to the cinema.	**Je suis allé au cinéma.**
I was born on the 10th July.	**Je suis né le 10 juillet.**

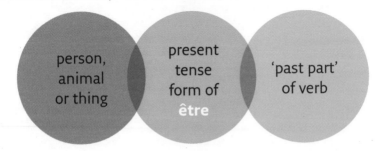

Did you notice? Some past parts are irregular. You will find the most important ones on the verb wheel. Use associations to memorise them. For example, the past part of **voir** (to see) is **vu**; you could link it to the expression 'déjà vu', meaning something that we think we've seen or experienced before.

Masculine, feminine, plural, the past and être

With the verb **être**, the masculine, feminine and plural pattern makes a comeback.

Following the same patterns as the regular descriptive words, the past part has either a masculine, feminine or plural form depending on **who is speaking** or **who we're talking about**:

Vincent came.	**Vincent est venu.**
Caroline came.	**Caroline est venue.**
Vincent and Caroline came.	**Vincent et Caroline sont venus.**
Caroline and Eloïse came.	**Caroline et Eloïse sont venues.**

Reflexives like it with être too

To make the past of the **reflexive verbs** (G) you learnt in Unit 12, you also use the verb **être**. The important thing to remember here is that the reflexive bit goes <u>before</u> **être**:

I woke up. **Je me suis réveillé.**
Julie and Constance hurried up. **Elles se sont dépêchées.**

Mental gymnastics 3

Join the beginnings of sentences on the left with the endings on the right to make some sentences in the past.

1	Franck et Pierre	a	sont rentrées.
2	Mylène	b	es tombée?
3	Julien, tu	c	est arrivé.
4	Carol et Ève	d	est née en France.
5	Stéphane	e	es sorti?
6	Annie, tu	f	sont venus.

Mental gymnastics 4

Fill in the missing letters to complete these sentences in the past:

1 ....l s'....st pr....p....r.....
   He got ready.

2 ....ll.... s s....nt ....rr....v.... ....s.
   They have arrived.

3 J'.... .... p....rd.... m.... cl.....
   I have lost my key.

4 N.... ....s ....v....ns h....b....t.... .... P....r....s.
   We lived in Paris.

5 V.... ....s n'....v....z p....s v....s....t.... l.... L.... ....vr....!
   You have not visited the Louvre!

6 ....ll.... ....st ....ll.... ....n ....str....l.... .....
   She went to Australia.

How to talk about what used to be

25

In Unit 24, you learnt how to say 'I have done' or 'I did' something. In this unit, you'll learn how to talk about what you used to do regularly in the past as well how to describe situations in the past.

I used to rule the world

When you regularly did something in the past but you don't do it any longer, you say:
'I used to go to the gym every day', 'He used to come with us', 'They used to listen to music'.

In French, the **tense** (G) used to talk about what used to be is called the **imperfect tense** (G). It works like the **present tense** (G) – you need 'I', 'you', 'he' or another **subject** (G), then the **verb** (G) with special endings.

Another tense with different endings

As with the present tense in Unit 10, choosing an ending depends on whether you are talking about 'I', 'you' or 'he'. For example, **j'aimais** 'I used to like' and **il aimait** 'he used to like'.

It's also quite useful to remember the present tense forms for **nous**. They will be the starting forms for this past tense. Check in Units 10 and 11 or on your verb wheel to remind yourself how the **nous** form is constructed.

Start off with the **nous** form of the present tense and get rid of the –**ons**:

finissons → **finiss**

 **ons**

then add the endings to the bit you are left with: **finiss–**

As with the present tense, each **je, tu, il/elle, nous, vous, ils/elles** calls for a specific ending.

eh, eh, eh: the sound of the imperfect

Here are the endings for the imperfect:

The endings for **je, tu, il, elle, ils** and **elles** sound the same: **eh**.

Did you notice? The endings for **nous** and **vous** are very similar to those of the present tense! Just an extra 'i' for the imperfect tense.

Mental gymnastics 1

Take two minutes to memorise as many endings on the previous page as you can.

How many endings can you now recall without looking back at the previous page?

Try to recall them again in **two hours**, in **one day** and in **one week**. The more you repeat them, the longer you will remember them.

The song we were singing

In English, we can describe actions that took place in the past like this: 'I was walking', 'he was working', 'they were talking'. In French, you use the imperfect tense for this, e.g. **il travaillait** he was working.

When one action is interrupted by another, the imperfect tense is followed by the perfect tense. For example, 'I was walking down the street when I bumped into a friend' is '**Je march<u>ais</u> dans la rue, quand j'<u>ai</u> rencontr<u>é</u> un ami**'.

Mental gymnastics 2

Join the halves together to complete the verbs, then match them with 'il', 'elle', 'je', 'nous', 'vous' or 'ils' using the prompts below.

-daient -nais -liez -tait -dait -vais -taient -ssions

1	.... pou–.............	I used to be able to ...
2	.... atten–.............	She used to wait ...
3	.... réussi–.............	We used to succeed ...
4	.... per–.............	They used to lose ...
5	.... télépho–.............	You (informal) used to phone ...
6	.... habi–.............	He used to live ...
7	.... vou–.............	You (formal) wanted ...
8	.... écou–.............	They used to listen ...

Mental gymnastics 3

Complete the words with their missing vowels to make the following verbs in the imperfect tense:
jouer, faire, devoir, réfléchir, étudier, rendre, prendre, vendre.

1   ....ls   r....nd.... ....nt
2   v.... ....s   pr....n.... ....z
3   j....   f.... ....s.... ....s
4   n.... ....s   j.... ....ns
5   ....ll....   ....t....d.... ....t
6   t....   d....v.... ....s
7 l   v....nd.... ....t
8   ....ll....s   r....fl....ch....ss.... ....nt

Mental gymnastics 4

Complete the criss-criss using the imperfect tense.

Across

3   Il ... (descendre) dans le salon.
6   Nous ... (habiter) à Lyon.
7   Tu ... (réussir) tous tes examens.

Down

1   Nous ... (marcher) dans le parc.
2   Vous ... (attendre)?
3   Elles ... (devoir) travailler.
4   J'... (écouter) de la musique.
5   Je ... (prendre) le train tous les jours.

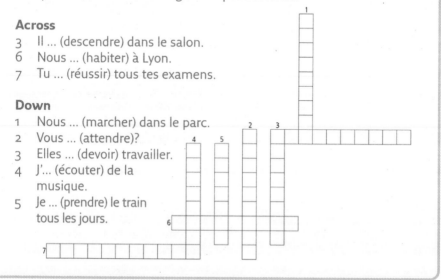

How to talk about what is going to happen

In this unit, you'll learn how to talk about what is going to happen.

In English, you could talk about the immediate future like this: 'I**'m going to** dance tonight' or 'She**'s going to** take the bus'. It's generally:

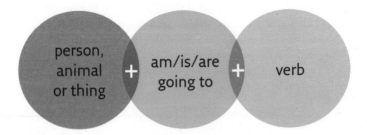

person, animal or thing + am/is/are going to + verb

Va va voom

In French, it's almost the same. You need to use **aller** (the equivalent of 'to go')in the present tense. You learnt about this **verb** (**G**) in Unit 11. Look on your verb wheel to remind yourself how **aller** works.

I **am going to** dance tonight	**Je vais danser ce soir**
She **is going to** take the bus	**Elle va prendre le bus**

The immediate future follows this structure:

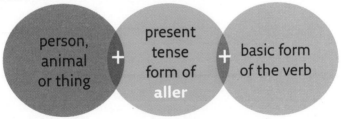

person, animal or thing + present tense form of **aller** + basic form of the verb

Leave 'be' out of it

Remember! Use **aller** only: no **être**, **suis**, or **est**. Literally in French, you say 'I go to call', 'She goes to take the bus' – so you don't need the 'am' of 'I am going'.

So rather than saying 'am going to' you just use 'go':
'I go to eat dinner' rather than 'I'm going to eat dinner'.
'He goes to call his friend' rather than 'He is going to call his friend'.

Not going to

So how do you talk about what you're not going to do? Just by surrounding the **aller** form with **ne** and **pas**.

I am not going to dance tonight.	**Je ne vais pas danser ce soir.**
She's not going to take the bus.	**Elle ne va pas prendre le bus.**

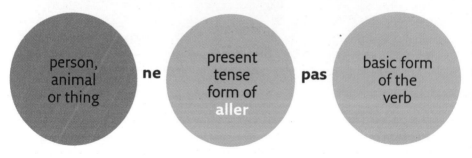

Mental gymnastics 1

Rearrange the words in each question to make a sentence about the near future.

1   ej iasv à riaPs ....
2   onus lansol repdenr eds stooph ....
3   leel av nevri ....
4   osuv lezla ua eusém ....
5   lsi vnot theranc ....
6   sav-ut à Neic? ....

Mental gymnastics 2

Here are some more mixed-up sentences about the near future to unravel:

1   n' – pas – nous – répondre – allons   ....
2   vont – réfléchir – ils   ....
3   Philippe – pas – ne – venir – va   ....
4   allez – est-ce – contacter – que – vous – hôtel – l'?
....
5   travailler – pas – vas – ne – tu   ....
6   pas – la – elle – va – cuisine – faire – ne
....

Stand-in fitting in
Finally, if you want to talk about the near future using stand-in words (the ones you learnt in Unit 23), here's how:

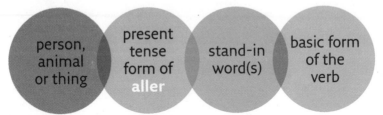

We're going to phone him.   **Nous allons lui téléphoner.**
I'm going to take it.   **Je vais le prendre.**

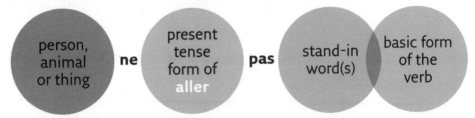

We're **not** going to phone him.   **Nous n'allons pas lui téléphoner.**
I'm **not** going to take it.   **Je ne vais pas le prendre.**

Mental gymnastics 3

How would you say in French:

1   You're going to live in Paris. (informal)

....

2   She's going to speak to her.

....

3   We're going to watch TV.

....

4   They're going to sell their house.

....

5   I'm going to make a cake.

....

6   Are you (plural) going to visit this castle? (visiter)

....

How to talk about what will happen

In this unit, you'll learn how to talk about what you will do in the future.

What will be, will be

When you intend to do something later or tomorrow you use the word 'will': 'I'**ll bring** some pizzas' or 'we **will go** to Canada next summer'. This is called the **future tense** (G).

In French, the future tense works like the **present** (G) (Unit 10) and **imperfect** (G) (Unit 26) tenses – you need 'I', 'you', 'he' or another subject, then the **verb** (G) with special endings.

rrr ... the sound of the future

To make a future verb, you start off with the **infinitive** (G), the form of the verb that you find in the dictionary – but **don't** remove the ending. Instead, you add to the endings directly at the end. This is why you'll recognise the future by the **rrr** sound, as there'll always be an **r** near the ending.

Let's look at some examples:
I **will bring** some pizzas.
J'apporterai **des pizzas.**
We **will go** to Canada next summer.
Nous partirons **au Canada l'été prochain.**

Endings sounding like avoir

As with the present tense, each **je**, **tu**, **il/elle**, **nous**, **vous**, **ils/elles** calls for a specific ending. Apart from **nous** and **vous**, the endings of the future tense look very much like the verb **avoir**:

Mental gymnastics 1

Join the halves together to complete the verbs, then match them with **je**, **tu**, **il/elle**, **nous**, **vous** or **ils/elles**.

−drez −irai −llerons −teras −ndrons −eront −nera −endront

1 .... rempl−..............   5 .... habi−..............
2 .... cherch−..............   6 .... att−..............
3 .... ren−..............   7 .... travai−..............
4 .... don−..............   8 .... répo−..............

Verbs with a different future form

For some very common verbs, the future tense is not formed using the infinitive. They have a special basis from which the future is formed. Fortunately, you can find many of these exceptions on the verb wheel, which you can use to memorise them.

Here are some of the most useful verbs with an irregular future form:

aller	**ir–**	**j'irai**	pouvoir	**pourr–**	**je pourrai**
avoir	**aur–**	**j'aurai**	savoir	**saur–**	**je saurai**
devoir	**devr–**	**je devrai**	venir	**viendr–**	**je viendrai**
être	**ser–**	**je serai**	voir	**verr–**	**je verrai**
faire	**fer–**	**je ferai**	vouloir	**voudr–**	**je voudrai**

Mental gymnastics 2

Solve these anagrams to find some irregular futures.

1 LI RAAU ....
2 LESEL TRIDONVEN ....
3 USON RURSPONO ....
4 EJ RARIVE ....
5 LEEL RAEF ....
6 UT RASSE ....

What you won't do

To talk about what you won't do, just surround the verb with the two fellows **ne/n'** and **pas**.

I won't come.   **Je ne viendrai pas.**
We won't visit the castle.   **Nous ne visiterons pas le château.**

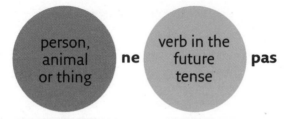

person, animal or thing **ne** verb in the future tense **pas**

Gee! y doesn't go with 'irai'

As the sound 'ee' would be too long, **y** can be omitted with the future tense of **aller**. You just say **j'irai** – and that implies **y** 'there' – 'I will go (there)'. Short and simple!

Mental gymnastics 3

Fill in the missing vowels to complete these future tense sentences.

**faire · choisir · attendre · téléphoner · réfléchir · vouloir
vendre · écouter**

1	....l t'....c.... ....t....r.....	He will listen to you.
2	....ls n.... v.... ....dr....nt p....s.	They will not want.
3	N.... ....s ....tt....ndr....ns.	We will wait.
4	T.... ch.... .... s....r....s.	You'll choose.
5	....ll.... n.... v....ndr.... p....s.	She won't sell.
6	J.... r....fl....ch....r....	I will think about it.
7	....ll....s l.... f....r....nt.	They will do it.
8	V.... ....s n.... t....l....ph....n....r....z p....s!	You won't phone!

Mental gymnastics 4

Future crossword

Across

1 Vous ... sur la lune. (aller)
3 Il ... ses clés. (chercher)
5 Nous ... plus tôt. (finir)
7 Elle nous ... (téléphoner)
9 Ils ... plus heureux. (être)

Down

2 Vous ... vos enfants. (voir)
4 Tu ... travailler. (devoir)
6 Je ... beaucoup de films.
   (regarder)
8 Elle ... venir. (pouvoir)

In this unit, you'll learn how to use a variety of negative forms.

The negative pair

In English, when you use negative words like **never** or **nothing**, you can use them on their own, e.g. **never!** or as part of a full sentence: 'I have never been to France'.

Likewise, in French, you can use jamais (never) and other negative words on their own, jamais! or in a sentence. The only difference is that you also have to use ne in sentences: **Je ne suis jamais allé en France.**

Questions and negative answers

Here are the negative words paired with their positive opposites:

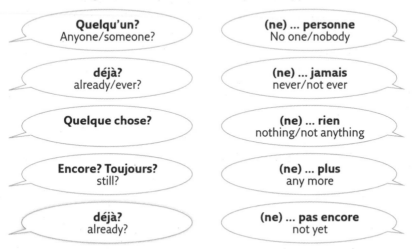

Quelqu'un?
Anyone/someone?

(ne) ... personne
No one/nobody

déjà?
already/ever?

(ne) ... jamais
never/not ever

Quelque chose?

(ne) ... rien
nothing/not anything

Encore? Toujours?
still?

(ne) ... plus
any more

déjà?
already?

(ne) ... pas encore
not yet

Have you noticed? **Encore** means both 'still' and '(not) yet'. Don't worry: you'll hear **pas** just before when it means **not yet**!

Mental gymnastics 1

Look for the negative words and some of their opposites in this grid.

```
S  E  N  N  O  S  R  E  P
E  J  A  J  E  D  P  E  I
P  A  S  E  N  C  O  R  E
I  M  E  S  U  L  P  I  C
N  A  E  I  P  E  R  E  J
C  I  R  A  U  C  U  N  I
E  S  R  U  O  J  U  O  T
```

Mental gymnastics 2

Fill in the missing letters to answer the following questions by using negatives.

1   Voulez-vous manger quelque chose?
    Non merci, ... e ....e ....eu.... .... ie..... (I don't want anything)
2   Tu connais quelqu'un ici ?
    Non, ...e ....e ....o.... ....ai.... ....e.... ....o.... ....e.
    (I don't know anyone.)
3   Achèteras-tu des souvenirs?
    Non, ...e ....'a.... ....è....e....ai au....u.... ....ou....e....i.....
    (I won't buy any souvenirs.)
4   Tu vois quelque chose?
    Non, ...e ....e ....oi.... ....ie..... (I see nothing.)
5   Elle fume toujours?
    Non, e.... ....e ....e ....u....e ....u..... (She doesn't smoke
    any more.)
6   As-tu déjà mangé? Non, ...a.... e.... ....o....e. (Not yet.)

Negatives and the perfect tense

For almost all of the tenses we have looked at, the negative words work like **ne ...
pas** (see Unit 13). However, in the **perfect tense** (**G**) and other 'two-word' tenses
not covered in this book, the negative words are divided into two groups:

- those that go <u>before</u> the past part: **pas (encore)**, **jamais**, **rien** and **plus**
  Je ne suis jamais allé au Japon.
  I have never been to Japan.
  Je n'ai pas encore mangé.
  I have not eaten yet.

- those that go <u>after</u> the past part: **personne, aucun**
  Je n'ai vu personne.
  I did not see anyone.
  Je n'ai envoyé aucune invitation.
  I didn't send any invitations.

Mental gymnastics 3

Rearrange the words in each question to make a sentence.

1   a – personne – n' – elle – téléphoné – à
....

2   jamais – venus – ils – ne – sont
....

3   nous – rien – préparé – avons – n'
....

4   n' – pas – fini – encore – vous – avez
....

5   il – aucune – vendu – n' – maison – a
....

6   vacances – parties – plus – sont – elles – ne – en
....

Mental gymnastics 4

How would you say these in French?

1 I have never been to Paris.

....

2 He doesn't want anything.

....

3 I don't know anyone in Montpellier.

....

4 We haven't eaten yet.

....

5 They are still at the cinema.

....

6 We won't come any more!

....

Key to Mental Gymnastics

Unit 1

Mental gymnastics 1
1. f.
2. m
3. f
4. f
5. m
6. f.
7. f
8. m.
9. m.
10. m.
11. f.
12. m.
13. f.
14. f.
15. m.
16. f.
17. m.
18. m.
19. f.
20. f.

Mental gymnastics 2
1. le
2. la
3. la
4. l'
5. le
6. la
7. la
8. la
9. l'
10. le
11. le
12. la
13. la
14. l'
15. le
16. la

Mental gymnastics 3
1. une femme
2. l'étudiant
3. une amie
4. la personne
5. un garçon
6. la voiture

Mental gymnastics 4
1. un homme
2. une fille
3. la souris
4. une question
5. un infirmier
6. une vendeuse

Unit 2

Mental gymnastics 1

-s	-x	no change
accusations	châteaux	nez
vendeurs	tableaux	époux
questions	genoux	
princesses		
chanteuses		
musiciens		
girafes		

Mental gymnastics 2
1. les vendeurs
2. les voix
3. les hommes
4. les châteaux
5. les amis
6. les infirmiers

Mental gymnastics 3
1. les carottes
2. les crocodiles
3. les bébés
4. les garçons
5. les personnes
6. les étudiants

Unit 3

Mental gymnastics 2
1. elles
2. nous
3. il
4. tu
5. je
6. elle
7. ils
8. vous

Mental gymnastics 3

```
J   I   E   T   I   E
T   V   L   O   U   S
N   E   L   L   E   S
O   N   U   S   J   E
U   V   O   L   E   L
S   L   I   L   S   L
E   V   O   U   S   E
```

Mental gymnastics 4

SI LJ EE
OU   LL
UN   EV
ST   OU
IL   SE
ES LL

Key to Mental Gymnastics

Mental gymnastics 5

1. vous	4. vous	7. vous	10. ils
2. nous	5. elle	8. ils	11. elles
3. tu	6. vous	9. il	12. je

Unit 4

Mental gymnastics 2

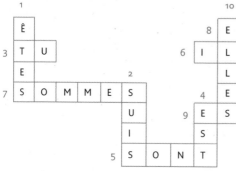

Mental gymnastics 3

1. Elles sont
2. vous êtes
3. il est
4. je suis
5. nous sommes

Mental gymnastics 4

1. tu es; nous sommes
2. il est; elles sont
3. je suis; elle est
4. vous êtes; ils sont

Mental gymnastics 5

1. He's in love.
2. We're late.
3. They're tired.
4. She's asleep.
5. I have to!

6. Are you comfortable?
7. They (feminine) are late.

Mental gymnastics 6

1. Je suis fatigué(e).
2. Nous sommes amoureux.
3. Elle est obligée.
4. Ils sont endormis.
5. Il est bien.
6. Tu es en retard.

Unit 5

Mental gymnastics 1

1. j	6. a
2. g	7. f
3. b	8. d
4. e	9. h
5. c	10. i

Mental gymnastics 2

1. woman
2. man
3. either men, women or a mix of men and women
4. a man
5. men or a mix of women and men
6. a woman or a man
7. a woman
8. women

Mental gymnastics 3

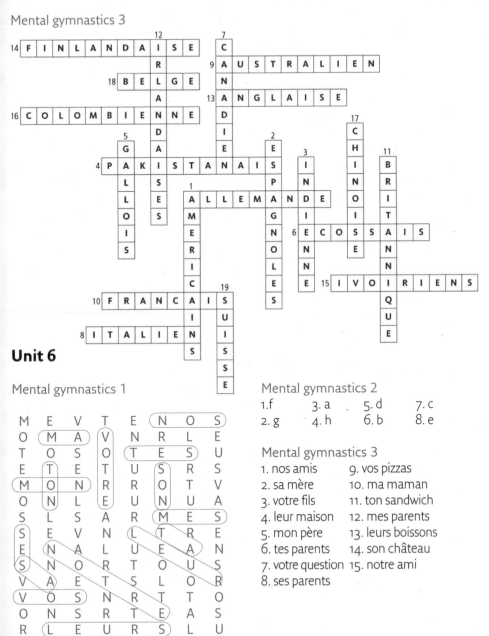

Unit 6

Mental gymnastics 1

Mental gymnastics 2

1. f   3. a   5. d   7. c
2. g   4. h   6. b   8. e

Mental gymnastics 3

1. nos amis
2. sa mère
3. votre fils
4. leur maison
5. mon père
6. tes parents
7. votre question
8. ses parents
9. vos pizzas
10. ma maman
11. ton sandwich
12. mes parents
13. leurs boissons
14. son château
15. notre ami

Key to Mental Gymnastics

Unit 7

Mental gymnastics 2

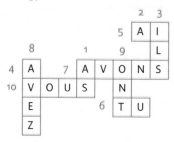

Mental gymnastics 3
1. nous avons
2. tu as
3. ils ont
4. elle a
5. vous avez

Mental gymnastics 4
1. a
2. e
3. b
4. d
5. c

Mental gymnastics 5
1. Je suis fatigué.
2. Elle a faim.
3. Nous sommes en retard.
4. Il est amoureux.
5. Vous avez 18 ans?
6. Tu as sommeil?
7. Ils sont endormis.
8. Elles ont froid.

Unit 8

Mental gymnastics 1
1. un joli château
2. une maison verte
3. le premier étage
4. une cité jolie
5. une grande ville française

Mental gymnastics 2

Groom	Bride	Both
impatient	belle	intelligents
élégant	joviale	tolérants
brillant	différente	intéressants
galant	patiente	grands
charmant	créative	adorables
	observatrice	sociables

Mental gymnastics 3
1. une histoire brève
2. une valise ronde
3. une souris grise
4. un homme étrange/bizarre
5. un bébé adorable
6. une jolie actrice

Mental gymnastics 4

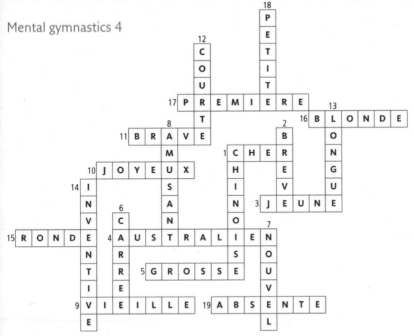

Unit 9

Mental gymnastics 1

1. C'	3. ça	5. ça	7. C'
2. Ça	4. Ce	6. Ce	8. C'

Mental gymnastics 2

1. cet	3. Cette	5. Ces	7. Ce
2. Cette	4. Ce	6. Ces	8. Cet

Mental gymnastics 3

1. celles-ci/là	5. celles-ci/à
2. ceux-ci/là	6. celui-ci/là
3. celui-ci/là	7. celle-ci/là
4. celle-ci/là	8. ceux-ci/là

Mental gymnastics 4

1. c, 2. a, 3. c, 4. b, 5. a, 6. b, 7. b,
8. c, 9. a, 10. c

Unit 10

Mental gymnastics 2

1. nous parlons	5. j'aime
2. vous regardez	6. ils habitent
3. nous écoutons	7. vous travaillez
4. tu donnes	8. ils marchent

Mental gymnastics 4

1. nous réfléchissons	5. il grossit
2. tu rougis	6. ils remplissent
3. elle grandit	7. vous finissez
4. je finis	8. je vieillis

Mental gymnastics 6

1. je réponds
2. ils vendent
3. nous attendons

Key to Mental Gymnastics

4. elle descend
5. j'entends
6. vous perdez
7. ils vendent
8. il rend

Mental gymnastics 2

1. nous prenons
2. vous pouvez
3. elles doivent
4. tu fais
5. je connais
6. elle veut
7. il sait
8. ils viennent

Mental gymnastics 3

1. nous devons
2. je fais
3. ils peuvent
4. il vient
5. vous connaissez
6. nous voulons
7. elles font
8. tu sais

Mental gymnastics 7

Unit 11

Mental gymnastics 1

1. il/elle peut
2. nous savons
3. ils/elles veulent
4. je/tu connais
5. il/elle doit
6. vous allez
7. ils/elles prennent
8. vous faites

Mental gymnastics 4

1. I play/am playing football.
2. She knows how to bake cakes.
3. We take/are taking the train.
4. They want to visit the castle.
5. Do you (formal or plural) play sports?
6. Do you know Bordeaux?
7. He goes/is going to the cinema.
8. They are coming/come tonight.

Mental gymnastics 5

Unit 12

Mental gymnastics 1

1. f	3. d	5. h	7. g
2. c	4. b	6. e	8. a

Mental gymnastics 2

1. elle se coupe
2. ils se dépêchent
3. tu t'habilles
4. vous vous maquillez
5. je me couche
6. nous nous préparons

Mental gymnastics 3

1. je me maquille
2. tu te fais mal
3. nous nous dépêchons
4. vous vous lavez
5. elles se réveillent

Unit 13

Mental gymnastics 1
1. Elle ne parle pas français.
2. Nous ne vendons pas notre maison.
3. Je ne joue pas.
4. Il ne prend pas le train.
5. Ils ne se lèvent pas.
6. Tu ne travailles pas.
   7. Vous n'êtes pas mariée?/
      N'êtes-vous pas mariée?
   8. Je ne parle pas italien.

Mental gymnastics 2
1. Elle ne vient pas.
2. Nous ne travaillons pas.
3. Ils n'ont pas de voiture.
4. Il n'écoute pas de musique.
5. Je ne fais pas de sport.
6. Tu n'as pas de clé?

Mental gymnastics 3
1. Elle n'est pas américaine.
2. Ils n'ont pas faim.
3. Nous n'avons pas d'enfants.
4. Je ne me lève pas à 5 heures 30.
5. Il ne se prépare pas.
6. Elles ne préparent pas de pizza.
7. Il n'attend pas à la gare.
8. Paul ne se dépêche pas.

Unit 14

Mental gymnastics 1
1. Vous êtes anglais(e)?/Êtes-vous anglais(e)?/
   Est-ce que vous êtes anglais(e)?
2. Vous habitez à Londres?/Habitez-vous à
   Londres?/Est-ce que vous habitez à

Londres?

3. Vous êtes étudiant(e)?/Êtes-vous étudiant(e)/Est-ce que vous êtes étudiant(e)?
4. Vous travaillez?/ Travaillez-vous?/Est-ce que vous travaillez?
5. Vous êtes en vacances?/Êtes-vous en vacances?/Est-ce que vous êtes en vacances?
6. Vous voulez boire quelque chose?/Voulez-vous boire quelque chose?/Est-ce que vous voulez boire quelque chose?
7. Vous restez une semaine?/Restez-vous une semaine?/Est-ce que vous restez une semaine?
8. Vous parlez anglais?/Parlez-vous anglais?/Est-ce que vous parlez anglais?

Mental gymnastics 2

1. Vous venez de Paris?/Venez-vous de Paris?/Est-ce que vous venez de Paris?
2. Vous avez des enfants?/Avez-vous des enfants?/Est-ce que vous avez des enfants?
3. Vous habitez à Sydney?/Habitez-vous à Sydney? Est-ce que vous habitez à Sydney?
4. Vous aimez cette musique?/Aimez-vous cette musique?/Est-ce que vous aimez cette musique?
5. Vous jouez au tennis?/Jouez-vous au tennis?/Est-ce que vous jouez au tennis?
6. Vous travaillez à Manchester?/Travaillez-vous à Manchester?/Est-ce que vous travaillez à Manchester?

Mental gymnastics 3

1. pourquoi?
2. quand?
3. est-ce que?
5. combien?
6. lesquels?
7. qui?

4. quelle?   8. d'où?

Mental gymnastics 4

1. Est-ce que vous parlez français?
2. Elle est d'où?/D'où est-elle?
3. Comment est-ce que tu fais?
4. Qu'est-ce que nous faisons?
5. Où est-ce que tu vas?
6. Pourquoi est-ce qu'il ne vient pas?
7. Où allez-vous?
8. Combien ça coûte?

Mental gymnastics 5

1. b   2. d   3. a   4. e   5. c

Unit 15

Mental gymnastics 1

1. Je peux venir ce soir.
2. Elle sait faire les pizzas.
3. Nous voulons prendre le train.
4. Il veut habiter en France.
5. Vous pouvez travailler en Grande-Bretagne.
6. Ils/elles savent jouer du piano.
7. Ils ne veulent pas faire du ski.
8. Il doit aller à Paris.

Mental gymnastics 2

1. Je ne dois pas être à l'aéroport à deux heures.
2. Nicolas ne veut pas venir.
3. Nous ne pouvons pas prendre des photos.
4. Vous ne devez pas faire le ménage.
5. Elles ne veulent pas prendre le bus.
6. Mes parents n'aiment pas faire du shopping.
7. Ces enfants ne peuvent pas regarder

Key to Mental Gymnastics

la télé.
8. Tu ne peux pas venir?

Mental gymnastics 3
1. Elle ne peut pas venir.
2. Ils veulent travailler.
3. Nous savons parler français.
4. Jérémy ne peut pas attendre.
5. Nous voulons finir à cinq heures.
6. Elle ne doit pas marcher.
7. Je n'aime pas faire le ménage.
8. Elles adorent prendre des photos.

Unit 16

Mental gymnastics 1

du	de la	des
vin	limonade	tomates
gratin	glace	carottes
coca	bière	aubergines
café	pizza	
gâteau	tarte	
champagne		

Mental gymnastics 2
1. de la sauce
2. des échalottes
3. du vin
4. du tennis
5. en
6. de voiture
7. de la pizza
8. du pain
9. de l'argent
10. du basket

Mental gymnastics 3
1. Sébastien prend de la bière.
2. Je fais du sport.
3. Michel fait de la guitare.
4. Louise vend des pizzas.
5. Les enfants veulent des gâteaux.
6. Mes parents font du golf.

7. J'aime faire de la natation.
8. Vous ne prenez pas de gâteau?

Unit 17

Mental gymnastics
1. Nous y allons.
2. Je n'y retourne pas.
3. Est-ce que vous y habitez?
4. Carine y passe ses vacances.
5. Mes parents y habitent.

Unit 18

Mental gymnastics 1
1. à la pharmacie   3. au Japon   5. à Rome
2. en Australie   4. au parc   6. au cinéma

Mental gymnastics 2
1. J'habite au Pérou.
2. Je vais en Espagne.
3. Ils sont dans le musée.
4. Nous allons à la boulangerie.
5. Elles sont à l'école.
6. Il est aux toilettes.

Mental gymnastics 3

à	Manchester – Hawaï – Paris – Delhi
en	Chine – Écosse – France – Bretagne
au	Pérou – Nigeria – Mexique – Brésil
aux	Antilles – États-Unis

Mental gymnastics 4
1. au
2. à
3. au
4. aux
5. à l'
6. à
7. en
8. au

Key to Mental Gymnastics

Unit 19

Mental gymnastics 1
1. Il faut venir ce soir!
2. Il faut faire du sport.
3. Il faut prendre le bus.
4. Il faut manger des fruits et des légumes.
5. Il faut des œufs et du lait.
6. Il me faut mon sac!

Mental gymnastics 2
1. Il nous faut du lait.
2. Il ne faut pas fumer.
3. Il me faut des vitamines.
4. Il faut des tomates, du thon et de la mayonnaise.
5. Il faut choisir.
6. Il faut pratiquer.
7. Il nous faut nos bagages.
8. Il faut essayer.

Unit 20

Mental gymnastics 1
1. regarde!
2. écoutez!
3. Vendez!
4. Soyez!
5. Va!
6. Prends!

Mental gymnastics 2
1. Allons au cinéma!
2. Jouons aux cartes!
3. Faisons du shopping!
4. Rendons visite à des amis!
5. Visitons un musée!
6. Prenons un verre au café!

Mental gymnastics 3
1. Ne venez pas.
2. Ne faites pas de gâteau.
3. Ne soyez pas en retard.
4. Ne prenez pas le train.
5. Ne vous faites pas mal.
6. Ne partez pas!

Mental gymnastics 4
1. Lève-toi!
2. Réveillez-vous!
3. Ne te coupe pas!
4. Dépêchons-nous!
5. Ne vous faites pas mal!

Mental gymnastics 5

Key to Mental Gymnastics

Unit 21

Mental gymnastics 1
1. la mienne   3. le leur   5. le tien
2. la vôtre   4. les siennes 6. les nôtres

Mental gymnastics 2
1. le nôtre   3. le mien   5. les vôtres
2. les leurs   4. la sienne 6. les tiens

Mental gymnastics 3
1. la sienne   3. les nôtres 5. la tienne
2. le leur   4. les miens   6. la vôtre

Unit 22

Mental gymnastics 1
1. plus
2. autant de
3. plus ... que
4. moins de
5. aussi ... que
6. moins de ... que
7. plus d' ... que
8. autant de ... que

Mental gymnastics 2
1. c   2. b   3. a   4. b   5. b   6. c

Mental gymnastics 3
1. b – moindre/petit   3. a – pire/mauvais
2. d – mieux/bien   4. c – meilleur/bon

Mental gymnastics 4
1. Il est plus sympa que Christophe.
2. Vous avez autant de clients que nous.
3. Ils ont moins d'argent que vous.
4. Tu es aussi grand que Carine.

5. Nathalie cuisine mieux.
6. Ces melons sont meilleurs.
7. C'est le meilleur gateau.
8. Je suis le plus vieux.

Mental gymnastics 5
1. Nous avons moins de vacances.
2. Ce fromage est meilleur.
3. J'ai autant de problèmes.
4. Les enfants sont plus grands.
5. Florence a plus d'humour.
6. Ils travaillent moins.
7. Les vins français sont les meilleurs.
8. Cette chemise est la moins chère.

Unit 23

Mental gymnastics 1
1. Je les connais.
2. Elle la prend.
3. Nous les adorons.
4. Il en veut.
5 .J'ai besoin d'elles.
6. Vous ne me connaissez pas.
7. Ils lui téléphonent.
8. Elle ne t'attend pas.

Mental gymnastics 2
1. la   3. les   5. en
2. l'   4. le   6. lui

Mental gymnastics 3
1. I answer him/her.
2. She dreams about you.
3. They need them/it.
4. He's thinking about it.
5. We ask him/her.
6. Are you afraid of them?

Key to Mental Gymnastics

Mental gymnastics 4
1. Ils me téléphonent.
2. Je suis amoureux de toi.
3. Elle lui parle.
4. Ils ont besoin de moi!
5. Vous? Nous ne vous connaissons pas!
6. Je le veux!

Unit 24

Mental gymnastics 1
1. parlé
2. réussi
3. vendu
4. rendu
5. aimé
6. fini
7. étudié
8. attendu
9. réfléchi
10. perdu
11. choisi
12. trouvé

Mental gymnastics 2
1. J'ai vendu ma maison.
2. Mon bébé a grossi.
3. Nous avons réfléchi.
4. Avez-vous attendu?
5. Ta mère n'a pas téléphoné.
6. Ils ont travaillé.
7. Vous avez choisi?
8. Tu n'as pas regardé la télé?

Mental gymnastics 3
1. f   2. d   3. e   4. a   5. c   6. b

Mental gymnastics 4
1. Il s'est préparé.
2. Elles sont arrivées.
3. J'ai perdu ma clé.

4. Nous avons habité à Paris.
5. Vous n'avez pas visité le Louvre!
6. Elle est allée en Australie.

Unit 25

Mental gymnastics 1
1. je pouvais
2. elle attendait
3. nous réussissions
4. ils perdaient
5. tu téléphonais
6. il habitait
7. vous vouliez
8. ils écoutaient

Mental gymnastics 2
1. ils rendaient
2. vous preniez
3. je faisais
4. nous jouions
5. elle étudiait
6. tu devais
7. il vendait
8. elles réfléchissaient

Mental gymnastics 3

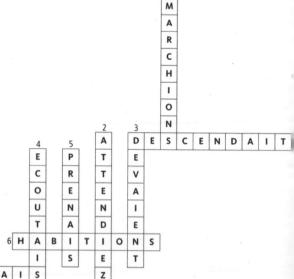

Key to Mental Gymnastics

Unit 26

Mental gymnastics 1
1. Je vais à Paris.
2. Nous allons prendre des photos.
3. Elle va venir.
4. Vous allez au musée.
5. Ils vont chanter.
6. Vas-tu à Nice?

Mental gymnastics 2
1. Nous n'allons pas répondre.
2. Ils vont réfléchir.
3. Philippe ne va pas venir.
4. Est-ce que vous allez contacter l'hôtel?
5. Tu ne vas pas travailler.
6. Elle ne va pas faire la cuisine.

Mental gymnastics 3
1. Tu vas habiter à Paris.
2. Elle va lui parler.
3. Nous allons regarder la télé.
4. Ils vont vendre leur maison.
5. Je vais faire un gâteau.
6. Allez-vous visiter le château?

Unit 27

Mental gymnastics 1
1. je remplirai
2. ils/elles chercheront
3. vous rendrez
4. il/elle donnera
5. tu habiteras
6. ils/elles attendront
7. nous travaillerons
8. nous répondrons

Mental gymnastics 2
1. il aura
2. elles viendront
3. nous pourrons
4. je verrai
5. elle fera
6. tu seras

Mental gymnastics 3
1. Il t'écoutera.
2. Ils ne voudront pas.
3. Nous attendrons.
4. Tu choisiras.
5. Elle ne vendra pas.
6. Je réfléchirai.
7. Elles le feront.
8. Vous ne téléphonerez pas!

Mental gymnastics 4

Key to Mental Gymnastics

Unit 28

Mental gymnastics 1

S	E	N	N	O	S	R	E	P
E	J	À	J	É	D	P	E	I
P	A	S	E	N	C	O	R	E
I	M	E	S	U	L	P	I	C
N	A	E	I	P	E	R	E	J
Ċ	I	R	A	U	C	U	N	I
E	S	R	U	O	J	U	O	T

Mental gymnastics 2
1. Non merci, je ne veux rien.
2. Non, je ne connais personne.
3. Non, je n'achèterai aucun souvenir.
4. Non, je ne vois rien.
5. Non, elle ne fume plus.
6. Non, pas encore.

Mental gymnastics 3
1. Elle n'a téléphoné à personne.
2. Ils ne sont jamais venus.
3. Nous n'avons rien préparé.
4. Vous n'avez pas encore fini!
5. Il n'a vendu aucune maison.
6. Elles ne sont plus parties en vacances.

Mental gymnastics 4
1. Je ne suis jamais allé à Paris. (best)/
   Je n'ai jamais été à Paris.
2. Il ne veut rien.
3. Je ne connais personne à Montpellier.
4. Nous n'avons pas encore mangé.
5. Ils sont encore au cinéma.
6. Nous ne viendrons plus!

Glossary

Grammar term	Related word	Definition
noun		A 'naming' word for a living being, thing or idea; for example: *woman, desk, happiness, Andrew.*
gender		Whether a person, thing or adjective is masculine or feminine.
	masculine	A form of noun or adjective that is used to refer to a living being, thing or idea that is associated with the masculine gender, for example: • le serveur – the waiter • le couteau – the knife • le restaurant italien – the Italian restaurant • le chapeau bleu – the blue hat • le socialisme – socialism
	feminine	A form of noun or adjective that is used to refer to a living being, thing or idea that is associated with the feminine gender, for example: • la serveuse – waitress • la table – table • la recette italienne – the Italian recipe • la chemise bleue – the blue shirt • la beauté – beauty
subject		The person or thing which helps us understand what a sentence is about. e.g. *I like cheese.* **They** *are late.*
singular		The form of a word which is used to refer to **one** person or thing, rather than many.
plural		The form of a word which is used to refer to more than one person or thing.
verb		A 'doing' word which describes what someone or something does, what someone or something is, or what happens to them; for example: *be, sing, live.*
	regular	A verb whose forms follow a general pattern or the normal rules.

Glossary

	irregular	A verb whose forms do <u>not</u> follow a general pattern or the normal rules.
	reflexive	A verb where the action 'reflects' back on the subject, e.g. *I wash myself (je me lave).*
adjective		A 'describing word' that tells you more about a person or a thing, such as their appearance, colour, size or other qualities; for example: *pretty, blue, big.*
negative		A word that is used to say that something is not happening, is not true or is absent, e.g. *not, never, nothing.* In French, negatives are usually made using *ne* before the verb and another word after the verb, e.g. *ne ... pas, ne ... jamais, ne ... rien.*
infinitive		The form of the verb with *to* in front of it, e.g. *to walk, to have, to be, to go.* In French, infinitives usually end in –er, –ir or –re, e.g. *travailler, finir, attendre.*
tense		The form of a verb which shows whether you are referring to the past, present or future.
	present	A verb form used to talk about what is true at the moment, what happens regularly and what is happening now; for example: *I'm a student; I travel to college by train; I'm studying languages.*
	perfect	One of the tenses used to talk about the past, especially about actions that took place or were completed in the past. For example: *I walked to school yesterday.*
	imperfect	One of the tenses used to talk about the past, especially in descriptions, and to say what was happening or used to happen; for example: *I used to walk to school; It was sunny at the weekend.*
	future	A tense used to talk about something that will happen or will be true.